Much of Madness

Much of Madness

The Conexus Chronicles, Book I

S. E. Summa

For more info:
Visit my website at sesumma.com

Printed in the United States of America

First Printing: February 2016
Inkmancy Press

Cover design by Seedlings Design Studio
Book design by S. E. Summa

This book is dedicated in loving memory to:

Melanie Therese Summa
October 1978 to August 2013
My cousin, my co-conspirator, my heart.

&

Charles Raymond Abernathy
June 1980 to November 2014
My friend, my champion, my brother.

Mel and Charlie were the closest thing I ever had to younger siblings. It is a tragic irony that neither reached the age of thirty-five. In my grief from Mel's passing, I rediscovered writing. In my shock from losing Charlie, I found the courage to publish.

That motley drama—oh, be sure
It shall not be forgot!
With its Phantom chased for evermore,
By a crowd that seize it not,
Through a circle that ever returneth in
To the self-same spot,
And **much of Madness**, and more of Sin,
And Horror the soul of the plot.

-Edgar Allen Poe, "The Conqueror Worm"

Part I: Sin

Chapter One

Marceau smiled as his finger caressed the cursed hourglass. It looked like nothing more than a novelty Halloween decoration with two skeletal hands and yellowed, fraying rope to hold the glass bulbs in place. But he wasn't fooled. Max wouldn't have sent them to steal the rustic timepiece unless it was priceless.

Breaking into Thibodeaux's stately Garden District mansion had been the easy part, despite the modern security system. Vespa was taking care of the final guards while Marceau took the greater risk.

This particular hex was a tricky one, and flickers of fiery crimson upon its cords warned Marceau a wrong move could be fatal. He knew one this complex must have cost Thibodeaux a pretty penny.

The voodoo priestess was crafty when she'd woven the hex into the threads of time itself. The very nature of the hourglass allowed for an unusual bond. Now, that he had identified the source of the curse's strength, it was only a matter of time before he discovered its weakness. Then he could begin his favorite part, unwinding her careful construction.

Thud! The distinctive sound of a body hitting the floor preceded the creaking of the study door behind him. High heels clicked against the hardwood floor.

Marceau exhaled, then said, "I cannot concentrate with all the racket you're making, Vespa. Find another guard to play with or better yet, sit down and be quiet."

Vespa wore her usual black working attire, a tight black cat suit and a thigh-high pair of leather stiletto boots that fit like a second skin.

"I'm fresh out of guards, lover. I bought some time, but you'd better break this one fast. The next scanning spell is due in less than five minutes."

Lover indeed. The thought made his flesh crawl.

Smudged lipstick framed her dangerous mouth. How many souls had she fed on tonight? Her forked tongue slid along her lower lip. Marceau often lost sleep after Vespa glutted herself during one of their jobs as if he then bore some responsibility for the twisted fate of her victims. Maximilian, his benefactor, and her boss, prized her little gift and used her macabre ability to his advantage.

Marceau said, "All the more reason for you to stop rubbing my arm. Go sit down."

Vespa sauntered to a chair facing him, sat, and kicked, sending expensive tchotchkes clattering to the floor before propping her boots on a table.

"Oops. You think it was a real Fabergé egg?"

Marceau gave her a look. "You call that quiet?"

Vespa raised a shoulder.

"I'll just enjoy the view, then," she purred, looking him up and down. "Oh, do stop rolling those baby blues of yours. What type of curse have we tonight?"

Marceau placed his hands back against the grim hourglass. His eyes closed in concentration as he searched through the hex's vibrations for a weakness.

"The hex is woven to kill anyone, besides Thibodeaux, who removes the hourglass from the curio with selfish intent." Marceau froze as he felt a loose thread, a tiny opening into the inner workings of the curse. "Ah, here it is."

"Four minutes."

"This part can't be rushed, Vespa. I'm close."

Marceau tilted his head and pushed more power into his palms.

"Got it! There's a loophole. You can remove the particular item for a very short time as long as your intention is not to use it."

Marceau lifted his hands from the hourglass and scanned the room. Not seeing what he needed, he turned to Vespa. "Where's the nearest bedroom?"

Vespa's eyes lit up. "Really, lover? I thought you'd never ask, but we are almost down to three minutes." One eyebrow rose as her eyes trailed lower. "Better make them count."

Working with her could be a real pain in the ass.

"Vespa. Focus. I need an item to replace the hourglass in the cabinet. Where is the nearest bedroom?"

"Just when things were getting interesting." She slumped back in her chair. "Second door on the left. The guard in there won't be a bother."

Marceau rushed to the bedroom. The sentry would certainly not be a bother. His corpse lay on the floor. What remained of his flesh was little more than a dry husk covering bones. Marceau stepped over the skeleton, grabbed what he needed from the bedside table, and refused to look at the withered remains on his way out.

Back in the office, Marceau raised his hand to grab the hourglass... and hesitated.

"Two minutes until the next security spell, lover. Do pull the trigger and get us out of here," Vespa urged.

Marceau took a deep breath. A miscalculation would be more than unpleasant because the priestess was renowned throughout the French Quarter for her savagery.

Grabbing the hourglass, he lifted it a few inches off the shelf. Power from the curse surged up his arm, contracting muscles and sending electric pulses into his chest in warning. Yet he did not release the precious item as the hex demanded; instead, Marceau removed it from the curio and willed the priestess' hex to take hold. He fought his reflex to drop it and repeated, "I will put you back in the curio. I will put you back..."

A long night of cat burglary and hex breaking had certainly taken a toll, but last night's challenges were child's play compared to the danger posed by Maximilian... who as luck would have it, was due to arrive any moment.

At ridiculous o'clock in the morning, only one thing could improve Marceau's mood. Closing his eyes, he inhaled: bold chicory coffee, powdered sugar, and fresh beignets. Perfection.

Sitting at a tiny round corner table, he scanned the green and white canopied patio again. He'd positioned his back to the wall and allowed the best angle for surveying the crowded café. In Marceau's line of work, safety was paramount. Besides, Vespa, Max's favorite serpentine pet, threatened to track him down and finish the seduction she'd tried last night.

Daybreak had only been a few hours earlier, but Café Du Monde was already bustling with activity. Tourists were easy to spot in their "I heart NOLA" souvenir T-shirts and colorful plastic beads. Business people hurried in and out, their attention focused on various electronics as much as their rushed breakfasts. A collection of aging regulars read newspapers and debated current affairs.

One motley group sat at a nearby table—a broad, muscled man with a handlebar mustache—a palm reader wearing the expected heavy layers of eyeliner and scarves—a street performer painted silver from head to toe. When an alluring, older woman joined them, she propped a weathered saxophone, with care, on the green chair beside her.

In any other city, a group like that would have attracted interest. In the French Quarter, their eccentricities were par for the course. They were probably heading to Jackson Square to entertain and swindle the tourists.

Max referred to the park attracting such diverse performers as Place d'Armes. Always old-fashioned, always formal, and certainly always punctual… that was Maximilian.

Another sip of coffee. This time, he let the rich, thick liquid swirl on his tongue before swallowing. Max had demanded a meeting, so Marceau insisted it be at the café, knowing Max was sure to ruin his morning. At least, he'd get breakfast out of the deal. In the meantime, Marceau endeavored to enjoy the small things. Watching normal people, humans with no ties to the supernatural, fascinated him. What would it be like to work a normal job, spend free time with friends and family, to not bear the weight of Maximilian's cruel demands?

At a nearby table, a couple seemed unaware of the growing audience. Their coffees and beignets sat cold and untouched. They stared at each other as if entranced.

How much entertainment could that possibly provide? The girl laughed, and the boy's eyes widened. He cupped his hand against her cheek. She leaned in.

Marceau tried to ignore them, but his eyes betrayed him again and again. One of the old men across the room had abandoned his newspaper to observe the couple, as well. He could not imagine loving someone, trusting with his heart. The vulnerability, the surrendering of one's self to another person with no guarantees they wouldn't turn power against you? It was absurd.

Girls seemed to like his dark hair, olive skin, and Mediterranean features. Max's money also probably didn't hurt the situation. His off-campus apartment and sports car were much nicer than those of his classmates. A sense of not belonging in his own life kept Marceau from making friends easily.

"Gah," Marceau said when a high-pitched shriek jolted him from his thoughts. Everyone in the café turned and watched as two laughing boys with powdered sugar mustaches darted between the small, crowded tables as a pretty girl chased them.

Marceau looked down and quickly closed his hand to hide the blue glow radiating in his palm. A rapid scan of those nearest him provided assurance no one else had noticed. He was still on edge from last night or summoning a hex wouldn't have been his first reaction.

Pull it together. Max was incoming. Calm, measured, control.

Taking a deep breath to center himself, Marceau visualized the immobilization hex trickling back up his arm, across his shoulder, and into his chest where his power over curses originated.

The babysitter grabbed one of the boy's arms just as he knocked into Marceau's table. She gaped at him a moment and her lips parted in a shy smile as she tucked a strand of hair behind her ear and said, "Sorry about that."

The blonde's shorts revealed tanned, nicely muscled legs. She appeared to be about twenty. Marceau was only a couple years older, yet his upbringing was such that they might as well be worlds apart.

"No worries. You'll be busy until the sugar rush wears off those two," Marceau responded with a wink. He reached for a napkin to wipe up the cream that had spilled across the table.

A blush flamed across the girl's cheeks as she tugged on the hyper boy's hand. Marceau paused to check out her assets while she walked away.

All movement in the crowded café halted, and the boy clutching the blonde's hand froze mid-leap. A momentary hush was Marceau's only warning before…

"Ever an observer of the mundane Master L'Argent?" asked a familiar voice.

Years of practice kicked in and without flinching, Marceau turned and raised a dark eyebrow. "Don't you ever bore of your tired entrances?"

"I must find merriment where I can these days," answered Maximilian, now seated at the table. He smoothed an impeccable gray pinstripe suit and twisted, attempting to settle into the café's uncomfortable green chair.

"You could drink your coffee at a fine establishment, one befitting a young man of your wealth, Marceau, though you'd have to wear more appropriate attire."

Marceau glanced at his jeans, sneakers, and college T-shirt, then shrugged. He'd looked out of place when he started at Tulane. Now, almost finished with a dual master's degree, he'd learned to dress like everyone else on campus. Anything to avoid standing out in the crowd.

Max continued, "I'd certainly prefer the comfort of a leather high back chair and a good cigar at the club."

"You know I have coffee here every morning. This café has history and the best people-watching in the city when they are allowed movement."

Marceau gave him a pointed look. A light breeze blew through the patio, sending thin paper napkins fluttering to the ground. None of the patrons were sentient to catch them.

Maximilian shrugged. "You've seen how these fragile humans react to my presence if I do not halt them. These people are attuned to me from the moment they are born into this realm."

A single nod was the only concession Marceau was willing to offer. If Maximilian did not mask himself, every human in the café would turn toward him in an almost magnetic, involuntary response. Certainly, a survival instinct buried within their subconscious would recognize him, even if they did not.

Max's penetrating hazel eyes, square jaw, and straight, Roman nose were worthy of an old movie star, but what lay beneath was anything but attractive. He often kept his sun-streaked, dark hair long in a ponytail, a contrast to the stiff formality of his suits worthy of a 1920s Gatsby party. He looked to be in his late twenties; appearances were quite deceiving when it came to Maximilian.

Marceau broke the temporary silence. "Can we forgo the usual banter and get to the point of this meeting?" He took another drink of his cooling coffee.

"A bit testy this morning? Feeling the effects of last night's acquisition, are we? Vespa came home pouting too. You make an excellent team. I assume you know she desires you." Max's face showed no emotion when he laid an ornate wooden cane across the small table.

"Vespa's desires are irrelevant." Marceau dared a quick glance at the cane. It was a sign of trust in Marceau that it had left Max's palm. Today, the cane's silver handle had morphed into a frightening mimicry of a feline face, complete with stones resembling tiger's eyes. The grotesque figure's lip peeled back in a snarl, revealing two long fangs.

Perhaps Max was stressed and territorial today?

Marceau's assessment took only a second or two. He looked away and feigned disinterest, hoping Max hadn't noticed.

With a simple twist of the handle, an eight-inch knife would spring forth from the cane's tip, but the sharpness of the blade was not the true danger. The rare venom coating the edge made the weapon deadly to all creatures, human or otherwise.

"You already know I procured the hourglass or we wouldn't be having this discussion." Marceau leaned back in his chair. "You did fail to mention the trinket came attached with a rather nasty death curse."

"True, but 'rather nasty death curses' are your specialty, are they not? Or did I waste a small fortune on your private tutoring? Besides, if the hourglass was not a priceless, occult instrument, Monsieur Thibodeaux would not have paid the Mambo to hex it, now would he?"

A conspiratorial smile did nothing to soften Max's severe expression.

"Tell me, Marceau, what clever trick did you derive to break it? I'm always entertained by your ingenuity. And I am confident this curse was masterful. I heard rumors it was a six-figure job for the Voodoo priestess."

Maximilian leaned in a little too far; his tone was also too sharp. He did not often agree to join Marceau in such a mundane location. Today, it served his purpose because he wanted answers.

"The Mambo wove the hex to kill anyone, besides Thibodeaux, who removed items from the curio for a selfish purpose."

Marceau swigged the last of his tepid drink. He preferred to enjoy coffee in solitude. Cold coffee was uncivilized.

"And the weakness you found?" inquired Maximilian.

"A crafty little loophole, as one could remove the hourglass without perishing if the intent was to not use the power of the hourglass, only to replace it quickly." Marceau pretended something across the café had caught his attention. Max leaned in closer, and Marceau hid a smile while withholding further explanation. As a boy, toying with Marceau's emotions had been Max's regular routine, a hobby even. More often than not, Max had left him stinging with the frustration of unanswered questions and unsatisfying exchanges. Theirs had been far from a nurturing relationship, but a slight shift had occurred as the years went by; Max taught him much, perhaps more than he'd intended. Marceau reveled when he had dominion over his benefactor, however temporary it might be.

"I thought we were foregoing our usual banter," quipped Maximilian. He pushed his hips back in the chair as if realizing his body language had betrayed his anticipation.

With a deep breath, Marceau's hand raised from the table in a gesture of peace. "We are, Max. My apologies."

Proper, uptight Maximilian hated nicknames.

Marceau finally explained, "The hex utilized a delay. An option only because the object being protected was a timepiece. This allowed the curse to stay dormant long enough for a maid or unaware admirer to not drop dead, provided it was their intent to put the hexed object back in the curio expeditiously." Leaning in, he smiled at Max. "One would hate to replace the cleaning staff each time the room needed dusting, after all."

"Indubitably, and your solution?" Max appeared as attentive as Marceau had ever seen him.

A blue glimmer of power danced in Marceau's eyes as he recalled the strength of the priestess' curse. The way she wove the hex with time itself was ingenious, a technique he'd have to practice. Deriving the means to break curses was not only his specialty, but he also relished the challenge.

"The solution was a simple matter really. I obtained a clock from a spare bedroom. As I removed the hourglass, I focused on my intent to promptly return the cursed object to the cabinet. I pulled the hex from the hourglass and released it down my other arm into the cheap, wind-up alarm clock I held."

Max's face split into a devilish smile. "Then, you only had to place the newly hexed clock into the cabinet and close the door?" He let out a bark of unrestrained laughter. "Well done, Marceau, quite well done indeed. Can you imagine Thibodeaux's face when he discovers a common alarm clock in place of his precious, cursed treasure?"

Max slapped his hand on Marceau's back. He tensed, unaccustomed to being touched by his benefactor. Maximilian simply did not give quick praise. Pleased, despite himself, Marceau said, "You will find the hourglass within your vault, sir."

Pulling a silver pocket watch from his gray tailored vest, opening it, and sighing, Max said, "Speaking of time, I must take my leave. The Nashville auction is Friday. Is your itinerary set?"

"Yes, I fly out Thursday morning. I'm booked at The Hermitage Hotel as you suggested."

"Excellent."

Maximilian's eyes darkened as he clenched his gloved fist. The figure on the cane's handle licked its lips in hunger. Longing? Max said, "Oh, and the adjacent Oak Bar prepares an exceptional martini, should you desire to imbibe in a celebratory cocktail."

Nodding, Marceau swallowed on reflex at the unspoken threat. Win the auction at all costs. He tensed while imagining the punishment Max would serve if he had even an inkling of how important winning the book was to Marceau, or why.

The silver figure on the cane turned to Marceau and inhaled. Control the emotion. Marceau was too close to losing this chance now. Pull it together. He adjusted his collar as a diversion and forced his shoulders to relax.

Max said, "I expect you at the manor this evening. A couple of new recruits are in need of your special skill set, and I caught Lynette eying my cane again at dinner last night. I believe an attitude adjustment may be in order."

A chill ran down Marceau's spine. More recruits? He'd just recovered from dealing with seven new corpses last week. "If I am to be at full strength for the trip, wouldn't it be better to lay the new cadavers to rest, Maximilian? I don't want to risk another backlash like the one I had after your experiment with the young actress."

"Yes, shame her spirit would not take direction. Ironic too, given her chosen field." Max smiled and shook his head.

"I need to pack and prepare for the trip. The risk…"

"I decide what to risk, Marceau, or do you need a reminder?"

Max's cane growled. Marceau could not help but glance. The tiger's lip curled in a vicious snarl, a forked serpent's tongue flicked between the fangs.

Danger.

Marceau willed his gaze back to his empty cup and traced his finger around its brim.

"You can adjust your plans. I'm sure she'll understand, whoever she is." Max glanced at the spilled cream on the table and smiled before tossing a napkin to Marceau. "No use crying over spilled milk is the saying, is it not?"

"Yes, of course, I'll come to the manor." Marceau stiffened at a faint tickle on the back of his hand. He fought the urge to look. Was that foul thing licking him? He pulled his hands into his lap with as much composure as possible, but Max's satisfied smile made him wish he'd stayed still.

"You'll have plenty of time to recover by Friday. My needs are manageable, a couple additions to my fold and a pinch of fear-induced cooperation from my dear Lynette."

Marceau's shoulders relaxed as the edges of Max's form wavered and then drifted away into a haze of smoke. Within seconds, Marceau sat alone, surrounded by a lingering odor of sulfur.

The boy clutching his babysitter's hand slowly landed on his feet as if the air was thick. People in the café began talking and moving as normal, unaware of their previous state, or of the dangerous being who sat among them only moments before. Their sudden noise grated on Marceau's nerves.

"Always with the grand exits, Max."

Marceau laid a generous tip on the table. He exited and turned toward his apartment. With no way out of visiting the manor tonight, he would need all day to prepare since it was a safe bet he'd be incapacitated later.

If everything on this trip went as planned, Marceau realized today might be his last day in his beloved New Orleans. The thrill of freedom would surely cure the ache that thought caused.

What did one pack for a trip to the self-proclaimed Music City? Nashville was home to the Grand Ole Opry, legendary Honky Tonks, and countless broken dreams. And here he was without a proper cowboy hat or boots. *Yeah right.*

Chapter Two

Bang, bang.

Seraphina jumped and whipped her head around to face the shop's back door.

Trouble.

Bone deep, her instincts warned her to exercise caution. The dimly lit apothecary had closed more than an hour ago, but the persistent knocking rattled the glass jars packed tight along the back wall.

Ugh, fine. Drunk tourist, superstitious human, or desperate supernatural?

She keyed up the apothecary's security footage. It had taken a moment before the shadowed figure backed far enough from the camera to reveal a scowling, old woman.

Seraphina pushed the intercom button and said, "Sorry, ma'am. We're closed. Our hours are…"

"I need help. I don't give a damn about your hours. This is an emergency. Why else would I come here… of all places?"

Ah, crazy and superstitious.

Seraphina rolled her eyes. Unseasonably hot, fall weather had Nashvillians testy as of late. She pressed the button again. "Ma'am, as I said, we are closed. You will just have to…"

"He promised he'd help when the time came. He gave his word. You must let me in."

Great. If she meant Finn, letting her scream in hysterics about his trade where anyone could hear wasn't good.

Seraphina leaned in to the mic. "All right, I'm coming." The unwanted visitor hit the door the last time. "I said I'm coming, lady."

Maybe drunk too?

After unlatching numerous man-made locks on the door, Seraphina whispered enchantments to unlock the invisible and more deadly ones.

The woman half barged and half fell inside the moment the back door opened. On instinct, Seraphina reached out to stabilize her. She received a dirty look for her trouble as the stranger jerked her arm away.

Well, she sure acted human.

Seraphina took in the woman's appearance and imagined the French twist in her hair stayed perfectly coiffed under normal circumstances. At present, it was in complete disarray with large swaths flapping around unbound. What remained of her makeup was traveling in slow trails down her cheeks, and she wore a misbuttoned, tailored jacket. Her hot mess appearance did not suit the way the woman carried herself.

"How may I help you, ma'am?" Seraphina asked.

Sensing the stare accompanying the question, the woman raised her hand and smoothed an elegant streak of white back into her dark hair. She lifted her chin and sneered. "Where is he?"

Seraphina didn't answer. She was not about to volunteer information to a possible human.

"The Sin Eater, you ignorant girl. I need the Sin Eater right away."

Ignorant girl? Seraphina bit back her retort. Technically, she was older than the condescending woman. But Seraphina was used to being treated as if she were in her early twenties.

The woman pushed past Seraphina and stomped farther into the shop. She searched the darkened apothecary taking in the long mahogany counter, the labeled drawers, and jar-lined shelves reaching the ceiling along every wall. She whirled, almost knocking into Seraphina again.

"I know he's here. So don't waste valuable time by lying or stalling. Just get him, now."

Oh, Finn was definitely going to have to come and deal with this one. Seraphina took a deep breath and said, "Yes, ma'am, of course. I wouldn't dream of wasting your 'valuable time.' Just let me lock up. I'll fetch him."

Proud that she'd managed to filter out most of her sarcasm, Seraphina gestured to an antique Victorian couch in the back of the shop. "If you care to sit, I will..."

The woman lunged and screeched, "Sit? I have no time to sit." She latched onto Seraphina's forearm and jerked her forward. Her putrid breath smelled of alcohol as spittle landed next to Seraphina's nose. "I'm not here to sit. Get me the damned Sin Eater. It is urgent."

"All right, that's it." Seraphina pried the woman's fingers from her arm one by one. Looking deep into her eyes, she tried to release a small trickle of power, but she was pissed off and her control slipped. "I cannot go and get the Sin Eater if you do not let... me... go."

The lady's arm dropped at once and swung into her body. As soon as Seraphina was free, she took the woman's bony shoulders and guided her backward until the sofa hit the back of her legs.

Maintaining eye contact, Seraphina whispered, "Sit and be quiet."

The stranger unceremoniously flopped onto the sofa and the antique gave a troubling groan at her sudden weight.

Seraphina rubbed her aching arm. "Ugh, seriously? That's gonna leave a bruise. Now, I'll be back in a minute."

As she started to turn, the first crimson drop fell from the woman's nose.

"Oh shit... Shit. Too much, Sera." She grabbed a box of tissues and waved one in the bewildered stranger's face.

"Here. Apply pressure." Seraphina took a calming breath. "You are bleeding, ma'am. Apply pressure to your nose, please, with this."

She put the tissue into the woman's limp, sweaty hand and pushed it to her nose. "I'll be right back."

Seraphina spun and ran behind the counter. She flung the door to the stairwell open and called, "Finn? Finn, hurry. Get down here."

A deep mumble, a crash as something hit the floor, and a muffled cuss word made her wince. She bit her lip. It was quiet upstairs.

"Finn, I'm serious," Seraphina yelled up the stairs. Raising her voice made it tremble.

A door creaked open above and hurried footsteps tromped her direction. As he started down the steep stairs, Finn ran his fingers through his stark white hair mussing it even further. Shirtless, he wore only a pair of low-slung pajama pants.

"What could possibly be worth all the commotion, love?"

Seraphina fidgeted. "A woman is here to see you. I think she's human, but I'm not sure..."

He stopped midway and said, "A human? At this time of night? Tell her to come back during business hours. I am rather busy at the moment."

Finn gave her the *look*. The stupid, condescending one Seraphina hated because it implied she didn't understand exactly what 'busy' meant. Why the hell did he think she was down in the shop this late anyway? Like bookkeeping and inventory reports were better than being in her comfortable room upstairs tucked in with a good book. She'd avoided their loft tonight because she was trying to give him a little privacy.

Men.

"She probably just wants a love potion or something equally ridiculous." Finn rotated on his right foot and made it back up one step.

"She's demanding to see the Sin Eater, Finn." He stopped his ascent. "I don't know how she knows about you, but she was quite insistent. I was afraid of what she might yell into the intercom, so I let her in. Then she started screaming, and she grabbed me and I..." Seraphina hesitated.

Finn froze. "What did you do, Seraphina?"

Seraphina winced. Finn turned back to face her. He only called her by name when the situation was serious.

"Well, I juiced her... a little," Seraphina confessed. "But she was hysterical." Seraphina raised her arm and watched as his eyes widened at the red welts blossoming on her freckled skin. "I just wanted her to sit down and shut up for a second, okay?"

"You juiced her? A little? How much is a little, Seraphina? Wait, you used your power on a human?" he asked incredulously.

Seraphina bit her lip and nodded.

"You know your magic is unpredictable at best on the living, especially humans," Finn called back toward his room upstairs, "Sparrow, we'll have to call it a night, I'm afraid."

A feminine whine of protest made Seraphina's eyes roll. Finn's guest, Kandy (with a K) as Seraphina always called her, must not have gotten everything she'd come for tonight.

Finn directed his attention back to Seraphina. "Fix our guest a cup of tea while I throw on proper clothes, would you? There's a red tin on the left in the back of the medicinal tea cabinet. It is marked Restorative Formula Eight. I'll be right down." The last few words were spoken as his long legs took stairs two at a time.

Seraphina glanced to the back of the shop at the unchanged state of their guest. Blood droplets trickled down her chin. Seraphina muttered under her breath, "Your fancy herbal tea is not going to fix that."

"Who said anything about the damned tea being fancy? Just make sure it's the red one that says Restorative. And only Formula Eight. Seven is much too strong for her kind," Finn called out from the top stair landing.

How does he *do* that?

Seraphina grabbed a teacup and saucer and began rooting through the stacks of multi-colored boxes and tins, finally locating an ornate red box with Formula Eight in Finn's elegant script, right where he said it would be. She removed a rather pungent bag, sniffed it, and recoiled.

Ew, bloodroot? Well, that would do it, all right. She poured hot water from the ever-present electric tea kettle. By the time Seraphina returned with the steaming cup, Finn was standing behind her extending his long-fingered hand.

"Bloodroot is poisonous, Finn. You're sure of this formula?"

"Of course, I am. Really, do you not trust me at—" He looked past Seraphina and gauged the woman's haggard appearance. Finn's expression tightened, and he cleared his throat.

"Well, it should straighten Phyllis right up, though she will pay for it tomorrow, I'm afraid." He set the teacup on the counter and raised Seraphina's arm, turning it outward as he examined the red welts. "On second thought, Phyllis Woodard deserves the herbal hangover she has coming. I'm sorry she hurt you, love."

He strode over to the confused woman rocking in a slow, uneven rhythm and humming a discordant melody under her breath. Finn dunked the tea bag angrily as he stared down at her.

Phyllis Woodard? As in *the* Woodards? Finn knew her by name, so this night had just gotten more interesting.

Finn knelt and pulled the bloodied tissues away from the old woman's face. She'd been holding them more on her cheek than her nose anyway. He laid the saucer and tea bag on the sofa next to her and placed the steaming cup in her hands.

"Drink up, Phyllis, come on now."

He guided her as she took a few sips, steadying her hands along the way. The old gal tried to turn away, but he told her to continue drinking. Another gulp and she retched, then took a deep breath, but still looked confused. At least she'd stopped humming.

A clicking sound echoed from the stairs and the stairwell door creaked as it opened again.

"You may want to wait in the loft until we leave, Sparrow." Finn quickly scoped out the scantily clad woman who'd come downstairs. "Ms. Woodard won't be here long."

The young woman jumped and fidgeted with her hair. She removed a couple pins and shook her head back and forth. Perfect caramel and blonde highlighted curls fell forward covering half of her face.

That should only be possible in slow motion TV ads. Seraphina wound her straight red hair around one of her fingers.

Kandy said, "No. I'm okay. It-it's okay. I'd rather leave. I'll just go on back to the club for a while."

Finn nodded. "I'll come see you tomorrow, and we'll spend the whole day together. I'll fix you up right as rain, promise."

She smoothed down her sequined skirt and walked to the back door. Her stiletto boots echoed with a clickety-clack against the hardwood floor.

Murmuring encouragement to the still frazzled Ms. Woodard, Finn coaxed her to take a drink of the tea. Another retching cough and the woman's wrinkled hands were noticeably less shaky. He was prompting her to take another sip when her gaze sharpened. Dark eyes bulged as she noticed his hands steadying hers against the blue, rose-patterned teacup.

"For the love of... don't touch me." Phyllis shrieked and threw her arms out. The teacup crashed to the wooden planked floor, shattering as the remaining noxious liquid splashed across her lap and onto the delicate silk of the antique couch. Kandy (with a K) froze a few feet behind the couch.

"Y-you touched me. You are unclean. Am I infected now?" Hysterical, Phyllis screamed and wiped her hands down the front of her expensive trench coat. She began praying, "Our Father who art in heaven… did you just p-poison me? …hallowed be thy name."

"Oh, bother. Victorian silk is so hard to clean," Seraphina mused, as she elbowed Finn's side.

Finn's unnaturally light blue eyes were beautifully framed by long, white eyelashes. Thanks to their rude intruder, they were full of sadness. When had even his eyelashes faded to pure white? Probably twenty years ago, though his handsome, young face was unchanged otherwise. Seraphina often worried about the sins her best friend ingested. It was clear they took a toll, both mental and physical.

His words broke the brief silence. "I always did like that teacup." Finn's quip was an attempt at humor, but the tightness of his jaw divulged his unease. This stupid woman's aversion to his touch upset him.

Seraphina bumped her hip against him, and he looked back down at her. She said, "I've always warned you that particular teacup was unmanly. She did you a favor."

His pale mouth tilted in a forced imitation of his usual wicked smile. He knew she was distracting him from the sputtering fool now digging in her purse while Kandy (with a K) remained frozen behind the couch.

The three of them stood perfectly still, a red-haired Spellcaster, an albino Sin Eater, and a well glittered, exotic dancer. Mesmerized, they watched as the hysterical woman—who easily spent their combined annual salaries on her clothing alone—squirted an entire bottle of antibacterial gel in her hands, down her arms, and onto her lap. She rubbed it vigorously on all exposed skin, even the tops of her feet. The clear ointment dripped down onto her designer heels. All the while, she vehemently recited the Lord's Prayer.

As if Purell worked on sin.

Humans.

When the contents of the bottle ran low, so did Ms. Woodard's prayers. Finally, as if snapped back into reality, she jerked her head up and flipped her attention to her audience.

"How dare you stand there judging me? It touched me. What if I die with its sin on me? D-Do I have supernatural sins now?"

"First, *it* is *he*," Seraphina snapped, "and second, I'm touching him right now, same as I did yesterday, and the day before that, and so on. You're not going to die just because he touched you. But if you keep on being a hateful, uppity bit…"

She didn't get to finish the cuss word because Kandy (with a K) snorted in amusement at Seraphina's rant, and Ms. Woodard turned and finally noticed Finn's guest.

"A whore? I am being laughed at by a whore?" The old woman's voice rose into an ear-piercing shriek. "You are nothing but a harlot. Is there no limit to the depravity? I'll not be judged by a bunch of degenerates, heathens."

Finn rushed around the small couch and stood in front of Kandy as if blocking her from view would protect her from the harsh judgments being made. Kandy's curvy body was half turned… hiding. Seraphina was surprised she'd care what this woman thought of her.

"Phyllis, enough," Finn commanded. It was his tone, more than the words, which seemed to reverberate throughout the darkened shop.

Kandy (with a K), as she had reminded Seraphina more than once, was probably the closest thing Finn had to a girlfriend in the last fifty years.

"Let me escort you to the door," Finn said. He turned and cradled Kandy under his arm, shielding her while they walked. He lifted her chin and whispered, "Tomorrow, Sparrow. I'm so sorry about her." He gave her a soft, lingering kiss and locked the door, leaned his forehead against it, and exhaled before turning back around, unsmiling.

"Now, Phyllis. I presume you require my services? I cannot imagine you would travel across town near midnight and sully your grand reputation with my company otherwise?" Finn didn't try hiding the acidic tone. "Collect yourself and stop being a nuisance or I'll put you out on the street myself. We've had more than enough of your theatrics."

Phyllis was once again tongue tied. Finn had matched her arrogant attitude with a dose of his own.

Some personal history existed there. Even though Seraphina knew his real age, it always struck her as strange when Finn—who looked to be in his mid-twenties—could so easily put others in a position of vulnerability, as if speaking to disobedient children.

Apparently, it worked on uppity Ms. Woodard because her demeanor changed right before Seraphina's eyes. She straightened and smoothed her hair back again, this time leaving an unladylike glop of antibacterial gel in her hair, much to Seraphina's delight.

"It's Virgil. He is dying even as I speak. He deserves to be cleansed before he passes and..." Phyllis stopped at Finn's white raised brow. "Okay. I know he's complicated and can be misunderstood, but it is not his..." Finn's brow raised even higher, causing her to stop once more and grimace. "Fine. My brother is a cold-hearted man who has lied, bribed, and forced his will on others his entire life." Her words snapped in the air like electrical impulses. Unsteadily, she began to rise. Finn started to reach out to help her, but he lowered his arm when she gave him a look to kill. "Begging? Is what you want to hear from a grieving old woman, Sin Eater? He did what he had to do to protect his family's assets. H-he had a lot of responsibilities. You promised. I was told you..."

Finn raised his hand. "You don't have to justify your brother's actions to me. I know his sins better than you, Phyllis. He is at Odol's home, I presume?"

"Odol has been dead more than twenty-five years Fi... Sin Eater." She huffed and met his eyes. "Yes, Virgil is there. Hospice sent him home to die weeks ago. I have paid the best healers, both human and supernatural, to do everything possible to keep him alive. The last Spellcaster left an hour ago. She wouldn't even try to help him. She said money couldn't buy more time."

"I'll be quick then. I trust you will have the offerings prepared? Red wine and bread?"

"Yes, of course."

Phyllis waved her hand at him and bent to collect the last few items thrown from her purse in her feverish pursuit of germ killer.

Finn asked, "Do you require a cab?"

"No. Addams is waiting with the car."

"I'll prepare and be there soon."

Seraphina watched the suddenly more formal exchange like a tennis match and felt relief as Phyllis Woodard headed to the door. The elderly client paused, apparently confused by the various locks. Seraphina rushed forward to let her out.

Phyllis turned as soon as she was outside and said, "Girl, you are far too young to understand. You mustn't touch the Sin Eater like that. Ever. He is a supernatural, an unclean demon. He will corrupt your soul."

Seraphina let a tiny trickle of power into her eyes. Not enough to hurt, just enough to make her green pupils glow with bright streaks of gold. She smiled wickedly when the woman gasped, clutched her chest, and stumbled backward.

Seraphina slammed the door.

"Love, anything wrong out there?" Finn called.

"Oh, not at all. Everything is just peachy." Seraphina locked the door and missed Finn's appreciative smile as he headed back upstairs.

Chapter Three

Trepidation plagued Marceau as he turned onto Max's private road. Thick Spanish moss swung loosely in the breeze from the low boughs of the old growth pecan forest along the path.

Marceau cringed as his headlights cast a spotlight on the first corpse of the evening. Even from this distance, something obvious struck him as unnatural about the footman—other than his outdated embroidered waistcoat, knee breeches, and white stockings. Rigid, old-fashioned formality reigned supreme in Max's household.

The footman was abnormally tall and broad shouldered, a powdered wig sat slightly askew atop his head. He was one of the lower levels of undead at Max's disposal, little more than an over-muscled puppet to raise and lower the bridge gate at Max's command.

Max maintained control over his undead workers through a hive mind. By joining their minds to his own, he was able to trap them into servitude. But Marceau wondered what other benefits Max reaped from the unnatural mental connection? How much did Max see through this undead servant's eyes, and was he watching even now? An icy chill shot down his spine at the thought.

As Marceau's Aston Martin approached, the corpse began turning a large, wooden wheel. The massive iron gate rose at a slow, steady pace, and Marceau's shoulders clenched as rusted chains screeched out into the humid night. Revving the engine of the Vanquish, he popped his neck side to side and forced his posture to relax.

The sentry was another cadaver not laid to rest and damned to walk the earth for eternity. All so Max's stupid gate would be raised by a uniformed footman who resembled a sick perversion of Masterpiece

Theater. No living human could raise a gate that heavy, for sure. Had Max even considered upgrading to an electric motor? Of course not. He enjoyed the pomp of his servants, hence their ridiculous attire.

When the corpse paused, Marceau drove under the gate and onto the long bridge. Thick fog rose from the swamp below, ebbing and flowing over the wooden planks while the car bounced rhythmically across the bridge.

Another screech as the footman released his hold and the imposing gate descended, trapping Marceau inside Max's compound. His breaths were shorter now, the familiar grip of imprisonment squeezing his chest. This place had once been his home. Marceau shuddered, remembering his childhood here, and the constant state of fear and longing that accompanied it.

Max monitored Marceau's every move. His studies, clothing, and even his food choices were all carefully managed. Every action he made from the age of seven had been cautious and calculated. Reprimands were swift and cruel. Marceau remembered the weight lifted when Max allowed him to move into New Orleans proper. Somehow he had convinced Max that living amongst humans while attending the university was to Max's benefit, as much as his own. He'd reasoned it was "an essential step in learning to function without undue notice in modern society." He could better carry out his duties while immersed, and, therefore, hidden, in the life of the city. Max saw through his arguments, but Marceau infused enough logic with his desperate plea to win.

For a few precious days, he'd thought he was free.

The bridge ended and Marceau continued onto the oyster shell drive. The mansion illuminated ahead was a glowing beacon of opulence and refinement in the center of the Bayou Sauvage. More than 24,000 acres of swamp, brackish marsh, and old growth forest surrounded Max's compound, all conveniently located within the very city limits of New Orleans.

Didn't the humans think it strange that every attempt made to tame this land and develop "New Orleans East," as they called it, had failed?

Max used Voodoo, untimely deaths, and well-placed hexes to retain control over the precious property the humans thought was a wildlife preserve. The inhospitable terrain also limited casualties that arose from stumbling into one of the undead.

While Marceau parked, another corpse approached in a foolish uniform. He could open his own damn car door, thank you very much. Marceau was quick to exit his sports car into the musky swamp air heavy with the smells of decay, brackish water, and earth.

Every angle of the mansion's spotless white exterior stood brightly lit, as if in defiance of the encroaching darkness of the surrounding swamp. Thin pillars along the porch stretched three stories, and a half-rounded portico served as a side gallery.

The haunting notes of a soprano opera accompanied by piano floated into the thick, evening air, contrasting with the night chorus of frogs and insects in the swamp. Lynette's angelic voice rang out from the large bay window of the ballroom. Someone else was entertaining, as well. Marceau spotted a lithe form dancing behind the lace curtains. Ballet? The piano stopped abruptly and Lynette's voice faded mid-note, about the same time a shadow ran forward and grabbed the spinning dancer. Marceau couldn't see what was happening, but Lynette's piercing scream made his blood run cold.

What hellish game was Max playing tonight? He climbed the rounded stairs of the Italianate plantation house two at a time.

The piano music resumed and Lynette's voice joined in, though not as controlled as before. She missed too many notes. Something was very wrong.

Benjamin, Max's head butler, opened the large, ornate door and bowed. His complexion must have been a rich ebony when alive, but death had faded his skin to a sickly shade of gray.

"Master Marceau. Master Maximilian requests your presence in the White Ballroom," Benjamin said in a gravelly monotone, gesturing to the ballroom.

"Thank you, Benjamin."

Marceau was halfway down the hall before the corpse closed the door and returned to the servant's quarters in stiff steps.

Marceau stopped in the doorway and looked at the white grand piano on his right. Max played while Lynette sang. Her empire waisted red gown draped her hips, and blonde curls in an old-fashioned up-do completed a formal look more befitting a fine opera house than an isolated home in the bayou. His eyes scanned around her. Everything appeared in order.

The imposing room had tall ceilings adorned with intricate plaster frieze work, Corinthian columns, and sparse furnishings. Everywhere Marceau looked he saw white: the ceiling, walls, draperies, and both the marble floor and fireplace mantle. The only color, besides the inhabitants, was gleaming gold leaf repeated on the chandelier, drapery ties, and elaborate gold frames of the Victorian mirrors and furniture.

Where was the dancer he'd seen in the window?

Lynette's head turned in small, jerking movements toward him, her haunting melody uninterrupted. Her operatic voice echoed throughout the sparse room accompanied by Max on the piano. Strange eyes, one a deep blue and the other a milky white, passed over Marceau and widened in fear as they stared at something in the opposite corner.

Reluctant, Marceau stepped inside and turned. A reaction from Lynette meant nothing pleasant awaited him across the room. He froze in shock, horrified by the grisly scene. A young woman in a pink ballerina tutu sat on the floor, her legs splayed at unnatural angles, her throat slit open from ear to ear. Dark blood poured down her body and pooled around her in hideous contrast to the white floor. Not far from her, a red gown matching Lynette's lay across a white chair.

The piano stopped again and Lynette's singing halted at once. Max finally spoke. "Ah, Marceau. So glad you could join us. I see you've taken notice of Lynette's new companion. Quite a striking resemblance, don't you think? I'm naming her Babette."

The corpse favored Lynette in every way except the sticky ringlets of her hair, where dry, were a darker shade of blonde. Well, and the gaping wound resembled a grotesque, low worn smile.

Marceau's fists clenched, asking, "Why, Maximilian? She had her whole life ahead of her. She can't be more than twenty-five years old. I-I won't raise her." Marceau waved his arm at the still bleeding corpse. "I told you no more murders. Natural causes only. I…"

Max interrupted, "And I warned you there would be occasional exceptions, did I not? I specially selected Babette, even lured her here to dance for our dear Lynette. It was such a lovely dance too. The girl had real talent, such grace."

Lynette flinched.

Max continued, "I mentioned Lynette's insolence this morning, remember? Well, I came home to find she'd wandered off into my swamp, foolishly deciding to escape while I was in the city. Can you imagine? Luckily, I had a secondary plan in case an attitude adjustment from you would not suffice."

"A plan? Maximilian, she was an innocent."

Max slammed the cover over the keys and Lynette ran around the edge of the piano.

"It's a pity my Lynette needed such a messy reminder," Max said while rising from the piano bench, "a visual aid if you will, to refresh her half dead brain of who exactly is in fucking charge here." Spit flew from his mouth as he fumed. Lynette cowered behind the piano.

"You've made your point, so please let her rest, Maximilian. Don't force me to raise the poor girl in this condition," Marceau pleaded. He was pushing it, but he had to try to stop this madness.

Max's voice lowered, asking, "Shall I procure a Marceau look-a-like and cut his throat open, as well? Would witnessing an innocent choke to death on his own blood still your tongue? His pulse slowing as jets of blood paint my floor with each heartbeat? Well, shall I?"

"No." Marceau's head dropped. "No, of course not."

"Then cease your little tantrum and revive her body. Be quick about it, Marceau. This one's spirit is strong. She is already trying to cross into the other realm. Raise her. Or I'll find another damn girl and start all over again."

Marceau saw no way out. Max was in a dangerous frame of mind tonight. He didn't doubt another Lynette look-a-like, and if necessary, someone resembling him, would be murdered. Better one unfortunate corpse than two more.

"It is harder when they have... when there are such wounds." Marceau winced at his own last words. Dropping to his knee, he forced himself to lift the woman's chin. Babette's body was still limber and her arm fell limply from her soaked chest. The back of her hand smacked into the pool of blood beside her... splattering a web of crimson droplets farther onto the white marble.

Marceau wondered what her real name was, certain it wasn't Babette. Did she have people who loved her? A family?

"Revive her and I'll have Benjamin take her to get her throat sewn. Problem solved," Max said in a tone more suited to mentioning the weather.

Lynette sobbed, the back of her fist pushed against her mouth.

Reviving her with the gaping wound still open was further punishment. Hopefully, the girl would be too confused at first to understand her body's present condition. It all depended on Max, of course, and how much of the girl's soul he chose to feed back into her corpse.

Please, just a little, Marceau silently begged. Don't give her as much as Lynette.

"Could she go see Doc fir…"

"Now." Max slammed the tip of his cane onto the marble summoning his henchmen.

Resigned and defeated, Marceau reached out his hand. Max approached, cane in hand peering up at the gleaming silver figure in the form of a scorpion.

Marceau placed his left hand on Babette's sticky, red chest. Steeling his nerves, he laid his right on the scorpion's back while dark magic seeped into his flesh from the head of the cane. The process made his skin crawl. Eyes closed, he focused on weaving a complex hex to reanimate the ballerina's body, envisioning her small dancer's frame, skin as pale as snow from blood loss and death, the torn gash in her… no, control it. *Life, focus on life.* Marceau drew a deep breath and tried again, this time imagining the girl dancing. Her strong arms and legs flowing in graceful, fluid movements as she spun and leapt around the stark room. He visualized the poise and grace of the finest ballet dancer and let the hex well in his chest… growing until the pressure made his heart pound. Focusing his mind deeper into her body, Marceau imagined blood pumping through her veins into her heart and out into her extremities. Next, in his mind's eye, he saw her brain lighting up as electronic impulses traveled through her nervous system. His hand slipped on her chest when her muscles contracted beneath his hand.

"Now, Marceau," Max demanded.

Exhaling, Marceau released the hex down both of his arms. His muscles contracted as biting, ice-cold power flowed, both into the corpse and the silver figure.

The scorpion reared back on its tail, striking, violently burying its stinger deep into his right hand. Marceau cried out as thick, hot blood trailed along his wrist contrasting the icy hex flowing through his hand.

"Reanimate. Forgive me, but I curse this flesh to reanimate and obey." Each word was accompanied with pain, and he knew it wasn't over. A venomous pulse traveled from the scorpion's barb into his flesh. Marceau braced. A wave of pure terror overtook him as the ballerina's spirit moved through his body and back into hers. Confusion, pain, maddening panic, and blind hatred poured into his mind. He couldn't draw a breath. What was Max *doing?*

Marceau's chest swelled as the pressure of the girl's soul pressed against his lungs. His ribs now expanded with excruciating pain as if his bones would snap at any moment. Max was letting too much of her soul in. Marceau had never felt such agony during a reanimation.

"S-stop. Too much," he wheezed. Marceau pushed with all his might. His thoughts screamed for release while forcing the girl's spirit down his left arm and into her corpse. Shaking his head, he fought the darkness threatening him. Losing consciousness now could be fatal. With only enough lung capacity for short, panting breaths, Marceau was desperate to feed the soul back into her body. The dancer was strong. Max had been right about that, but her soul was resisting. After yanking his hand free from the scorpion's sting, Marceau thrust it onto her chest as well. Screaming, he used all his effort to expel the soul from his body. The corpse seized in a full body spasm and drew a long, gurgling breath.

Marceau fell onto his side and rested his temple on the cool marble of the spinning room. Tiny stars flashed before his eyes, swirling in the darkness, limiting his vision. He coughed as a wave of nausea rolled over him.

Babette jerked upright and looked down at the blood covering her. She reached for her neck and moved her hands in rapid, frantic pats over the separated flesh below her jawline. Her eyes bulged in terror.

Two sets of heavy, lumbering footsteps entered the room.

"Ah, perfect timing, Benjamin, take her to the infirmary at once and have Doc sew the wound," Max ordered. "Oh, and do tell her to try to minimize the scar, would you? I can already see this one is a prized addition. I'd meant to merely strangle the girl but got carried away by the intensity of her performance. I didn't sever her vocal chords, though, so no permanent harm done."

Sweat dripped across the bridge of Marceau's nose onto the floor. She was aware. Babette had a conscience and would be more like Lynette than the lower level undead Max used as mere servants. She truly was the ultimate punishment for Lynette… and for him, as well. Max had damned her to an eternity under his control.

Babette managed to get to her feet. Frantically, searching left to right and back, she watched Benjamin and another large footman approach her on both sides, as though she was a wild animal loose from her cage. Her small hands held tight over her ravaged throat one on top of the other, trying to hold the gaping wound closed. She opened her mouth and began to scream. At first a frantic liquid whisper, then she coughed and dark blood flew from her blue lips. After a deep inhalation, she shrieked, this time with more power, sounding like someone blowing very hard to fog glass.

Marceau pushed himself up and said, "Please. They have to close your wound. Please, don't fight. They can do no more harm to you. I promise."

Babette's head snapped down, and she glared at him. The next time she inhaled, her rage produced a blood-curdling scream that echoed against the walls.

"You must go with them," Marceau yelled this time.

She ran to the door, but Benjamin grabbed her left elbow, and the other footman caught her right. Babette's struggling was futile since she was too afraid to let go of her throat. They picked her up by her elbows and carried her toward the exit, her feet scissoring in wild kicks. Fruitless attempts to break free did nothing to slow their pace, but a bloody ballet slipper fell from Babette's foot as they reached the doorway. It splatted, thick and wet, upon the white marble floor.

Lynette fell forward, her knees hitting in awkward angles, one at a time. She tried to swing her arm to catch herself, but the coordinating muscles did not cooperate, and she collapsed onto the floor. Smacking her hands against the marble in frustration, she wailed in hysterics.

"Oh, are we all just going to fall and hang out on the floor this evening then?" Max asked. Again, he slammed his cane against the marble to summon more servants.

Marceau drug himself a few feet and propped up against the wall. "You put too much of her spirit back into her. I didn't think you could take much. Babette will be a whole new level, she..."

"Yes. Well, I have been practicing, my boy." Max stroked the figure atop his cane.

Practicing how? Practicing on whom?

"Did you see how graceful she moved, Lynette?" Max walked over and bent, grabbing Lynette by her chin and wrenching her to face him. "Did you see her grace? How she moves without your awkward, robotic jerking? Your stiffness? She may be a fine companion for us both. What do you think of that?"

Lynette sobbed harder, short gasps of breath coming between sniffles. Max pushed her away, disgusted. "Why does she not move like the rest? What exactly did you do different this time, Marceau?"

Marceau fought exhaustion, but even he had noticed her fluidity. He thought it was because Max funneled such a large portion of her soul into the corpse, unless... "Dancing," he answered. "To reanimate her corpse, I imagined her body graceful and poised. I pictured her dancing around the room full of passion and life."

"Ah, can it really be that simple?" Max tucked his cane under his arm and clapped his hands loud and slow. Marceau winced with each celebratory clap, seeing nothing worth applauding in this new development. "What an interesting revelation. Why this may be the breakthrough I've been waiting for all these years. Do I have the key to fluid, cognizant reanimation at last? You must visualize not only their internal biological movements but also their physical prowess?"

Waiting all these years? Key? Marceau frowned.

Max looked down at Marceau and stroked the scorpion atop his cane with one finger. Cocking his head, he said, "Well, I see you are not up to celebrating, or anything else for that matter. Really, Marceau, I did have two others. And I had thought a little siphoning off of spirit would serve

Lynette right for her petulance and weak escape attempt." Max glanced at Lynette. Tears streamed down her face. "However, I guess maybe seeing her new companion's lithe exit was enough punishment after all." When no one moved to acknowledge or dispute, Max waved his hand. "Fine. I will let the other two lie at rest. It is a shame, though. One was a boxer with an impressive physique. I meant to put him on gate duty. Oh well, no matter now." Max turned and walked to the doorway. "Vespa? Vespa. Come at once and see to Marceau. He's in need of your care."

Marceau's heart thumped with panic. His chest tightened. He was too weak to protect himself.

"N-no Max... imilian. Not Vespa. I will—" He tried to raise himself farther up the wall, but his arms shook with violent spasms. He pleaded, "Vespa mustn't feed." Blackness threatened to overtake Marceau. He would not stay conscious long. How could he stop this? "Sir, the auction. I will not be able to recover in time if she... if she feeds on me." Marceau's arms were giving out. He sat back against the white wall and listened to the click-clack of her heels as Vespa approached the ballroom. "Please."

"Oh, all right. I suppose I am pleased with my new ballerina. Vespa, you are to nurse and care for him only. Absolutely no feeding. Am I clear?"

Vespa's whine of protest was the last sound Marceau heard before the pressing darkness won.

Chapter Four

Seraphina sat in the classic GTO, rubbing her hands together while the engine warmed. An unexpected cold front was moving in and the howling wind pelted heavy raindrops against the windshield. She was surprised Finn had asked her to drive him to the Woodard house because he never wanted her to come along for his jobs. She'd always wondered whether he feared her magic's affinity with the dead, or if he thought she'd see him as more normal somehow if she didn't witness his power in action. Seraphina hated the contempt other supernaturals showed him, at least until it was their turn to ask him to eat the sins of their loved ones.

Cold air interrupted her thoughts as Finn opened the door and climbed in the car. The slight shake of his hands was unusual. Finn rarely acted nervous about anything.

"Sorry I took so long. All set now, love."

Finn had changed into his usual Sin Eater outfit: a black V-neck T-shirt, black jeans, and black Doc Martens. His pale skin was a stark contrast to his attire.

Years ago, she had made the mistake of asking why he "went all Johnny Cash every time he had a job?"

She'd never forgotten his response, "Death is messy, even for supernaturals, black hides the blood."

Finn gave her a few directions and once they were on the interstate, he cleared his throat and turned to her.

"I need to make sure you understand what happens when I eat sin. I wish I didn't need you on this job, but it is a troublesome situation."

"Why is this one so different?"

"I'll explain in a moment. First, the basics. You probably know most of this, but I need to be sure since this will be your first time witnessing what I do in person."

Seraphina nodded.

"Evil enough deeds in life, when left unatoned, create a spiritual vacuum in supernaturals. Upon death, the body can become an empty vessel. It lies vulnerable if a supernatural in the shadow realm is strong enough to take hold."

Seraphina knew all about the Possessed, but they were a taboo topic for supernaturals. Plus, Finn almost never opened up about being a Sin Eater, so she nodded and listened.

"Possessed are unpredictable and deadly. Sometimes they've waited decades, even centuries, to cross back into our realm. They don't usually understand modern society or care for our rules, whether human or supernatural. Possessed threaten the anonymity of the supernatural community through their reckless actions and could garner the attention of the Conexus. Obviously, no supernatural wants to be on their radar."

She asked, "So is that why the families seek out your services? For fear of Conexus reprimands?"

"Fear and also pride. Possessed aren't easy to recognize, and humans certainly don't know of them. They often tarnish the reputations of both the dead and their remaining family."

Finn was silent a few minutes. Seraphina glanced at him as he pulled on the strap of his seat belt while lost in thought. He took a deep breath and continued, "As a Sin Eater, I ingest the unatoned sins of the most evil supernaturals. With my aid, their bodies lie at rest. My power pulls their negative energy into a chalice and knife. I channel energy into the bread and red wine. When I consume the sins, I relive each one from the perspective of the sinner. Actually, I think most supernaturals understand much of what I do, but there's more to being a Sin Eater, Seraphina. I also witness the consequences suffered by any victims. I relive the sin from their perspective and experience any pain or emotion they felt, for only then is true penance paid."

As his words sank in, Seraphina's heart ached for him. "Finn, I didn't know. I cannot even imagine what you must have suffered all these years."

For a long time, she'd worried about losing Finn to the sins he consumed. His moods swung without warning. One moment he could be joking and like his old self, the next he could shut down and spend days barely speaking. But he'd seemed better lately. His sense of humor had returned. In fact, his pranks were getting a bit out of hand. He had become less prone to violent mood swings. What had changed?

Kandy. He'd been spending more time with Kandy (with a K) lately.

Finn was silent again, only giving directions here and there. "Turn left just ahead. This is the road and the Woodard Manor is a few miles down. You'll see a large iron gate banked by lion statues."

They'd reached Belle Meade. The land of antebellum mansions, country clubs, and old money.

After a couple miles, she said, "Almost all these houses have gates and statues. How can I tell which one it is?"

"Trust me, this one will stand out to you."

"Well, that's certainly mysterious." At the next bend in the road, ripples of dark magic flowed ahead. "Oh." Seraphina turned onto the drive and stopped abruptly. She leaned forward and pressed her chest against the steering wheel to see up past the car's roof. Finn was right. No supernatural would ever miss the red glow of spelled markings ingrained on the large marble gateposts. When turning the windshield wipers to their highest setting, lightning lit the sky and for a moment, and she could clearly see the expressions on the frightening, snarling lion statues atop the spelled gateposts. Imposing, spike-tipped gates stood open, revealing a long winding, cobblestone driveway. She eased on the gas and the hair on her arms rose as she neared the statues. At the iron gate, Seraphina gasped, shock traveling all the way down her body, making her squeeze the steering wheel and curling her toes painfully under as dark, stinging magic slapped against her skin.

Finn wrapped his arms tight around his own waist and exhaled. The dark magical barrier was barely restrained from harming visitors, for now at least.

She looked at Finn and raised her eyebrow. What if they were trapped *inside?*

Finn answered her unspoken question, "Old Man Woodard, Phyllis and Virgil's father, was a bit... territorial. His name was Odol and he was a Possessed. His body was held by something ancient and without mercy. He was one of the most evil, psychotic bastards I've had the misfortune of meeting. In my line of work, that's truly saying a lot."

"A Possessed? In Nashville? So that's why the gateposts had such strange markings? What if we can't leave?"

The GTO's left front tire ran slightly off the edge of the long driveway, the pounding rain-fed streams of runoff and fallen leaves making it impossible to tell how deeply the ground dropped off along their path. This was definitely not the place to get her car stuck.

"We won't be trapped here. Odol disappeared a long time ago. And Virgil is on his deathbed, or trust me, we wouldn't be here. Phyllis has no active powers. She knows of our community but keeps her distance because she fancies herself to be more human, and, therefore, better than the rest of us."

Seraphina interrupted, "If we're so safe, then why has your leg been bouncing the whole car ever since we left? And why did you finally ask me along? I've offered to assist before and you always refused. Why are you so nervous about this one, Finn?"

"Because evil is as deeply rooted here as these old oaks. Don't be deceived into thinking Virgil is anything other than dangerous, no matter how weak he seems. Odol fed his tainted blood to his son before Virgil ever had a chance to nurse from his human mother. One drop insured Virgil was as close to Odol's natural born son as possible, despite the weaker supernatural body Odol possessed during the conception. Virgil's lesser DNA suppresses some of the power from being the offspring of a Possessed, but he's lacked none of the brutality."

"And Phyllis? You said she's human?" Seraphina swallowed, thinking about how she had basically hexed the woman earlier.

"Not fully, no. Phyllis was spared only because Odol felt a female child was unworthy of his *gift*. In fact, her human mother took her away at birth, and Phyllis never met her father. She was raised in a convent. Hence, her propensity toward religious fervor." Finn smiled, but it didn't reach his eyes. "By the time Phyllis returned to this house, her father had disappeared. And good riddance. The death count in Nashville took a considerable dip after Odol was gone."

Seraphina pulled to a stop in a circular drive. The six-columned antebellum mansion should have been beautiful. It was reminiscent of the Parthenon replica downtown. Closer, however, the limestone mansion's beauty was marred by grotesque figures coiling around the columns and perched along the roof.

She turned and stared, but Finn would not meet her eyes. Instead, he reached back to get the old-fashioned leather satchel he'd thrown in the back seat. He opened the bag and drew out a black hooded cloak. The car's interior lights reflected off a curious assortment of silver implements inside. Seraphina again broke the momentary silence. "What aren't you telling me here? I can tell you're holding something back."

"It was rumored Virgil could absorb powers, could feed on the abilities of other supernaturals."

"How is that even possible?"

Finn shrugged. "I don't know for sure it is. Virgil could've started the rumor himself to invoke fear in the supernatural community. After Odol's disappearance, Virgil began running an underground mafia of sorts. He leads a syndicate of criminals who traffic occult items and offer dark magic services. He's ruthless. I fear he has more sin than ten ordinary supernaturals, and it will take a lot out of me to perform this ceremony, love. If there is any truth to his ability to feed on power, I need you here to watch my back."

"Then why are you taking this job?"

"I promised Willa, Virgil's mother, and I have to honor that obligation. I feel responsible for her meeting Odol because I didn't know he was a Possessed when I sent her here on an errand, just a simple pick up of some herbs for one of my experiments. It was back when you were… you know… gone."

Seraphina nodded.

Finn continued, "Anyway, it should've been a quick in and out. Willa wasn't a supernatural, so the barriers here wouldn't hurt her. She stopped coming around, but I thought little of it. You know how flighty humans can be. A few weeks later, I ran into her and knew something was off. I asked around and soon realized she was living here. I tried to warn her, but being human, she didn't believe in possession, well, until it was much too late. Then one day, Willa came with baby Phyllis in her arms and begged me to do what I could for her son. I helped her and Phyllis escape Nashville and arranged for her to stay at the convent. Virgil grew up here and was a cruel, heartless bastard all his life. I couldn't change what he was, but I promised his mother I'd do what I could to ease his sins at death."

Seraphina let his words sink in. Typical Finn... to shoulder the responsibility for someone else's poor choice. Look at all he'd endured because of her. "So you're risking everything because you feel guilty? I get that you promised her, and I can even see why, but this sounds really, really dangerous."

"I'm hoping the rumors of Virgil's deeds and powers are just that, rumors. I asked you along in case he tries to attack me before I can finish. You can use your power to hold him. He's already dying, so your magic can't backfire and hurt him. Together, we can make sure his evil ends tonight. Everything will probably be like normal, maybe just a longer hangover, right?" He winked at her.

Finn's little *hangovers* knocked him on his butt when the sins were strong enough. The thought scared her.

He continued, "Virgil is dying. I called and confirmed Phyllis' story. That's what took me so long earlier. Audra, Nashville's favorite witch-for-hire, confirmed Phyllis has been throwing money at any healer brave enough to come out here for the past month. She was surprised Virgil was still alive, given how unnaturally frail he was when she was here a few days ago."

"All right, I'm here. You're here. He sounds weak—despite his scary pedigree—so let's just get it done and over with. This place is creeping me out."

Finn nodded. "Thank you, love."

"Come on then." Seraphina raised the hood on her jacket and opened the car door. She had to grab it tightly with both hands when a gust of wind threatened to take the door off its hinges. She slammed it closed and ran up the stairs as fast as she could. The black robe whipped around Finn's body as he put it on while ascending behind her.

The monstrous figures snaking up the mansion's posts seemed to watch Seraphina. Wait, did one just *look* at her?

"Don't make eye contact with them," Finn warned.

Seraphina snapped her eyes downward and didn't dare ask why. She was scared enough. The towering cherry wood door opened as they approached, and a solemn man gestured for them to enter.

"Addams," Finn said.

"It is good to see you again, Sin Eater." Addams's distinct, Southern voice was so deep it rumbled like thunder.

Just before crossing the threshold, Finn paused to raise the hood on his robe and hide his face.

Phyllis waited inside. To Seraphina, the rooms of the ornate mansion were a blur as they were rushed through the foyer. Phyllis led them up an elaborate carpeted staircase accented with gold scrolls and blood red roses.

Because she took quick glances around at the lush surroundings instead of paying close attention, Seraphina caught her foot on the runner. She would have fallen if Finn had not caught her elbow and kept her upright. He'd never lifted his hood or turned his head, and yet he caught her. When her footing was secure, he released her elbow.

"Thanks," she whispered.

He did not respond as they hurried down a long hallway and turned through a set of golden doors covered in carvings so detailed she imagined plucking a piece of fruit from the engravings. They stopped in a dark, wood-paneled parlor. Marble busts of men she did not recognize sat between full bookshelves. The smell of leather, old books, and cigars was oddly comforting. Above a black marble fireplace, almost as tall as she, hung the portrait of a man with so much intensity in his expression, Seraphina took in a sharp breath when studying his face. She'd never seen a painting so detailed and realistic. The effect was startling because the man had both a look of keen intellect and a complete lack of human compassion. She silently hoped was *not* Virgil Woodard.

Finn whispered, "If this is too much, you can wait out here."

"No, no… of course not. I'll assist you. I can warn you if I feel energy pushing between the realms. When the veil opens. I'm sure it would help you to know. I'll even lay out the wine and bread, whatever you need." Besides, there was no way she was staying out in the creepy, dark parlor with that maniacal painting staring at her. She had goosebumps but found it nearly impossible to turn away from the eyes in the painting.

Finn's comment broke her concentration. "What I need is for you to be safe. I'm second-guessing you being here at all. Do you feel the dark magic pouring off that damned painting?"

Swallowing, almost choking, Seraphina nodded. She forced herself to turn her back on it. Her senses were messing with her, and she rolled her shoulder, trying to ignore a tingling sensation crawling up her spine. The painting was really staring at her.

"I'll handle the ceremony. I want you focused on protecting yourself," Finn said. Sensing her incoming protest, he raised a hand. "Your full power should be on shielding. Only help me if I directly ask you for assistance. Is that clear?"

"Yes, of course, Fi…"

"Here I am the Sin Eater. Don't speak my name where the veil is this thin and those of power may overhear. I'm in death's presence too often to be known by my given name." He reached over and quickly squeezed her hand. "S'alright, love. I'm not cross. I realize now, I shouldn't have asked you to come. But it's too late. Your job is to shield yourself."

She argued, "If I see he's hurting you, I can try to shield us both." Seraphina locked onto Finn's gaze. Her chest tightened as she recognized true fear and a hint of desperation. She hated seeing such terror in the beautifully pale eyes of her brave, steadfast friend.

"Only try if I ask, and even then if it goes badly, I want you to pull back from me and focus on yourself. Remember, I am a Sin Eater. I can endure much. Strength is gained from my suffering. Promise me."

"I promise… Sin Eater."

The tall double doors next to them creaked open, and together they entered a grand master bedroom, the likes of which Seraphina had never imagined.

Chapter Five

Splitting pain throbbed with each beat of his pulse. Marceau rolled over and pressed his palms against his forehead. He expected daylight when he opened his eyes, but the room was dark. Looking for his phone, he turned to his side.

What *day* was it?

His bedside table wasn't there. Marceau sat up and searched for signs of familiarity. The room was too dark to make out much, but he wasn't in his apartment, that much was for sure.

A door in the far corner opened, and someone entered.

"Hello?" Marceau called. He pressed fingers against his temples. Note to self: Noises *hurt.*

The silhouette approached with quiet footsteps.

"Who are you? Where am I?"

"You woke up too soon. I haven't had any fun yet," whined Vespa.

Marceau scooted farther on the bed until his back pressed against the headboard. "Vespa, turn on the lights."

With a click, a light came on, blinding him. Marceau squinted. Patches of darkness clouded his vision, but he recognized the room. He was still at Max's mansion.

Vespa stood at the foot of the bed wearing Marceau's Tulane University T-shirt and little else. She was beautiful. All of Max's chosen were breathtaking creatures. He had an eye for feminine beauty and unashamedly collected dangerous women like fine art. Vespa's unusual serpentine qualities made her one Max's favorite little pets. Her body and voice were weapons. Every move she made was sensuous and hypnotic to entrance her victims, reminding Marceau of a deadly cobra charming her prey. But Vespa's beauty was only skin-deep, Marceau knew, beneath the sexy façade, she was a cruel, heartless bitch.

Marceau shifted the covers, relieved to feel his boxers.

"You must be thirsty." Vespa rounded the bed and handed him a glass of water.

Marceau accepted the offering, and asked, "How long have I been here?"

"You slept all day. It's a little after nine. You missed dinner."

Marceau did a feelings check. He seemed normal. A bit weak, but otherwise okay. He took a drink. "You left me alone?"

Vespa rolled her eyes and sat on the side of the bed. "I was a good girl. Just put you to bed as Maximilian ordered. He made me promise to let you recuperate without interference."

Marceau nodded and noticed a patch of reptilian skin showing on her upper thigh. She hadn't fed for a while. Hunger was letting her true nature peek through. He took another drink. "Thanks for that. I fly out tomorrow afternoon."

Vespa smiled. "I hoped we could have a little fun before your trip to Nashville."

She knew where he was going. Marceau hadn't told her, must have been Max. Vespa's face stretched. Her head lengthened like a balloon.

"Wha…"

Light and shadow swirled. Marceau dropped the glass and slapped his hands against the bed as his head rocked back. He was spinning. The room tilted.

"Sorry, lover. I kept my promise and now you've recuperated. But I want more snuggle time before you leave."

"N-no."

Chapter Six

Everything in the room was either black or a deep red. Red damask with black trim covered the walls. Ornate black furnishings, large vases of red roses, and a library of books filled the shelves—each bound in aged red or black leather. Flames cracked and popped in an equally impressive black marble fireplace casting dancing light around the otherwise dimly lit room.

Seraphina's eyes were drawn to lit curio cabinets in each corner. Most supernaturals had a similar, though smaller, curio to hold their magical devices. Here, four huge ones were the main focal point in this one bedroom. She'd bet money that dangerous spells existed to protect the daggers, scrolls, cloudy bottles, and strange bones visible behind the glass. Wincing at a jar with fleshy contents she did not want to identify, she was afraid to ask. Eyes? No, stop thinking about it. Do *not* look back at that cabinet too closely.

Unbridled magic caused blood to thrum in her veins. Each corner of the room pulled at her. Seraphina's insides felt as though they were being stretched. She tried to breathe against the weight squeezing her chest. Her long, red hair rose from her back, undulating in the waves of power.

Whispers.

She tilted her head and listened. Promises of pleasure, pain, or of both if she would only caress the magical instruments. Ecstasy, if she would only unleash them.

Seraphina took a step toward the nearest cabinet. Quick as a flash, Finn's hand shot out and grabbed her shoulder in a crushing hold until the pain was sharp enough to temporarily clear her head.

A figure lying on the huge carved bed in front of them jerked violently. Phyllis sobbed at the bedside and pressed her fist to her lips.

"Now." Finn jerked Seraphina's shoulder. "Shield right now. His collection has grown to nightmare proportions. If he is sensing your ability..."

Seraphina locked down her thoughts and focused only on her skin. She squeezed her eyes shut and visualized a glowing layer of power coating her skin. Starting in her hands, the shield danced across her fingertips as soft as a feather and gained strength as it spread to her elbow and over her shoulders. It climbed, covering her face, caressing her eyelashes, up higher, circling her head. Seraphina's hair fell back onto her shoulders as the shield cut off the wild magic swirling through the bedroom. The magic whooshed downward swirling firmly around her torso, and finally down each leg to her toes. With her shield closed, Seraphina's power settled against her flesh while she mentally pushed outward and fed it more strength until it heated her skin. She opened her eyes and looked at the bed in front of her.

Virgil spasmed again. The red sheet that had covered him fell back as his skeletal torso arched upward and his heels dug into the mattress. The emaciated body took a wheezing breath.

"What the hell did you do, Phyllis?" Finn asked. "His body's been eaten away while you tried to stop his death... It's unnatural. It's an abomination."

Seraphina's shield flared as if reacting to a desperate power grab. Looking down at the dying man should have upset her, but instead, she felt disconnected from the scene playing out around her. She normally sensed emotions and intentions from others. Sometimes she could even predict their movements, but now she seemed adrift in her own body. Fear had driven her to infuse her shield with more power than ever before and the effect was dizzying. Confusion clouded her mind and dulled her senses.

Virgil collapsed back onto the four poster bed. With a long, rasping exhale, his body went slack.

"Hurry and get the offerings ready, he's dying." Finn's tone and physical expression matched. The situation was dire.

Phyllis did not move.

"Phyllis," he shouted.

She jumped and snapped her head up.

"It has to be *right now,*" ordered Finn.

Seraphina watched dispassionately as Finn ran to the right side of the massive bed. The satin sheets glimmered in the firelight. He threw his bag on a marble bedside table and almost knocked over a lit candelabra. Tearing open the flat bottomed satchel, he grabbed a wide-mouthed silver chalice. The runes etched along the vessel's base flared bright white at his touch.

Seraphina swayed slightly. A dark shimmer formed in the air above the bed. Cold, stale air blew across her face, and she recoiled at its damp stench.

"Veil," she said.

Finn's shoulders tensed under his flowing cloak. He whispered something to Phyllis, and she looked up at Seraphina, who cocked her head. She could not hear them over the thundering pulse in her ears.

Phyllis poured red wine into the chalice and spilled it all over her own shaking arm in her haste. She shook her head and tossed the bottle over her shoulder behind her, caring nothing for the opulent rug on which the half full bottle landed.

A dark wave of energy flowed across Seraphina's shield. It breached her defense and stroked her cheek. Her throat constricted when a feathery voice whispered, "Drink."

"I'm so thirsty," Seraphina said and stepped nearer the bed.

Finn used a matching runed silver knife to hack a jagged slice from a loaf of bread.

"Eat," whispered the seductive voice. The word echoed in her ears as if from a deep canyon.

She lifted her face and inhaled. Seraphina was overwhelmed with the earthy scent of freshly baked bread. The smell of the yeast dough was so intoxicating, she could almost taste it on the back of her tongue. Her mouth watered as she imagined biting into the crusty outer edge. She swallowed, thinking of how the soft bread would melt against her palate and groaning as the warm, slightly sweet taste flooded her senses. Unknowingly, she'd taken a few steps forward.

Finn threw back his cloak's hood and yelled at her, "Shield. Step back and shield yourself, Seraphina."

She didn't hesitate, but stepped forward rather than back.

"Get her out of here. Something's wrong. She shouldn't be drawn to eat the sin," ordered Finn.

Seraphina sensed, rather than saw, commotion around her. A flash of black fabric distracted her as an arm tried to grab her.

No.

Why would anyone try to stop her from tasting the bread? Why shouldn't she quench her overwhelming thirst with the rich, velvety wine?

Addams tried again to wrap himself around Seraphina and pull her back to safety.

Don't *touch* me.

Angrily, her mind pushed him away even harder. A heavy weight landed behind her after she heard a masculine grunt and glass crashing to the floor.

Addams lay unconscious, as crumpled as a broken doll against the wall. Seraphina hadn't even blinked when she cast him back with such violence.

She had almost reached the black wooden bed post.

The voice promised, "Nothing you've ever drunk could possibly compare to the rich wine in the silver chalice. No bread could ever equal the thick slices cut with that beautiful, silver knife."

Seraphina braved another step. Just one sip. Only one bite. She would be forever sated. Her skin flushed as she imagined feasting on the bounty before her. A wave of dizziness made her reach out blindly and grab the bedpost for support. Her shield shuddered against a powerful, familiar energy. The veil was open.

On the bed, the corpse inhaled a sudden loud breath. The dead man shook violently on the huge mattress. He sat up and locked glowing eyes with hers. Sagging skin exposed the pink inner flesh of his eyelids. His stiff arms extended slowly outward and forced his sleeves up, revealing impossibly thin arms. He was so pale and opaque that blue veins corded beneath his skin. The maw of the skeletal face opened and revealed blackened gums with teeth sharper than any normal man should have. His eyes had already clouded over with a slight pallor of death, yet the opalescent pupils were intently focused on Seraphina's green eyes.

The corpse ripped the neck of his damp pajamas open and exposed an age-spotted chest. He appeared so frail that each unnatural beat of his heart fluttered frantically, visibly beneath his skin. His ribs creaked as they expanded and contracted to draw deep breaths. A noise wheezed from his throat, at first, whisper soft, but it grew stronger with each breath. The echoing, hollow sound increased into a screech.

He screamed, "Free me, girl. Eat the bread, drink the wine, and free me."

Seraphina shook her head and tried to focus. The man before her screamed with such ferocity that long lines of spit dribbled down from his chin. His body shook in the moments before he inhaled deeply, followed by another scream. Veins stood out on his neck in unnatural ways and his head tilted back as he shrieked, "I am Odol. Eat. Drink. I command you to release me."

Phyllis cried in terror at her brother's transformation.

Seraphina took a long step back.

With a loud crack, Virgil's jaw broke from the intensity of his screams. The bottom half of his face drooped against the rise and fall of his bared bony chest.

His gray tongue flicked from side to side as if it had a mind of its own. He had lost the ability to form distinguishable words, but his blood-curdling screeches continued.

A faint thread of fear made Seraphina step back again. But it was as if someone else stood in the opulent room witnessing the terrible scene while she observed from a safe distance. Her head rocked back as another wave of dark magic pulsed through her. She was reminded of the thick, velvety wine the woman had poured into the chalice and the browned, buttery crust of the bread. Seraphina leaned in and inhaled, pushing her senses beyond the smells of sickness, sweat, and death that emanated from the unfortunate man on the bed. She wanted to find the intoxicating aromas of the wine, the yeasty notes of the bread.

The possessed man continued to scream as Finn and the corpse's sister looked on in absolute horror. Finn supported Phyllis's weight. She was too gripped by terror for her previous aversion to his touch now. When he let go of Phyllis, Finn snatched the ceremonial silver knife from the bed and plunged it deep into the corpse's chest.

Seraphina screamed and clutched her own chest.

Dark blood sprayed across the dead man's chest and onto Finn's pale face in fine droplets.

The darkness gripping her mind slipped, and Seraphina pushed against it with all her might.

Virgil's possessed heart slowed when the magically blessed silver dagger had penetrated its chambers. Congealed blood spurted from the wound with each heartbeat.

A thick sucking noise came from Odol's throat as his scream lowered again to a moan, and then to a mere whisper.

The corpse shot Finn a final look of hatred before it fell backward, blood flowing down its ribs onto the bed.

Seraphina dropped to her knees… gasping for air… the fog in her mind clearing. "Wh-what was that?"

Finn answered, "Odol tried to possess Virgil's body, but in its weakened condition, he could not keep his hold. I believe he was trying to get you to ingest his sins and somehow possess you." Finn helped her up. "I've never seen anything like it. Are you okay?"

"I think so. I wanted to——"

Finn interrupted, "I want you to leave. Now. Go. Wait outside. I still have to finish here, but you should go."

"No, Finn. I understand this now. I was able to expel his grip on my mind. We have to hurry, but I think I can shield us both for a short time."

"Sera…"

She grabbed Finn's left hand and began reconstructing her shield, this time sending the energy over and around them both. When the force was in place, Seraphina focused all her energy on strengthening it.

Now, Finn.

Finn's hand tightened, and he turned to her, his eyes wide. *I heard you in my mind, love.*

She nodded. *I hear you too. Just do it while I have the strength to hold the shield in place. A black mist is swirling around the body. It's darkening. I think Odol's coming back.*

Finn shook his head. His eyes pleading. *I can see his sins. Innumerable ones have transferred from Odol and now fester on Virgil's corpse. You might feel them too.*

Seraphina said out loud, "There's no time for this. The mist is flowing back into his body. Eat his sins now. Drink the wine, hurry."

Phyllis grabbed the chalice of expensive, French wine and held it out to Finn. "Here, drink of my brother's sins. Please, lay him to rest like you promised our mother."

Finn sucked in his lower lip and nodded. His anguish was tangible to Seraphina as he made his decision. He raised the black hood back over his head. She understood. He wore the hood to hide the pain he suffered during the ceremony.

Finn took the chalice and held it over the body. The runes on the silver cup shifted their glow from white to bright red. Raising it to his lips, he knew he'd have to drink far more than just the sins of Virgil now.

The dagger would not hold Odol for long. Already, the wound was trying to close and push the dagger out.

Finn choked as he drank the thick, viscous wine. Thoughts of Seraphina kept him swallowing despite the wine's rancid taste. Long ago, he had sworn to protect her. He'd already gone to extraordinary lengths to keep his word, and now he gathered his strength to finish the putrid brew.

Extraordinary lengths? Seraphina asked.

Finn's posture stiffened as he lowered the chalice while Phyllis placed the ceremonial black cloth on her brother's bloodied chest and laid a piece of bread on the cloth.

"Better make it two slices." Finn coughed beneath his black cloak. His shoulders quaked as he fought to not heave and choke. His hand tightened on Seraphina's. She was gagging too.

Phyllis placed the second piece of bread on Virgil's corpse and stepped away.

He and Seraphina both shuddered, sharing the thought of how the bread would taste. Finn glanced at her. *The wine only creates the link with the sinner. The bread holds the sin. I will not let you experience that. Release me. I will finish the ceremony alone.*

She shook her head side to side.

Release my hand or we leave and the corpse lies unprotected. I will not have you ingest his sins, Seraphina.

"Are you sure you can?" Seraphina whispered.

"Only one way to find out."

He squeezed her hand, then pulled his away.

Seraphina took one long stride away from the bed. But instead of severing the shield, she pushed more power toward him, adding a wall around her own thoughts to keep Finn from knowing she still shielded him.

With a deep breath, Finn bit into the first piece of bread. Images flooded Seraphina's mind. They flashed like images on a screen. Men had been beaten and hung from a second-story patio of this very house in the pursuit of Virgil's illicit business.

The roof of Seraphina's mouth ached, and she realized Finn's was burning and blistered as if scorched by hot molten liquid. Through the opening in his hood, she watched his throat convulse when he choked down yet another bite. Violent images of people being tortured flashed through her mind once more. Manacles, whips, red molten brands, Virgil had enjoyed torturing his enemies.

Finn had swallowed three large bites before the horrified screams of the victims forced his gag reflex to kick in. The echoes of their screams overwhelmed Seraphina, and she pressed her hands against her ears. She wanted to drop her shield from Finn, anything to stop the ringing screeches of pain, but she held fast.

Finn's body lurched forward as he continued to force down the bread.

More images flashed before their eyes—explosions, pools of blood, corpses, and a beautiful, young woman with bruises and torn clothes.

Poor Willa. Finn couldn't imagine her pain even now, experiencing it second-hand. He managed to finish the last bite as her shrieks echoed through his mind. Miraculously, he'd completed the first piece of sin-laced bread.

Seraphina checked the corpse. The dagger was free and lay at the body's side. Blood streamed up the ribs and back into the wound. Odol was recuperating.

Finn had to hurry to consume the second piece of bread before the corpse recovered from the dagger wound, or all would be lost.

Seraphina wanted to collapse from the effort of holding her shield around them both and the horror of seeing the sins Finn had ingested. She locked her knees and reached out for the bedpost to keep herself upright. Fearing the worst was yet to come, Seraphina pushed even more power into their protection.

By then, Finn had picked up the second piece of bread. He took the first bite and swallowed it with minimal chewing.

More gruesome images of torture played in their minds with so many victims burned, the faces blurred together in a torrent of pain. The tools of torture were older, more severe. These sins were much too old for Virgil to have committed them. The sins of the father now flooded their consciousness. How many sins had Virgil siphoned from his father during the brief possession?

Seraphina felt Finn's internal struggle. He'd eaten countless sins and relived the most evil, desperate deeds of the supernaturals he serviced. But never had he struggled so much to complete his duty.

Again, he pictured Seraphina and drew strength from his promise to her. Tears flowed down her cheeks when she realized he used his love for her and their friendship to hold his sanity while he consumed the evil of others. Another bite and one of Finn's teeth loosened as his gums were singed by the blazing sins he consumed.

Atrocities throughout the ages flooded Seraphina's mind until she honed in on a medieval dungeon. Desperate pleas rang out from men whose hope for survival had been abandoned long ago. The disfigured prisoners begged for the mercy only death could provide.

Finn swallowed down the sin. One more bite and he would finish his task. Steeling himself for the worst, Finn placed the now rotten, blackened bread on his tongue and groaned as images of children sprang before his eyes.

The corpse breathed in a long choked breath and exhaled in a gleeful, hissing laugh. It was too late for Odol to survive, but he was laughing at the immense pain the Sin Eater endured.

Seraphina gagged. Her thoughts and senses were overwhelmed by the past evil deeds of Virgil and Odol. The Possessed had fed on the innocent to sate his hellish hunger.

How had Finn been able to endure this? She wasn't eating or feeling the sin, merely witnessing it, and she feared she would never be the same. Horrified, Seraphina's shield finally collapsed. She fell to her knees and sobbed. No strength left.

Finn swallowed down the last bite and grasped his stomach. He slowly lowered himself onto the floor, easing near where she knelt and curling into a ball, wracked by full body retching. He fought off the waves of nausea.

Seraphina had never deluded herself into believing his power was pleasant, but in her worst nightmares, she never comprehended the extent of his suffering.

Finn's body convulsed and his muscles clenched. He cried out, unwilling to release evil back into the world, containing the sin at any cost.

Their link was severed, but she understood Finn must be feeling the sins from the perspective of the victims by now. He'd told her it was the final step before atonement.

Seraphina gently pulled him into her lap and rocked, comforting him the best she could. She whispered soothing phrases hoping he could hear her. At last, Finn's body stilled and he drifted into merciful unconsciousness as the penance was paid. The energy and power from the sins had dissipated.

She pulled back his hood and wiped away the tears streaming down his face.

Virgil's body was finally at rest, and Odol was cast out. They were all safe.

Seraphina spoke around the knot in her throat, "Phyllis, we would like to go home now. But I'm not sure I can drive."

The tearful woman stood and pushed away from the wall she'd been using for support. She smoothed back her hair and shook Addams' shoulder. He awoke and started to stand. "Help Finn to the car. Take them home and see they make it safely."

Addams rose on shaky legs, also using the wall for support.

"Should I drive them myself?" Phyllis snapped.

"No, of course not, ma'am." Addams shook his head. He carefully picked up Finn, cradling him in his arms like a child.

Phyllis helped Seraphina to her feet.

Addams drove them back to the apothecary and carried Finn, unconscious and burning with fever, to his room.

Seraphina's thoughts replayed the images and sounds from Virgil's bedside. She feared she was going into shock because it seemed like a dream or a movie she had watched more than actual events. Already, she'd forgotten the worst images in self protection. But those sins had nearly destroyed her best friend.

Finn needed her full attention now. She had nursed him on many occasions after eating heavy sin, but his current condition was obviously more dire than she wanted to admit.

Seraphina tried to ignore the temptation she'd felt deep in her bones to open herself to the Possessed. Tonight, she would let her mind stay busy and distracted.

In the light of day tomorrow, however, she'd have to face the temptation. The overwhelming desire she'd felt to her core had called for a surrender to evil. What had she almost done? Yes, she definitely had questions for Finn, if he survived and was sane enough to answer them.

Chapter Seven

Marceau awoke when a body pressed against his chest. His arms felt heavy, like lead, yet were suspended above him. He moved numb fingers, opened his eyes, but couldn't focus well in the faint light. Something dug into his wrists, and he tried to pull his hands up to his face, but his shoulders lifted instead.

Restraints.

Vespa.

Marceau jerked against the manacles on his wrists. The heavy wooden headboard rattled but nothing else moved.

"Sh, be still, Marceau," a voice whispered.

The person on top of him shifted slightly, and the binding of his left wrist loosened.

"Lynette?"

"I said to shush," Lynette said. "I'm not supposed to be in here."

Marceau pulled his hand free. She moved across his chest, tugging, trying to find slack in his other restraint. He reached up to help and was able to slip his hand out.

Lynette slid off him and murmured, "Hurry. Everyone else is still asleep. Vespa went out to feed, but I don't know for how long."

Marceau rubbed his wrists. "She must've drugged me. Something in a glass of water."

Lynette whispered, "You should have known better than to trust her." She stood after her second try and threw a pile of clothes at his chest. "Dress. Hurry. I'll meet you in the hallway."

Opening a curtain as she left, he noticed the sun rising. It had to be Friday. There was no way Vespa would risk angering Max by keeping Marceau from his trip to Nashville.

Marceau slid on a white T-shirt and winced. He lifted it and ran his hand across his skin. Finely lined cuts traced down his stomach, some circled in red lipstick. Vespa hadn't fed in her preferred way, but she'd found a way to taste him anyway.

Slipping into jeans and buttoning them as he stormed out, Marceau met Lynette down the hall. She held up an old pair of his shoes. He hopped on one foot while pulling on each tennis shoe.

"I owe you one, Lynette."

"At this point, you owe me ten."

She held out his car keys and smiled. Marceau started to take them, then paused. She was probably right. Lynette was certainly not anything near a maternal figure for him, but she had been a constant presence in his life. And she'd been there when it truly counted, helping him get out of trouble. He'd tried to return the favor when he was younger, but in the past few years, he avoided the manor as much as possible.

Marceau asked, "The ballerina?"

"She's resting in my room. But I'd stay clear of Babette for a while if I were you. She's blaming you as much as Maximilian for what happened. I'll explain things after she's had more time to accept everything. I think she has some kind of power, Marceau. We'll need her as an ally."

Marceau nodded and finally accepted the keys. He stared at them, deciding. "Max's punishments are getting worse, but you still try to escape. Wherever you try to go… you know he will find you."

Lynette's smile dropped. "I know I'll never be free from him. Honestly, I gave up that dream long ago, but I have to keep trying. Otherwise, I'll go insane. I'll be like him. I know I'll never get far, but to feel freedom for just a little while… to walk alone in the city… see humanity and normal life… have time to myself where he isn't nearby. That's why I run."

Marceau's decision was made. He grasped the key and twisted it free of the key chain. He'd carried it every day for three years. His own secret little insurance policy.

Marceau held it out to Lynette.

"What's that for?"

"For helping me."

She took the key and turned it in her palm. It seemed only a mundane skeleton key, tarnished and nicked. She blinked at it and took a breath. "I feel it. It's charmed. Magic is tightly wound around it."

Marceau said, "It was costly. You must use it only in an emergency, Lynette. This key will only work once. If you ever need to escape. Put the key in my workshop's door and turn it to the left three times."

"What will it do?"

"When you walk through the door, you will enter my apartment in the Garden District."

Lynette gasped. She grabbed Marceau and hugged him tightly. "Thank you. You can't believe what it means to have an out. Just knowing I have it will help me so much."

He hugged her back and leaned away, looking into her mismatched eyes. "Only in an emergency, Lynette, and you must promise to never reveal where you got it. Max has no idea it even exists. It took me years to construct the right hex, and I had to hire the Mambo to bind the other door. She's the only other person who knows the doors are linked. Max would punish me for that, severely."

Lynette nodded and whispered, "I promise." She grabbed his arms and pushed him toward the door. "Now go, Marceau. Go to Nashville and enjoy every moment you have away from this place, away from him."

Marceau kissed her cheek and left.

If the Blackthorne Grimoire held the answers he hoped, Marceau would try his best to free Lynette.

And the ballerina too. He owed her that much.

Chapter Eight

Seraphina wrung her hands as she looked out Finn's bedroom window. It was Friday. His fever should have broken by now. For the last two days, she'd applied cool herbal compresses, given him small sips of cold water and his favorite teas to keep him hydrated, and did countless healing spells.

Finn's shivering had finally slowed, but he still suffered with occasional waves of uncontrollable shaking that rattled his teeth together and spasmed his whole body. His face remained flushed and his skin burned with fever. Previously, he'd never lost consciousness after taking sins.

What had eating Virgil Woodard's sin done to him?

Seraphina's heart ached each time she thought about their night at the Woodard estate. She'd certainly never believed what he did was a cake walk, but after witnessing the suffering Finn endured up close and personal? Seraphina realized what a miracle it was for him to still be sane and have retained who he was inside. She had decided not to share the horrors she had witnessed through the link her shielding created. Even though she had seen the sins, Finn had to experience them fully, and she would not remind him of that pain unless he started the dialogue. Any conversation would be welcomed at this point, however, even a difficult one. Why wasn't he awake yet?

She couldn't take Finn to a human hospital. They certainly didn't have a healing protocol for a sin overdose. Besides, who knows what effect human medicines would have on a nearly immortal Sin Eater?

Seraphina consulted every spell book she owned. She had tried incense and burned three different colors of candles. But Finn's only response was a coughing fit from the smoke. She had chanted, performed

Reiki, and even covered his pale face and chest with a green, noxious herbal poultice in a moment of desperation. Yet nothing broke his fever.

At nearly noon, Seraphina left his side for a moment and started straightening up Finn's bedroom. His clothes were thrown around on the floor. The guitar lay across a chair just as he had left it. She carefully picked it up, plucked a note, and placed the instrument on the guitar stand in the corner.

Seraphina had to make a decision about the upcoming auction soon. Tonight she was supposed to attend the Music for Youth Masquerade at the Schermerhorn Symphony Center, but she couldn't leave Finn in this condition. On the other hand, she simply had to win the book. For years, she had dreamed of an opportunity to even read it, let alone having an unbelievable opportunity to own the powerful Blackthorne Grimoire.

Could it restore her magic to the way it was *before*? What if it held the key to breaking their curse?

If anyone else in the magical community was aware the mysterious, legendary book was about to be auctioned for charity, Seraphina feared she was in for a hell of a fight. But she had a plan. Luckily, it was a silent auction.

She had been working on a spell to help her win, but her magic for such things was unreliable at best.

Now if someone had hidden the book before they died or left it guarded by a horde of vengeful spirits, that she could work with. Death magic was a real bitch sometimes.

Seraphina straightened a stack of philosophy books that seemed ready to tumble from Finn's nightstand.

Who could she possibly trust? Anyone from the local covens would not be inclined to care for a Sin Eater. Besides, they were comprised of weaker Spellcasters, and those with less power often combined their efforts. And Spellcasters were nothing if not superstitious. Spells were weaker than curses and had to draw on outside energies to sustain their power. Nature's energy, karma, and even the power derived from the mere belief in superstitions all fueled spell magic. Well, for normal, unhexed Spellcasters anyway. Most Spellcasters would treat Finn as an *untouchable* for fear of negative psychic transference and other such nonsense.

A young Miasma's vapor magic may help. She frequented the apothecary and seemed stable enough, though quiet. But the Miasma always paid cash so Seraphina didn't know how to reach her. Besides, Miasmas could be too unpredictable for something as important as this.

Seraphina could not be in two places at once. Leaving Finn alone was certainly out of the question. What if he woke up confused or his condition worsened?

And yet, the grimoire was her best chance at finally finding answers, breaking the cycle. What if it held a way to ending to this curse madness once and for all? An end to the heartbreak and death was almost too much for her to hope, after so many years. Almost.

Tears stung her eyes as Seraphina's fingers traced a Hatch Show print for an old Ferlin Husky concert hanging on the wall. She released a slow breath and relaxed her shoulders. One choice remained, and Seraphina had to force herself to admit it. Then she could stop questioning herself and get on with it.

"Finn," she whispered.

Of course, she would choose Finn. The book would just have to wait. She frowned, thinking about the mysteries, the knowledge, everything she had hoped to find within the book. Just getting an invitation to bid had cost her dearly.

As if by divine intervention, Finn's cell phone rang.

Seraphina paced in front of the shop's back door. Kandy (with a K) was due any moment. She'd called in sick from her shift at Absinthe & Alchemy, also known by the locals as "the triple-A." The AAA was the hot spot and local den of iniquity for supernaturals in Nashville.

The girl always wore heavy makeup, sequins, and little else, but Seraphina's intuition told her there was more to Kandy than met the eye. They had even shared a few playful observations about Finn to fill awkward moments, much to his chagrin.

Uneasy about leaving Finn under someone else's care, even though his fever had lowered slightly about three o'clock, she'd made her decision. She knew he'd insist she go if he was able. At last check, he seemed to be resting more comfortably. The desperation grew with every passing thought of getting the grimoire.

It's not as if he could *die*, Seraphina reminded herself for what seemed like the thousandth time. At least, she didn't think so. Still, Finn was suffering. She worried.

Her thoughts swirled and bounced all over the emotional map. Finn was a Sin Eater. He just, well he overdid it, that's all. She paced. He's weak now, but he'll be stronger than ever if he wakes up. *When.* When he wakes up. As long as Finn eats sin regularly, he's a powerful immortal and boy, oh boy, he gorged himself on sin at that damned mansion.

Knock, knock.

Seraphina started unlocking the door before the soft raps even ceased. She almost didn't recognize the woman who stood before her.

"K-Kandy?"

"Yeah, sorry if I'm a little late. Dance class ran over and then I had to walk from SoBro. The tourists are out thicker than usual today, now it has finally cooled off." She shifted a large bag from one shoulder to the other, nervous.

"No. You're not late. I'm so glad you..." Seraphina trailed off, unable to complete a thought.

Kandy looked up at her and smiled. "You all right, girl?"

"You look so different, that's all." Seraphina realized she may have sounded rude and began to backpedal, "N-not bad, different. I like it. I mean you look really pretty. Oh, but not you don't usually. It's just, you..."

Seraphina gave up and waved her hands up and down.

Kandy (with a K) was almost unrecognizable. She wore a light yellow T-shirt with a smiling pink cupcake silkscreened on the front. Seraphina snorted a laugh as she read the shirt, "Hope you like my new recipe. They're called Shut the Fucupcakes." Her well-fitting jeans had a hole in one knee, and black Converse completed her fashion statement.

Her clothes were not the main cause of Seraphina's shock, however. When had she changed her hair to brown? Soft highlights contrasted with her darker curls and stood at all angles accentuating her delicate facial features. Her face was shocking as well. For once, she had very little makeup on. The usual shimmery glitter was there dusting her brown skin, but otherwise only a touch of mascara and a light pink lip gloss? Or perhaps, her long eyelashes were naturally well-defined.

Seraphina had never, ever seen her without long blonde, teased hair and what was likely ten pounds of makeup. She usually blushed from Kandy's outfits too, all skin and stilettos.

Their eyes met and they both laughed. "It's all right, Seraphina. Honestly, I know you're used to seeing me all slutted up for work. I can understand your reaction. I'm not exactly proud of how I make my living, but I've supported myself since I was eighteen and won't apologize for it either."

"K-Kandy, I never meant…"

"Since we are making nice and all, my real name is Khatereh. Khatereh Woodard."

Seraphina stuttered, "Khatereh W-Woodard? Wait, you aren't related to…"

"Um, yeah, but just call me Khat. Imagine my surprise to see the old biddy here the other night. Aunt Phyllis can be rather dramatic, probably from growing up in the convent. I was just glad she was too worked up from thinking I was a *harlot* to stop and recognize me. I don't exactly go home for the holidays, ever, and it's not as if she's issuing invitations to her illegitimate, biracial niece anyway. Look, are we good? I wasn't expecting the chill today and forgot my jacket. Can I come in?"

"Oh jeez. Kandy—Khat. I'm so sorry. Come in, come in." Seraphina had been blocking the doorway this whole time.

"Look, I know where you and Finn went the other night, but I admit I was surprised when you asked me to come take care of him. What happened? He'll be okay, right?"

Seraphina turned from locking the door. "How do you know where we went?"

"It wasn't exactly rocket science. My judgmental bitch of an aunt was here, hysterical, and my father was dead by the next morning."

"Your F-Father? Virgil Woodard is, was your Father?" Seraphina should have made the leap in logic after the Aunt Phyllis comment, but this conversation was moving too quickly for her to follow in her tired, frazzled state.

"Yeah, I don't exactly go around bragging about that one either. If you met him, then I'm sure you understand. I hadn't seen him in years and am not mourning the abusive jerk, so spare me from any 'sorry for your loss' type junk, okay?"

They had reached the top of the stairs and entered the loft. Khat tossed her bag on the gray loveseat. "So, was Finn beaten up? It was one dear old Dad's trigger happy guards, wasn't it?"

Seraphina's worry must've been written all over her face because Khat laid a hand on her chest. "Wait. Finn didn't get shot or stabbed, did he?"

Seraphina snapped out of it and said, "No, no nothing like that. We didn't even see any guards. Just your aunt and Addams. It was the sin. Things went kind of crazy that night. I almost thought Virgil came back from… Well, it was really confusing, but I do know Finn ate your father's sin, and then he collapsed. He has not woken up since."

"I don't understand. My old man was a terrible person, believe me, I know better than anyone. But why would that make Finn sick?" Khat leaned and looked behind Seraphina, down the hall to Finn's door. "I knew something was wrong when Finn never came to see me the next day. He never breaks his promises."

Seraphina wasn't sure how much to explain. She didn't want to sound overly dramatic, but if Khat was going to take care of Finn, she needed to understand how serious this was. "Sins that powerful can be difficult for him. But I've never seen him so bad after a job. I have done all I can for him the past two days, but he has not awakened."

"Did you use your magic?" Khat asked.

"Yes." Seraphina tilted her head. "I wasn't sure if you knew about that."

"Oh, I see it on you. Pretty potent stuff, right? Shadowy though. You feel a lot like the veil."

Seraphina stared down at her arms. She sees *what?* How the heck does that work? Her father was a powerful, supernatural, so it means she is… a *something*.

Khat asked, "So, is Finn in his room?" She was halfway down the hall before Seraphina realized she'd been asked a question.

"Um, yeah. In his room," she answered no one.

Seraphina was so exhausted from this past week; her mind was processing slower than normal. She was already walking to Finn's room when she heard a sharp cry.

"Finn," she gasped as she ran through the open doorway.

He lay in his bed, still unconscious. His body was shaking softly again, but otherwise looking unchanged from her last check.

"Oh, I thought the worst when I heard you cry out." Seraphina pressed her hand over her frantically beating heart as she glanced over at Kan... Khat. The name change was going to take some getting used to.

"What the hell is wrong with him?" Khat demanded from his bedside. "Is it because of the whole Possessed lineage? Or is this a spell of some kind?"

"Oh, no Finn is completely immune to all supernatural maladies. He can't be spelled by magic. I've tried a small spell here or there just to test it out." Seraphina laughed, a bad habit when she was nervous. "As a Sin Eater, he's immune to almost all supernatural abilities. He cannot even be charmed by a djinn."

Khat had jumped at the mention of the djinn. Seraphina understood the reaction. Djinn were the most unpredictable of the non-human world since so few of the usual rules applied to them.

"I think the sin hasn't left his body yet or it has taken a lot out of him," Seraphina said in a whisper. "I've cared for him before when he was sickened by sin, but he's never been unconscious after a session. The aftereffects have never lasted this long."

"Sickened by sin? He's a Sin Eater. Eating junk is what he does. Besides, he said it keeps him strong. He looks awful, but I've never seen sin make him sick at all." Khat reached down and felt his head. "He's burning up."

Seraphina was taken aback by Khat's reaction. She knew Khat liked Finn, but she hadn't guessed how much... apparently.

Finn moaned a faint whisper.

"His power siphons off the sin of supernaturals, but the sin doesn't magically disappear. The evil must be faced, relived. The full consequences of the sin must be felt." Seraphina squinted while thinking about the last sentence.

Khat's eyes were wide as she raised her hand to her mouth. "Consequences? He feels the sins?"

"Yes, I didn't understand it fully myself until the other night, but Finn feels every sin he takes. From the perspective of the sinner. And for the atonement to work, he must also relive the pain felt by whomever the sin was against."

Khat frowned down at Finn and then back at Seraphina. "No. That can't be right. He should—Finn would have told me." Slumping into the chair by Finn's bed, she sat staring at him for several minutes.

Seraphina didn't know what to say, so she busied herself walking around the room straightening up again. Cleaning settled her nerves.

Khat sniffled, and when Seraphina turned, she was wiping wet eyes.

"Khat, I didn't mean to upset you." Seraphina grabbed a few tissues from the dresser and handed them to her. She was a walking, talking tissue dispenser these days.

After wiping her face, Khat took a deep breath and met Seraphina's worried eyes. "He's known all along. I tried so hard to hide things, despite that, he's known everything about me all along."

Seraphina began to understand. "You said you'd never seen sin make him sick before. He's eaten yours, hasn't he?" she gently prompted.

She'd always wondered but knew better than to ask Finn. He was defensive about his relationship with Khat.

"Yes, I sought him out back in January and asked him to help me. I thought it would make me feel different, happier, I guess. It worked, and my life has really changed for the better this year, but not because he ate my stupid sins. He's become such an important part of my life." She grasped his hand. "Finn can see sin on victims too, can't he?"

Seraphina closed her eyes and blew out a slow breath in acknowledgment.

Damn, damn, damn.

Seraphina nodded. "Yes, I think so. I've seen him react strongly to people who have experienced crimes. If a sin is strong enough, I'm pretty sure he sees some trace of it on the victim."

Finn's illness, Khat's transformation and lineage, and her own *little issue* as she often referred to the curse… it was all just too much.

Khat turned away.

Seraphina didn't know what to say. The two girls had never formed a real friendship, but Seraphina sensed a new closeness. Khat practically oozed sexiness in every movement, but it had almost seemed like an act.

Seraphina always believed something deeper existed below Khat's war painted exterior. Now she knew.

Finn groaned and writhed on the bed. His sallow, pale forehead scattered with drops of sweat from the fever again. He began to shake and kicked the covers lower, even as his teeth chattered.

Seraphina grabbed a cool rag from the basin at the foot of the bed and scooted closer. It was too soon for another healing spell. What could she possibly do to ease his fevered chills this time?

Khat reached out. She laid her small, trembling hand upon Finn's chest. His limbs instantly went still.

The frightened girls made eye contact, and their focus met on Finn at the same time. He lay still, except for labored breathing. His chest wheezed, panting, drawing haggard breaths.

Khat rose and then lay down beside him. As she wrapped her arms around him, Finn's breathing slowed, and the wheezing stopped.

The sudden silence in the room was startling. Finn's face started losing its red flush as if it had only been a momentary blush of embarrassment.

Khat propped herself on her elbow. Leaning in, she cautiously kissed Finn's cheek and then his pale lips.

Seraphina looked away and quietly headed to the door. She didn't want to intrude on a private moment. Plus, after so many cursed years, it was her natural reaction to look away when people kissed. "I'll give you some privacy. Being with you seems to be helping him." Seraphina softly closed the door, then leaned back against the hallway wall, shutting her eyes, thankful Khat had come. She went to shower... the best place for another good cry. Some shampoo wouldn't hurt her at this point either. The last two days had been a blur of concern and fear... and no showers.

When had she last eaten?

The hot, cleansing water improved Seraphina's mood and brought with it as sense of optimism. She was wrapping her hair back in a towel when Khat called for her. Whipping open the door, she hurried to Finn's room, followed by a cloud of steam.

Finn's color was back to his normal pallid white. He no longer shook and his breathing was even. He appeared peaceful for the first time in days. The creases on his forehead had disappeared.

Khat said, "He said my name and his eyes opened for a second."

Both girls gasped as Finn's eyes snapped open.

He blinked rapidly and looked around the room. Finn swallowed with difficulty and in a gravelly voice asked, "W-what is going on?"

First, he focused on Seraphina, who had hiccupped on a deep sigh of relief. "Love, is everything all right? Sparrow?" he asked, the strength of his voice improving.

Seraphina had not realized how little hope she had left until she heard his familiar little nicknames.

"It is now," both girls answered in unison, and they laughed in relief.

Seraphina had to rush to get ready for the Music for Youth masquerade gala. Luckily, Khat was absolutely masterful and helped. Her makeup was light since the mask would cover half her face. Seraphina turned in front of the mirror and did a final inspection. She could have never pulled her long hair into such a beautiful, complicated style. It was piled atop her head in a frenzy of loose curls secured with jewel-tipped pins glimmering in the light as she moved. Khat left long, red curls trailing down Seraphina's back and the contrast against her black dress was as striking as Khat had promised.

The original plan had been for Finn to be her escort. He was awake and his color had faded to what, for him, was a healthy white pallor. But he clearly did not have the strength to wear a tuxedo, watch her back while she cast the spell, and play arm candy for the next several hours. It was a shame too; Finn had teased Seraphina about how handsome he looked in his rented penguin suit. She'd been curious to see him all dressed up because it was nearly impossible to get him out of his standard jeans and combat boots.

Inwardly pouting over losing her best friend's company, she would never show it. He was awake. That was all that mattered now.

Highbrow social climbers were definitely not her preferred company. But at least, it wasn't a sit-down dinner. The Music for Youth fundraising gala was one of Nashville's premiere social events of the year with a rare Nashville Symphony and Nashville Opera combined performance.

It had taken her two weeks just to figure out how to get one of the coveted invitations to the Schermerhorn Symphony Center's most prestigious event. Seraphina learned there would be two separate silent auctions, one for the general public with the expected country music memorabilia of signed guitars and boots, concert tickets, and backstage Grand Ole Opry tours with the flavor of the month star. She had no interest in those prizes.

The Blackthorne Grimoire would be up for bid in the more expensive VIP silent auction.

Seraphina donated one of her most prized possessions to the event, and her donation had been deemed valuable enough to garner her a VIP invitation. She'd hated to part with her precious Moonstone cameo because it had been a gift from Finn many, many years ago. But it was Finn who'd insisted she use the treasure to gain entry. He argued that breaking the hex was worth far more than a sentimental trinket.

She didn't think Finn understood what the Moonstone cameo meant to her. The gift had been one of her last pre-curse memories. It reminded her of much simpler and happier times, but in the end, she relented. Freedom held more appeal.

The trinket, as Finn called it, was now worth five figures and a donation of that magnitude had been required to secure an unknown, young woman such as herself access to play with the Music City's big dogs. She prayed she could pull off her spell, win the book, and make it home without getting bit.

Seraphina carefully descended the stairs. Left, right, left… She could walk in heels, but it had been a while since she'd tried, and the stairs were steep in buildings this old. Breaking her ankle before even leaving home would be bad.

"Um, love? Your ride just arrived," called Finn as she walked into the shop.

The apothecary had been closed due to his illness. Finn was propped up on the antique sofa reading and drinking one of his medicinal teas by the fire. He'd retreated downstairs after commenting on how much giggling and chatter came with Khat helping Seraphina get ready.

"Why do you sound so apologetic?" she asked.

"Well, I had thought we would be going together, you know. I figured you'd be nervous about your spell. And seeing as I never blend in, in a crowd anyway, I thought we might have a bit of fun on the way and make a rather grand entrance."

"What did you do, Finn?" She tried to control the whine creeping into her voice… but failed miserably.

"I secured us a, well a carriage, to take us to the gala and you may as well still use it. You'll never be able to drive your GTO Judge in that getup, and it's too late to cancel the carriage anyway."

Khat smiled at Seraphina apologetically and pointed to the front window.

"A carriage?" Seraphina peeked through the lace curtains and sighed. "Oh, no, no, no. Really?" She turned back with pleading eyes. "Finn, it looks like something from a fairy tale. I'm not freaking Cinderella."

"That was actually the point, love. I planned to lighten up the seriousness of the evening by playing up the fairy tale a bit. Can you believe functional glass slippers are really hard to find, even on the internet? The driver was supposed to move the carriage and leave a pumpkin—"

Seraphina stomped her foot. "Finn."

"Oh, don't worry. I was able to cancel the Fairy Godmother singing telegram. Besides, none of my other little surprises can take place without me being present."

"Fairy… Godmother… singing telegram?" Khat choked out between fits of laughter.

"Quite, Sparrow. It was going to be a perfect fairy tale event. Why do?" began Finn.

"…when you can overdo," finished Seraphina rolling her eyes. "It's kind of his personal motto," she told Khat.

"Thanks for the warning." Khat sucked in her lip and took a calming breath. She smiled and said, "It's not too bad, girl. The carriage is kind of romantic."

Finn cleared his throat. "Icksnay on the omanceray."

Khat smirked at him, and he shook his head discreetly, much more serious all of the sudden. She started again, confused, "Well, didn't you say the auction started in just over half an hour? I'm sure lots of folks will make grand entrances with every trust fund diva in the city trying to make her mark, right? Maybe it won't stand out so bad."

"I do need a ride." Seraphina's shoulders slumped. "There's no way I can walk there in these heels, survive the gala, and walk back." Flaring out her long gown, she stared at the carriage. "Finn's right. I don't think I can drive the GTO in this and forget trying to find parking near the Schermerhorn tonight." Seraphina exhaled in defeat and Finn beamed. She looked back out the window. "But it's just so... flashy."

"Your carriage awaits, milady," he replied in his happiest voice.

Chapter Nine

Marceau sat on one of the unforgiving, marble benches next to a fountain outside the Schermerhorn Symphony Center. The round, bubbling fountain featured an illuminated bronze sculpture depicting Apollo, God of the Arts, as a muse playing a horn. From his vantage point, Marceau watched Nashville's elite emerge from rented limousines, Hummers, and all manner of comically elongated vehicles with their jewels and finery on full display. He'd even laughed, despite himself, at the first Tom Ford tuxedo paired garishly with flamboyant, rhinestone Cowboy boots. Nashvillians certainly had an interesting range of fashion choices, but then again, he never batted an eye at the flair in New Orleans.

He adjusted the tie of his matte black masquerade mask. It covered most of his face and the curved horns added several inches to his height.

The slow parade advanced. A sparkly couple caused a barrage of camera flashes while exiting yet another excessively large vehicle for two.

Something caught Marceau's eye, and he leaned forward, squinting as an ornate white frame came into view over the line of vehicle roofs. Was that really a horse-drawn carriage? One worthy of a fictional princess? He started to laugh at the absurdity until the carriage driver shifted to speak behind him. Marceau's laugh caught in his throat when the passenger was revealed.

A stunning young woman sat alone in the carriage. Several bystanders in the crowded entryway turned toward her. Their elaborate masks did little to hide their snickers as they gossiped about the new arrival.

The girl raised a black-gloved hand as if to cover her already masked face. She appeared to be pleading with the carriage driver, and he waved his arm at the surrounding vehicles rather dramatically in return.

"This night may not be so droll after all," Marceau murmured as he rose and quickly closed the distance to the woman in distress.

"I...really, really meant what I said, sir. You should have let me out farther back. I did not require front door service. I..."

"Listen, Miss, I'm doin' all I can here. I'm fixin' to let you out, but it ain't like I can just cut through all these here limos. This ain't no Prius. It takes a certain amount of space," the driver said.

He sounded apologetic enough, but Marceau had a feeling the driver could be more accommodating if he tried.

"Okay, then perhaps I could just get out here? I could—"

"I can't climb down when the line's 'bout to move again. You ain't goin' nowheres 'til I get the door and fold that there step down. There ain't no inside latch, you see? Ol' Smokey Joe here is right nervous with this crowd and needs a steady hand on the reins with all these folk a'congregatin' here. Can't swear he won't start if'n I let go."

The white and gray horse shifted restlessly and jerked his head upward against his bit. He snorted and his metal shoes clanged against the pavement.

When the line was beginning to inch forward, Marceau raised his hand and signaled the driver to wait. He trailed his hand along the horse's jaw and soothed him for a moment.

"I'll assist the young lady with her exit. If you'll hold up the line for just a moment. Your horse is showing signs of distress."

The driver started to protest, but Marceau gave him a pointed look. The gentleman nodded and Marceau stepped forward and flipped the step down. He released the latch, opened the ridiculous carriage door, and extended his gloved hand to the lovely, red-haired stranger.

Looking down at him with a mixture of relief and shock, the young lady opened her mouth to speak. "I am..." she started but seemed to have lost her train of thought.

"If I may, I believe you wished to exit?" Marceau was thankful his voice remained steady and confident. From the moment her bright green eyes had met his gaze, his heartbeat had gone rather erratic.

She wore an intricately constructed sugar skull mask decorated with Victorian scrolls and framed with fresh dahlias.

The carriage lurched forward and the driver yelled, "Whoa, Joe, whoa. If'n you're goin', ya better get movin', ma'am."

She reached out and grasped Marceau's hand tightly as she took a cautious step onto the carriage's stair and then to the ground. The woman was taller than he'd expected.

Marceau did not want to let go of her gloved hand so soon, but he had to release her to close the carriage door and secure the step. He nodded at the driver and stepped back from the road.

In a pleasant Southern accent, she said, "Thank you, sir, for the ride. I apologize for this traffic upsetting Smokey Joe. I won't need a ride later, so please take him on home to rest."

Marceau was surprised she thanked the driver after he had seemed rather uncooperative.

She turned and looked up at Marceau. "Thank you, as well. I am pretty embarrassed by the spectacle of this." She waved at the carriage. "Anyway, thanks."

Crimson curls bounced down her back as she turned and rushed away adeptly through the throngs of people. Many stopped to take notice of her, but she paused only to show her invitation at the door and then she disappeared.

Marceau hadn't even introduced himself. But he made a silent promise to correct that error before the night was over.

When he showed his invitation, a muscled man in an ill-fitted tuxedo removed a red velvet rope and gestured to the right. "VIP is that way, sir."

Marceau nodded and proceeded forward in hopes of finding the mysterious woman in the VIP area. He barely took notice of the two-story columned Main Lobby. Running a quick scan, found no sign of distinctive red hair. Normally, he'd have paused to critique the architecture since he had never been to this particular music hall. Tonight included only two goals: procure the Blackthorne Grimoire and learn more about the intriguing young woman who had captured his interest.

Weaving through the slow progression of patrons into the spacious West Atrium, he looked up only momentarily to notice the skylight and impressive marble. His pace did not slow. Once inside the columned West Lobby, he again surveyed the crowd and exited. Marceau made an expedient loop around a finely landscaped courtyard and, frustrated, he re-entered the lobby area and scanned the upper balcony. Nothing. He noticed a sign directing patrons upstairs for the VIP Silent Auction.

Well, he did have to go there, either way, so he started up the steps, pausing along the way and marveling inside at the elegant, hardwood paneled Founders Hall. Long, antique tables formed a line down the length of the room holding the various items available for bid in the special auction.

There.

Marceau exhaled a long breath as he watched her from the doorway. Why was he so relieved to see her? He knew nothing about this young woman, and yet he could not deny a desire to be near her.

Stepping aside, he allowed others to enter the opulent hall. The room was quite large, but with rich, wood tones and well-chosen antiques, it managed an intimate feel and reminded Marceau of Max's beloved club.

Max.

Marceau's spine straightened as he remembered why he was there in the first place.

Maximilian wanted the grimoire and Marceau needed to focus. Failure to procure the book would result in punishment, and Max's discipline ranged from simply severe to absolutely grotesque.

As he walked along the line of tables on the opposite side from the woman in black, Marceau looked for the book. But with each step closer, his attention was focused more and more on her than the contents of the tables.

Her presence had a wistful, longing sense to it. She reached out and touched something small that lay on the cream-colored table linen. What object did she desire? She pulled her gloved hand back and turned without catching his stare, then walked farther down the hall.

Marceau stopped in front of the small object she'd handled. An intricately carved cameo surrounded by blue and white stones was up for auction. Diamonds and sapphires, judging from the way the facets captured the light. Moonstone, Marceau decided, as he bent to further examine the figure on the cameo. The carving was almost three-dimensional. Upswept curling hair and delicate features on the cameo reminded Marceau of the woman from the carriage. He looked farther down the table. She'd stopped again.

Marceau moved to join her but froze at a tinkling laugh that grated against every nerve in his body.

"Marceau? What a pleasant surprise."

Making sure his face represented only arrogant disinterest by the time he turned, his raven-haired, blue-eyed partner was an unwanted complication. She'd gotten the better of him while he recovered from raising Babette. Marceau would not let happen again.

"Vespa, I highly doubt it's a surprise at all, but you look stunning, as always."

"Not surprisingly, you're delicious too, Marceau. I was very unhappy when I found you'd slipped out of my bed. I thought your hesitance might be lower after some quality time. I was a good girl too. I didn't even kiss you."

Her kiss held a venom that pacified her victims.

"Nice mask." Her eyes traced up to the tip of his black, horned accessory. She leaned in and Marceau forced himself to stay still. Vespa whispered, "Feeling horny?" Her forked tongue tickled his ear.

Her smell was intoxicating. Marceau stopped mid-breath and leaned back, rolling his eyes.

Vespa said, "Glad to see you recovered after reanimating Maxie-Waxie's little ballerina."

"Hmph. Do me a favor, would you? Call him Maxie-Waxie to his face, just once. I beg you." Marceau sneered. "But make sure I'm around to see it."

Vespa leaned her right shoulder forward, a gesture that made her large breasts move against each other beneath her scandalously low cut dress.

"Oh, now, now, lover. You'd miss me. Just think of our little kiss last year." She raked her teeth across her full lower lip. "Tasting your blood brought back memories. I was reminded of our good ol' days. Like when we stole that silly, little film."

Marceau's skin crawled. On job in California, his self-control slipped for only a moment and had he ever paid for the lapse. Whew. He fell victim to Vespa's demented appetite for one brief kiss. He'd never forget the mixture of extreme pleasure that had rippled down his body straight to his groin and the freezing, agonizing pain immediately following.

Memory of the kiss gave him nightmares for weeks afterward, all the more horrifying as his body ached for her.

At the time, Marceau had needed a female distraction to keep an aging film archivist's attention while he stole the original 1922 film reel of the infamous Nosferatu.

The Djinn Faction in Manhattan paid Max two trunks filled with precious stones for the job since they did not bother to keep up with modern currencies. The faction wanted the original copy of the film to ensure modern film restoration techniques would never reveal that Max Schreck was not a human actor, after all. There had always been rumors of his authenticity as a vampire, which was ridiculous since the foul tentacled Sanguine were the closest thing that existed to them. But Schreck was a ghoul, a lower form of djinn, and he'd fed on the camera. Schreck disappeared not long after the Djinn Faction learned of the movie, but they had been unsuccessful in stopping its release.

Marceau had needed a djinn's help to resist the temptation to go to Vespa. His body shivered involuntarily, and she giggled again.

"So, you do remember."

"Enough, Vespa. Why did you follow me here? I thought after your Louisiana visit, you would be hungry for the Los Angeles crowd again."

Marceau maintained strict eye contact. He would not give her the satisfaction of looking elsewhere.

"Mm, I was. They do take such good care of their bodies there… vanity is delicious."

Vespa fed not only on her victim's life force but their desires too. She reached up and traced her finger along her collarbone, trying to draw his attention lower.

"There are so many pretty boys in Hollywood, but they'll have to wait. I've hungered for a rather tasty morsel in a cowboy hat ever since I saw his moves at the Grammys." Vespa tilted her head back slightly, indicating the tall man a few feet behind her. "Maximilian sent me to Nashville in case you needed me, so I finally got to taste my cowboy. Sadly, I'll be finished with him tonight, tomorrow at the latest. He isn't holding up very well."

Marceau looked around her and recognized the country music star leaning against the wooden column. A casual observer might assume he was slightly intoxicated, but Marceau knew better.

Vespa pouted her lips. "Wanna take me out, lover? We could go Honky Tonking." She giggled and chills ran down Marceau's spine. Several heads turned in response to her seductive laugh. "Aren't Southern words just so cute? The nightlife is intoxicating down on Broadway. Desperation hangs so thick you can taste the lust in the air."

Her current victim listed to the side behind her, only standing with help from the wall. Marceau noticed lines that did not belong on the young man's face and a vacant expression in his heavily bagged eyes as he stared at Vespa's exposed back.

Marceau's lip pulled back in distaste as a line of drool fell from the man's lip. The cowboy was going down and soon. Maybe he could convince Vespa to let him go.

"Cowboy's not looking so good. If he dies here, it will disrupt the auction and Maximilian will be furious. Perhaps, you should be finished with him now."

It was worth a *try.*

Vespa stomped her stiletto. "Oh, no way. Not this one. I'm taking all of him. He actually tried to sneak out first thing this morning, can you believe it? I caught him tiptoeing toward the door with his boots in hand. He actually thought he could leave me in some damned hotel and go back to his boring, human wife. As if she could ever bring him the pleasure I had."

Marceau tried to mask his disgust and sound indifferent when he said, "He must love her very much to have even remembered she existed after a night of your feeding, Vespa. Why not cut him loose? Surely, there's another boy toy here you could devour tonight."

"If you're offering..." Vespa licked her cherry red lips.

"I certainly am not," Marceau answered. The muscles in his jaw ticked in anger at the mere thought.

"Pity, Marceau. One day, though mark my words. That kiss was just the beginning. I want you to cry out my name in ecstasy. Come willingly and I won't make you beg for my touch."

Vespa ran her manicured hands up her slim waist, around the sides of her full breasts, and into her shiny, black hair. She paused to see if Marceau was reacting to her pose.

He raised his brow and shook his head.

She dropped her arms. "Fine, whatever. I guess I'll just have to go back to my cowboy then. Oh look, he's drooling over me, at least someone is."

Vespa turned and sashayed back to her unfortunate escort. A normal woman would have dislocated her hip trying to put so much sway in her walk. Men in all directions gawked, several women, too.

Marceau was unimpressed. He'd seen it all before, so he turned his back to Vespa and looked for his mystery woman once more.

His eyes narrowed and his fists clenched.

What in the *hell* was she doing?

Chapter Ten

Seraphina knelt and lifted the tablecloth.

"Are you ready?" she whispered.

"Yeah, thought you'd never get here, Miss Sera. I been sitting still a long time."

"I know, Rolf. Thank you for helping me tonight. We have to hurry. Remember how we practiced it?"

Rolf's little head nodded. He scooted to the edge and raised his small, ghostly hand.

Seraphina only felt the barest indication of his touch as she grasped his hand. She said a silent prayer.

This spell had to work. She couldn't deal with it if little Rolf were hurt. *Please pull from Rolf's loneliness and pain, and leave only warmth and love in its place.*

Seraphina set her other hand on the grimoire and began chanting the well-practiced spell. Her desperation for the book supplied the nerve to cast a spell in a room crowded with humans.

Her incantations worked better when connected to the dead. That was where Rolf came in. She'd found a way to use his anguish to fuel the power in it even when she wasn't nearby. Spells faded. Hers sometimes faded too quickly. This one had to hold its strength for several hours.

Rolf promised to stay under the table until she returned, and she'd vowed to take him to a place filled with children for a day of fun and let him stay in her room at night. She planned to cross him over the veil as soon as she figured out how. Hopefully, the grimoire would hold some clues about that problem too.

At last, she felt the tie between her little ghost and the book's binding.

Chapter Eleven

Marceau looked back. Luckily Vespa and her cowboy were too engaged in what some might call soft core porn for her to notice.

Waves of turbulent magic ebbed from where the redhead stood. Any moment now Vespa would detect her, she would dump her man in boots and jeans in a heartbeat and go after the woman if she got a taste of her mystifying power.

A few quick strides and Marceau stood opposite her. Marceau's eyes widened as intricate red scrolls crossed her palm and curled up her wrist before disappearing. A faint red glow faded back into her skin.

She jumped and quickly replaced her silk glove. Guilt, fear, and then determination, flashed in her deep green eyes. Marceau yearned to pull the sugar skull mask from her face and see her full expression. Who was she? Instead, he followed her gaze downward. His mouth fell open. The Blackthorne Grimoire lay between them on the table. The object she spelled was the very book he'd traveled all the way from New Orleans to procure.

She bent and quickly wrote on the book's auction sheet, then locking eyes with Marceau as she firmly laid the pen back down. Without a word, she turned and walked briskly toward the stairs to the West Lobby. Slowing only when she passed the Moonstone cameo, she brushed her hand against the table's edge and disappeared through the hall's wooden doors.

What did she *do?* Damn it to hell.

Marceau rounded the end of the long auction tables and rushed to stand where she had been only a moment before.

Seraphina Pearce, $6,000 was written on the auction sheet in curving, feminine handwriting. The bid above hers had only been $1,000.

Marceau's muscles contracted painfully. Electricity jolted through his flesh as the spell blossomed and frenetic magic took hold of his senses. When he looked at the ancient grimoire, he now saw a tattered, ugly book, knowing only a moment before the Blackthorne Grimoire had sat in very spot. He closed his eyes and struggled to picture the grimoire as it had appeared before the spell.

Moments earlier, thick, red leather binding had covered the weighty volume. A golden latch secured the corded black leather strap that held the book closed. Complex golden patterns of Celtic knots branched out from each corner culminating in a Tree of Life medallion in the center of the cover.

The grimoire was a beautiful tome. Marceau exhaled and opened his eyes focused on seeing the book as he remembered. Trying to push through the spell, all he saw before him was a dilapidated journal lying limp on the table. Torn bits of yellow stained paper stuck out from the edges. He closed his eyes and focused on how he needed the grimoire to appear. The spell flared stronger. He staggered, overwhelmed with revulsion. This time, he didn't want to even open his eyes and look at the ugly, insignificant book.

Painful pin pricks in his fingertips electrified at the mere thought of touching the disgusting thing, and he drew his hands into fists. With each breath, he smelled the rot of musty, damp pages thick with dust, mold, and age. His stomach rolled while the noxious odor increased.

Powerful. An impressive spell.

Fine, if Marceau couldn't get through her spell, he'd work around it. He wouldn't touch or even look at the damned book. He'd just make a bid and get the hell away as fast as possible.

Breathing through his mouth, Marceau snatched up the pen to write a higher bid than the troublesome Spellcaster's. The moment he tried to put pen to paper, a debilitating wave of melancholy, a heart-wrenching grief as strong as the mourning of a new death, overtook him.

Stunned, Marceau swayed. His eyes closed on their own and started to tear up. He tried to take a deep breath and clear his mind, but the crushing weight of indescribable misery constricted his chest.

Dropping the pen, he fell forward and grabbed the edge of the table. His firm grip was the only reason he could stand.

"I don't want the book," Marceau said aloud, trying to release the hold of the spell.

His stomach rolled with nausea. He swallowed rapidly again and again as he fought to keep back the acid sliding up his throat, but it wasn't helping. He was going to throw up right there if he didn't put some distance between him and the nasty grimoire. Stumbling back two steps, his arms raised as if in protection.

"I said I don't want the damned book," Marceau repeated with more conviction.

Another step back and he was able to take a clear breath.

Someone's throat cleared nearby and Marceau opened his eyes. An older woman lowered her mask and looked at him questioningly.

"Just s-something I ate, ma'am," Marceau forced out.

"Indeed. Should I get you some help?" she asked in a weathered voice, her Southern accent heavy in his ears. "I said, do you need help, young man? You are swaying like a drunkard and look the worse for wear."

Marceau's ears thrummed, making it difficult to process her words. He took another longer step back.

"No, no thank you, ma'am. Please don't trouble yourself." Marceau's voice was louder, steadier.

He straightened his spine and, with trembling hands, smoothed his lapels. Marceau ran a hand through his unruly, black hair causing a strand to fall on his forehead. He faked a smile and nodded as the older woman walked past him, still glancing around, concerned.

Marceau looked back down at the pen. A wave of nausea and a panicked sweat formed on his brow at the thought of touching it again. His body trembled with a racking chill.

His knees would give out before he could manage a bid. The mystery woman's spell would render him unconscious prior to writing his name, let alone a dollar amount.

Marceau looked up. Vespa was eyeing him. Cowboy licked her neck, oblivious to the judgmental stares he received. She arched her dark eyebrow, surely questioning Marceau's actions.

When he stepped back, even more, he could lean against the cool, exotic hardwood paneling. With Vespa waiting to pounce, unconscious and vulnerable was definitely not an option.

What the hell had the Spellcaster done to the grimoire? From this distance, Marceau could think again. It was not a hex, that much he could tell right away. He had a sixth sense about curses and would have felt drawn to the object, not repulsed. His instincts would be intact, and he would have seen a faint glow around the book. Even if the purpose of the hex were to repel others, he would not have felt more than an irritating prickle against his skin. Such was his talent.

No, this was definitely a spell.

She'd levied a baffling, powerful spell to have affected another supernatural as strongly as it had. Her dominance in the air seemed familiar, similar to the dark magic Max used.

The enigmatic young woman in black had somehow managed to make sure no one else could possibly bid on the Blackthorne Grimoire. At least, he knew her name now, Seraphina Pearce.

Maximilian was not going to be pleased, not pleased at all. Marceau sighed.

Unless.

Perhaps, he could get the book another way. He straightened from the wall with new determination and found Seraphina sipping a glass of champagne in the moonlit courtyard. A heavyset twenty-something with a thick mustache was talking to her, his short arms waving around like a cartoon walrus as he spoke.

Seraphina's body language spoke volumes. Her arms were tightly crossed in front of her. The almost empty champagne flute in her left hand was tucked against her right elbow. She leaned back from the man, and her gaze darted from side to side as if contemplating her escape. The man leaned closer. Her eyes met Marceau's across the courtyard.

He walked toward her, slowly winding through the other patrons. Marceau grabbed two flutes when a waiter conveniently turned in his direction, but he didn't break the gaze he shared with Seraphina until a girl no older than twelve stepped into his path as he rounded a fountain.

"Pardon me, Miss." Marceau winked. She bounced to the side with a nervous giggle. He bowed. Marceau approached and held out the champagne to Seraphina with a half-smile. "With the mask, it's difficult to be sure you're old enough to drink this. I'll not be arrested, will I?"

Seraphina returned a sly smile, "I'm older than that, trust me. Besides huma... I mean people overlook much."

She accepted the offered drink but acted confused for a moment with the two flutes, one in each hand. Marceau took the empty one from her and turned, setting it on a nearby waiter's stand.

The pompous walrus was so busy bragging about his bar exam score, he hadn't noticed their exchange.

"Ahem." Marceau cleared his throat. "My dear, Seraphina, I do apologize for the delay."

She startled when he said her name.

"I had unexpected difficulty in placing my bid. I do hope you're not cross with me." His smile grew wicked as her eyes widened and her mouth formed a perfect little O.

The lawyer-to-be had finally come up for air and shut up long enough to look annoyed.

"Ah, I see you made a friend in my absence. Marceau L'Argent." Marceau extended his hand politely. "I am Miss Seraphina's escort for the evening, and you are?"

"Gene Buford."

They shook hands.

She interrupted, "Well, Gene, it was nice to meet you. If you will both excuse me, I need to go to the powder room." Seraphina gave Marceau a pointed look as she said *both* and walked away.

"She never said she had a date..." began Gene.

"No harm, no foul. Enjoy your evening," Marceau replied as he walked away.

He'd been chasing after Seraphina half the night. Well, this time, he had a hunch about exactly where she was headed.

As he predicted, she walked directly to the stairs leading back to the grimoire. He didn't bother to follow her. Instead, he finished his champagne while she checked on her bid.

When she emerged from the stairs appearing reassured, Marceau stepped into her path.

"Look, I really don't like to play games," Seraphina said.

"Oh, I think you might."

Marceau gestured for her to join him in a less crowded area, a corner of the hall. She didn't move.

"Unless you wish to discuss your spell here in the main thoroughfare?" Marceau waved his hand at the people around them.

Seraphina took small, measured steps to the corner as if trying to stall and come up with a plan.

Marceau said, "Considering the magnitude of your spell on the grimoire, I'd say you can relax and feel secure you'll win."

"So, it worked?" Seraphina sounded surprised. She stepped back and lowered her voice. "Oh, I meant what spell? I don't know what you're talking about."

"Yes. I'd definitely say it worked. A little too well for my taste." He pulled his collar away from his throat at a momentary flashback of the spell's choking despair.

Seraphina stood, arms crossed. He expected her to step back again, but she surprised him by inching closer this time.

"I'm sorry if it hurt you. I wasn't sure how strongly to—" She stopped mid-thought and studied him for a moment, inspecting from the tips of the horns on his mask down to his feet.

When her eyes came back and met his, Marceau let out a sharp bark of laughter. "Like what you see, Seraphina?"

Marceau bent in a mocking half-bow.

"You wish." She frowned. "I was just making sure you were... intact."

"Intact?" He laughed again. Her response was so unexpected. "You really were unsure about the strength of spell, weren't you?"

She did not reply.

"We have a dilemma. I must have that book. I'm willing to offer you fifty thousand dollars to transfer ownership to me as soon as the auction ends. You will make quite an easy profit. However, the sale must be finalized *before* you take possession of it. That part is non-negotiable."

"No, *you* have a dilemma, because the grimoire is not for sale. Assuming I even win it in the first place, I'm certainly not selling it."

The lights flickered. A male voice asked everyone to take their seats in the main concert hall.

Marceau said, "Seventy-five thousand."

"Not even for a million dollars. It's priceless to me. Now if you'll excuse me, the music is about to start. My invitation was costly, and I intend to enjoy the concert."

Seraphina brushed past him and blended into the stream of people filing to their seats.

Marceau looked at his invitation. It indicated his seat was in the East Loge, Box 2. Seraphina had turned toward the West Loge. Rolling his eyes, he followed her.

Seraphina had arrived in that ridiculous carriage alone. He was gambling she had an unused *plus one* on her invitation. At least, Marceau hoped. How else would he be able to sit near her?

She went into Box 9 and took her seat. Most of the other seats were already filled. Marceau waited until the lights were lowered and the audience began an anticipatory applause before he claimed the empty seat beside her.

"You have some nerve."

An older man behind them leaned forward and shushed her.

"Only being a gentleman, Seraphina, I wouldn't want you to fall prey to that lawyer again," Marceau whispered.

"Gentleman, my a..."

"Shhh." This time, it was an older woman two seats to her right.

"Oh, chill. Would you? The music hasn't even started yet." Seraphina sat back and crossed her arms.

Marceau had won his seat.

He smiled as the symphony began their performance with the "Hamlet Overture" by Tchaikovsky. He found it difficult to concentrate on the tune, however, his attention remaining on the woman to his right and the predicament at hand.

Max expected him to bring the grimoire and that was reason enough to feel stressed. But he also needed the book for himself. The Blackthorne Grimoire was rumored to contain a wealth of magical knowledge.

If there were a way to subdue Max's powers or undo his evil deeds, the grimoire was his best chance. Plus, Marceau wanted to know if curses were included in the mythical volume. He had studied them since he was a boy but had not yet found a way to secure his own freedom. He needed a way to mask his presence, to be shielded from even Max's power.

And then there was the rumored hex on the book. Max either had not heard of the ownership hex on the grimoire or had not believed it. Marceau had certainly not pointed it out.

His plan had been to outbid any competition and take ownership as quickly as possible. If true, the book's hex prevented it from being taken by force from the owner. If he'd won the auction, the grimoire would have belonged to him, not Max.

Marceau surmised the only reason the volume was up for auction was because an heir to the book was clueless about its true value, meaning most likely, the beneficiary was human.

A terrible thought pushed its way forward, and he looked at the young woman beside him. If she died…

No. He couldn't even finish the thought. That would have been Max's solution to this situation. Despite all of the lessons, Marceau was determined to not ever become like Max.

Absolutely not.

Marceau had lied, conned, and stolen. Sure, that was what Max required of him. And Max was very persuasive. Marceau was not, however, capable of murder. Especially not of such a beautiful woman.

Max, on the other hand. Well, Marceau needed to keep Max in New Orleans and far away from her.

The audience applauded. Marceau was unsure what the symphony had just played, but he clapped along. He peeked at his watch. He'd zoned out for longer than he thought.

"Bored?" she whispered as he checked the time.

"Not in the least," he replied.

Marceau caught her sneaking glances at him several times during Mendelssohn's "A Midsummer Night's Dream, Op. 61, Nocturne."

Seraphina smiled and rolled her eyes when she caught him staring during Sergei Prokofiev's "The Death of Tybalt." He was trying to gauge her reaction to the piece. It was one of his favorites.

The stage darkened and spotlights illuminated a large four-poster bed on the left side of the stage. Marceau glanced at the program and read "Selections from Verdi's Othello, Act IV." The finale of the evening.

A charismatic opera singer playing Desdemona sang a haunting rendition of "Ave Maria." Seraphina shifted forward as if entranced by the opera. She held her hands tightly in her lap, then reached underneath her masquerade mask to wipe her eye.

Marceau quickly found his handkerchief and held it out to her.

"You would have a handkerchief, wouldn't you?" she whispered and sniffled.

He was puzzled by her statement.

Seraphina reached behind her head and untied the silk strings of her mask.

Marceau's breath caught as she lowered her mask and he saw her face for the first time.

Seraphina was lovely with the mask, but without it? He was mesmerized. Her eyes were even more striking, long eyelashes framing bright, almond-shaped green eyes. Freckles, by the hundreds, dotted across her nose and onto her fair cheeks. She wiped a tear as the singer portraying Othello entered for Desdemona's death scene, but Marceau had eyes only for her.

Enthralled by the performance, she wrapped the handkerchief around and around her left hand squeezing it tightly when Othello killed his bride.

The stage went dark and the audience erupted in applause. Seraphina shot up from her chair, clapping. Most of the audience stood, as well.

Marceau rose to his feet and clapped.

Seraphina turned and a deep, rosy blush covered her cheeks.

"You must think I'm silly for getting emotional, but it was beautiful. So heartbreaking."

"No, I think it was... charming that the performance had such an effect on you." And Marceau was surprised he meant it. After a childhood with Max, emotion in public settings usually brought out his inner snob.

The people sharing their box filed out. Marceau didn't want the evening to end so soon.

"I must look a hot mess," Seraphina said. "I bet I have raccoon eyes."

"No, you look beau..." Marceau did not finish. He'd spoken without thinking, something he rarely did.

"Is there mascara on my face?" she asked as if covering the awkwardness of his unfinished compliment.

"Only a small spot."

Marceau took the handkerchief from her hands, slowing raising his hand and dabbed at the outer corner of her eye.

"Just here," he said softly.

They stood there staring at each other for several moments.

Seraphina raised her hand to where he had touched the handkerchief to her face. She breathed in a sharp breath and took several steps back.

The moment was gone. She was visibly upset.

"Thank you. I, um, I should go make a final check on the auction."

She walked away, certainly the theme of the night. But this time, just before she left the box, Seraphina glanced back at him over a shoulder.

Marceau waited by the exit. He could already predict how the auction had ended. He called and instructed his hired driver to have the luxury SUV waiting at a nearby corner to avoid the slow loading zone of the exiting crowd.

Seraphina approached, smiling to herself but stopping short when she saw Marceau was again in her path.

He asked, "I take it you were successful?"

"Yes. They stopped taking bids halfway through the performance."

"I wish you would reconsider my offer."

"There's nothing you could offer that would—" Seraphina blushed.

"I see," Marceau said with his most wicked smile. "Well, it is a shame."

Her blush deepened and spread across her cheeks. She held the mask and fiddled with one of the strings.

"Shall I escort you to your princess carriage?" Marceau's tone was playful again.

"No, I told the driver I didn't need to be picked up, remember? One ride in the Cinderella Carriage of Doom was more than enough. I'll just walk home. It's only a few blocks."

Marceau frowned when he noticed her high heels. "In those shoes, I would venture a few blocks is longer than would be comfortable." He stepped forward. "I'm happy to give you a lift, rest assured, I have a driver so you wouldn't be alone with a relative stranger."

She said, "Um, no. That's okay."

"It's no trouble, really."

"I don't want you to know where I live," Seraphina blurted. "Relative stranger and all, like you said," she added quickly.

She was correct, of course, and Marceau was strangely glad of her caution. "I see and I completely agree."

Marceau could easily find out where she lived with one phone call or an internet search, but it would be ungentlemanly to point that fact out.

Instead, he said, "I'm staying at the Hermitage Hotel on Sixth. I could have the driver drop me off first? And then he can take you to wherever your home may be. Normally, that would be against my chivalrous nature, but I want you to feel safe."

Seraphina looked down at her feet as she considered his offer. She stifled a light yawn. "Well, as long as there is a driver, then yes, I guess. It would be really great, actually. The truth is I'm exhausted. I've had very little sleep in the last few days."

Seraphina smiled.

"Ah, and a smile too. Come on then, Miss Seraphina. The car is just down this way."

Marceau extended his arm, and she hesitated before carefully placing her gloved hand into the crook of his elbow.

"Are you always so formal?" she blurted and then winced.

"Are you usually so direct?" he asked and made a mock wincing expression.

"Yes," they both answered after a long pause.

They looked at each other and laughed.

"It's not always my best quality."

"Actually, I find it refreshing," Marceau answered. "And I suppose I am more proper than most my age. I was raised by an aristocratic benefactor who required absolute formality at all times, even when I was a child."

Seraphina frowned. "Makes sense. But it couldn't have been a very happy childhood, could it?"

"Indeed. Here's the car." Marceau was grateful for the distraction. He'd not meant to disclose anything about his upbringing at all. Seraphina had a disarming effect on him. Marceau opened her door with his mind on how to see her again and made small talk during the short distance to his hotel. As the driver pulled up to the Hermitage, Marceau turned and asked, "Will you have dinner with me tomorrow night, Seraphina?"

"I can't." Her posture stiffened. "I already have plans."

Marceau had expected a *yes* answer. Had he misread the signs? He needed access to the book, sure, but he also wanted to see her again.

"All right, lunch, then?"

She shook her head no.

"I would like to further discuss the book you purchased tonight."

She fidgeted with her seat belt and said, "I told you, it's not for sale."

"I understand that now and am no longer interested in buying it."

Seraphina looked unconvinced.

"I'd like to discuss a business proposition. Access to the book in exchange for my services."

Her eyes narrowed. "Your services?"

"Yes, which must be discussed in private." Marceau looked at the driver and back at Seraphina. "So, lunch tomorrow? I'll even let you choose the place if makes you more comfortable. Anywhere you like."

"Fine." Seraphina took a breath as she decided. "All right, one o'clock at the Arcade."

"The Arcade?"

"Google it." She smiled mischievously.

He laughed. "Okay then. Good evening, Seraphina."

"Good evening, Marceau," she replied, mimicking his serious tone.

Marceau's heart did a very unmasculine skip as he exited the vehicle and closed the door. It was the first time she had said his name.

He saw no point in putting off the inevitable. Once in his room, he pulled off the horned mask. He'd felt ridiculous in it at first, and as the night took an interesting turn, he'd forgotten he was even wearing the strange mask.

He'd failed to get the Blackthorne Grimoire at the auction. Max would find out, of that there was no doubt. Marceau wouldn't be surprised if he already knew.

Max picked up on the second ring. "I assume you have an explanation."

Marceau took a deep breath, loosened his tie, and sat on the bed. "I was unable to procure the grimoire. I've already made contact with the party who won the auction. We're meeting tomorrow to discuss a mutually beneficial arrangement."

Marceau kicked off his shoes. He knew a fancy explanation would get him nowhere with Max.

"I did not send you there to flirt with a fiery haired girl and let her win the book, Marceau."

Marceau's spine stiffened. "Checking up on me, Max?"

"You know how I abhor nicknames and now is not the time to test me. Steal the blasted book. Have your way with the girl if you must, but get it out of your system and get me the grimoire."

Max assumed Seraphina had no more value than a plaything to be used and thrown away. But then again, Max treated everyone that way. He continued, "As luck would have it, I am quite occupied at the moment or I would come and remedy the situation myself."

Something in Max's tone alarmed Marceau. He sounded pleased, satisfied even, despite Marceau's failure.

Marceau asked, "Occupied? I was aware of no other pending jobs, Maximilian." Max was up to something. "I could use the jet and commute back and forth if you require my specialized skill set."

"No, that will not be necessary. Enjoy your tryst, see the sights of Music City, and procure the book."

See the *sights?* Max was *definitely* up to something, something big. Marceau made a mental note to warn Lynette.

Marceau replied, "Of course, I'll keep you updated. But there may be a complication."

"I care not about complications. Fix this." Max hung up.

Marceau ran his fingers through his hair. He opened the internet browser on his phone, wondering what exactly was "the Arcade?"

Part II: Curse

Chapter Twelve

Seraphina said, "Rolf, you're going to have to come out from under the bed eventually. Why not sit up here with me? I won't use any magic. No trying to open the veil. I promise. We'll just chat."

"Pinky swear?" a muffled voice asked from below her.

"Yes, pinky swear. Our spell worked well last night. I won the book and am so thankful for your help. Let's just celebrate with a nice cuddle."

A slight scratching noise came from under her bed as he scooted closer to the edge. Her only response was straightening up the pillows behind her back and waiting. Nothing.

"I'm all alone up here. I could be scratching someone's back if only some itchy, little ghost would join me," Seraphina sang.

Immediate scooting sounds and grunts. Yep, worked.

Seraphina bit the inside of her lip to stifle a laugh as a translucent, scruffy head popped up from the end of her bed. Two small, hairy hands slid up onto her quilt. Rolf was in pouncing mode today. His moods could be so unpredictable. Slowly, he rose until she could see his eyes. He squinted and the corners turned up slowly.

All smiles, so brace. Here he comes.

Rolf leapt onto the bed and crawled quickly up to where she sat. He hesitated only a moment, and she nodded. He flopped onto his stomach and lay across her legs. A wave of cold power washed over her the moment he made contact.

"Good thing you're a ghost, my little wolf boy, or my legs would be bruised after that." Seraphina laughed and started scratching the area where his back would be. "Feel it yet?"

"Nope."

"Okay, concentrate harder. Remember to picture in your head. I'm touching your back."

She knew when Rolf could feel her touch because he exhaled a long, relieved sigh. He'd been so desperate for physical contact when she first found him. Seraphina had been researching the famous "Thing of Nashville" and had expected a much scarier culprit than poor, little Rolf. He'd latched onto her waist and had not let go the entire way after she promised he could come home with her.

Seraphina knew how painful it was aching for physical contact. To see everyone around you take something essential for granted while you were denied such a small comfort? Yep, she was happy to snuggle Rolf because she understood exactly how his loneliness felt.

His long-term solitude and fear provided her spell with an immense power boost. The poor little guy. But she'd cast the magic to pull those pent-up emotions from him. She hoped he would feel lighter from now on.

He giggled and squirmed when she strayed too close to his sides. A ticklish ghost, who knew?

Rolf had hypertrichosis and, when living, had traveled with a freak show as "Rolf the Frightening Werewolf Boy." Though how he had ever pulled off the frightening part was beyond Seraphina's imagination. He acted like a canine as much as he did a human. The leader of the traveling carnival sideshow had rewarded all dog-like behavior and punished Rolf when he acted too much like a normal little boy. Rolf died when he was only seven years old, and the violence of his murder scared him so badly he failed to cross over the veil when it opened for his spirit, leaving a very confused little ghost trapped in the mortal realm.

"Miss Sera? Will you sing me a song? How about the one with the little songbird?"

"I will in a little bit, Rolf. First, we have to talk. Remember when we discussed the house rules?"

"But Miss Sera, I didn't remember how the jars went. I tried my best to put 'em back in order. Really, I did. And I didn't drop 'em this time. I was super-duper careful. See, first I put the one on with the smelly green goop. And then the black powder smells like licorice but makes me sneeze.

And then the one that rattles like old bones when you shake it really, really hard…"

Seraphina shook her head, and her shoulders drooped. She hadn't realized Rolf was down in the apothecary messing with the jars again. The purpose for the chat was only to get him to stop pestering Finn because he was losing his patience with her *little ghost pet.*

"Rolf," Seraphina interrupted.

"… I like to put some in my hand and then spit on it cause it fizzes up something awful."

"Rolf, enough."

He would go on and on at this rate. How many of the apothecary jars had he gotten into anyway?

"Are you mad, Miss Sera?" Rolf turned and looked up at her.

"No, of course not. However, when we are done here, you do have to go down to the shop and show me every single jar you touched. I need to put them back in order before Finn has a coronary."

"Finn's gonna have a canary bird?" Rolf's voice rose.

"No, Rolf. A coronary. Um, before he gets real upset." Seraphina tried not to laugh. She wasn't very good at this whole discipline thing, clearly. "What I needed to tell you was no more rubbing on Finn's legs, or anyone else's for matter, while you are here."

"Aw." Rolf whined and made sounds like a mewling puppy.

"Come on now. We are talking like people. You don't have to act like a doggie with me, Rolf. I like you just the way you are."

Rolf stopped his puppy whining and smiled.

She said, "Remember, I explained this before. Others cannot see you the way I can. You scare them when you come out of nowhere and rub against them."

"Dat's the whole point. I like to scare them, Miss Sera." Rolf laughed. "You shoulda just seen how high the Sin Eater jumped. He said worty-dirds after that, though. I covered my ears."

"Worty-dirds?"

"You know. Cusses," Rolf whispered and then much louder, "He knows a lot of them too."

Rolf's eyes were big, but his tone implied he was impressed by Finn's colorful vocabulary.

"Yes, he does, doesn't he?" Seraphina shook her head. This was exactly why this whole situation was so difficult. He was so young and had the attention span of a hyperactive cocker spaniel. "Rolf, I bet you will have so many new adventures after going behind the veil."

Rolf stiffened and scooted his belly across her legs. He rose and sat by her, picking at his nearly transparent shoe laces. "I thought that was what I wanted, back when I died. And again when Ms. Allen left me behind."

Seraphina said, "We talked about that. She died too, Rolf. I'm sure she looked for you and tried to keep her promise. Most humans only have a short window of time to cross over. Besides, you said you had followed some children to the park that day."

"They were playing and the little boy wasn't being fair. He peeked while he counted, so I pulled down his britches when he found the pretty girl with the blue dress." Rolf snickered.

Seraphina nodded. She'd heard the story, at least ten times. He must have really thought his trick was funny.

"Focus, Rolf. We're talking about the veil, remember? You helped me with my spell on the book and it worked perfectly. I was able to link your emotions, the sadness you used to feel, to the book. Thank you for sitting so still under the table until the auction was over. I really appreciate your help. Now, I want to help you. You should have crossed over the veil a really, really long time ago. I don't want you to ever feel lonely or afraid again."

"But I'm not lonely anymore, Miss Sera. Cause I gots you now. I reckon you're even a better friend than Ms. Allen was. She got all old. Plus, she could only hear me, but you can see me too. And you lemme sleep in your closet on your soft stuff. I pretend I'm a handsome prince…"

And here she was again, the exact same place they wound up every time Seraphina tried to convince Rolf it was time to cross over. She sighed.

Rolf stopped and said, "It's Finn, right? Grumpy Sin Eater don't want me here no more? We can just leave him behind. We don't need him and his nasty ol' cusses anyhow."

"Rolf, I cannot leave Finn. Ever. I explained that to you. The curse, remember? Our only chance of breaking it is if we stay together."

"I know, I know." Rolf crossed his arms over his chest and his lower lip pouted. "If I promise to stop touching the Sin Eater, I can stay here?"

"Only until we get you across the veil." Seraphina ruffled his hair. "Did you feel that?"

"Like a wind blowing on my head." Rolf smiled. "Do it a'gin."

"Okay, concentrate. I'll do it again."

Rolf giggled and shook his head under her hand.

Seraphina wasn't sure she could open the veil on command anyway, but once she figured it out, Rolf had to be ready. Convincing him to go was yet another complication.

"All right, buddy. Miss Sera needs her coffee and then we have to straighten out those jars. Remember, I'll be out most of the day so please be good for me, okay?"

Rolf nodded, but his mischievous grin worried her.

Seraphina took a sip of her coffee as she looked over the shop's inventory report on her laptop. She'd ordered the usual items tourists would buy next month: shaped candles, a few costume accessories, colorful sugar skulls, and books on Samhain, Halloween, and Dia de los Muertos lore.

Stacks of boxes sat ready to be unpacked and stocked on the seasonal shelves, but she knew she'd forgotten something. Oh, the masks. She had another box ready to pick up at the Arcade's post office.

The thought of masks and the Arcade brought a fresh wave of butterflies to Seraphina's stomach. Last night seemed like a dream, maybe a whirlwind—dressing up, her spell, the auction, the music, and the mysterious Marceau. What a night. She'd been wrapped up in the moment, Seraphina told herself, and was caught in the thrill of the spell working and winning the auction.

Seraphina used to believe, with her whole heart, she would be free to experience love one day. Now, after so long, her hope was a fragile, flickering flame. She'd almost given up entirely, but then Seraphina discovered the Blackthorne Grimoire had resurfaced right there in Nashville. Maybe, just maybe, she was meant to find a way to free herself. It might have been fate that put the mythical book in her path. If it did, then surely the grimoire would have an answer. Seraphina had risked exposure by doing the spell at the auction. Magic was not to be practiced in front of strangers, especially among humans, but she'd taken the chance because of her desperate hope that something, anything, in book would finally help. She had to break free from the curse that had held her prisoner for so long.

Was Marceau someone she could love?

The stray thought was dangerous. No, she chastised herself. Even if the grimoire contained an answer, it could take months, maybe even years, to find. She could only imagine the mysteries the book would reveal. Thorough, dedicated study of it could be her only focus now, not dark blue eyes and stolen glances.

Seraphina reassured herself things would feel different when she met with Marceau. The spark last night was from the excitement of it all, right? Beautiful masquerade costumes and the intoxicating music made anything possible last night.

Today, in the harsh sunlight and hot, humid air, she could not afford to indulge in romantic fantasies about handsome strangers. She knew where the kind of feelings she'd had last night could lead. For her, unfortunately, they were fatal.

Taking another sip, Seraphina refocused. One step at a time. Today would be all business. First, check the jars Rolf messed with. Then a trip to the bank and the Schermerhorn. She had made arrangements to pay her bid and pick up the book.

Assuming all of that went well, she was meeting Marceau at one o'clock. He said he wanted to offer his services. What could it mean? Well, he had some sort of magical ability, that much was clear.

Seraphina would politely, but firmly, decline his services, whatever they were. Marceau tempted her, but no help he could offer was worth the risk, so she would say "no thanks" and that would be that.

She hadn't even seen him without his horned mask. Maybe he was ugly. Surely, his forehead was huge. Or his nose could look like a beak. Perhaps, his eyes were too close together.

His eyes. They were a deep shade of blue and had sparked with both intellect and humor. His dark hair had been a little long on top. A lock had fallen forward and rested against his mask when he confronted her about the spell. Seraphina had fought the urge to reach up and touch it. He'd had a hint of a five o'clock shadow on his defined jaw. His mouth...

"What's with that look, Seraphina?" Finn asked as he poured a cup of coffee.

She jumped so high she tottered and almost fell off her stool.

Finn regarded her beneath long eyelashes, trying to read her. "You look guilty," he said while adding a copious amount of cream and three sugars.

"Yeah, well, you drink coffee like a girl," she replied. Seraphina tried to appear cross but wound up grinning.

"Okay. Nice try, love. What gives? You were strange when you came in last night too. Said you won the auction, but that's not what you were just thinking about, was it?"

Finn leaned back against the counter and peered over the rim of his mug as he sipped.

No. She was most definitely not talking about Marceau with Finn. If he found out she was meeting a strange guy for lunch, whom she had just been daydreaming about no less, Finn would blow it all out of proportion. He wouldn't understand. He'd read way too much into it already and might flip out and try to stop her from ever laying eyes on Marceau again. Plus, he would worry. *Needlessly* worry, she amended. No reason to even go there. She needed to deflect. Now.

"So, I have been thinking about Kan... Khat," Seraphina was quick to correct herself.

Finn squared his shoulders and frowned, defensive. "I have told you before, love. My relationship with her is not something I want to discuss. I will not..."

"No, Finn. Seriously. I'm not trying to pick a fight here." Seraphina raised her hands. "I'm beginning to understand now. She told me a little about her past, and said you ate her sin, but I'm not sure she understood much about how it all worked before last night."

"Khat told you I ate her sin? You two talked about what I do?" Finn's voice slid up into a whole other register in disbelief.

"Yes, we sort of, um, bonded a tiny bit when you were sick. She told me about Virgil being her father, the stupid jerk face."

Finn stood, sipped his coffee and started pacing. "I hope her feelings for me haven't changed. She never mentioned any of this last night. I've held back on the less attractive realities of being a Sin Eater. It felt improper to discuss it too much at first when I was a relative stranger to her. And then, well, as things changed and we grew closer, I figured we were only a more physical pair. Less talking and more action."

Seraphina fidgeted. "Yeah, moving on, please."

"Oh yes, of course."

"Mm-hmm. Well, I figured she wouldn't know how to bring up last night." Seraphina shrugged. "So on the bright side, she seemed kind of fascinated and open to learning more about what you do. I guess things will be easier now. I saw how much she cares about you, and it's obvious you care about her."

Seraphina flipped her spoon over and back, over and back, on the counter. Her words were not coming out well. She'd given this a lot of thought as she tossed and turned last night.

"Look, I think you should invite her to dinner tomorrow. I know you limit your time together here in the loft, and I don't want you to do that anymore. You two have been together since the beginning of the year. It's awkward with you tiptoeing around, trying to protect me from seeing you together, in love, whether you admit it to each other yet or not." She stopped to give him a *look*. Finn lifted a shoulder in response, not committing to the idea, but not arguing it either, so she continued, "I appreciate the kid gloves, Finn, and I guess I did need it that way for a long time. I'm sorry if that's made it hard for you to have normal relationships, but I think I can handle being around the two of you more now."

"I just never thought you'd feel comfortable, would be okay, with being around a couple type situation. I would never, ever want to hurt you, love. I wouldn't want you to feel..."

"Like a third wheel? I'll be okay, really. She's growing on me. Khat's actually kind of sweet in her own way. It would be so nice to have a girlfriend I could talk to about everything. Someone who could know our full situation, you know? She handled the sin stuff really well, and I think with time I could open up. There's something about her." Seraphina smiled.

"Tell me about it," Finn agreed.

"Khat was really confused when she realized how sins could make you ill. I think she wondered if you had eaten her sins at all." Seraphina shifted her weight and straightened her shirt.

"Her sins are so minuscule. They didn't even weaken me."

"You need to tell her that, Finn. I think it would help her understand."

The grandfather clock downstairs chimed.

"Oh, I have to hurry. I'm picking up the book today." Seraphina ran down the hall to get dressed. She needed to be at the Schermerhorn in barely more than an hour.

Seraphina made it to the Schermerhorn with a few minutes to spare. She paid her bid with a certified check and was handed a leather pouch that held the large book. It was heavier than it looked. Seraphina allowed herself one quick peek before hugging it to her chest as she walked out into the sunny morning. She took her prized possession home and locked it in the apothecary safe. The shop and their loft had enough magical enchantments to rival Fort Knox, but she wanted to be cautious. She checked her reflection one last time and sternly reminded herself. All business. Pick up the mail, eat a quick lunch, and resist Marceau... ugly. He'll definitely be ugly. With that thought repeating in her mind, Seraphina left for their rendezvous.

The Arcade felt like 350 feet of sauna today. Located between Fourth and Fifth Avenue North, the Arcade was a glass-roofed, two-story shopping district that had seen better days.

In 1903, it was the first shopping center in Nashville. Although the glory days were behind it, Seraphina loved the bones of the old building and thought it had character. She loved the art deco post office decorated by a round bronze seal of a mail carrier on a speeding horse. She walked there every day, except Sunday, to check the shop's mailbox.

Art galleries lined the upper level. While small shops of all kinds, and restaurants, popular with the hurried lunch crowd, lined the mall's lower level. Colorful state flags lining the Arcade hung limply in the humid air. A row of small, iron tables lined both sides, the perfect place to sit and watch people from all walks of life: transients, struggling musicians, blue-collar workers who kept the city running, and even wealthy executives in expensive suits.

Seraphina always came when the lunch crowd was dwindling, but there was still a hint of hustle and bustle. Another hour or two and the place would be like a ghost town. Where was the fun in that?

She went inside the post office and waved at the clerk behind the counter. Bob nodded and went to the back room to get any packages the small rented box could not hold. She met him at the counter with a few envelopes in her hand and they exchanged the usual pleasantries. He handed her a medium-sized box, her masks, and a thick padded envelope.

"Thanks, Bob. See you, Monday."

As she stepped back into the breezeway, Seraphina noticed the clock hanging above the middle of the second level connector. It was one o'clock.

Her mouth went dry. Maybe Marceau wouldn't come. She hadn't been rude, but she also hadn't accepted his dinner invitation. She turned toward one of the exits as two homeless men traded enthusiastic hellos.

"May I assist you?" asked a masculine voice from close beside her.

Chapter Thirteen

Sneaking up on her wasn't planned, but it had been easy. Marceau hadn't meant to scare her. Well, maybe just a little.

Seraphina whirled and a padded envelope flew through the air. "Oh."

Marceau stooped and picked up her discarded packet. "I didn't mean to frighten you, Seraphina."

He stood perfectly still. Seraphina's eyes widened.

"I-I think you did. Why else would you be trying to hide a smile?"

Busted.

Marceau let the smile form. "Ah, direct. I remember now."

"Ah, old-fashioned. I do, as well." She tried to fight it, but she smiled too.

Seraphina walked over to an empty table and sat down with the box and stack of mail. When she looked back up at him, her smile had faded.

"I was pleasantly surprised when I googled this place, as you suggested, and saw it was a charming, historical landmark and not a place with video games. Why, may I ask, did you choose here? I would've taken you anywhere in the city. Nashville has much trendier places."

"I come here every day." Seraphina gestured behind her to the post office. "The Arcade has character. Plus, I like to people watch. And the spanakopita is great."

Marceau laughed, surprised by how relaxed he was around her, "Luckily, I like spanakopita too."

Greek Touch was just ahead. A quaint little restaurant with blue-lined windows, and a bust of an ancient Greek sitting on a pedestal in one window, a cartoon profile covered the other. Marceau held the door and waved his arm.

The place was tiny, with a few small tables sitting to the left and the cash register on the counter to the right, a small grill directly behind. Large frames held napkins on which customers had written friendly reviews of the food and helpful tips on what to order.

Behind the counter, a cheerful looking man with a white goatee winked at Seraphina. "I know what you like." He asked Marceau, "What can I get for you?"

"The same," Marceau replied without hesitation.

"Two Spanakopita lunch specials with potatoes and lemonades it is."

He turned to prepare their food.

"Where are you from?" the man asked over his shoulder as he worked a flattop grill overflowing with potatoes, onions, and peppers.

Marceau saw no reason to lie. "New Orleans."

Seraphina peered at him over the box she'd refused to let Marceau carry.

"Good eatin' down there. Been there a time or two myself," said the man.

"Yes, sir, I don't often complain. Though, this smells promising, as well."

As soon as their order was ready in white Styrofoam to-go containers, Marceau stepped forward to pay. Seraphina opened her mouth to protest, but Marceau shook his head. He carried their lunches and followed her to one of the small tables outside. Eating in silence for several minutes, they each stole glances at the other between bites.

She fidgeted, a lot.

The silence was making him nervous. He usually enjoyed it, but he wanted to know more about her. Finally, after taking a drink of the fresh squeezed lemonade, he said, "Okay, the spanakopita was an excellent choice. I was prepared to tease you for selecting such a casual place. This, however, is delicious." Marceau tilted the cup to her, indicating the lemonade met his approval too.

Seraphina smiled. "I had enough fancy last night to last me for a while. Don't get me wrong, I like a night out as much as anyone, but last night was, well, intense."

"That it was." Marceau stabbed a potato with a plastic fork.

"Look, let's not dance around this. I meant what I said. The book isn't for sale. I don't want to waste your time." Seraphina paused to sip her drink. She was giving him an out.

"I also meant what I said, I'm no longer trying to purchase it, or take it either."

Her eyebrows rose at that.

Marceau continued, "I believed you when you said money wouldn't persuade you to part with the grimoire. And unless I am mistaken, taking the book from you now would be impossible."

Seraphina put down her drink and leveled a suspicious frown at him.

His thoughts were a jumble. Marceau wasn't setting this up right. Clearing his throat, he tried again. "I'll explain. You picked the book up this morning, I assume?" She nodded. "Then you have taken ownership. The book is now yours and yours alone."

"What are you talking about?" She took a bite of the flaky spinach filled pastry.

"I believe the Blackthorne Grimoire has an ownership hex attached to it. If true, you're now tied to the book," Marceau explained.

"Not another freaking cur—" she started. Seraphina huffed and blew a lock of hair away from her face.

Marceau leaned in. "Not another what, Seraphina?"

"Nothing. Just why does every old thing have to have stories and rumors of doom? Can't some things just be... normal?" Seraphina spoke very quickly.

The fans blowing an artificial breeze into the Arcade freed some of her red hair from her high ponytail, and Marceau watched the stray lock as it blew near her face. It reminded him of the bright red design he'd seen flash across her skin last night when she finished her spell. There had been something familiar in the delicate curves of scrolled design on her flesh.

Seraphina's hair wafted again and so did something else. A thread that didn't belong caught his eye, a pale, thin trace of old magic.

Marceau regarded her differently. His eyes no longer focused on her features. He looked around her, through her. He sat still as stone watching as she began to fidget, rolling a small potato from side to side with her fork.

"Seraphina?" Marceau whispered. "Do be still for a moment, please?"

She froze.

Gone was Marceau's formal, confident tone and smile. He was not being playful. Something was *off* about her.

Several minutes passed by, with her not moving and him looking right through her. He hadn't moved, hadn't even blinked.

Then Marceau jumped and drew a loud, deep breath. He shook his head and wiped his damp brow with a napkin, refocusing his eyes on hers.

Seraphina appeared extremely uncomfortable. "Look, I think I'll go." She closed her lunch container. "This is all a little too strange, and I have to work this afternoon."

Marceau said, "You're cursed."

Her mouth dropped open and she almost knocked her lemonade over. Marceau caught it mid-fall and set it right.

"I don't know what you are talking about," Seraphina snapped. She ducked her head as she placed the strap of her bag back across her chest.

"Seraphina. Stop." Marceau reached his hand out to touch her, but she recoiled.

"Rule number one with me. No touching. Ever. You got that?"

He withdrew his hand and nodded.

She added, "Non-negotiable."

"Yes, forgive my familiarity. But give me five more minutes, please. Allow me to explain how I know. Then I promise I won't try to stop you from leaving."

"Five minutes." Seraphina leaned back in her chair and stilled. She gazed around the area and swatted at the air near her face though Marceau couldn't see what had bothered her. She took a long swig of her lemonade.

"Last night, I mentioned my services. I'd planned to trade use of my gift in exchange to access parts of the grimoire." He waved his hand as if that was far from important now.

"And what is your gift?" Seraphina asked as she tucked the same loose piece of hair behind her ear.

"Curses."

She leaned in and he did too, mirroring her action without even realizing. Marceau said, "I have a gift with curses. I can see them. Read them. Often, I can find a way to break them."

Seraphina drew a sharp breath and asked, "How?"

"Every hex is as unique as a snowflake. They each have nuances pulled from their creators and intricate ties are fed by the object," he said, nodding at her, "or person to which they are bound."

Marceau closed his lunch container and paused. He wanted her to understand his fascination with curses.

He continued, "They're like a puzzle to me. Each requires careful examination. Sometimes the nature of the hex is straightforward, other times it's more like unraveling a complex web. Also, they vary in strength. The price a person pays to bind a hex determines the curse's intensity."

"What type of price?"

"A tithe of pain, usually. I see traces of yours. But they are faint, much lighter than they should be. How long have you had it?"

Her shoulders drooped. She drew in her arms and tucked them over her stomach. Marceau wanted to comfort her, to hold her hand. He lowered his hands into his lap instead.

"A lot longer than you might think." Seraphina's monotone voice trailed off into a whisper. She looked behind him with an empty stare.

He waited for her to say more, but her mind was somewhere else. "I'll make no promises, Seraphina, but I am willing to try. I may be able to help with your curse." Marceau's hand moved on its own. He reached for the stubborn lock of hair blowing in front of her face again. Seraphina shifted back and lifted her eyebrows in warning. His hand dropped. "I apologize. I don't know what came over me. No touching, non-negotiable." He forced a smile.

After moving her own hair behind her ear, Seraphina pressed her forehead with her fingertips as if she had a headache. "I guess I could let you see inside the grimoire. I don't know…" Seraphina hesitated.

"It's okay. Take time to think it through. Are you still unavailable tonight?" Marceau's confident air was gone.

"I, yes, I have plans."

"When can I see you again?" He hated the vulnerability in his voice, but if not tonight, when?

"I'm not sure. I need to think." She stood. The table screeched as its metal feet slid against concrete, and she held her head and said, "I-I need to go. Thank you for lunch."

Marceau sighed. "Of course. It was my pleasure."

Seraphina waited, the to-go container in her hand looking down at the box of masks and then around her.

Marceau took the Styrofoam box from her, careful his hand was nowhere near hers. He stacked his own lunch on top and walked to a nearby trash can. He had an idea of what was going on and it wasn't good. Seraphina was already distrustful of him. He'd shared too much about his power with curses, and now this?

"May I carry your box to the apothecary for you, Seraphina?"

She stepped back. "How do you know about that? I never mentioned the shop to you." Her voice raised louder and louder while checking the area behind her again.

"Seraphina, breathe, it's going to be okay." Marceau held his hands up. "I think you may be feeling disoriented? Unwell?"

She pressed her lips together and her brow wrinkled.

Marceau continued, "I believe your hex has reacted to my power. It's difficult to explain. It flared brighter right before I pulled my control back, almost like a built-in defense mechanism. Your curse seems tied deeply with your emotions. This unwanted side effect should be very temporary. I do apologize but couldn't have known it would react so vibrantly to my power. I only want to walk with you until I'm sure you're okay. I meant you no harm. Truly."

"If you mean no harm, then how do you know about the store? Are you *stalking* me?" Her voice had turned demanding.

"Your mail. The box and the envelopes all have the same address for the apothecary? On Second Avenue?" He pointed to the peeling mailing label on the package. "I remember spotting a clever sign with same name a few blocks from here. On an old Victorian fire station?"

Seraphina nodded.

"You have several pieces of business mail and mentioned you were working this afternoon. It wasn't a challenging mystery. I assure you I'm not stalking you. I only met you last night."

Her shoulders lowered as he spoke. "Sure. I guess I could use a hand since I'm… I seem to be a bit… I'm discombobulated." She covered her mouth to stifle a hysterical laugh.

Marceau frowned. "Discombobulated indeed. Yes, that about covers it." He picked up the box and tucked her mail under his arm. "Shall we?"

He made light conversation as they approached Broadway and walked past a line of legendary Honky Tonks. Marceau read each sign aloud and peered in with curiosity as they passed. "Legends, Tootsies, Robert's Western World, The Stage." It was early afternoon and already a steady stream of tourists filled the sidewalk lining the famous landmarks and gift shops. This was the heart of the Music City.

He asked about living in Nashville. Hoping the easy-going conversation about her home would help her feel grounded again. By the time they turned onto Second Avenue, she sounded more like herself.

"It reminds me of New Orleans in many ways. The tourism, the music pouring from bars, and the street performers. Of course, in New Orleans, it's beads, Mardi Gras, and the music is zydeco and jazz."

"And here it's honky tonks, cowboy hats, and boots, The music is mainly bluegrass and country. Though Nashville also has gospel, rock, and all kinds of music, really. But the crowds? They come to pay homage to the Opry."

"You love this city." It wasn't a question.

"I do."

Seraphina stopped in front of the Victorian fire station. It was a beautiful, three-story brick building complete with a turret. "Here we are. Thanks for walking me and carrying the mail. I am feeling better now."

Marceau didn't want to leave her. The sign on the door read CLOSED, but he wished she'd invite him inside. "I want to help with more than your postal deliveries, Seraphina. Will you let me try? To help you? I'd like to examine your curse further, whether you decide to share the grimoire or not. Your hex is quite complex."

Seraphina bit her lower lip and finally said, "The shop is closed until Monday. Finn's doing inventory. We're having Italian tomorrow for dinner." She looked up at him. "You could come. I'd like you to meet Finn. I want to get his opinion about your offer."

"Finn?"

"My best friend and roommate. And he's tied into the curse. So that makes whether we accept your help his decision too."

"I'd like to meet him. And I happen to love Italian." Marceau's eyes peered up at the old building. "So, you live upstairs?"

"Yes. Dinner at seven? I'm making pasta. Finn is fixing his sinful garlic knots." She giggled.

Marceau's eyebrow rose, an unspoken question.

"Oh, uh, a little inside joke." She paused. "You could bring wine if you like? I prefer red. Though I'm not sure about Khat."

"Your cat has a preference on wine, as well?" Marceau's brow furrowed.

Seraphina laughed again and Marceau's eyes closed for a moment. He enjoyed her amusement.

"No. No, Khat is Finn's girlfriend. I meant I'm not sure what type of wine she likes. Finn will drink whatever. He's more of a beer guy anyway."

"Okay, I'll be sure to cover the bases. Until then…" Marceau reached into his back pocket and pulled out a business card. Engraved in elegant print were his name and phone number. No title or other information. "In case you need to reach me before seven tomorrow."

Seraphina blushed as she carefully took the card, mail, and box from him without touching his hands.

"Bye, Marceau. Thanks again for lunch." She took a couple steps toward the door and turned back. "For the offer too. No matter how things turn out tomorrow night. Thank you for offering to help me and Finn."

"Seraphina, I saw death in your curse," Marceau admitted.

"Oh, I know. It was really scary the first time I died." She smiled, spun on her heels, and entered the store.

Marceau's mouth hung open as she closed the door. "The first time you died?" he asked no one.

Chapter Fourteen

"I invited someone to join us for dinner. And I want you to have an open mind, Finn," Seraphina said as she chopped vegetables for a salad with a large chef's knife.

"An open mind? I'm the very picture of acceptance and charitable nature." Finn laughed, pleased by his own ridiculous answer, but when he met her unsmiling eyes, he stopped kneading the dough under his hands. Suspicion was now written all over his face.

"Okay, let me start again. Someone else wanted the grimoire the other night. And when my spell prevented them from bidding, they recognized my magic."

"Why didn't you tell me about this when you came home? You only said you were tired and you won the book. Was it a human? You know the dangers these days with their smartphones and video websites."

She grabbed a tomato and gave him a look. "No, of course not. I'd have told you right away if it was a human. And try *not* to sound like an old man, Finn."

Finn usually smiled when she caught him sounding his age, not today apparently. "I thought you'd been acting strange since the auction. So who was it and why exactly did you invite them to our home?"

"Well, first, I was tired when I got home that night. I'd had a stressful week, remember? Second, I didn't quite know what to say about being caught. I'd already agreed to meet them yesterday. I wanted to see how went before I…" she sighed. "I'd planned to wrap up any loose ends at lunch and send them on their way."

"At lunch? And that didn't happen, I take it, or she wouldn't be coming to dinner?" Finn scrunched up his face.

"He." Seraphina looked up in time to see his jaw tighten. "*He* is coming to dinner."

"He." Finn resumed kneading a little harder than necessary. "And what does *he* want exactly, love?"

"He knows about…" She put down the knife. "He knows about the curse, Finn."

Finn smacked his hand on the dough and leaned forward. "You told some stranger about that? Why the hell would you do that, Seraphina?"

Crap. He said her name. Finn was upset. Big surprise.

"I didn't. You know I wouldn't just go tell someone I barely know all about our curse. Jeez, give me some damn credit." Hands on her hips, she glared at him. "He saw it, Finn. He figured it out on his own."

Finn leaned back, took a deep breath, and washed his hands. He dried them slowly. By the time he turned back to face her, he seemed calmer.

"I'm sorry. Really, I apologize." He rubbed a hand down his unshaven face and the white stubble made a scratchy sound. "I'm still on edge from my *sin overdose,* as you call it. I… You do know I don't mean to snap, right? I know it's no excuse that I'm on edge." He paused and tilted his head, "Wait, you said he *saw* it? He saw what?"

"I understand, Finn. But don't snap at Khat like that at dinner tonight. She's not used to your moodiness after a job."

Finn nodded.

"Anyway, he has a gift for seeing—no, that's not what he said—for reading curses. He was talking to me one minute and the next moment it was as if he were looking right through me." She added the chopped tomatoes to the salad bowl. "I felt a brush of energy or power. But not on my skin, against something around me. It's hard to describe."

Finn stared around her as if trying to see what she meant.

"I felt confused. Anxious. He said it was my hex reacting to him and it flared at him, some kind of a defense thing. He seemed surprised, but I don't really know what that means. It was unpleasant, though. I felt dizzy."

"Wait, did he drug you? If the bas—"

"No, no. I swear, Finn." Seraphina shook her head. "It was nothing like that. When he realized how it was affecting me, he stopped right away. I felt his power pull away. I was sort of in shock, I think because I wanted it to come back. I missed it. He could've tried to take advantage of the situation but didn't. He, well, he was gentle and kind."

"Oh, hell, Seraphina." Finn crossed his arms. "You don't have a crush on him, right? Do you care about him? You know we cannot risk what could happen."

"No. I don't even know him. It isn't like that, okay? Besides, I know better, Finn."

"All right, then tell me he is a wrinkly old man. He's a warty, rather ugly fellow who smells like moldy cheese. Tell me he is repulsive."

"Who smells like cheese?" Khat asked as she came in swinging a grocery bag. When she heard Finn and Seraphina were both cooking, she quickly assigned herself dessert duty and left for the store.

"No one smells like cheese," Seraphina muttered.

She and Finn stared at each other across the kitchen island. "And he is not old either. Twenty-five, I'd guess? I didn't exactly ask to see his driver's license.

"So ghastly ugly then? I was right about the warts?" Finn sounded hopeful, desperate almost.

"No. Jeez, Finn. I didn't see any warts. He isn't bad looking, I suppose. But that's not what matters here at all," Seraphina said. "Pay attention to the important part, would you? He claims he finds weaknesses in hexes. He doesn't just weave them. He can break them too. You know how rare that is?"

Marceau had sounded sincere, but she'd never met anyone who had a similar gift. Many others created curses. Travelers and those who practiced voodoo specialized in them. Seraphina had sought help from members of both, but no one had been either able or willing to help. A curse weaver was easy enough to find, but a curse breaker was extremely rare.

"If it's even true." Finn folded his arms across his chest.

"Of course, if it's true. Which is why I invited him to dinner tonight. We have to, at least, check his claims out. But he did figure out I'm hexed without a hint at all from me, so that's something, isn't it? He said he wants to try to help us."

Finn asked, "Help us? And what does he want in return, love? Why would some irritatingly wart-free stranger who isn't bad looking, you suppose, want to help break our curse?"

Seraphina hated this side of Finn. He was usually so open and carefree with her, and now with Khat. But Finn had taken in countless sins. He'd seen—no he had personally experienced—the absolute worst, most vile deeds of others. When it came to outsiders, he was not trusting by any definition of the word.

"Finn, please try to have an open mind. I understand why you're leery. He's offered his help, but it's not as though I have accepted it yet. I invited him here so you can meet him, and we can decide together. I know we both have a say. We share the curse."

"You did not answer me, love. What exactly does he want from you in return?" Finn emphasized each word.

"The book. He wants access to the Blackthorne Grimoire."

"See? I knew there was something he wanted. Well, that better be all he wants. I'm not going to lose you again, Seraphina." Finn slapped a towel over the dough and walked away. From down the hall, he added, "Next time, there may be no way of pulling you back from the dead."

"Are you all right?" Khat asked and put her hand on Seraphina's back. "I've never seen him like that. I don't understand."

"Ugh, I'm okay. Just pissed off. Finn's different with outsiders, Khat. He does not trust easily. It's a side effect of what he does."

"Oh," Khat said, tilting her head, "that does make sense. I guess I wouldn't either if I'd felt so much sin and could read it on others."

"Yeah, I just hope Marceau's sins are of the more mundane variety. Or this dinner could be a complete fiasco."

"Marceau, huh? Ooh la la. Is he as sexy as his name?" Khat giggled.

"Unfortunately," Seraphina grumbled and she started chopping again. "And don't think for a moment, Finn won't point it out."

The grandfather clock downstairs chimed. Seraphina put the salad on the table. Khat set the table. It looked lovely. Fragrant purple and white flowers in small, low vases and tea candles cast their flickering light on the mixed plates. The whole scene resembled a fancy tablescape from a magazine.

Seraphina jumped and almost knocked over a wine glass as the buzzer rang for the door. "I got it," she called out and headed toward the stairs.

As she passed the hallway, Khat's voice soothed, "…trust her judgment. You never know this may be a great opportunity…"

Earlier, Finn had come back to the kitchen to finish his contribution to dinner. Garlic rolls were baking in the oven now, filling their home with the aroma of fresh bread. Seraphina didn't enjoy the aroma nearly as much as usual. She had to force replays from her night at the Woodard mansion from her mind.

Finn had barely spoken to her all afternoon. He'd finally stopped slamming things around, which was good, but he was closed down. It hurt when he acted so distant.

Seraphina hoped she hadn't made a mistake by inviting Marceau. It wasn't because Finn was jealous or territorial. Or even that he was a controlling jerk, which was how he'd acted earlier. Finn was afraid. And he was trying to keep her alive.

She opened the door. "Hi," she started, but it died in her throat.

Flowers.

Oh, *come on.* Not good. Not at all.

Marceau stood there looking too handsome in a black sweater and dark, snug jeans, a canvas bag in one hand and in the other held a small bouquet of vibrant dahlias. Her favorite.

Damn it.

"Come on in." She backed up without taking her eyes off him.

"I hope you like dahlias," Marceau said as he handed them to her.

"Yes, they're actually my favorite." Seraphina frowned at the bouquet.

"If you like them, then why is your forehead all wrinkled like that?" As Marceau stepped inside, the smell of him enveloped her space, and she was struck silent by how intimate the sensation became. She inhaled, but discreetly because she didn't want to look like a weirdo.

"Oh, um."

"It's okay, Seraphina. What's wrong?"

Marceau took another step, and his closeness was overwhelming. Seraphina shuffled back and the familiar smells of the herbs and essential oils in the shop helped clear her mind.

"It's just that, well, Finn is a little concerned about your intentions. I reassured him you only wanted access to the book for helping me, for helping *us*. That you had no interest in…"

"I see. So he may question my motives if he sees the flowers?" Marceau interjected.

"Yeah, probably. But it was so nice of you to bring them."

"Relax. It's okay, really."

Marceau held his hand out for the bouquet and she bit her lip while giving them back, careful not to touch his hand. He walked over to the sales counter and laid the flowers near the register.

"Let's leave the dahlias down here, for now. I'd prefer to not upset your friend before I even have the chance to meet him."

"He…" Seraphina realized her shoulders were so tensed they almost touched her ears. She took a deep breath and centered herself. Her shoulders lowered as she exhaled. "Finn is just really protective. Thanks for understanding."

Marceau turned, surveying the apothecary. "This is quite a place, Seraphina."

He walked along one of the long shelves, surveying the dark blue hermetic bottles, each labeled and organized. Stopping at a tincture made of a scarce dried Amazonian flower, he made an appreciative whistle. "Impressive."

"Thanks. I'm glad you like it. We've been collecting them for many years. Finn is quite an herbalist." She was an accomplished herbalist too but preferred to brag about Finn's talent. He'd studied so hard. "We get orders from all over the world for the rare specimens and tinctures."

Seraphina turned the door's three deadbolts. Her hand glowed and illuminated a red circle against the door as she activated the magical locks.

Marceau raised a brow.

"Oh, they are designed to keep beings out. Like I said, we have some very valuable items here that would be quite dangerous in the wrong supernatural's hands. I'm not taking you prisoner or anything creepy."

Marceau's laugh echoed, deep, masculine.

"Hungry?" Seraphina asked in a high pitch voice trying to deflect from what she'd just said.

"Famished. Something smells wonderful. I brought beverages as requested." He lifted the canvas bag. Glass bottles clinked together.

"I'm starving too. I've been smelling dinner for the last hour. Come on then." Seraphina started up the stairs. She stopped and turned without notice. The bag's contents clanged together again as Marceau stopped short to avoid walking into her.

She said, "Finn is my best, my dearest, friend. He's wonderful, really."

"But?"

"But, he does not trust you. Well, not yet. So, I just wanted to." She hesitated.

"To warn me?" Marceau smiled. "Seraphina, it's okay. I'll be fine. I'm sure he will be too. I can understand him being protective of you."

She took a deep breath, started up the stairs. "You're right. I'm probably worrying over nothing. Let's go see what you brought. I think I could use a drink."

He chuckled again causing goosebumps on her arms.

When they arrived in the large open area of her loft, Seraphina was relieved Finn had come out of his room. He was taking steaming rolls from the oven. Finn turned, locked eyes with Marceau, and slowly set the hot pan on a trivet on the dark marble counter. "Well, you were right, love, he did come."

"Love? I didn't realize the two of you were…."

"Oh, they aren't together like that at all. He calls me Sparrow. It's a Sin Eater thing, I think." Khat said as she bounced into the room and smiled appraisingly at Marceau before going to Finn and leaning into his side. Finn broke eye contact with Marceau long enough to kiss the tip of Khat's nose before resuming his glare.

Marceau took a sharp breath.

Finn raised his arm and Khat snuggled into his hold.

"A Sin Eater and a djinn?" Marceau turned to Seraphina, incredulous. "I assumed your Finn would be of the magical community, but my, my, what interesting company you keep." He bent, "Let me guess, you keep an exoskell as a pet?"

Huh? Exoskells were monstrous tentacled skeletal creatures. "Of course not, an exoskell would be ripping away your flesh by now… Wait, a djinn? What are you talking about?"

"Me," Khat said. Finn stiffened and his arm was holding her in a more protective way now. "I don't know how he could tell so easily. But, he's talking about me."

"Glamours don't work well on me. My work requires I travel in some exotic circles and the Djinn Faction granted me the gift of Sight so I could complete a task for them."

"How convenient." Khat's smile was forced.

"Hold up. Let's just back this train up, shall we?" Seraphina said. She was gaping at them, her head bouncing back and forth like a tennis match.

"You are a djinn?"

Khat nodded. "A djinn halfling."

"Halfling?"

"I'm at least a quarter Spellcaster on dear old dad's side, and my mother is a djinn, so yes. I'm not sure how the quarter Possessed affects my genetics, but I can't rule it out."

"That is quite some pedigree. And you knew about this?" Seraphina fired the question squarely at Finn.

Finn was still staring at Marceau, his jaw set.

"Oh, quit with the stupid stare off. Look at me, Finn. I'm the one you are catching hell from, not him. Did you know?"

Finn stared down at the floor and shifted his weight, then raised his eyes to meet hers. He swallowed and gave the tiniest nod.

Seraphina crossed her arms over her chest and said, "You did, Finn. You knew she was djinn. And you were hiding it from me?"

Finn closed his eyes and took a pained breath. In a soft voice, he said, "I was planning to tell you, love. I just wanted you to get to know Khat a little better. To trust her before..."

"You conniving jerkface." Seraphina got almost in his face. Her fists clenched at her sides.

In a louder voice, Finn said, "I know, Khat. She would never use her power against either of us, love, and I trust she wouldn't..."

"Oh, give me some damned credit. I know that, Finn. I'm not mad for what she is." Seraphina waved her arm at all of them. "We're all, who we are. I doubt any of us had a damn choice in it, did we?" She looked around. "I'm pissed off because you were hiding it from me. You've been manipulating me. Waiting until I was friends with Khat while you withheld the truth. You didn't trust me enough to know the truth and to still give her a chance."

"Love, I…"

"Oh, don't you *love* me right now. Finn McKenna, I've been tiptoeing around here all day. Worrying and feeling, well, guilty for inviting someone to dinner who might *possibly* upset you. Even though I don't think he poses a threat…"

"Maybe I should go." Marceau took one long stride back.

"No. You, stay put." Seraphina pointed and glared at him.

Marceau's eyes opened wide, but he halted his retreat. Finn and Marceau exchanged a look. The irritating guy look. The "I know women can be kind of crazy" look.

"Stop it, you two. You can bond in a minute, right now I am busy having a hissy fit."

Finn laughed. Marceau and Khat jumped and looked at him confused. Seraphina's mouth twitched.

"Nuh uh, it is not going to work, Finn." Seraphina sucked in her lower lip and bit down.

"Are you finished with your hissying?" Finn had managed before he began shaking from holding his laughter.

Seraphina stomped her foot and gave in. "Oh, damn it," she said as she burst into uncontrollable laughter too.

Marceau grinned at Khat, "Do they do this often?"

Khat's shoulders raised and dropped. "I have no clue. This is my first time invited to dinner too."

Seraphina's laugh died down. She pointed her finger at Finn and said, "Look you. We don't keep secrets like that. I told you what Marceau's power was right away and you still pouted and acted all pissy. I put up with you stomping around and slamming things half the day. I needed you to trust *my* judgment in inviting him here, but you didn't."

"You are absolutely right, love." Finn put his hands up. "Can I safely call you love again?" He raised an eyebrow and smirked.

Seraphina nodded but crossed her arms.

"Okay, love," Finn said. "I apologize. I should have trusted you both with Khat's," he said with a lifted shoulder, "unusual pedigree as Marceau put it. And I should've trusted your judgment on your new... *friend.*" He emphasized the friend part a bit too hard, but it was clear the drama was over.

Seraphina's arms dropped, and she smiled. "Okay. I accept. Now let's stop behaving like children. We have company for a change. We both worked hard on dinner. Smelling your garlic knots has been making my mouth water all day, and Marceau was about to offer us a drink."

Marceau stood still. Neither he nor Khat had moved an inch since she had ordered him to stay put.

"Ahem, that's your cue, Marceau," said Finn.

"Oh, yes, of course." Marceau approached the counter and set his bag down. He pulled out a pricey red wine, a white wine she didn't recognize, and a bottle of Gentleman Jack.

Finn nodded at the Jack and asked, "On the rocks?"

"Please," Marceau responded.

"*Men.*" Seraphina blew out her breath puffing her hair off her forehead.

"Red for me," Khat said, laughing.

"Me too," Seraphina added.

Seraphina walked around the counter, pulled a corkscrew from a drawer and slid it across the granite counter to Marceau. She turned and gloved up before pulling two deep-dish lasagnas from the oven and placing them on the stovetop.

"Fifteen minutes for the lasagna to rest." She turned and took the wine Khat offered. After a long sip, she asked, "So, how did you know Khat was a djinn?"

"Well, she's kind of shimmery for starters. As a Spellcaster, you should be able to see that, right?" Marceau said and took a sip of his whiskey.

"I thought that was... I thought you just liked to wear a lot of gold glitter." Seraphina looked at Khat and *yes*, she had her usual slight shimmer.

Finn rolled his eyes and Khat snorted.

"Glitter?" Khat laughed. "I'm not twelve, Sera. Why would I wear glitter from head to toe?" She looked insulted, with a smile, though.

"I thought it was a stripper thing?" Seraphina added grimacing.

Khat stuck out an inhumanly long tongue. Whoa, Gene Simmons had nothing on her.

"Also, there are the ears, of course," Marceau added.

Seraphina stared at Khat's ears. They looked perfectly normal to her until Khat shrugged and dropped her glamour as a golden shimmer traveled down her body. Her small ears came to points at the top, just like every genie character Disney ever made.

"You can see why they might get unwanted attention. But on the bright side, I can be ready for a Renaissance Festival in two seconds flat." Khat giggled but sounded nervous.

Marceau tried to stifle a laugh.

Khat's brown skin had almost a sparkle to it as the kitchen light reflected on her face. Her features were more angled, sharper. Her heavy lidded eyes were sultry and surrounded by thick, full eyelashes. Her pupils elongated and looked feline, a striking shade of teal. They reminded Seraphina of a prism as they switched between silver and blue tones in the light, both shades much too bright to be human. Her smile revealed teeth just a tad sharper than normal. She was beautiful but definitely otherworldly.

Seraphina's mouth fell wide open.

Finn looked at her without any shock or surprise. He had obviously seen her natural form before.

Khat's smile fell and her gaze dropped down quickly. She shook her head from left to right. Her glamour shimmered down her body and fell into place once more.

"Well, all right then," Seraphina said, proud her voice was even. "On that note, let's eat."

Khat's head jerked up and Seraphina smiled. "Oh, I'm shocked all right, but Finn cares about you, and I like you too. The way I see it? You're one of us now."

Khat was the only one who appeared shocked.

"However, it's *so* not fair that you're even more beautiful than you let on. Thank goodness you tone it down a bit or no man would ever be able to look away." Seraphina winked. "Now, who else is hungry?"

Chapter Fifteen

Marceau picked up Seraphina's wine glass, then followed everyone else to the table. He didn't have much experience with being an invited guest for dinner and usually broke into other's homes rather than coming through the front door.

They all sat and eagerly passed the salad and rolls around the table.

"Two lasagnas?" Marceau asked.

"This one is vegetarian. That one has beef," Seraphina answered as she scooped a piece of the vegetarian pasta onto her plate. "When much of your power is focused on death, meat is… less appetizing. Let's leave it at that." She smiled and bit into a roll.

The conversation stayed light because the information divulged earlier had created a vacuum which only lighter subject matters and casual banter could balance.

Khat started the topic of music. Marceau was impressed by her knowledge of classical and that she took ballet lessons four days a week, which made Marceau cringe at the thought of another ballerina in his mind.

Sounding much older than he appeared, Finn debated whether folk music should retain its title when electrified. His pallor hinted he'd been a Sin Eater for quite some time. Marceau was curious but confident he'd learn more about him without asking, especially, if they agreed to share information about their curse.

"My favorite has to be blues, though. Not the dressed-up fancy kind, mind you. I like it to have sorrow and grit like the blues in the bayou." Of course, Marceau would relate the topic back to New Orleans.

Seraphina raised her glass in approval. "You should check out my favorite blues club on weeknights then, Bourbon Street Blues and Boogie Bar. It's in Printer's Alley, a couple doors down from the AAA club."

"I read a piece about Printer's Alley when I was looking for the Arcade. A seedier area of downtown, is it not?"

"The AAA is there, so supernaturals of all kinds hang out in the alley. But it's tourist-friendly even late at night." Seraphina sounded sad, which seemed odd. "Zeke, a spectre, runs Printer's Alley and the club with a transparent, yet iron fist. All nefarious activities are strictly limited to the inside of his establishment."

"I've never heard of the AAA. I thought Absinthe & Alchemy was the main supernatural gathering place downtown."

Khat chimed in, "Yeah, it is, but locals call it "triple A" rather than Absinthe and Alchemy." Khat added, "We Southerners are famous for our abbreviated speech patterns, you know."

"Okay, I get the first two A's, but what's the third?" Marceau asked.

Seraphina winced but looked up quickly when Khat burst into laughter.

Khat answered, "Why it's for *Ass,* of course. The first floor, Absinthe, is the bar. Despite the cloaking spells outside to make it look like the nastiest dive in town, humans do occasionally wander inside. The second floor, Alchemy, is strictly for supernaturals. It's where the gambling and negotiations for magical services take place. Money holds little value in Alchemy. The stakes are much higher than human paper and coins. They mainly gamble magical services and paranormal items. And then there's Ass, the unofficial name for the third floor, where I work as a dancer."

Marceau kept his expression neutral as he nodded. "Interesting, well it does make more sense now."

Finn laughed and Marceau relaxed again. "Printer's Alley is famous, so why haven't the supernaturals there garnered the attention of the humans in the city?"

Seraphina chimed in. "Oh, there was an incident a few years ago, a tourist snapped a few unfortunate photos when cell phones first took off. A curseweaver was a little too specific when she cast her hex to cause cameras to malfunction in the alley, but not all devices capable of taking photos. Zeke cleaned up the scandal and punished her in a quite public fashion. It made his point, though because Printer's Alley has been much more respectable ever since, but boy was it fun when it was seedier." A wide grin accompanied the last word.

"Now I get your joke yesterday about Finn's *sinful* garlic rolls," Marceau said as he took another from the basket. "They are delicious."

Khat laughed and tried to cover her amusement by shoveling in another huge bite of lasagna. She was already on her third piece.

Finn said, "Well, you know what Khat and I are, supernaturally speaking. And Seraphina has obviously shown her power since you caught her casting the spell on the book. I believe it's your turn to share, Marceau. Curses are your specialty?"

"Yes. I have an affinity for them. When I focus, I can often read them. Find weaknesses when possible, and I can manipulate them in many ways. It's all dependent on the power and nature of the specific hex."

Finn put down his fork and spun his whiskey glass on the table. "And what exactly does a hex look like?"

"Each is unique. They wind around the person, or thing, to which they are attached. Sometimes in elegant thin ribbons or thick binding chains. They vary in size and in color too like complex webs. And they usually hold traits from both the person who wove the hex and energy from the cursed object or person in their strands. Curses are fluid. That's why they last far longer than spells. They can react to emotions, environment, weather, any number of factors. It all depends on what the hex entails."

"Fascinating. I've never heard of anyone with the power to read a hex before." Finn looked at Seraphina and back at Marceau. "What makes some strong and others weak?"

"Most often, the intensity is determined by the skill and tithe paid by the curse weaver."

Seraphina asked, "Have you always been able to read them?"

"Yes, since I was a young child. Though I didn't understand what I was seeing or that everyone else couldn't see them. I was… misunderstood." Marceau cleared his throat. "I have no memories of my early childhood. But I was told, I wound up in a rather unfortunate facility until my ability came to the attention of my benefactor. He took me in and helped me to understand what I saw."

Marceau sat straighter. His relaxed demeanor evaporated when he talked about his past. Max wouldn't like his openness about how he learned his trade, so he was careful with what he shared.

"Is your benefactor a curseweaver too?" Khat asked.

"No, but he found private tutors to educate me—Travelers, Hoodoo rootworkers, and later a Voodoo priestess. They taught me to channel my powers into weaving and hex creation. Those same teachers also wove hexes for me so I could practice unraveling them, a talent he paid them well to keep secret."

"What an unusual childhood," Finn said. "Were curses all you studied?"

"I had access to a world-class magical library and was privately tutored in traditional studies, of course, but my primary education was of the art and nature of curses. I've studied them intensively since the age of seven."

Finn said, "And how fortunate you just happen upon a cursed woman."

"Finn, relax. Open mind, remember?" Seraphina said softly.

He stared at Marceau, but his eyes were unfocused and not on his face, an expression Marceau recognized.

"It's all right, Seraphina. I'm familiar with the abilities of Sin Eaters. You are also reading me, for lack of a better term, right? Assessing what my sins are." Marceau leveled his gaze on Finn. They stared across the table from each other.

"Indeed," Finn responded through tight lips. His whiskey glass sat still on the table now.

Marceau knew he shouldn't rock the boat, but he was curious. If Finn could truly see all of his sins, why did he let him still sit at his table? He risked asking, "And do I meet with your approval?"

"I'm reserving judgment." Finn sat back and raised his glass. "For now." He knocked back the last of his drink.

"Men." Khat rolled her eyes.

"When I noticed Seraphina's hex, I tried to read it right away. I was surprised at how faded it was. Until it reacted badly to my powers, that is."

"And why exactly did it react badly? What did you do to her?" Finn's gaze returned intense. He leaned toward Seraphina as if searching for any signs she'd been hurt.

Marceau wanted to explain, but it had become clear that Finn did not care what anyone had to say at the moment, except Seraphina. She said, "Like I said before, Finn, I was disoriented. Well, a little more than that. My emotions were all over the place—sad, scared, and confused."

"Elaborate," Finn said.

"Marceau said the hex flared brighter, so I think it was kind of like a magical hot flash. I had trouble breathing as if the air was really thick with humidity. And my mind felt cluttered. I was overwhelmed, vulnerable, and angry, all at the same time. It's hard to describe."

"And yet you invited him here?" Finn asked.

"It caught me off guard before. It's not often that people figure out I'm cursed over lunch, Finn. Plus, Marceau said the hex is tied to my emotions. So, it would make sense I'd have that kind of a reaction if my curse acted up, right? I want… Well, I'm hoping you might let him try to see what he can read from you."

"How does looking at the hex differ from how you are looking at me now?" Finn asked Marceau.

"Much in the way you looked at me moments ago as you searched for my sins, I suspect. I focus on you differently and look at the space around you until I find a trace or strand. Then I follow it until I can concentrate on the weave of the hex. It doesn't always affect the person I'm reading. Just depends on how powerful the curse is and the nature of it. However, if your emotions are in play as strongly as Seraphina's, I can make no promises."

"I will take it into consideration," Finn said.

Seraphina lightened the tone. "I could use some more wine. Anyone else want anything?"

"I need to check on dessert," Khat said. "I hope y'all saved some room."

Khat's lemon cake with raspberries was delicious and closed out the meal perfectly. When their plates were clean, Finn stood and started gathering the dirty dishes. Marceau joined him.

"After we get the dishes soaking and our dinner settles a bit, Marceau can have a go at reading the hex on me. I admit I'm interested in what he will find."

Khat reached over and squeezed Seraphina's hand, as if surprised Finn had relented.

Marceau smiled at the girls and cleared the table faster. He wanted more information about their curse. Hoping he could trade his skills for the grimoire was definitely a factor, but he also wanted to free Seraphina.

Chapter Sixteen

Seraphina seemed to dance her way around the room, turning on every single light. She even flipped on the stove hood light, just to be safe.

Marceau had pointed out the bright sunlight streaming on her from the glass roof at the Arcade helped him notice a trace of her hex. Finn's hex was tied hers, so he reasoned it would be faint as well.

Finn sat in a wooden dining room chair opposite Marceau in the center of the room. Khat and Seraphina perched a few feet away on the gray loveseat while Seraphina picked at the strings hung from the bottom hem of her jeans.

What would Marceau see? The weight of a thousand unspoken wishes pressed upon her chest. Would he find a way to break the curse? Would Finn get upset the same way she had? So much rested on this moment. After all these years of desperately clinging to hope, could this be when she finally found her freedom?

Finn sat relaxed. His fingers splayed on his lap and his face neutral. He watched Marceau, but his expression gave no hint as to his emotions, and he breathed in long, slow breaths.

Marceau mirrored Finn. A casual observer would find it curious seeing two young men sitting a few feet from each other. . . staring without conversation.

After what seemed like the longest minutes of Seraphina's life, Marceau's head cocked slightly to the side. "Ah, there we are," he said softly as if afraid he'd scare away whatever he'd seen. He leaned in closer.

Khat bit her nails, caught a glimpse of Seraphina, and forced a smile. Seraphina reached over and squeezed the hand Khat wasn't chewing.

Marceau's head slowly turned toward Seraphina, his gaze appearing out of focus. She felt heated as if hot air swirled around her, yet there was no breeze. He was reading her hex again.

Stay calm. Seraphina repeated like a mantra. She needed to keep her emotions locked down so Finn would not order the session stopped. Seraphina put up a mental barrier in hopes it would help protect her from the emotional backlash she'd felt at the Arcade.

Finally, Marceau spoke, "Fascinating, yours is similar in design but silver and gray." His eyes moved back and forth at her and then slowly to Finn. "Would you mind moving over to the couch, Seraphina? Walk slowly, please."

"Sure." Seraphina rose and rounded the coffee table and sat at the opposite corner of the couch, nearer to Finn.

Marceau studied an area between Finn and Seraphina as she sat.

"The strands connect you. When you were farther away, they were thinner. The closer you moved, they thickened and twined around each other." He sat back for a moment absorbing the change. "Okay, now would you leave the room, Seraphina? Go downstairs, perhaps."

"Okay." She turned and headed that way.

"Slower, please."

She obliged, looking back at Marceau when she started down the first few steps. He nodded for her to continue.

"I'll call for you in a moment." He was again following something only he could see between Finn and Seraphina.

She went downstairs and stopped to admire the dahlias by the cash register. Seraphina stroked the delicate purple petals of one. It was really sweet gesture by Marceau. Finn brought her flowers sometimes, but this was different. She pictured him standing in the door holding the bouquet, with a new type of smile. A shy one. Her stomach tightened as she pictured him.

Stop it, she chided herself before going to stand in front of the door.

After a couple of minutes, Marceau called for her. At his request, she returned to the loveseat with Khat again.

Marceau was concentrating on her with his brow furrowed. "The strands separated when you were far enough away from Finn. However, there was a tail, of sorts, left. A long bunch of strands undulated as if they were seeking to reconnect with you as you got to the bottom of the stairs, but then something changed." Marceau looked from Finn to her. "What did you do when you went downstairs?"

"I walked to the door and waited."

"You went straight to the door?"

"No. I stopped by the cash register for a moment." Her focus dropped to the floor and she began to pull at the strings on her jeans again.

"What did you do when you stopped, Seraphina?"

"I touched one of the..." Seraphina started. After taking a deep breath, she finished, "One of the dahlias you brought."

Crap.

"What dahlias?" Finn asked, no longer sitting back in his chair.

"Marceau brought some flowers." Seraphina met his pale gaze. "As a hostess gift," she added as if that would wipe the frown from Finn's face.

Finn's agitation was growing. "What happened when she touched the flowers? How did you know she did something down there?"

"The hex appears slightly translucent, sort of like a web in the sunlight. When I tried to examine Seraphina's hex in the Arcade, it flared to a brighter color, more of a pinkish tone and it became more distinct."

"And tonight? What did you see when she was downstairs?" Finn pushed.

"The strands glow brighter when the two of you are close to each other. When she sat across the room, it was a pale pink, and then when she moved closer on the couch, it deepened to a richer rose." Marceau rubbed his hand through his hair. "As she went down the stairs, it gradually lightened again. And when she was about halfway down, it whitened as the connection severed."

"You have not answered my question. When she touched the flowers?" Finn was sitting straight, hands clenched in his lap.

"The strands on your hex were reaching for the stairs, toward her, curled in on themselves. Then they snapped back in your direction like a whip. They changed to a shade of purple."

"Damn it, Seraphina." Finn leapt from his chair. He paced between the table and the clear area with the two chairs. His fists clenched and unclenched.

"Finn, it… it's okay. We don't know what it means." Seraphina started.

"Don't we?" Finn yelled. He put his hands on the back of his chair and leaned in, glaring at Marceau.

"Finn, please," Seraphina said.

"Do you realize what you are doing? Do you know the danger you are putting her in? Flowers? Stupid flowers." Finn rounded on Seraphina. "You know better, love. You know what the curse will do if you engage even in silly, puppy love foolishness."

"Silly, puppy love foolishness? You have some damned nerve, Finn." Seraphina jumped up from the loveseat returning his glare. "You are embarrassing me. And you are wrong."

Finn walked around his chair.

Khat stood and placed her hand on Seraphina's arm. "Maybe we should all sit down and…"

"Sit down. She is going to die again and you want me to, to just sit down?" Finn raged.

Khat took a step back, obviously hurt. "What is wrong with you, Finn?"

"Finn. Seraphina. We know the answer to one of the keys of the curse now," Marceau said.

Finn stepped closer.

Khat came to stand between the guys, a hand extended in each person's direction. She said, "Let's take a moment and calm down so we can talk this out."

Finn took another step closer to Marceau and said, "Lies and deception, thievery, arrogance, such regret, and, of course, desire. Your sins broadcast to me like radio waves. I can taste the flavors of them in the air." Finn inhaled deeply. "Greed. Wrath. Pride. Lust. Envy. You have five of the seven deadly sins written on you as plain as day. Why should I trust you? What is it exactly you want here? She is off limits."

"The book. I want to examine the grimoire. I seek a freedom of my own. I need a way to stop even worse deeds from tainting my soul." Marceau did not drop Finn's stare. "Can you not taste sincerity as well, Sin Eater? Or are you limited to recognizing only the evil in a person?"

Finn took another step. His body rigid with barely contained violence.

"Stop it. Both of you. Right now," Khat demanded.

"She's right." Marceau ran his hand through his dark hair. "I apologize. You're reacting like Seraphina did, Finn. Your emotions were affected. It's the hex reacting to my power. Back down, and we can discuss this like gentlemen." Marceau raised his arms placating Finn, but he did not step away. He stood his ground.

"He's right, Finn, please come sit down," Seraphina said. She sat back and patted the couch beside her. When no one moved, said, "Finn, look at me."

Finn looked down.

"This is exactly how I felt yesterday—angry, sad, confused. Sit down, and for heaven's sake, stop looking for a fight. It will pass if you give it a few minutes."

"I-I need space." Finn stormed from the room.

Marceau pushed back in his chair and leaned forward. He put his fingers on his temples and rubbed. As they sat in silence, the emotional charge of the room slowly drained.

"He will be okay, right?" Khat asked as she stared down the hallway.

"Yes. I already feel it fading. He'll be all right," Seraphina said. "He didn't mean to snap at you, Khat. It's an overwhelming feeling like everything hits you all at once."

"I know. He's never yelled at me before. I just wonder if I should go after him."

Brave girl. Seraphina was once again struck by how much Khat cared for Finn.

They sat in silence, not knowing what to say in Finn's absence. His bedroom door finally opened and Seraphina held her breath.

"I'm fine. Well, heading back in that direction anyway," Finn said as he reappeared in the room. "I want to apologize." He looked at the girls and then said to Marceau, "To all of you. I don't know how to describe how intense that felt. An emotional sucker punch."

"That's it exactly. It is like all your pent up feelings suddenly slam into your chest," Seraphina added.

"It's okay, we all knew it wasn't the real you," Khat said.

Finn stood beside Khat, hesitating and then bent to rest his forehead against hers. "No, it is not okay, Khatereh. I should have never snapped at you. I'm sorry," he whispered.

She leaned away and kissed his pale forehead.

"Well, now we've confirmed the hex feeds on the emotions of you both. I saw more details in the hex too. Some things I understand but a lot I don't, not yet. I could spend a week trying to decipher what it all means, or I propose a little experiment if you're willing."

"Experiment? I thought we just did that." Finn's jaw clenched.

Marceau jumped in before Finn had a chance to refuel. "That was only a reading of your hex. I've spent the last three years working on a scientific theory. A way to revolutionize how curses are examined. It could lead to a means of treating those hexed, by the few curseweavers brave enough to try."

Seraphina asked, "Brave enough? Why is it most curseweavers turn me away the second I ask how to break a hex?" She'd always wondered why you could pay most curseweavers to weave you a small hex without even sharing your motives, but mention you want to break one and they skedaddled as though you suggested raising the dead.

"Because there can be a backlash of power. Dangerous consequences are involved for those who get tangled within someone else's hex."

Finn poured another drink and sat, pulling Khat closer. "And this theory? What is it exactly?"

"A way to reduce the potential for mistakes while unraveling a hex. Merely hearing about who hexed someone and why is often not enough. There are clues hidden within a curse's origin story, even if those telling the tale don't recognize them."

"Makes sense, but could you get around that?" Seraphina asked.

"Curse Regression. I've been practicing for years. If a curse is strong enough, and I believe yours is, I enter a meditative state while combining my power with the hex through touch."

Finn sat up and shook his head at Seraphina.

Marceau continued, "Seraphina made her *absolutely no touching* rule quite clear the day we had lunch. I have no intention of touching her. Khat, as a part djinn, I believe you have some ability to amplify the magic of others, is that correct?"

Khat nodded but chewed on her fingernails.

"Then I propose we join hands. I will hold Finn and Khat's hands only, of course. And we can see if a Curse Regression is possible. I've been successful in roughly half of my attempts."

"And what exactly do you see if it works?" Seraphina asked. She had been a different person before her death... with problems, sure, but in hindsight, they'd been mostly trivial. Thinking about it made her miss the carefree, impetuous girl she was then.

Marceau continued, "It depends on how well I'm able to travel along the curse's timeline. I've been able to witness a curseweaver in action and have seen the moment a hex took hold of its victims. Both provided invaluable clues. It does have limits, however. I'll need someone to help me decipher the clues—who I see, events, and places. I cannot hear during the regressions, only see shadowy images so I would need to ask questions as images came to me. If you're both willing, it wouldn't have to be tonight. You should think it over, of course."

Seraphina raised her shoulder and focused on Finn. She was more than willing, but Finn was a very private person and this sounded more intrusive than he would allow.

"I think he needs to know," Finn said. "All of it. I say we go ahead and try it. Tonight."

It felt off that Finn was willing to try a regression so soon. He hardly knew Marceau. In truth, neither did she. Seraphina suspected Finn's unusual candor was because he wanted Marceau to understand the danger he posed.

"Fine, but Finn will probably need to answer most of your questions. He knows more about what happened... after. I'll fill in as needed." Seraphina's expression was more serious than Marceau had seen before.

Marceau rubbed his hands together. "Excellent." He gestured toward the table. "Shall we?"

Chapter Seventeen

Marceau took a drink of his whiskey and waited at the table. Seraphina sat across from him. Khat had asked for a moment alone with Finn before they started and the two had disappeared down the hall.

"This has certainly been a more eventful dinner than I intended." Seraphina smiled.

"The evening exceeded my expectations, as well." A huge understatement. Marceau tried to maintain a calm demeanor, but inside he was brimming with nervous excitement. He'd overstated his success rate by a significant margin. He was actually only successful in maybe a quarter of his attempts at regression. But he needed them to try, their curse was powerful. It was very difficult to find willing participants. And the ones who agreed to let him usually had insignificant hexes lacking the power required to fuel a satisfying attempt. Finding two willing participants with a curse as strong as Seraphina's and Finn's? Well, there was a first time for everything, right?

Seraphina fidgeted in her chair. Would she be disappointed in him? What if he was unable to see anything? Marceau didn't want to let her down. In fact, he hoped to impress her.

Khat came back into the room and joined them at the table. Her smile was sheepish, and she picked at her fingernails as a very serious Finn joined them. She spoke up, "So we need to talk about my abilities before we proceed. I hadn't been completely upfront with Finn before. Now, having just fixed that, I need to explain part of my magic... before we try this." Turning to Seraphina, she continued, "I know this whole djinn halfling thing came out of left field for you tonight. I've never even met my mother. All I know of djinn magic has been learned on my own, by rumors, or from even less trustworthy sources, like my father. But this isn't tied to being part djinn. I hope you'll still feel comfortable around me once you know about the ability I inherited from my father."

"Oh, I'm sure— Seraphina started before Finn cut her off with a slight shake of his head.

Marceau's interest was definitely piqued after that little exchange.

Khat exhaled. "I feel vibrations, the frequency of other supernaturals' powers. I'm able to mimic their fluctuations and can adapt my power to align with others."

Marceau sucked in a breath. It was unheard of. It was *powerful.* His mind reeled with the possibilities.

Seraphina tilted her head. "The rumors Finn told me about were kind of true then, about Virgil?"

"What rumors?" Khat asked Finn.

Finn gave Seraphina a hard look before answering, "Rumors that Virgil fed on the powers of others. He absorbed their powers and left them weakened. I had some idea Khat might have inherited Virgil's ability some time back. But I didn't understand how it worked until now."

Khat stared. "Before we even started dating, you'd heard my father weakened and fed on people? And you suspected I might do it too? Then why on earth did you ever ask me out?" Khat chewed on her thumbnail. "Why did you trust me?"

"Sin Eater, remember?" Finn pointed to himself. "I see people's sins. And you, Sparrow, would never feed on me or anyone else for that matter. Now, on to how your ability may affect the experiment."

Khat swallowed, watching Marceau's expression. "If you use your power while holding my hand, I'll feel the frequency of your power. Sometimes it's hard not to mimic. It's a natural reaction, I don't understand why."

Marceau grinned. "It could be an unknown adaptation for survival, Khat. Think about it. If you can mimic those around you, that is rather like a camouflage. What better way to blend in with other supernaturals? It's quite fascinating, really. I'd prefer you not hold back at all. Allow your powers to sync with mine. If you do share my *frequency,* the djinn's amplification power may well come into play too." He rubbed his hands together. An unheard of supernatural power, one of the most complex hexes he'd ever seen fluctuating with power on not one, but two supernaturals, and the possibility of a djinn power boost as well? He couldn't have constructed a greater Curse Regression Theory experiment if he'd tried.

Finn frowned and stared at him. Marceau schooled his expression back into one of calm, confidence and only slight interest. Then he laid his hands on the table, palms up.

Moment of truth. Would they go through with it? After exchanging a long look, Finn and Khat grasped his hands and then Seraphina's.

"What do we do now?" Seraphina asked.

"Just relax. I must slip into a deeper level of consciousness. Bear with me. Try to stay as still and quiet as possible. If I'm able to make a connection, I will see flashes of images. I'll describe what I see and ask questions."

Marceau tried to clear his mind, but it was difficult. He was losing hope when he felt a tug. The muscles in his hands jumped as his mind traveled back along a stream of power. The hex seemed familiar after examining its patterns on both Seraphina and Finn. Marceau tightened his hands. With an answering squeeze from Khat, a pulse of energy flowed into his hand and he gasped. It usually took time to follow the path of a curse, but now he was being dragged backward at mind-numbing speed. Vertigo set in and Marceau fought through the dizziness as pure, warm power flowed through his body. It was an amazing sensation as if he'd been wrapped in a cloak of thick, unfamiliar magic.

"Too much?" Khat whispered.

Yes. "No. It feels wonderful, actually," Marceau answered and this time, Finn's hand tightened a little. "Please, give me a moment to acclimate."

Marceau took several deep breaths and tried to focus on his body. He methodically traced his consciousness from his feet to the top of his head. After the familiar mental exercise, Marceau felt a measure of control again.

"Please continue, Khat," Marceau said.

More magic pulsed from Khat's hand and flooded his senses. His nostrils flared as he breathed in and smelled something new—smoke and lemon, mixed with a chemical odor. Grain alcohol? Marceau opened his eyes but saw no sign of Seraphina's loft. He stood inside a dimly lit room with a long counter to his right. When he shook his head a static, white noise dissipated. Music. A piano played an old tune he recognized from The Great Gatsby. One voice sang out, "Every morning, every evening, ain't we got fun?" Marceau turned and saw a young man playing an upright piano. "Not much money, oh, but Honey, ain't we got fun?" The guy wore a coarse cotton, buttoned shirt with his sleeves rolled up. A girl with short, finger-waved hair danced beside the piano, the fringe of her flapper dress flared outward as she spun.

"When were you cursed?" Marceau whispered afraid that speaking would ruin the crystal clear vision.

Finn responded, "It was 1925."

"And where were you when the hex took hold?"

"In a speakeasy called The Phantom," Finn answered.

Marceau looked around for any sort of name or identifying features. During the few successful regressions he'd managed, flat, shadowy images flashed through his mind. Now it seemed as if he was actually in the scene around him. Marceau lifted his foot. He was *there* in a body. He took a step and approached the bar. Never before had he retained any physical features during a vision, and certainly never had the ability to move where he wanted.

A translucent man behind the bar turned. His form wavered, but when Marceau focused, he could make out the bartender's facial features. The man seemed to look right through Marceau as he wiped the inside of a small glass with a white towel. Then, the bartender smiled and said, "Wondered when you'd show up, Miss Sera. You're all dolled up today."

Marceau turned and froze.

Seraphina was certainly not ghostly. She was more solid than the others in the room and walked straight toward him, only something was off. He tried to figure out what made her look so different. She wore a lace-covered dress, but Marceau couldn't make out the color. He realized as he looked up at her usual fiery, red hair that everything else appeared in shades of black and white. Her hair was cut in a short bob.

She waved and said, "Hi Rex. Everything's jake now. But Daddy had me parading around entertaining the mayor's wallflower of a daughter all day while he negotiated their monthly bribe. She was a real wet blanket, I tell ya. Positutely drab."

Marceau kept waiting for her to react to his presence, but she didn't even slow before stepping right through him. Marceau gasped and shuddered.

"Are you okay, Marceau?" Khat whispered. Her voice pulled at his mind, a sudden reminder he was not really there. He sat at the table in Seraphina's loft.

Marceau said, "Yes, I just had an interesting encounter. Please tell me more about this speakeasy, The Phantom. Describe it to me."

It was Finn who answered, "Long wood bar with high windows along the ceiling because it was in a basement. Had round tables and an upright piano."

Marceau looked around him. Everything matched Finn's description. Dust motes swirled in the sunlight drifting in from rectangular windows set high in the walls. Squat wooden tables sat mostly empty though he did see a shadowy group of men playing cards at a table in a far corner. "What kind of floor did it have?"

"Don't remember," answered Finn.

Seraphina jumped in and said, "Concrete, rough and grooved. I had to be careful not to catch the heels of my shoes and trip."

Marceau scooted his foot across the floor. The sole of his shoe scraped across ruts in the floor. Fascinating.

"Tell me more. What did you do for a living? Why did you come to The Phantom?" Marceau asked.

Finn cleared his throat. "Prohibition was in full swing and I made my living as a bootlegger. I ran moonshine from a few choice stills in Appalachia down to Georgia. Filled up my trunk with rum in Savannah, for the return trip."

Seraphina said, "He's being modest. He was the go-to bootlegger on route."

Finn laughed. "Yeah, those were fun times. I was never caught, never lost a load. No one else moved much hooch without losing cargo. Back then, they'd rather drive the car into a lake and watch it sink than to let the law drink it. I spent most days at The Phantom when I wasn't driving."

He paused and Marceau watched the regression form of Seraphina as she joked with the piano player and did a few dance moves. A Charleston? She clapped and bowed to him before climbing up and sitting right on top of the bar.

"And what was Seraphina's tie to this bar?" Marceau asked.

The vision's Seraphina swayed as she sipped from a small glass and listened to another song.

"It was one of the few places I could be myself, free from my father's prying eyes and the societal demands of being the judge's precious daughter. At The Phantom, I was amongst friends."

"The Judge?" Khat asked.

Finn said, "Judge Pearce. He was Savannah's most powerful judge and just happened to run the bootlegging and gambling underground. His position helped keep the entire city of Savannah under his control. All who crossed him were either run from town or jailed. And those who worked for him weren't even questioned by the police."

"How convenient that your father could decide who went to jail and who walked free," Khat said. "Mine had to spell or kill anyone who threatened the family business."

In the present, Seraphina laughed, but it sounded hollow and without humor. "Convenient. I guess that's one way to look at it. Daddy also controlled most of the upper brass in the police force and placed several leading politicians in office."

"So, you and Seraphina met through Judge Pearce?" prompted Marceau.

Finn said, "No, the Judge didn't like his only child associating with his employees. But she was strong-willed even then. My reputation as a driver drew his attention, and I started running routes for him. Seraphina spent most of her evenings singing and playing cards at The Phantom. I rented a room in the upstairs boarding house that disguised the basement level bar. We became quick friends."

Our lives were simpler then. I played the good daughter and Finn drove like a madman, until Daddy forbade our friendship, at least, that was when the trouble started."

"Why would the Judge try to keep you from being friends?" asked Khat.

"He thought we were sweethearts and it didn't fit into his plans. No one dared cross Daddy in Savannah. But for men like him, there was never enough power. He wanted to expand his territory and, for that, he planned to use me as a pawn. A marriage would forge a stronger bond with the Callaghans."

"Who were they?" Marceau asked.

As soon as he said the name, the scene in front of him changed. He stumbled forward, tripping on an uneven wooden slat. In the regression, he tried to throw out his arms to catch his balance. The weight of Khat and Finn's hands in the present was confusing.

"What is it? Why did you jump?" Finn asked.

"I've moved to a different location. I was in The Phantom with Seraphina, but now I'm on a wooden deck? There are some..." Marceau stopped speaking as Finn walked by farther down the pier. He too appeared more solid in form. Finn wore a light, Oxford shirt, a buttoned vest, and dark pants. His sleeves were rolled up and even with the absence of color in the vision, it was clear Finn's hair and skin were darker. There was a relaxed ease, a calm, the future Finn no longer possessed. Finn took off his cap and shook hands with a tall, broad man. The man gestured toward Marceau.

"Some what?" present Finn asked.

"Sorry, this is a bit confusing. It's as if I'm in two places at once. Some barrels. Near a stack of large ones, I see you, Finn, talking to a man in his late twenties. He has short, dark hair, and a large frame. Something about his demeanor tells me—he's in charge."

"Kieran Callaghan. You just described one of the docks where the Callaghan rum was unloaded. But Kieran rarely came on shore. He preferred the safety of his ship."

"Tell me more about him."

Finn replied, "After the fall of the McCoys, the Callaghans became the premiere rum runners to Savannah. The McCoys were famous for refusing to pay off politicians or gangsters, and also for never sampling their merchandise. The Callaghan brothers shared none of those hang-ups. Aedan Callaghan, the younger brother, was a brilliant captain. But he was reckless. He gambled, and his quick temper wasn't helped by drinking from morning until night. Kieran was the older and more serious brother.

He ran their smuggling business. Together, they made a formidable team. They ran a fleet of three ships into Rum Row and made money by the fistful."

"Rum Row?" Marceau leaned forward in the present. Several men approached in his vision. They each tipped a barrel and rolled them down the pier. The barrels bounced loudly across the uneven wood planks.

Seraphina answered, "Ships anchored three miles offshore in neutral international waters. Daddy would send out smaller boats and sneak rum in through the swamp. Drivers, like Finn, loaded up and drove the hooch into town. Daddy had a good thing going with the Callaghan group, but he wanted them to stop selling to his competitors. Plus, he wanted to expand into the Florida panhandle, so he needed even more rum. That's where the bargain for my arranged marriage came in."

"Arranged? To marry who?" Khat asked in a high-pitched voice.

"Aedan Callaghan," Finn answered.

"Aedan Callaghan," repeated Marceau testing the regression's power.

Once again a wave of dizziness overcame him. Marceau stood in a narrow cobblestoned alleyway between two buildings.

Shadowed figures moved farther down the dim lit alley. Sounds of a scuffle and a thick thud, followed by loud coughing, set Marceau in motion. Ahead, someone kicked a man lying on the ground with enough force to raise the victim from the ground.

Marceau asked, "Was Aedan prone to fights? Lighter hair, and a wiry frame? Taller than his brother?"

"Yes," Seraphina said, her voice soft.

"Tell me about him."

Marceau could do nothing for the man Aedan was beating senseless, but he still flinched with each blow.

"Kieran knew his brother liked me. He'd come listen to me sing at The Phantom. Tried to impress me with his money and charm, but I saw through him." Seraphina added details to what Marceau was envisioning. "Aedan had a deep, inner cruelty. No handsome smile could hide that. I refused his advances, especially after he beat up a friend over a stupid poker debt."

In the regression, Aedan laughed and spit at the now unconscious man before walking down the alley. Marceau followed.

Finn said, "Kieran agreed to sell rum only to Judge Pearce if Seraphina married Aedan. Thought his reckless brother would finally settle down and stop gambling every night. His transgressions hurt business and Kieran needed Aedan's focus back at sea."

"Okay, so the booze brothers had you cursed when you refused to marry the meanie then?" Khat asked.

"The Booze Brothers?" Finn chuckled. "No, the Judge arranged the hex with Mirela Dufrene." Finn cleared his throat. "Young and half crazy, she was the most powerful curseweaver in Savannah. Well, other than her older sister, Liv. But Liv didn't use her powers for dark curses, so the judge paid Mirela to hex his own daughter."

Khat said, "But why? If he needed Seraphina to marry this Aedan guy, why hex her to die?"

"The hex was supposed to make me fall in love with Aedan and stop resisting the marriage. Daddy thought I'd be a rich wife and he'd get his precious rum. I have to believe he didn't know more. He gave Mirela the perfect opening for exactly what she'd been dreaming of, revenge."

Marceau interrupted, "Give me a moment, I'm somewhere else now."

He'd followed Aedan down a darkened street where the guy had hitched up his pants and ran his fingers through his disheveled hair before walking into a small, ramshackle house. A woman with tangled, long hair stood from a rocking chair beside a lantern. Her expression was guarded, vacant.

"Miss me?" Aedan slurred. "Don't I even get a smile?"

She peered at Aedan for a moment before answering with the requested smile and a nod. The woman took a small step toward him. Aedan stumbled forward, kicking up a cloud of dirt from the floor. Her smile dropped. Aedan grabbed a half empty liquor bottle from the table and took a long drink. He laughed and fell back on a bed next to the table.

Marceau turned and walked out of the shack. He stood on the dirt road and wondered where he should try to go next. "Okay, I am trying to… Well, for lack of a better term, navigate again. Please tell me more about the judge. Let's go back just a little, before Mirela. You said the judge tried to forbid your friendship and set the curse in motion? Why did he to want to keep you two apart?"

Finn cleared his throat. "He thought Seraphina was in love with me after an incident he'd misunderstood. He thought a little love hex would fix all his problems in controlling his daughter."

"An incident?" Marceau asked.

"A car accident. I was determined to leave Savannah to avoid the marriage, so I begged Finn to teach me to drive." Seraphina's brow wrinkled.

Marceau focused his mind and tried to visualize Seraphina driving an old-fashioned car. Nothing happened. He was still outside the house of Aedan's female friend.

"During one of our lessons, Seraphina was overconfident around a curve and drove the car into a ravine. I was ejected, but Seraphina was trapped by the steering wheel. The engine caught fire. I managed to pull her out, but she'd stopped breathing from smoke inhalation. One of the judge's goons drove up and saw me giving her mouth to mouth. The idiot reported back he caught us kissing."

"So naturally, Daddy believed some jerkface over me. He forbade me from ever seeing Finn again. When that didn't work, he came up with the idea to use a curse."

Marceau didn't like picturing Finn's mouth on Seraphina's. "I'm stuck," he said. "I'd hoped I could get back to either of you or to the judge. Let's try Mirela. You said she wanted revenge?" Marceau needed to see her weave the hex. He whispered her name. His head began to ache, but he tried to push his consciousness toward the curseweaver. Again, nothing.

This time, Finn answered, "Mirela misunderstood the nature of our relationship, in that she thought we had one. She and I had some good times, but I was clear from the start there'd be nothing more. She was jealous and believed the rumors about Seraphina and me."

"A woman scorned," Khat said.

Marceau's head was beginning to pound. He said, "And what do you know of the curse? So far, I am unable to see Mirela."

Finn said, "From what we know, Mirela hexed Seraphina to love Aedan, but she also wove it to kill anyone Seraphina touched if she was in love with them."

If the judge and Mirela were both beyond his reach in the regression, Marceau needed to find a way back to Seraphina. He tried to visualize her, but nothing happened.

Khat asked, "So she fell instantly in love, touched this Aedan guy, and then died?"

"No, I killed her," Finn said.

Real life Seraphina exhaled and sounded tired when she responded, "Finn, we've been over this a thousand times. You didn't kill me and neither did Aedan."

"Seraphina's death," Marceau whispered. His chest tightened. He didn't want to watch her die, but he needed more answers to help her in the present. He pictured the way her red hair had blown around her face in the Arcade. The air spin around him and Marceau's head rolled back as he fought vertigo. Shapes swirled. Marceau blinked, trying to get his eyes to focus.

A shadowed Finn grabbed Seraphina's elbow. She glared at him and wrenched her arm free.

Marceau's energy was slipping. He asked, "What did you feel when the hex took hold? What did you do?"

Seraphina ran her fingers along the back of a wooden chair as if she wanted to sit, then paced in front of The Phantom's door. She smoothed her dress down and paced again.

"It's hard to describe. I was drawn to Aedan, and it seemed as if I had to be near him or I'd hurt forever. I thought I'd go crazy while I waited. The love hex was so strong, I ached. I was convinced only his touch could soothe me. I couldn't eat. I couldn't even sit still. Finn and I argued. He didn't understand my sudden need to be with Aedan, someone I'd always disliked. I didn't understand it either but knew I had to be with him. Finn tried to reason with me, but I couldn't think straight." Seraphina reached up and patted along her short hairline. The door opened. She cried out and ran right through the shadowy Marceau.

Aedan appeared confused until she collided with him and wrapped her arms around his neck. Then he smiled a cruel, predatory grin at Finn as if he knew about the hex.

A complex web flashed over Seraphina's body when her hex activated. Thin strands floated from her body and reached out to Aedan. Seraphina gasped and her body went stiff.

Marceau asked, "When you hugged him, what did you feel?"

"A cold burn. It traveled through my veins and squeezed. The only way I can describe it was somehow my insides were being constricted. Even then, I recognized what it meant. Death."

Finn stumbled forward into a nearby table. He held his sides and knocked over a chair. A dark web surrounded him, his hex reached for Seraphina.

"Finn, what did you feel? Why did you stumble?"

"A blast of cold had seized me. Freezing pain all the way into my bones." Finn winced while remembering.

Seraphina's body shook. Tears streamed down her face as she gasped for air. Aedan was restraining her, too busy reveling in his triumph to see something was wrong.

Finn stumbled forward and grabbed her arm. He tried to pull her free from Aedan.

"We each held one of her wrists. I felt a connection the moment I touched her. A link and something unnatural, dark. I realized later it was death under her skin. I didn't understand it at the time, but I think Seraphina could have pushed darkness into either of us. I could have died, or Aedan. Either way, she would have been free of the curse. Seraphina would have lived. But of course, she didn't."

Seraphina tucked her head down and tried to pull her wrists to her chest. Finn said something Marceau couldn't hear. Seraphina shook her head and grimaced.

Aedan grabbed Finn's shirt and jerked him forward.

Finn let go of Seraphina's wrist to pull free.

Seraphina's body crumbled to the floor, Aedan's grip on her wrist still holding her up.

Finn dropped to his knees and cupped her face with his palm. He whispered something and leaned in, his forehead against hers.

Then Aedan kicked Finn's shoulder and let go of Seraphina's wrist. She fell back.

Finn screamed her name. He dove forward and caught her shoulders, but the back of her head hit the concrete floor.

Finn gently laid her back on the floor and spoke to her, but she didn't move. He leaned one ear on her chest to search for a heartbeat.

Aedan grabbed Finn and pulled him to his feet, but Finn swung and punched Aedan so hard the crack made Marceau jump, both in the regression and in the present.

Aedan flew backward, landing on a table. The legs collapsed, and Aedan crashed to the floor.

Finn was already back on his knees listening at Seraphina's chest. He looked up. His expression a mask of outrage and pain. The scene froze.

A deep, grinding jolt of pain through Marceau's head made him cry out. He jerked his hands free and pressed hard against both of his temples. Rocking back and forth, he took a couple slow breaths before opening his eyes. His head was only inches above the tabletop.

"Are you okay, Marceau?" Seraphina asked.

"Yes. Fine." A lie. "It's over. The regression stopped. Your death must have ended it. I'm... disoriented."

"You watched her die? How I killed her?" Finn demanded.

"Stop it, Finn, I mean it. My father sealed my fate. He took my free will when he paid Mirela to weave that damned hex. It was my father's actions, whether he understood them at the time or not, that led to my death."

Marceau said, "From what I saw, she's right. You were the only one who realized something was wrong. I'm still unclear why, though. Why did you feel the curse too?"

"I've wondered for more years than I've cared to count. I felt a jarring, cold pain the moment Seraphina touched Aedan. Yet I can touch Khat, and Seraphina feels nothing. If we are bound by the same hex, then why can I touch Khat without consequence? Without dying?"

Seraphina looked at Finn and then to Khat. She seemed surprised. Finn had just basically said he was in love with Khat. That fact had been obvious to Marceau from the moment he'd seen Finn and Khat together.

"I may be able to answer that. Your hex is darker, shadowed. It lacks the color and vibrancy most active hexes have. I believe you're linked to

Seraphina, but the curseweaver wasn't actually trying to hurt you." Marceau was slowly understanding more about the situation.

He visualized the scene again. Finn had stumbled forward *before* he touched Seraphina. Finn's hex reached out for her, but her hex had reached only for Aedan. "Finn, I think your curse is dormant and has only one path to activation and becoming deadly."

"And what would that be?" Finn sat straight in his chair.

"If you and Seraphina fell in love and touched, I believe your hex would then flare with power and it would kill you both. I'm pretty sure the curseweaver intended to punish Seraphina no matter what and make sure she never knew love with anyone. But you said Mirela wanted a relationship with you, right Finn?"

Finn nodded. His eyes widened as the pieces of the puzzle fell together in a new way. "So, Mirela left me free to experience love, hoping I'd eventually be in love with her."

Seraphina looked away.

Finn sat quietly a moment, tipping his glass from side to side, then shook his head. "But something else doesn't make sense. She disappeared. I never saw Mirela again."

Marceau shook his own head. It made perfect sense after examining the strength of their combined curse. "I'm almost positive Mirela died the day she wove the hex. Curse power of this magnitude is unusual. It demands a hefty tithe." Seraphina stared at him. He exhaled and said, "You each bear the strongest and most intricate hexes I've ever seen, and I have examined many."

Seraphina's palm hit the table. "All of this pain. This stupid curse. All because of petty jealousy and people trying to control others. It's just more than I can sometimes take." She sucked in her lip and bit it.

Finn reached over and held her hand. "All these years I wondered why I survived. I have blamed myself, thinking I caused your death. I never understood until now." Finn stared, eyes vacant as if lost in his memories. He downed his drink and sat back. "It's all so clear."

"Sum it up for me then, 'cause I feel like I'm missing something," Khat said. "Why'd you think you were dying when she touched Aedan?"

"I felt her pain only because the curse linked us, not because I was dying too. The pain was an echo of what she felt. If Marceau's right, I was never in danger of dying at all."

Marceau explained, "Well unless she chose to let you die. You were both touching her. I believe she could have transferred death into either of you. If I'm right, Seraphina had only a matter of seconds to decide which of you would die. It appears to be the only sliver of free will she has in the curse. Can you describe how you felt, Seraphina? When you touched Aedan?"

"The cold started in my hands, then burned up the veins in my arms. Aedan never reacted, didn't even seem to notice. But I made the connection or link to Finn right away." She stood and walked to the window. "Part of me wanted to push it out, cold, biting death. I was desperate to release the pain, but I fought against my own instinct to survive. I understood if I let the darkness go, it would take Finn or Aedan. So I held the hex deep in my chest. I kept it until I was no more. I remember falling. One moment Finn was screaming my name, and the next, nothing. A pain exploded in the back of my head and I was gone."

Finn winced.

"You really died?" Khat said, wide-eyed. "And to free yourself, you have to kill someone you love. It's all so *tragic*."

Seraphina turned back and nodded. "I could choose to let them die. I'd be mortal and free, but how could I ever live with the consequences? I'll never give up on a cure for the curse, but I'll never take the life of someone I love, either. So I'm stuck. Alone."

"For how long?" Khat asked.

Finn leaned forward and rested his head in his hands. "Seraphina hasn't aged a day since she came back from the veil."

Marceau said, "This is the part I don't understand. Exactly how long were you dead, Seraphina, and how did you come back?"

"I was dead for fifty years."

"How is that even possible? Why didn't you, you know, decompose?" Khat asked confused.

"My body wasn't in this realm. Both my body and soul crossed the veil. I was suspended there until the curse let me cross back, fifty years to the day after my death. I awoke in 1975. You wanna talk about a culture shock."

It made no sense. There had to be more.

"I saw your body in The Phantom," Marceau said. "The hex rested against your skin. It was satisfied by your death. So why would it cast your physical body across the veil? And how? And where did it find the energy to bring you back again? Why after fifty years? Death is quite controlling and punishes those who try to cheat fate."

An idea occurred to Marceau, a terrible thought he wanted to put to rest. "Were you always a Sin Eater, Finn? Even before the curse?"

Finn's eyes locked on Marceau's. His posture stiff.

It wasn't Finn who answered. "No, Finn was a Spellcaster. He manipulated luck and chance, which helped him win at poker and perfect bootlegging record. It was the hex that turned him into a Sin Eater." Seraphina's head tilted as she noticed Finn's change in demeanor. She rejoined the group and stood beside him. "You okay, Finn?"

"Yes, just remembering my time while you were away," Finn replied tight-lipped.

Marceau asked, "Is that when you became a Sin Eater? After the curse brought her back?" He knew of only two paths to becoming a Sin Eater and neither involved a curse.

Finn didn't respond.

Seraphina answered, "No, he'd already been affected by then. When I died, he had dark blonde hair and golden, tanned skin. His eyes used to be a deep, cornflower shade of blue. His new appearance took a while to get used to when I awoke. The hex killed me and changed him into a Sin Eater. Daddy really messed up our lives."

Marceau started to open his mouth. Finn stood abruptly. "All this talk of the past has put me in the mood for another drink, anyone else? I think we've solved enough mysteries for one night."

The subject was far from closed, but Marceau dropped it, not wanting to push his luck.

Chapter Eighteen

Seraphina stared at the chair where Marceau had sat last night. So many revelations left her mind spinning, and she'd barely slept. Khat was part djinn. Finn's reaction to having the hex read had been as emotional as her own. Marceau brought her dahlias. She followed that thought with an admonishment to stop treading in dangerous territory. The flowers were just a simple hostess gift.

Last night as Seraphina tossed and turned, she'd thought about how Finn seemed better lately. Not counting last night's outburst, which was magically induced and had mirrored her own initial reaction to Marceau's power. During the past few months, Finn was more stable, lighter somehow. The strain around his eyes and in his jaw had almost disappeared, and he seemed to breathe easier. His attention didn't wander off as memories of other's sins haunted him. It was as if Khat grounded him. She seemed to anchor Finn to the present more than anyone or anything else had in years. The realization came that not only did Finn need Khat, but she also needed him. They seemed to balance each other very well.

Finn entered the kitchen and poured himself a cup of coffee. "Well, last night was certainly interesting."

"You can say that again."

"Were you able to get any sleep?"

"A little."

"Look. About that Khat. I should have told you..."

Seraphina held up her hand to stop him. "We covered all of last night, Finn. With so much happening in the past week or so, let's just drop the djinn part, okay?"

Finn raised an eyebrow and nodded. He sipped his coffee.

Seraphina retreated back into her thoughts and spun her mug on the dark marble counter. She knew what she wanted to say, but it would be a very big change, for all of them. After so many years together, her endless fidgeting was a nervous gesture Finn recognized. He reached over and stopped the noisy mug mid rotation.

Finn took her cup and freshened the coffee. "What's going on in that head of yours, love?"

"I think Khat should stay. Here, I mean."

Finn spun and coffee sloshed over the rim of her cup. He shook the hot droplets off his wrist. His light eyes widened in disbelief. "You're proposing she live here? We've always kept it just the two of us."

"I think Khat should be here with you. She said she lives in a one-bedroom studio apartment. I can't imagine living all alone, and, when I couldn't sleep last night, I was thinking about everything. I'm sure my insomnia was helping rehash the past, but it really hit me how much the curse has taken from us. I'm unable to have romantic relationships, but you aren't, Finn. You should live as normal a life as possible."

Finn ran his hands through his white hair and looked puzzled, unsure.

Seraphina straightened her spine and nodded. It just seemed right and the words came much easier. "It's like we talked about yesterday." She paused. "Was that really only yesterday morning?" She shook her head with an uneasy laugh. "You don't have to hide or try to protect me from your relationship. Khat is growing on me, even more after last night. I see why she is right for you. Hell, she even wanted to go after you when you went all nuclear from Marceau reading your hex. She loves you, Finn, as do I. I worry so much about you and everything you go through as a Sin Eater. Khat seems to help ease your struggles, and I want you to be happy."

Finn stood silent.

"Plus we could use the help, right? She rearranged the new Samhain/Dia de los Muertos display and it looks fantastic. We're constantly shorthanded in the apothecary, and she has offered to help. So, I think you should ask Khat to live here. She helps keep you feeling more stable, more plugged in to the here and now. I'm right, Finn." Seraphina took a deep breath because the words had just rushed out.

Finn didn't hesitate answering, "I know you are, and I would love to have her here… if she would want to stay, that is." He looked down the hall and blushed, angelic almost, as the pink rushed across his fair cheeks.

"I think you've sacrificed more than enough for me. I want this for you and Khat, if she thinks she can put up with the two of us." She smiled. "Actually, I want it for me too. So go ask her to move in, okay?"

Finn smiled again looking past her. "I believe you just did, love."

Seraphina turned and saw Khat standing in the doorway. Her beaming smile was answer enough. But then Khat clapped and nodded so fast she looked like a bobble-head. "Really?" she squealed.

"Really," Seraphina and Finn answered in unison.

Khat skipped over and kissed Finn. They leaned into each other so naturally it was as if they were built as each other's perfect match.

That must be nice, Seraphina thought. An ache tried to take hold in her chest, but she quickly pushed the negative feeling away. Finn and Khat had both been through so much and deserved this happiness. She wouldn't let her own yearning interfere. No, she would choose to feel happy too.

"Well, there we go. I know you'll probably spend most of your time together, but frankly, your closet space sucks." Seraphina laughed as she stood up. "Tonight we'll spruce up the spare room so Khat can have a space of her own too. Hey, we could add some large mirrors on the back wall to make it your own little dance studio."

Khat beamed. "I would love that, Seraphina."

Finn looked from Seraphina to Khat and back. His face broke into a glorious smile.

Seraphina hadn't actually planned to bring up Khat moving in that morning, but she thought the time had been right. Now her best friend looked happier than he had in quite some time. "Well, that's settled then. Don't forget it's your turn tonight, Finn."

Later that evening, Seraphina stopped trying to decipher a passage in the Blackthorne Grimoire after Finn ran up the stairs and called, "Movie Night."

Finn's excitement was infectious. He held a plastic bag with a yellow smiling face in one hand and a six-pack of beer in the other. Chinese takeout perfumed the air as he approached the kitchen counter.

Seraphina warned Khat, "You know we could be in trouble, right? Since it was his turn to choose the movie. So what is it, this time, Finn? Macho one-liners? Rabid aliens? Chainsaws?"

"In celebration of our new roommate," he winked at Khat, "I chose one of her favorites."

"Oh goody. Whatcha got?" Khat pulled at the DVD tucked under his arm.

"Who you gonna call?" Finn started.

"Ghostbusters," Khat cheered. They laughed and started pulling the Chinese containers out of the bag, setting them on the counter.

Seraphina gestured toward her room. "Fitting, considering my ghostly little friend is still hanging around."

Finn asked, "Ah, no luck shooing him across the veil today, love?"

"I'm working on it, promise. In the meantime, Rolf is curled up and napping on the floor of my closet. He has promised to stop rubbing against you, and I made it very clear he is *not* allowed in the shop anymore. I had to rearrange some bottles..."

Finn stopped opening takeout boxes and frowned at her.

"I know, Finn, I fixed them. Anyway, I only turned my back on him for two seconds and a customer shrieked and ran out of the shop. Rolf chased after her, but all she saw was a floating sugar skull mask. She was a tourist, but young. So I imagine we'll end up with yet another haunted apothecary story on the internet. Luckily, they seem to cause a boon in business, especially this close to Halloween. I got onto Rolf. I threatened if I catch him messing with a customer again, he'll have to leave, period."

"Is that why he's in your closet? He's pouting?" Khat asked.

"Well, partially. He's also made a pile of every silk or satin thing I own on the floor of the closet as a bed. He seems to be intrigued by modern women's clothing."

"As am I," Finn said in a seductive tone as he shamelessly checked out Khat's cleavage. She was bent over putting plates and silverware on the coffee table.

"Oh, please." Seraphina rolled her eyes and tilted her head. "Though they are rather impressive aren't they?" Seraphina poked his side.

"Well, I'm mostly settled," a rosy cheeked Khat chimed in, to change the subject. "Since I had a furnished studio apartment, there wasn't much to pack up."

Later, as the actors in the movie discussed Twinkies the size of a school bus, Seraphina's thoughts were on Marceau. He made her nervous. Part of her wanted to push him away, the other believed Marceau could figure out their curse. She had to decide if she'd share the grimoire in return. Plus Finn would need to agree to work with Marceau, too. It was only fair.

A giggle drew Seraphina from her thoughts. Finn reached over and stole a piece of broccoli from Khat's plate. Khat nudged him with her shoulder and pointed an egg roll at him as a threat, but her smile was playful. Jeez, they were even cute when they ate. Seraphina went back to eating her Schezuan Tofu.

Seraphina felt a little third-wheelish and didn't know when to look at them and when not to, not that they seemed to mind. At the same time, she wanted to work through her feelings. Her new shyness would subside. She didn't want to be petty or bitter.

Finn was her best friend and had made so many sacrifices for her. He was the most loyal and loving person she had ever known. Khat made Finn happy, and he would be good for her. It was bittersweet to see how easily they could touch, though, she couldn't deny that. They seemed to move in unison, automatically, as though they were both directed by some invisible force. Anyone could see they loved each other, even if they hadn't admitted it to each other yet.

Seraphina thought of her curse and a familiar ache blossomed in her heart. *Love.* She could never allow herself to fall in love. So many seemed to take it for granted, but she'd never really felt the touch of someone she loved. Not in a romantic way, at least. Those sudden feelings for Aedan had not been her own. His arms held her only for a moment, and she couldn't even count one embrace since her free will had been taken by her father's plot. She had made out with a boy or two before the curse, but that was more curiosity and thrill.

Finn laughed at the movie. He certainly loved her, but that was different.

On long nights when there was nothing to do, and no distractions to occupy her mind, Seraphina was sometimes overwhelmed by the weight of the curse. She read, watched old movies, and tried to be content with her life. But sometimes the pretense of acceptance she wove around her heart would tear and her loneliness would pour out, wracking tears and grief consumed her. At times like that, she allowed herself to wallow in sadness for only so long, just the time it took to let out enough of the pain, so she could again think clearly and reaffirm who she was and who she refused to be. Seraphina never had, would never, allow the curse to win. She would not break. And she'd never give up. She would endure and somehow, someway, she'd find a reprieve from her punishment. Hope sustained her.

Now, she had both a mysterious curseweaver and the Blackthorne Grimoire. Seraphina believed that after all the waiting was a new chance at freedom. She'd be able to feel the embrace of someone she loved, one day. She would finally be able to let someone into her heart.

What had Marceau said? Every hex had a weakness. They just needed to find the weak spot. But that was his specialty, not hers, and he was dangerous. Marceau was also frustrating and unpredictable and pretentious and intelligent and handsome and oh, who was she kidding? Maybe she wanted the infuriating Cajun's help after all… and she knew that was exactly why she should push him away. But her remaining flicker of hope would never let it happen.

Chapter Nineteen

Marceau waited each day anxiously until it was time to work with Seraphina. They'd settled into a comfortable daily routine. She worked in the shop until early afternoon. He arrived promptly at three with two coffees from Crema, her favorite local coffee house. He was careful to always set her toffee nut soy latte on the counter to avoid touching her hand.

They would put the Blackthorne Grimoire on the corner of the coffee table and sit on the floor, so she and Marceau could both see the book while maintaining a safe distance. With practice, Seraphina said it was getting easier to shield her mind and control her emotional reaction to his powers. She read through the pages of the book, which gave her something else to focus on while he examined her hex. Many of the grimoire's passages required translation, so her laptop and a growing collection of reference books were required. It was slow going, but Marceau was impressed by her analytical approach. She was steadily filling a binder with detailed translations, drawings, and notes.

Marceau also spent time with Finn daily. Finn was more relaxed with him when Seraphina was not around. But he still had emotional outbursts during examinations, though Finn recognized them now and didn't pick fights. Usually.

When Marceau had the two of them together to examine the hex, Finn was watchful, too watchful. Marceau often asked Seraphina and Finn to touch, then step back, to cross the room, anything to examine the hex's reactions to its hosts.

The hex was different now too, or maybe Marceau was.

Unsure whether it was his growing familiarity with it or if the hex was indeed evolving, Marceau could find the Seraphina's strands in an instant now. The variation in the coloring of her hex had changed from translucent to a faint pink and seemed to darken each time Marceau examined it. He was hesitant to discuss the changes. Finn's moods were unpredictable, even more so after he'd been on a job. Marceau decided to withhold that information until he had a better understanding as to the cause.

Seraphina slammed the book shut and blew upwards fanning her red hair from her eyes. "All right, all work and no play made Jack attack his family with an ax."

"Jack? An ax?" Marceau was at a complete loss.

"Torrance. And *yes*, you know redrum and all jazz?"

Marceau just stared at her. Was this a new reaction to his power? Delirium?

"Really, Marceau, have you not seen *The Shining* either? The list of reasons you're culturally deprived grows." She filed away her current notes and closed her binder. "In other words, I need to get away from this dusty grimoire and go have some fun. We've been at this every afternoon for weeks now. I'm *bored*."

"Of course, I'll take my leave." Marceau stood. The thought of returning to his lonely room at the Hermitage earlier than usual was not appealing. The hotel was historic and comfortable, but after several weeks of staying there, it resembled a well-decorated cell… with room service.

"I didn't mean you should go. Why don't we get out of here for a while and have some fun?" She blushed. "Um, for the curse. Yeah, that's why. You can examine my hex while we are out in public and see if it's any different than here at home. I didn't mean it was a…" Her blush spread deep red across her freckled cheeks.

"An excellent idea." He almost wanted to let her flounder for another moment or two so he could enjoy her reaction, but his chivalrous nature wouldn't allow such rudeness. "Where would you like to go?"

"Hmm." She stood and stretched like a cat who had napped too long on a windowsill. "I know. We can play tourist." Her smile beamed.

"How does one play tourist?"

"By starting with the meccas of all Nashville tourism. How else? Give me two minutes to change and off to the museum we go, then we can visit the Mother Church."

"A museum does sound like a nice distraction though I'm not exactly dressed for a church." He looked down at his jeans and crisp white T-shirt. Marceau wondered what art exhibits were currently on display at The Frist Center while he waited.

Marceau shielded his eyes from the sun as he stared up at the impressive, if unusual, building in front of him. The curved structure's windows resembled piano keys and a large triangular mast, similar to a radio tower, rose from a circular end.

"The Country Music Hall of Fame," Marceau read aloud and looked at her with no shortage of skepticism.

Seraphina smiled in return and nodded. Not what he pictured when she said museum, but it explained her wardrobe change. She now wore a big smile along with a pair of cowgirl boots and a denim jacket over her sundress.

Marceau was willing to try almost anything to keep that carefree smile on her face, even country music. He was beginning to doubt the "Mother Church" she'd mentioned was comparable to the cathedrals in New Orleans.

She said, "Yep, tourism ground zero. See how the building curves? It's actually in the shape of a giant bass clef. And look how it juts out at the end there? That's to emulate the tail fin of a 1950s Cadillac." She approached the glass doors. and he rushed to open one for her. "Part museum and part archive, any day of playing tourist must start here. Come on."

Inside, Marceau insisted on purchasing their tickets. They spent the next two hours wearing headphones for the audio tour and exchanging funny faces and remarks between the displays. He had to admit the instruments, crazy vehicles, and garish clothing of the country stars were interesting.

"Ah, finally, here is my favorite room of all. The Hall of Fame Rotunda." Seraphina slid the headphones off and entered a round, impressive room.

WILL THE CIRCLE BE UNBROKEN was printed in large letters separating rows of inductee plaques from the large windows atop the room. A huge, triangular mast, identical to the metal framed one jutting from the roof outside, dropped from the center of the ceiling. An old woman walked around slowly as she read, but otherwise, the rotunda was empty.

"Aren't the faces sculpted on the plaques great? Ferlin Husky, Hank Williams, Sr., Johnny Cash. *This* is the goal of every dreamer who comes to Nashville to be a country music star. They all want to have their names displayed in this very room one day."

She and Marceau circled the room and scanned the inductees.

"Where do you wanna go next? We could grab a bite to eat or go listen to some live music. I have a friend at the Ryman so we can take a private tour." Seraphina headed to the center of the room.

A large ring of contrasting marble was positioned in the middle of the floor. Seraphina walked into the circle and turned slowly while reading the words inscribed there. She raised her arms and spun faster with a laugh. "We don't have all day, Cajun. Come on, where should we go next?"

Cajun? A laugh barely escaped his throat before the metal structure above crashed down and impaled Seraphina's chest.

Her torso stopped spinning instantly, but her arms swung completing their momentum.

The radio antenna replica pinned her like a butterfly in a glass case. Seraphina was suspended in a grotesque backbend a few feet off the marble floor.

Wh-what happened?

The woman screamed hysterically behind him.

Marceau could only stare at Seraphina. Her mouth opened and closed though no sound escaped. Tears fell, pulling in swirling red hues as they mixed with the fine droplets of blood on her cheeks. Her green eyes went blank with death.

All breath left Marceau's lungs as his mind finally understood the macabre scene before him. Marceau dropped to his knees and covered his mouth. He turned his head away as dark blood fell from her bottom lip in a steady stream.

Above her, the metal structure was fully revealed. The two radio masts were one huge, diamond shaped murder weapon. Sunlight streamed in, circling her body, from a hole in the ceiling where the sculpture had been anchored.

Marceau reached forward and tenderly wrapped his fingers around a long curl of her red hair. It ran through his fingers even silkier than he'd imagined. He had wanted to touch her hair so many times. What could be the danger now?

Pulling his hand back and pressing it against his chest, he tried to hold in the pain. His body shuddered as the screeching sounds of the tourist continued. He couldn't think, couldn't even draw a breath.

This can't be. I don't understand.

Gasp.

She was just spinning. And teasing.

Breathe.

She called me a Cajun.

His thoughts stuttered through his mind, even his inner voice rocked to its core.

A new noise pounded against his eardrums.

The shrieking stopped mid-scream and now an echoing, repetitive sound grated on his nerves.

Clapping. Slow, steady clapping.

"Now that is one hell of a way to die, is it not Marceau?" Max asked.

Terror shot another round of adrenaline through his heart as Marceau turned to face his mentor.

"M-m..." Try as he might, Marceau could not force the name from his trembling lips.

"Oh, do pull it together, Marceau, or I shall leave her that way simply as a lesson in fortitude."

Leave her that way? *Wait.* Then there's a chance this is one of his threats. Maybe, he will reverse her death. Is this real?

Marceau pushed every ounce of his will into his spine as he rose and straightened himself. He smoothed down his white shirt, now misted with crimson, to stall another moment while he centered himself. "A lesson in fortitude shall not be required, I assure you, Maximilian. I was simply caught off guard. You do have a flare for the dramatic. I am myself once again." Marceau forced his voice to stay as even as possible.

"Oh," a small voice exclaimed right beside him.

Marceau's body betrayed the calm facade he struggled for, by jumping much too high.

"A tear. May I have his tear, Max?" the high pitched voice continued.

"Of course, my sweet," Max replied, in a tone Marceau was sure he'd never heard before. Max hadn't even bristled at the use of his nickname.

Babette, the undead ballerina, reached for the tear on his face. She was dressed in a light, blush pink tutu that matched the jagged, raised scar across her throat. Her other hand held Lynette's tightly.

Lynette was dressed in a formal corseted gown in the same pink shade and shook her head only enough to catch Marceau's eye. It distracted him long enough to not flinch as Babette's cool hand brushed his cheek.

Babette slowly pulled back her hand and his tear hung from her dainty, index finger. She giggled. Chills ran down his back. Babette raised the finger to her mouth, licked the tear and closed her eyes. "Pain, fear, and oh. Affection. Such delicious longing."

She licked her lips.

"Affection? Longing?" Max laughed. "My Babette has quite an interesting little talent you see, Marceau. She's extremely sensitive to emotions… and has visions, as well."

Marceau said, "Maximilian, I've been sending you copies of our transcriptions of the grimoire. I speak with you every couple days and am always available when you require me. I hardly think such a graphic threat was necessary to garner my attention."

"It may not be a threat. Her fate is yet undecided. I am bored by your slow progress on the book. I had a feeling your pace was impeded by," he curled his lip in distaste as he said, "growing affection. If I end her life here and now, could you not simply take possession of the grimoire?"

Marceau needed to concentrate. Seraphina's life depended upon his next answer and he knew it. What could he possibly say to save her?

"She has a curse," Marceau blurted out. "I've never seen one of this complexity. I've been studying it while letting her do the tedious work of transcribing the grimoire. You know how obsessed I can become when I can see no way to break one. This hex is quite involved. The affection, the longing, Babette senses are no more than my desire to break the curse. I admire the curseweaver who wove it."

Marceau turned and let desperation sink into his eyes as he stared first at Babette and then Lynette. Neither changed their expression in the least, but he thought Lynette's hand tightened on Babette's a moment before the ballerina said, "A curse."

Babette sniffed deeply in his direction and then in Seraphina's. She guided Lynette's stiff steps, before reaching a cold hand out once more.

Marceau cringed as this time Babette pulled a crimson drop of blood from Seraphina's, now blue, lower lip. She tasted the drop of blood and closed her eyes and groaned a sexual and primal sound. "Mmm. Yes, there is terrible suffering here. Long felt pain and deep loneliness." Babette locked eyes with Marceau and held out her hand.

He hesitated, but Lynette's mismatched stare urged him forward. Marceau took her hand as his thoughts screamed—*Save her.*

It seemed as if his bones would break from the tension, when Babette finally said, "Yes, I agree. His obsession for this curse drives his actions here. She is much too delicious to waste. Enduring suffering this long has tainted her blood like the aging of vintage wine. Do bring her back so I can taste her again someday, will you Max?" Babette lowered her head and her mouth formed a seductive, dangerous smile, which made Max's eyes widen.

"Ahem, yes. I believe my message has been received loud and clear, has it not, Marceau?" Max slammed the tip of his cane into the marble floor and a droplet of blood froze inches below Seraphina's mouth. "My Ettes and I will take our leave, for now."

Lynette turned her body away from Max and mouthed, "Danger. Stay here."

Marceau frowned. What could be more dangerous at home? Nothing could be worse than what Max had done here.

The Ettes joined Max, and they each raised their free hand and placed it on his shoulders forming a circle. Max slammed his cane once more into the floor and as if a video played in reverse, the blood droplets began to slowly rise back into Seraphina's mouth.

"Thank you, Maximilian." Marceau dropped his eyes and focused on the floor, his posture the definition of subservience.

"I expect more pages by the end of the week then. I shall also expect you'll be finished tinkering with this curse before the next full moon. Do not try my patience, Marceau. There are many opportunities for a grisly death in this city. Now Babette has a taste for the woman, she may want more."

"Yes, sir." Marceau did not look up until Max and his Ettes had completely faded. Then he rushed forward in time to see the tip of the metal spire as it left Seraphina's chest. Her wound closed and she stood upright.

The sunlight above was muted as the ceiling was again intact. The woman who had been screaming was now quietly reading plaques again.

Seraphina stopped abruptly after half a rotation. She cried out as she pressed against her heart and looked at Marceau with an expression of sheer panic. Her prior levity forgotten.

Marceau froze. Seraphina shouldn't feel anything with Max gone and his punishment reversed. What did she sense? He reached toward her instinctively, and she flinched back.

"Yes, sorry." He lowered his arm. "You seem alarmed. Are you all right, Seraphina?" His voice was steady, but his eyes raked over her looking for any sign of her previous injury.

"I-I want to go home. Right now." Seraphina rubbed her sternum and started forward at a clipped pace. Once outside, she turned. "I need to be alone, Marceau. I need space."

Marceau didn't want to let her out of his sight for even a moment but knew he had no right to argue. The farther she was from him, the safer she would be.

Seraphina turned and walked away, her steps quickening as she left the area. Marceau watched until several blocks down, she turned out of sight.

The events of the afternoon reeled through his mind on his way back to the hotel.

He had until the next full moon, less than a month, to free her. Then he would leave and never see Seraphina again, for her own safety.

Chapter Twenty

Marceau chatted with Khat while Seraphina tried to work out a series of troublesome Celtic symbols. Her concentration was shot, however, between hidden glances at the way Marceau's black T-shirt clung to his body and flashbacks of the biting cold she'd felt in her chest the last time they were together.

She hadn't mentioned her sudden unease at the Country Music Hall of Fame to anyone, especially Finn. But something frightening and familiar jarred her subconscious in that bitter cold—a hollowed out emptiness set her nerves screaming and kicked her flight reflex into high gear—ruining an otherwise fun afternoon.

Finn walked in and paused to kiss Khat before heading to the refrigerator.

"Interesting. I don't know why it didn't register before," Marceau said. He looked back and forth from Seraphina to Finn and Khat. "Do you mind kissing Khat again, Finn. For science?"

"Well, if it's for science, then you'd better make it good." Khat laughed and laid a lingering kiss on Finn that made Seraphina's eyes drop. She faked concentration on the book.

"Huh." Marceau stared at the air around Seraphina.

"What?" Khat asked after she came up for air.

"Seraphina's hex doesn't recoil when you touch Finn. I had assumed it was a natural reaction to touch, but apparently it's purely one sided. The hex only reacts when Seraphina touches objects *she* feels an emotion toward."

Seraphina blushed. Marceau was referring to when she touched the dahlias he brought her.

She couldn't help but feel a little jealous her hex showed no reaction when Finn touched Khat. Seraphina was happy for her friends and wanted them to enjoy a normal relationship, but it was still difficult at times. Finn was cursed but still free to experience love, to touch Khat and be touched.

Cut out the petty thoughts. She scolded herself. Snap out of it. She went back to scanning an index of ancient pagan symbols on her laptop.

"There. Go back to the last page, Seraphina." Marceau pointed at her laptop.

She hit back on her browser. Marceau's arm hovered over her shoulder as he started to point out a symbol they'd been searching for. He hissed and jerked his arm back, tucking it tight against his chest.

"What? What's wrong, Marceau?" Seraphina asked.

"N-Nothing just an arm cramp." He got up quickly. "I've just been sitting too long without stretching." Marceau paced and shook out his arm, not looking at any of them.

"Arm cramp, huh?" muttered Finn. He looked back and forth between Seraphina and Marceau. "I think it's my turn. Don't you? I want to try playing my guitar as a distraction while you work on the curse. May help damper my emotional response. Let's go try it in my room."

"Sure." Marceau followed Finn down the hall still rubbing his arm.

"What was all about?" Khat asked.

"I have no idea," Seraphina answered and turned back to her translation to hide her worry.

Beautiful music filtered out of Finn's room, but it was one of his more melancholy songs. One he played when something was troubling him.

The guys stayed in Finn's room the rest of the evening. Seraphina gave up on the grimoire around seven when she and Khat decided to watch TV for a while.

"I need my comfy pj's," Seraphina said, rising. "I'll be right back."

She headed toward her room. The music had stopped a while ago, but she hadn't thought much of it. Finn often preferred to stay secluded in his room while working with Marceau to prevent hurting anyone's feelings when his emotions got out of control. He hadn't acclimated to Marceau's power as well as she had. Seraphina hadn't thought anything was wrong until she neared Finn's door.

"I… haven't seen any signs of that. I mean she always stays focused on our work. Seraphina is well aware of the dangers…" Marceau sounded upset. She couldn't help it. It was wrong to eavesdrop, but the door was cracked open and they were talking about her. Seraphina was human, well, sort of.

"To be safe… don't touch her. Sit farther away. Wear damned gloves. I don't know. Just don't ever dare touch—"

"Ahem," Marceau interrupted.

Seraphina's heart leapt to her throat.

She rushed the rest of the way to her room and quickly closed the door. Leaning back against it, she tried to take deep breaths. Finn was warning Marceau not to touch her. How humiliating can you get? This stupid curse. Seraphina's eyes stung with unshed tears. She wanted to throw herself on the bed and start bawling, but that was silly and would fix nothing. It wasn't as though Marceau had ever touched her anyway. They sat together every afternoon and talked for hours, but he followed her rule and was careful. He understood her hex meant touching had consequences. She flipped through a book and tried to distract herself, too embarrassed to rejoin the others.

A little while later, Finn knocked softly on her door. "We need to talk, love." He opened the door and stepped inside when she did not protest.

Seraphina sat propped on her bed pretending to compare an herbal diagram in her notes to a more detailed illustration in a wilderness field guide.

"Oh no, oh please, Rhett," Seraphina said, exaggerating her Southern accent. She threw her arm across her face over-dramatizing. "Don't break up with me today. My poor, delicate heart could not take the rejection."

She raised her head in synchronization with her arm dropping. "Let me guess, it's not me, it's you?"

Finn sat on her bed and didn't take the comedic bait.

Uh, oh.

Seraphina tried to deflect. She did not want to participate in what she knew was coming. Maybe Finn would catch the hint and leave it alone. "What's going on, Finn? Trouble with Khat?"

"No. Khat's fine. We're fine. You know what this is about. I know you overheard, well, some of what Marceau and I were talking about earlier. So we must talk about your feelings for him." Finn looked at her, his expression softened. "I see the signs, love. I know you as well as I've ever known anyone. You care for him."

"Finn, I do not. I mean I like him, of course, just look at all he is doing to try to help me. To help us. But, I'm keeping my distance. I remind myself every day we're working toward a way to break this curse and not to get too emotionally attached."

"That is exactly what I mean, love. You shouldn't have to remind yourself every day not to get"—he raised his hands and emphasized the next words with his air quotes—"emotionally attached."

"You know I hate it when people do those." She crossed her arms, sullen.

"Whether you're ready to admit it or not, you are falling for him. I see the way you look at him when he isn't watching. I see the way he looks at you too, by the way."

"But—"

"He does, believe me. Marceau's affection is written all over his face when he's around you. You two are in very dangerous territory here. I think you need to stop working together."

"Stop working with him? Isn't it enough you're telling Marceau I care about him and he better not touch me? Like that's not humiliating enough? Thanks so much for that. But to just give up? To stop even trying to break the curse? Are you crazy, Finn? This is the closest I've ever been to an answer."

"And are you willing to risk death to find it? I'm not saying he has to stop working on the curse, or even that you should. You just need to stop working together. He can work off what he has gleamed from your hex already. I'll work with him whenever he likes, but you must distance yourself."

Even the thought of distance made her sad. She would miss him. That realization alone was proof enough Finn was right. Seraphina placed her hand on her chest against the growing ache. Finn nodded at her subconscious reaction.

"Damn it, Finn." She fell back on the bed. "We're close. I can feel it."

Finn lay back beside her, and they stared at the ceiling of her bedroom. "I know, love. I feel it too. I told Marceau to wait for me downstairs. I'll set up a time to meet him tomorrow. He and I will keep working on the curse. Meanwhile, you figure out what you can from the grimoire."

"It may be silly at this point," Seraphina sighed and said, "but I don't want you two to talk any more about why I'm keeping my distance. It's bad enough you both spoke about it today. Feelings are a distraction. Marceau needs to stay focused on the curse. Maybe one day I will be free to tell him more, but until then, don't go there. Okay?"

"Of course, love. I understand. We'll just make sure you're otherwise occupied." Finn sat up. "And the two of you don't touch. Ever."

"Curses suck, Finn."

"That they do, love. They sure do."

A little later, Khat knocked on her door. "Um, Sera? The guys just left. Look, I don't know what happened, but Finn kind of hinted I should check on you. So, yeah. Are you okay?"

Seraphina opened her door and met Khat with a deep sigh, her eyes filled with tears.

Khat nodded. "Worse than I thought. Okay. Junk food or whiskey?"

Seraphina looked at Khat and sniffled. "Both?"

"You read my mind. Come on, a hot fudge and bourbon sundae it is."

"A what?"

"Trust me. They're magical. No djinn powers needed." Khat grabbed Seraphina's hand and pulled her toward the kitchen.

Chapter Twenty-One

Downstairs Finn opened the locks on the shop door and followed Marceau into the alley behind the apothecary. "Want to grab a beer?" Marceau asked.

He was on dangerous ground. If he didn't continue sending transcriptions from the grimoire, Max would retaliate. That was the last thing they needed.

Finn rubbed the back of his neck. "May as well, I asked Khat to check in on Seraphina. I'll catch hell from her later too, so I'm not in any hurry to go back upstairs."

As much as Marceau hated to admit it, he felt compelled to break the curse that bound Seraphina and Finn. Marceau wanted to be the one to free her... for once to be the good, valiant guy who rescued the damsel in distress. Marceau snorted a laugh and tried to hide it.

"I hardly see what is amusing in this situation, Marc." Finn started pacing. "There's no telling how long she'd been listening. I had hoped to keep our conversation private. She is sensitive about what we discuss without her present, understandably so."

"Indeed, my mind wandered for a moment. I agree about wishing our talk had been more discreet. And just in case she does feel anything for me, we'll work on greater diligence when we're together."

"If you work together." Finn walked back toward Marceau his jaw set.

If?

Finn hadn't seen her hex's reaction, but he was suspicious.

Careful.

"My best chance of understanding how to unweave the hex is to continue working with you both. Just tonight, the revelation that Seraphina's hex shows no reaction to your physical contact with someone you…"—Finn's brow raised and Marceau hesitated, searching for the right word—"…admire, was a new piece of the puzzle. It would've been impossible to recognize distinction without Seraphina's presence."

"Look, I want her freed from the curse too, but not if it risks her life. Better to be cursed and alive, than to lose her completely." Finn turned. "Perhaps we could find another curseweaver to help us, a woman maybe? Surely you know of another who could take over?"

Tension weighed down his shoulders. It wasn't only arrogance that made the answer to Finn's question a resounding *no*, but that was part of it. "No one else approaches curses as I do. My life has been devoted to the exploration of the science behind them. I know others. Older curseweavers who are quite powerful. But none who could be trusted to not hurt Seraphina. Or to not capitalize on her circumstances. Their means are questionable and often involve trickery or superstitious nonsense. Besides, breaking hexes is not a talent we're willing to advertise—"

Finn's phone interrupted Marceau. The ringtone sounded like antique alarm bells and Finn's posture stiffened. He pulled his phone from his pocket and held up a finger. "Excuse me."

Finn answered his phone with a curt, "Speak."

Marceau's phone vibrated in his pocket. Was it Seraphina? Very few people had his direct number. Instead, it was a text message from Vespa… *Come get me.*

Yeah, he'd get right on that. Marceau put his phone back in his pocket and crossed his arms.

"How many does the term *pile* refer to exactly?" Finn snapped. "Well, if they're already dead, you know there is nothing I can do." He paused. "Administer first aid, CPR, apply pressure. I don't know, I'm a Sin Eater, not a damned EMT. I'm on my way. Three minutes." He hung up.

Marceau's phone vibrated in his pocket again. *Need you, now.* Give it a rest, Vespa.

Finn said, "I have an emergency, a job. I don't mean to be rude, but I prefer you not linger when I'm not home until we finish this conversation."

Marceau nodded. "Of course. I'll just call it a night."

His phone vibrated yet again. Marceau sighed and took out his phone. Another text from Vespa, *TROUBLE. You can help or Max. Hurry.*

What had Vespa done now? Marceau texted, *Where?*

"Goodnight, Marceau." Finn hurried toward his black motorcycle. The engine roared to a start, and he yelled, "Tomorrow, we'll finish our talk." He put on his helmet and was gone.

Marceau checked his phone. Vespa still hadn't responded. If she called in Max, his problems had just escalated. He repeated his text, *Where Vespa?* and then climbed into his rented SUV and hit the steering wheel. This night had certainly gone downhill.

AAA. Hurry.

Marceau turned onto Second Avenue and headed toward ground zero for all supernatural activity in Nashville, Absinthe & Alchemy.

A sign spanned the alleyway with PRINTER'S ALLEY illuminated in bright letters. Between the words, a red circle had been drawn around the white image of a print boy. A more welcoming sign than he'd imagined, given the reputation of Nashville's former red light district of speakeasies, gambling, and brothels.

Several young men stumbled around the corner, two holding one up between them. Their unconscious friend's feet drug the sidewalk as they worked to move him out of the alley. A stream of blood tinged drool fell from his lip. One of them stared at Marceau with the eye not rapidly swelling shut, before slurring, "Man, I'd go somewhere else if I was you. AAA is shut down while they clear out the bodies."

His drunk friend was rambling, "I should've hit him even harder. You see the dude's face? A fire Spellcaster too. I knocked him out cold before he could even light a damn match. Let's wait. I'll kick his ass again."

Marceau walked past them with only a nod.

The friend argued, "Shut it. We're taking my brother home. I bet he's got a concussion from that crazy bitch. She kicked him right in the head."

Sounded like Vespa's usual tricks.

Marceau approached the club and was stopped by a large framed security guard. "Club's closed. No one goes in."

"I'm here to pick up an acquaintance, I believe she is inside."

"Third floor's on lockdown, no more girls dancing tonight. Move along." The guard flexed his shoulders.

Marceau noticed a familiar black motorcycle parked in the alley. *Not good.* But he saw an opportunity. "I'm here to assist the Sin Eater. I suggest you let me pass. Or should I explain to him that you hampered my progress?"

The guard's lip curled in distaste. "Should've known you were with him. You the cleanup guy? Go on in, mind the blood. Zeke's up on three. Whatever's left of the girl when Zeke's done with her, will be up there too."

Marceau hurried past and entered Absinthe. He was surprised by the distinguished appearance of the place. A long, elegant wood bar lined the right wall. Victorian sconces illuminated each booth along the left wall. Halfway down the narrow room, a man's shins lay atop a booth table. His cowboy boots glistened with blood. The man stuffed into the tufted leather seat had a deep puncture through his left cheek through which Marceau could see a few of his upper teeth. Marceau sincerely hoped the hole wasn't from one of Vespa's designer heels.

An antique elevator door slid open at the end of the bar. Two men wearing black shirts with SECURITY printed on their muscled backs carried out another body by its wrists and ankles. This one was an older man in an expensive suit with a pencil mustache. His eyes were open but unseeing.

"Does this one still go to the Sin Eater? Think he stopped breathing halfway down."

"Naw, he's toast. Zeke's gonna be hot too, had a big ol' tab," answered the other guard. "But take him in there. I ain't waitin' to see if'n he gets possessed, no ways." The guard with the thick accent nodded at Marceau as they carried the corpse through an exit door.

Marceau stared at several pairs of feet lined up on the floor of the back room. An ominous figure in a flowing black robe turned toward the guards. Although Marceau saw only his chin, combined with his rigid posture and a flash of his pale hand, it was enough. Finn.

Rushing into the empty elevator, he slid the heavy, iron gate closed. He pushed up the antique lever and the elevator began to rise.

As the second floor came into view, he lowered the lever and it stopped. Alchemy, the second floor, was a wreck. Round tables lay on their sides. Cards, poker chips, small bottles and vials of various colors, and chairs covered the rich, green damask carpet. The walls were draped in black. Round booths were shielded by draperies along the walls. At the far end of the room, several wait staff dressed in crisp white shirts and black slacks were righting tables and stacking chairs. They paused when the elevator stopped, turning to stare at Marceau. An imposing bartender, muscular and covered in tattoos, stepped forward. He tilted his head and ran a hand through long, blonde hair that was shaved tight on the sides. Something vaguely familiar about his blue eyes made Marceau wonder who he was, but he did not want to be delayed.

Seeing no sign of Vespa, Marceau raised the lever again and the elevator ascended. The instant the next floor was revealed above him, Marceau could hear her. He pressed his temples and centered himself as the opening lowered.

By the time the third floor of the club, *Ass* as Khat had called it, reached his eye level, Marceau stood calmly ready to soothe whatever situation Vespa had caused. He had a plan: be sharp, be composed, and take control. Anything to keep Max from getting involved.

Vespa argued, "It's not my fault they started fighting. Maybe you shouldn't serve so much alcohol. Ever think of that? Probably because your dancers weren't keeping them properly entertained. I could show them a thing or two, to help satisfy your guests."

A man's voice boomed. "And maybe whatever you released in a crowded bar caused a riot. Every man in here went berserk. What the hell were you thinking?"

Marceau slid the iron gate open. "Oh, I'm sure a few women went berserk as well if she released her pheromones in such an enclosed area. They overcome both sexes with fervor when she's this careless."

Two guards parted and the semi-transparent form of an angry man turned toward Marceau. "Who the hell are you? I called in the cleanup crew."

Marceau stepped over the body of a Sanguine. The pale, nightmarish creature was dead though the bloodsucking tentacles that made up its mouth still moved. One reached out near his leg as he stepped over it.

Marceau's lip curled in disgust at the black blood oozing from the monstrous skeletal head.

He said, "Mind your manners, spectre. You should be thankful it was me she summoned, or the mess in your club would be the least of your troubles."

Vespa was secured upon a raised stage. She was on her knees with her arms bound to the long metal pole behind her. Her skirt was pulled up too high. A dark shadow colored her cheek and her eye was swollen.

Someone had hit her. Max would not be pleased if he walked in on this scene, not at all.

"It's about damned time, lover. Tell these idiots to let me go." Marceau fought to hide a grin.

"Who the hell do you think you are? You can't talk to the boss like that," said one of the muscled guards standing beside Vespa. At least, he'd taken his eyes off her body long enough to look up.

Marceau ignored the muscles and addressed the ghost, "The boss? Excellent, saves time. You're Zeke?"

The ghostly form turned to face him, forearms folded over his chest. "This had better be good."

Marceau maintained eye contact as best he could with the semi-solid club owner and walked forward. Zeke was imposing despite his present state.

"I am Marceau L'Argent." He leaned to the side and looked at Vespa. Straightening to full height, he shook his head and tsked. "Ahem, yes. And the woman you have chained to what I believe is an exotic dancer's pole is Lady Vespa. While we generally prefer to maintain our anonymity, this situation is forcing undesired introductions."

"As in *the* Vespa?" a guard asked.

Relaxed, composed, in control.

"I doubt she has waited this long to introduce herself." Marceau put his hands in his pockets and glared at the guard.

"Did she tell you her name?" Zeke asked.

The guard raised his hands "Well, yeah, Boss. She said all kinds of things, but I didn't believe none of it. Audra's spells keep charms and powers from workin' as strongly on us. I figured she was just trying to talk her way outta trouble. I mean we all know the stories. The real Vespa ain't gonna just show up in the AAA unannounced."

"Silence," Zeke snapped at guard.

Marceau noticed a slight tremor in the man's baseball glove sized hands. Zeke turned and stared at Vespa for a moment, nodded, and said, "You should've let me know you were coming. I have a private area set up for those with unusual appetites."

Vespa's face split into an evil grin, "Where's the fun in that? Who wants to be locked away from the fresh meat?"

"Release her." The moment Zeke barked the command, the second guard jumped and stepped back. "But boss, it took six of us to chain her. She kicked a hole right in Mac's cheek. I carried him down to Absinthe myself, but the Sin Eater said it was too late. What if she comes after us?"

Zeke turned and floated into the guard's face. "Make me repeat myself and I will take your eyeballs out with a jagged spoon and feed them to her."

Vespa giggled and licked her lips.

The first guard's eyes bulged at her forked tongue. He ran and grabbed Vespa's chain. "She *is* Lady Vespa. The key. Give me the damned key, idiot."

Guard number two handed over a large round key ring filled with a mixture of new and old keys. Vespa sucked in air from his direction and his knees buckled. He caught himself on the edge of the stage and backed up while holding out his hands. She laughed and made a biting gesture with her teeth.

The original guy freed her hands and held out his own to assist her.

"I highly suggest you step away, slow and steady." Marceau came forward and offered his hand to Vespa.

She pouted, her signature look for Marceau, then crawled toward him seductively and made a noise like a low, rumbling rattle. Lifting herself slowly back to her knees, she placed her hand on his. With the added height of the stage, Vespa's breasts were at eye level, but he maintained eye contact while she stepped off the stage. Once standing, she ran her manicured hand down the side of her thigh, sliding her short skirt back to an almost socially acceptable length. "Thanks, lover."

"I assure you I meant no ill will to you or your employer, Lady Vespa." Zeke bowed. "You've made quite a mess of my club. I lost customers and a guard in the melee of your power. Please accept my apology for the manner in which my guards detained you. But in the future, I ask you adjourn to the VIP area. Or at least, allow me to clear a floor of the club to minimize the damage."

Vespa threw her black hair back over her shoulder and laughed.

"You mentioned damages," Marceau began.

"Nothing for which you need worry yourself," Zeke answered. "It's part of owning an establishment like this. My employees will have the club cleaned by morning."

Marceau nodded. Perhaps Zeke hadn't yet seen the chandelier that lay in ruins on the second floor. Better not to dawdle. He turned toward the elevator, with Vespa's arm linked in his own, and froze.

Finn leaned against the far wall beside the elevator. His arms crossed over his chest. How long had he been there? Did anyone ever mention Max by name? By occupation?

Vespa squeezed his arm. "Everything all right, lover?"

"Why do you insist on calling me that?" Marceau asked between clenched teeth.

"A yoga guru I dined on taught me the power of positive thinking. He called it an affirmation. Oh, he also taught me this position where one leg was behind my neck and he would put his—"

"Enough." Marceau's volume and tone of voice indicated he meant business.

When they reached Finn, he spoke first. "I thought you were calling it a night, Marc." He nodded at Vespa. "Friend of yours?"

Marceau exhaled. The ease with which Finn had spoken earlier was gone. Now, he looked distant, angry. Finn's eyes widened at the multitude of sin on her flesh. Marceau could only imagine.

"Feeling hungry, Sin Eater?" Vespa cooed. "I'm delicious."

Marceau was mortified. If Vespa picked up on his desire to have Finn's respect, she was likely to use it against him. It wasn't only that she was cruel, it was also in her nature to use whatever weapons were at her disposal.

"Finn, may I introduce Vespa. Vespa, this is Finn."

"As in Lady Vespa of the Serpentine?" Finn asked, incredulous.

Marceau started toward the elevator, pulling Vespa along. If he could just get her inside before she said anything...

"Oh, time to go back to the hotel, lover?" Vespa smiled.

...else. She never gave up.

Finn pushed off from the wall and blocked their path. "Funny, you didn't mention you had such an infamous roommate while you were in town, Marc."

"Vespa is hardly my roommate or my lover either, for the record. We are acquainted by profession only. I'll be by tomorrow at three as usual to resume our agreement."

"Sure thing, I'll be waiting with bells on." Finn walked around them without giving Vespa another look.

Finn would be waiting, meaning no Seraphina. Usually, in the early afternoons, it was just Marceau and Seraphina. This night had taken quite a turn for the worse. Marceau led Vespa into the elevator and they rode back to the first floor in silence.

As they left, the security guards bagged up the bodies in the back room. Vespa certainly left her mark on this place. Well, Seraphina did say she missed its seedier days, didn't she?

"Seraphina's picking up a shipment at the airport, so you're stuck with me again." Finn walked to the refrigerator and pulled out a beer. He held it up offering one to Marceau.

"Sure, thanks. Seraphina has been busy ever since that night at the AAA. It's obvious she's avoiding me. Was it her decision or yours? Did you tell her about my association with Vespa?" Marceau took the beer from Finn and sat stiffly on the couch.

"Can tell you've spent a lot of time with Seraphina. Her direct manner has rubbed off on you." Finn took a long drink. He set his beer on the counter and fidgeted with the buttons on his shirt cuff.

"Bluntness seems to get the most direct answers from you."

"I suppose that's because I'm so used to it. And no, I haven't shared your *friend* with her. She has enough to worry about without adding a psychotic girlfriend."

"First, not a girlfriend. Not even a friend. A work associate forced on me, whom I'd much rather not know at all." Marceau maintained eye contact as Finn examined him for signs of a lie.

After a long moment, Finn nodded and came to sit across from Marceau.

Marceau continued, "In the spirit of direct conversations, I need to be honest with you about what happened the last day I did work with Seraphina. The real reason I pulled away after pointing to her laptop."

Sharing what happened with Finn was a risk. He'd not planned to tell him at all, but after a full week of not seeing Seraphina, Marceau figured it was worth the risk. Worry over what Finn may have shared about Vespa preoccupied Marceau the first few days. But now he simply missed working with Seraphina so much he was ready to push the issue.

Finn said, "I assumed you saw her hex react in some way to your closeness. With the way you jumped, it seemed like an unexpected event."

"I should've realized you'd put it together. And that's why she hasn't been around. You asked her to stay away, then?"

Finn tilted his beer in a toast as an acknowledgment. "Well, in all honesty, your familiarity and association with the infamous Vespa confirmed the need for that request too."

Marceau took a long drink and exhaled. "Once again, a forced work situation I've had to endure for many years. I'm sure you're known to some of the less than savory supernaturals in this area, as well, Finn. Yet I judge you only on who you are, not your associates."

Finn stared at him for a long moment and nodded. "Touché." He took a drink of his beer. "So elaborate on the unexpected event that made you jump halfway to the ceiling."

"When my arm was over her shoulder, the strands of her hex reached out. They—I don't quite know how to explain it—when they touched me, a jolt of raw power flashed up my arm."

"Damn it." Finn rubbed his hand down his face. "Her hex touched you? How is that even possible? Was that the first change you've seen in its behavior?"

Truth time.

"No. It has been getting brighter. The details have grown crisper and more defined. I've noticed the closer I am, the more it glows. I was working on a theory that the curse was feeding on my powers and was the reason for the change, but—"

"But?"

"But, I've been examining your hex all this time too. Your emotions change, but your hex shows no reaction at all to my power. It should behave the same as hers, yet it doesn't. So that weakens my theory about the curse feeding."

Finn's hex was not getting brighter or reacting in the same way. That could only mean one thing. One wonderful, terrifying, awful thing. Seraphina loved him, or she was beginning to at least. What other explanation could there be? "I have come to care for Seraphina. It wasn't planned. I think I pose a danger to her now." Marceau rubbed his hand through his hair and an unruly lock fell against his forehead.

Finn stood and started pacing.

"Seraphina doesn't want me to discuss this with you." He stopped twice and looked at Marceau and then resumed. "I pushed her to talk about you. I've seen signs. She's usually more distant with strangers, with men in particular. You cannot really blame her for that, now can you? If I knew simply touching the wrong woman could kill me, I'd live in a damned monastery."

"You've never struck me as the celibate monk type, Finn." Marceau smiled.

"Indeed. I'm very glad I'm not subject to that part of the curse, selfish as it may sound." Finn sat back down and picked at the label on his beer. "I noticed little things at first. Seraphina acted nervous when you were coming. She'd spend more time on her appearance. She'd fidget until you got here." Finn looked at Marceau as if sizing him up, then continued, "I confronted her. She's admitted there is some danger. Any feelings must be controlled and not allowed to grow. We agreed I would work with you, alone. You are the best chance we've ever had at finding a solution, but it's not worth her dying over. Not again."

She'd come back from death, but neither of them would discuss how. Seraphina said her death was hard on Finn. And she didn't like to talk about her time in the veil or how she returned.

Marceau needed to know everything. Any details held back could prevent him from finding the answer to their curse. He would have to push one of them to share. The real question was which one should he ask? Of course, if he never saw Seraphina again, the decision would be made for him.

Marceau nodded. "I understand. She must be protected. I'd thought the feelings were... one sided. My affection has been growing for a while."

When had she developed feelings for him? He thought back, searching for some sign. When had he first seen changes in her hex? She had been touched by the dahlias to some extent, and after that, her hex did start to glow brighter and—

"Wait. Why didn't I think of this before?" Marceau leapt from the couch. It was becoming clear to him. He visualized a dahlia. Yes, it made sense. It all made sense now.

He paced in Finn's former trail. Finn might not go for it. It was all or nothing stakes. What if Finn said it was too dangerous? What if Finn lost his temper and kicked him out? Marceau had to convince Finn of the potential here. The danger would be worthwhile if an answer could be found. If no solution could be found, Marceau would walk away and he'd vow never to see Seraphina again. No matter how much it hurt. He would not endanger her if the curse truly was unbreakable.

"You planning to fill me in or are you going to wear a groove in my floor?" Finn asked after several minutes.

Marceau spun to face him. "Her hex changes. I've been looking at yours and hers repeatedly. Yours has always stayed the same, with one exception. When she had an emotional reaction to the flowers, your hex recoiled. Otherwise, yours lies *dormant...*"

Finn sat stock still. Was he putting the pieces together too? "You said now Seraphina's hex is glowing brighter and brighter. You said it gains definition. It reached out and touched you."

"Yes. Her curse was dormant in a sense too. Whether because of age or because it had been so long since her feelings activated it. Her curse has awakened as her feelings have. Now, her hex is more visible and showing intricacies that were hidden before. Don't you see? It's like a blossoming flower, you cannot see the true shape and colors of the petals until the flower has bloomed. Think of a dahlia."

"So, if she is in love..."

Marceau ran his hand through his hair. "I might *finally* be able to find the key to the curse. To see the full detail."

Finn set down his beer. "So basically, you're saying she has to be in love, in full mortal danger, before you can see how to save her."

"Yes."

"I barely brought her back the last time she died. I almost lost her," Finn whispered, then his voice gained strength, "But I already know what she'll say. She has to be given the chance."

They agreed. Seraphina would work with Marceau again under strict conditions:

Rule number one was obvious, no touching, ever. In fact, Finn insisted Seraphina and Marceau both wear long sleeves and gloves to insure there would be no accidents.

Rule number two, Khat or Finn should be present to make sure they never slipped and forgot rule number one.

Rule number three, no more secrets. Not related to the curse, how the hex changed since Marceau's arrival, or Seraphina's death.

Finn and Marceau debated before agreeing on the last one. Marceau had questions about her death, but he'd let them wait. He was going to see Seraphina again and that was enough for now.

Chapter Twenty-Two

Seraphina's original plan for helping her little ghost friend involved taking Rolf to a hospital or hospice and waiting until the veil opened on its own. Where better to find someone dying?

She'd never been able to call the veil into her presence though she could often sense it was just out of her reach when she meditated. But now she had a plan B, after spending the last week practicing a conjuring spell translated from the Blackthorne Grimoire.

Seraphina's powers had mutated during all the years she was suspended across the veil. She used to have an affinity for elemental magic. In fact, she had abilities with air, fire, water, and earth, though some were minor.

Her father had bragged of her elemental affinities since her childhood. She'd wondered if that was a safe choice. All Spellcasters could produce magic, but not all had elemental powers. Aedan Callaghan had certainly been aware and made it clear he found that part of her powers attractive. He may have been more drawn to her power, than to her.

In her last few attempts, she'd summoned the telltale shimmer of the veil while funneling energy into the incantation. But each time the faintest undulation appeared, her energy failed and she nearly collapsed from exhaustion.

Finn's answer was to make her a noxious herbal tea that made her jaw tighten with each foul sip. She had to admit his herbal concoctions strengthened her, however, and she was ready to try yet again.

Seraphina sat cross-legged on a bright, cheerful rug on the floor of her bedroom. She faced the tallest window in the turret. The curtains were open to cast as much light as possible. Otherwise, the veil was too difficult to see. She closed her eyes and focused on the sunlight's warmth on her face. A light breeze blew her curtains and made long strands of hair tickle her neck. Seraphina's hands were centered over a wooden bowl of rough grained salt. She started the incantation, repeating the ancient words over and over. Instinctively, her body began to sway forward and back in rhythm with the words. Her mind slipped into a meditative state and the spell flowed freely from her lips.

A shadow gradually fell over her. No longer did sunlight illuminate her eyelids to a reddish hue. Instead, a stale, distinctively aged smell replaced the fresh air that had flowed through her open windows. Deep in her meditative state, Seraphina did not stop reciting the spell's melodious words. Her body's swaying changed on its own. No longer did she rock back and forth, instead, she was turning in a counter clockwise circle. Her head moved in a widdershin direction as well, but much slower than her torso.

A door creaked open behind her.

"Miss Sera?" Rolf's translucent form peeked around her closet door. He repeated louder, "Miss Sera?"

Rolf walked through the door he'd hid behind and cried out, "Miss Seraphina."

A faint red glow lit under her skin as Seraphina whispered the enchantment. She was unaware of Rolf's presence, unaware of the blood dripping from her nose, down her chin and pooling on the cheery rug, and unaware of the imposing black-clad woman who stood just inside the veil that opened wide in front of her.

The woman wore a tightly corseted dress of a heavy, dark material, made of a strange hide with a geometric pattern as if scaled. But this leather had very little in common with mundane cow skin.

When the mysterious woman looked up at Rolf, a terrifying smile split her blood red lips. "I have waited long. The girl will finally free me."

The horrified ghost ran through Seraphina's bedroom wall and only his echoing growl remained in the now darkened bedroom.

"Mongrel," she spat.

Her long skirt twisted around her legs. The faint red light cast from Seraphina's skin reflected off iridescent scales when the woman whipped her long, flowing skirt behind her to reveal bare, bloody feet. She tried to step forward. Her victorious smile fell into a cruel snarl when her progress was impeded by an invisible barrier. "This cannot be," she howled. "You are not pushing hard enough, girl. I command you to release me." The woman raised her pale arms and started an enchantment of her own.

Seraphina's voice cracked as she transitioned from a whisper to a shout in an instant. Her recitation sped up and the blood flowing from her nose splashed against her breath from the ferocity of her words.

The bedroom door slammed open. Khat paused only a second to take in the scene before her. She rushed to help and dropped to her knees behind Seraphina as a crack splintered across the air between them and the woman.

A stale, foul wind came through the crack in the veil and blew papers all over the room from Seraphina's neat desk.

Rolf ran to their side and squatted, putting his furry face right in front of Seraphina's. "Miss Sera. You gotta hush. That lady gonna come through if you don't stop. She ain't no ghost. She ain't supposed to cross."

Khat grabbed Seraphina, hugging her tight. She squeezed her eyes shut in concentration and a golden, metallic light illuminated and flowed down her skin in a shimmering trail. Khat's misty, metallic magic blanketed against her friend and she cried out, "Rolf, if you're in here, I need your help. I'm going to try to save Seraphina, but you have to keep her from getting through." The moment Khat's magic covered Seraphina completely, the fissures splintering out from the crack in the veil ceased growing.

"No. I am the Mistress of Death and will be trapped behind this veil no longer," the figure screamed. She beat against the fractured veil with both fists. "You have finally harnessed the magic, the necromancy over the spirit. I fed you all those years, and when you were mine." Each word was punctuated by a punch. "I shared my power over death so you could free me. I will have my vengeance."

Another thick crack formed and the foul wind shifted, no longer blowing outward, now a vacuum had formed. Debris in the air pelted against the shattered barrier, further weakening it. The shift in the air pressure of the room shook Seraphina from her trance. Her hair whipped forward, and a comforting, lush warmth covered her arms. Seraphina looked down at the unfamiliar golden magic blanketing her skin. She turned her head and realized Khat was the one holding her. Khat's chin rested on her shoulder, tears streaming from her closed eyes.

"Khatereh?" Seraphina yelled into the maelstrom that was her bedroom.

Khat's eyes flew open, "Wow, Sera, I thought I lost you." She looked up. "The Mistress of Death there is about to break out. Close it up. Seal the cracks."

The woman's fists continued to pound against the veil leaving bloody marks from her effort.

"The who of what? I-I don't know what to do. I don't know how to close the cracks."

Rolf leaned forward and grabbed Seraphina's chin. He nodded to himself, and she felt the faintest touch as he kissed her forehead.

"I gots an idea, Miss Sera. I love you bunches. You was my bestest friend ever, but I gotta go now." He stood and clenched his small fists.

"No Rolf." cried Seraphina. "She'll hurt you."

Rolf turned and winked. "I'm a wolf boy, Miss Sera. No crusty old Death Lady is fast enough to catch me." He ran to the back wall of the bedroom and braced his hands against it. "I always wanted to be a super hero. I'm gonna save you." Rolf ran full speed toward the veil. He leapt and slipped through the cracked wall as if it was only made of fog, landing against the Mistress's chest and knocking her down. Without stopping, Rolf sprang to his hands and feet, running on all fours, much faster than a normal child could travel. His ghostly body disappeared into the darkness beyond within mere seconds. The cracks and fissures in the veil started closing with a piercing, high-pitched screech as if crystals of glass had to grow to fill in the veil's weakness.

The Mistress jumped up. Her beautiful face contorted into a mask of pure hatred and rage. "No."

She launched her body against the veil as it sealed, then shimmered back out of sight.

The air in Seraphina's bedroom was weighted once more. Debris rained down on the floor, and the curtains fluttered back against the wall.

Exhausted, Khat flopped onto her butt.

Seraphina scanned Khat's tear-streaked face to make sure she was okay.

"You look like one of those damn idiots in the vampire TV shows, Sera." Khat grabbed a T-shirt from the floor, wadded it up and threw it at her. "Wipe all the blood off your face, so I can see if you're okay under there."

Seraphina did as Khat asked and realized the lower half of her face was covered in thick, sticky blood. She couldn't resist laughing at the absurdity of it and then a second later began to cry.

"You are gonna have to explain this mess and crazy lady to me in a minute, but first come here." Khat pulled her friend into a tight hug and sobbed right along with her.

When they both had released enough tears to clear a path for rational thought. Seraphina said, "I don't think I can explain anything. How did things get so out of control? I was practicing the veil summoning spell, same as I have every morning this week. And the next thing I know my room is like a hurricane, you have smoky magic all over me, some frightening woman is beating her way into our world, and Rolf..." Seraphina shuddered and fresh tears flowed down her cheeks.

Khat said, "I thought that was him."

"You could see him?"

"No, but he led me up here. I was working down in the shop and almost didn't make it to you in time. And I could only shield you and help you wake up. I didn't know what to do to send woman away. One minute she was breaking through and the next she landed flat on her ass. It was Rolf, right? What did your ghost boy do?" Khat rubbed Seraphina's back softly.

"Rolf ran through the veil and tackled her." Seraphina laughed and sniffled. "He bounced right back up and took off into the other realm. His passing through must have reset the balance of the veil and closed it."

"Now that was one brave kid." Khat smiled. "I wish I could have met the little wolf boy."

"Oh, he's been following you around like a lost puppy for weeks. He had quite a crush on you. Puppy love, he called it. Rolf said he always wanted a kitty for a girlfriend." Seraphina laughed again before swallowing hard and sucking in her lip to try to stop another round of tears. "Wait, but who the hell was woman?"

"She called herself the Mistress of Death. She was controlling you..." Khat stopped.

"What is it, Khat?"

"She said..." Khat's head turned, lost in memory. "She said she had fed you necromancy. Yeah, that's what she called it, necromancy over spirit."

"Fed me? Necromancy over spirit? No Spellcasters can harness spirit. It's the element we cannot reach in this realm. And besides, I've never seen that insane bitch in my life."

Khat just stared at her. Her brow creased with worry.

"Spill it, Khatereh."

"I don't think you have seen her in your *life*, but you did in your death. I think she fed you spirit power all those years you were with her... in the veil."

Seraphina shot to her feet. Khat got up too, but stiffly as if she was exhausted. She went to sit on Seraphina's bed but had to push papers and clothes off the edge to make room.

"I was dead. I wasn't awake on the other side, Khat. I was..." Seraphina stopped. "I don't know what I was over there do I? I don't remember a single thing between my decision to die for the curse and waking up."

Seraphina sat down next to her new friend.

"Aedan and Finn had me by my wrists." She held out her wrists staring at them while lost in memory. "And the next thing I knew, Finn was a pale, white Sin Eater carrying me into this very bedroom. He was upset, really emotional. In fact, his intensity frightened me. It had seemed like hours before he calmed down enough to explain. He said I'd been dead for fifty years, and he told me the story of our curse. Then we began our lives here. What if he didn't... tell me everything?"

"We will figure this out. We'll get to the bottom of it." Khat rose and swooned while almost falling back onto the bed again.

"Are you okay?"

"Yes, I used a lot of power. It will take me some time to recover, but I'd rather keep moving. It helps. Besides, we need to get your room cleaned up. And neither of us want to hear Finn's bitching if he sees the apothecary right now."

Seraphina stood. "What's wrong with the apothecary?"

"Finn had to go cultivate some more herbs, so I was on shop duty. A certain little ghost was so desperate to get my attention he threw things around like a pint-sized madman." Khat shook her head. "He got my attention all right, but I was picking up what he had thrown, so he grabbed jars and started pouring their contents in a path to lead me back upstairs into the loft. Then, I heard you screaming and figured out he was leading me to you. He was a smart kid, that's for sure, but the shop is trashed."

"Screw my room, shop first," Seraphina said. Going to her bedroom door, she saw a red powder line down the length of the hallway and an overturned jar. She squatted and ran her hand through the rare herb infused clay. Small, bare footprints running through the red powder were all that remained of her little Rolf.

He'd saved her. Seraphina thought she was meant to save him, but the brave little ghost actually saved her life.

Rolf had stopped the Mistress of Death from crossing over. What havoc would she have reeked in the mortal realm? And why was she trapped in the veil?

Seraphina whispered, "I'll miss you forever, Rolf."

Part III: Death

Chapter Twenty-Three

Today, Marceau was meeting both Finn and Seraphina at three o'clock. He hoped Finn had kept their run-in at AAA to himself, but Marceau had a plan to deflect, if necessary. Questions. Lots of them. He had a feeling Finn had been holding something back from Seraphina, as well. Finn seemed very reluctant to discuss how had he brought her back when she died.

When Finn answered the door to let Marceau in, he avoided eye contact. "Um, so Seraphina is feeling a bit testy. She didn't like not being included. I've already caught hell for it. Just thought I'd throw you a warning." Finn took the stairs two at a time.

Great.

Well, at least, Marceau was going to finally see her. Seraphina had become so important to him, and her absence seemed to have thinned the oxygen he breathed and dimmed the colors around him.

"Hello, Seraphina."

She stood in the loft's kitchen, leaning against the counter with her arms crossed in front. Wearing jeans, a simple, white buttoned shirt, her beauty overwhelmed him. The ponytail added charm.

"Hello, Marceau," she mimicked.

"It's nice to see you again. Finn has been helpful, of course, but I've missed our work on both the curse and translating the book."

"Cut the formal crap." Seraphina dropped her arms and stood straight. "This is awkward enough. Let's just get on with it, please. Where do you want me?"

"Direct as ever." Marceau smiled. "Perhaps, you could take a seat at the table. I'll sit across from you."

She walked to the table, scraped the chair legs across the floor as she scooted, and sat. Khat came in, waving before even heading to the refrigerator.

Marceau sat across from Seraphina in silence. He wondered where to begin. Tread lightly. He'd imagined what he would say over and over in his mind and thought a level of sensitivity should be used, maybe he should…

"So, my hex is glowing brightly like a red freaking marquis of my innermost, personal feelings, huh?" Seraphina blurted.

Marceau could not stifle his surprised laugh. Finn managed to cover his mouth, where he sat behind her on the arm of the love seat.

"Seraphina, I…"

"You should have told me. *Me*, Marceau. Not Finn. I mean it's bad enough as it is, but to know the two of you have been talking about my most private feelings behind my back like that? It should have upset your gentleman sensibilities, shouldn't it?" Her gloved hand was fisted against the table. Even while pissed as hell at him, Seraphina was the most stunning and frustrating girl he'd ever known. Her freckled cheeks blushed.

"I apologize, Seraphina. You're absolutely right. I should have discussed the changes I detected with you, but I was working on a different theory when last I saw you and didn't want to alarm you."

"Alarm me, how?"

"I thought your curse was feeding on my power. That maybe it was drawing its newfound strength from me."

She bit her bottom lip, considering his words. "And you still came here day after day when you thought I was somehow feeding on you?"

"Yes, I did."

"Why Marceau?" her tone had softened, vulnerable.

"Because even if you were drawing strength from me, it was well worth the risk. To spend time with you and see your smile, to hear your laughter, to be caught off guard by your charming candor… I would risk much for that."

Finn rubbed his hand through his white hair and slouched, defeated.

Khat said, "Whoa, okay. Hold up here. Mister Finn, you are coming with me." Khat pulled Finn up from the love seat. Finn stood, but started to protest. Khat lowered her chin and put a hand on her hip. "Don't even try it, Sin Boy. They deserve privacy for this talk. You can babysit later like a cranky mother hen, but for now, we are going to our room. Now march." She pointed to their bedroom. No one wore a bitchy expression better than Khat.

"Fine. Then put these on." Finn picked up a pair of dark gloves from the coffee table. He tossed them in front of Marceau before walking out. "And I'll be back in five minutes whether you're finished talking or not."

Marceau pulled on the supple leather gloves and winked at Khat. "Thanks, Khatereh."

"You're welcome. Now, you were just telling Seraphina how you would risk everything just to be in her presence. Carry on then…" Khat waved her hand at Seraphina and sauntered out whistling.

Finally alone, Marceau found once again, he was dumbfounded.

Seraphina said, "I don't know what to say." She looked down at the table and picked at a fingernail.

He smiled at their shared thought. "Seraphina, look at me, please."

When she did, her light green eyes were brimming with unshed tears.

"Please, don't be afraid of me. I will *not* touch you. I'll keep my distance and be ever careful. Finn or Khat would probably tackle me if I even tried to get too close to you. I won't endanger you. Please don't cry."

"Don't you understand, Marceau? That's exactly why I'm crying. It hurts to feel this." A tear fell. "So much emotion. Feelings I've denied myself all these years. It hurts to finally feel love and know you'll be perfectly careful and vigilant. I know you'll never touch me. I've watched Finn and Khat and hundreds of others in love. I've seen the comfort and pleasure they take from the most simple touch. But we'll never know what feels like."

"When we break the curse, when you are freed, we can…"

"If, Marceau, *if* we break the curse. I worry it's unbreakable. I'm afraid I can never run my fingers through your hair, never brush my cheek against your five o'clock shadow, or kiss the bow of your lip. It might be worth dying to experience the caress of love, just once." She looked away. "I've been wondering… If I died and stayed that way, Finn might be free to live a normal life too. Maybe he could stop eating sins and grow old with Khat."

"No." Marceau slammed his hand on the table. "If you truly care for me at all, then you have to *believe* in me too. I will find a way, Seraphina, but you have to keep your hope. You have to trust in me."

Seraphina sat, silent, staring into his eyes. She took a breath as if a heavy decision had been made and her body was responding at a deep cellular level. Her hex whipped forward, reaching for him. It glowed so brightly that Marceau instinctively skidded his chair back, shielding his eyes.

"Finn. Khat. Get back in here," Marceau yelled as he shot to his feet. Finn was beside the table in an instant.

"What? What the hell is it?" Finn looked from Marceau to Seraphina and back again. "What's wrong? Why are you hiding your face and why is she crying?"

"I've decided to trust him. I am giving him my hope. All the hope and yearning for the freedom I have left within me. No more walls. No more self-protection or hiding away from what I want most."

Marceau lowered his hand and squinted to look past the hex to Seraphina. It pulsed with red and amber light, flowing toward him and undulating in hypnotic waves. The intricate scrolls and webbing reminded him of flames both in movement and intensity. His face felt warmed as if by fire. Marceau cautiously sat down and scooted back up to the table. He placed his gloved hands on the surface, palms up.

"Do not move, Seraphina," he whispered.

Another tear traveled down her cheek when the hex reached forward again, and a single tendril touched Marceau's bare wrist just above his glove. It stroked his skin as light as a feather before rearing back and flaring brightly like molten lava. The smoldering tendril shot forward and wrapped tightly around his wrist, soon joined by another and another. Marceau's eyes widened and a sharp inhale bit his lungs as a shock of pure, freezing cold power traveled up, spasming the muscles of his forearm. Intricate blue scrolls and spirals fired, glowing and trailed up his arm.

"Oh shit," cried Finn. "What the hell is that?"

"Marceau?" Seraphina stared at his arm.

Marceau rotated his wrist and flexed his arm. "You both see it too?" She said, "Y-yes. What is that?"

"This is precisely what your hex looks like, only yours is in fiery shades of red. It started clear and thin, so faint it was almost like moving water. As we have worked together, it's been growing brighter and more colorful. Pale pink at first, then rose, and today it is red and amber, like a burning flame."

"And mine? Mine looks like this?" Finn was staring at Marceau's arm and then he looked at his own arm.

"Yours is always gray and black. It is shadowy. That's why I can usually see hers more easily. But yes, you carry the same patterns."

Marceau hissed as cold marks spread across his chest. He jerked his head to the side as the hex traveled up his neck.

"Is it hurting you? Should I move? Leave? What do I do?" Seraphina asked.

"Just stay still, please," he whispered.

Cold energy traced his face along his hairline. Marceau's chest muscles were spasming, and when he exhaled, his breath was visible as if the room was freezing cold.

"Your lips are turning blue, Marceau. Are you okay?" Finn asked.

"Y-yes. Let it f-finish." His teeth chattered.

"Finish what, Marc?" Finn asked. He moved closer to Marceau's end of the table.

"I'm not sure yet. But whatever it's doing is important. I can't explain how I know, but I feel it. This is what we've been waiting for. Her hex is blooming." His teeth chattered louder.

He felt light, free. And then everything faded to black.

When Marceau regained consciousness, he was on the couch with several blankets tucked under his chin and a hot water bottle behind his neck. His arms and legs were heavy and stiff, and he held his palm to his pounding forehead.

"He moved. He's waking up," Seraphina said.

"Marceau? Can you hear me? Are you awake?" Finn asked. He placed his warm hand on Marceau's cold forehead.

"Yes," he managed as a chill racked his body. "C—c-cold."

"I'll get another quilt," Seraphina said.

"You scared her, Marc. Hell, you scared me," Finn added.

"Wh-What happened?"

"When those blue swirly marks covered your whole body, you shot to your feet and your eyes went back in your head. You stood with your arms held out wide. Your hair and clothes blew around like you were in a wind storm, but there wasn't even a breeze. I was trying to decide whether to tackle you when finally your eyes rolled forward. They were glowing bright blue."

Marceau fought to stay conscious. "I don't remember any of that." Another chill. Marceau bit down on his lip in an attempt to stop his teeth from chattering.

"Here." Seraphina flung two more heavy quilts over him. He realized every blanket they owned probably covered him and yet he was freezing.

"Your lips are still blue," she said softly.

"Well, at least, he's finally awake and we can't see his breath anymore." Finn tucked the quilts tighter around him.

"How long was I out?"

"More than three hours now, I would have called an ambulance, but I didn't know how exactly to explain the marks all over you."

"Marks? They're still there?"

Marceau started to pull his arm from the blanket.

Finn held his arm. "Best to stay wrapped in for a bit. They seem to be fading now you are awake."

Seraphina's nose was red and her eyes were puffy. "I'm so sorry, Marceau. I don't know why or how, but I think I almost killed you."

"I'm okay. Really. I'm not sure what happened, but something is different. We'll figure out what it was later, okay?" Marceau scooted his shoulders back until he was partially sitting up. "Could I have something hot to drink? Coffee or tea or anything? I feel cold down to my bones."

"Oh, of course." Seraphina was in the kitchen and putting on the tea kettle in record time.

"Try the black tin of chai, love. The clove and cinnamon will help warm him up," Finn said as she stood looking blankly at a cabinet filled with colorful tins and boxes. "Middle shelf, right side."

"I'll help you sit up better." Finn grabbed Marceau's elbows and pulled, propping several pillows behind his back.

A few minutes later, Seraphina held out a steaming mug to Marceau. He reached to take it and Finn yelled, "Stop."

They froze.

Seraphina's hand was inches from Marceau's and hers was illuminated. Red, orange, and amber scrolls traced her knuckles and up her wrists. Identical electric blue, turquoise, and pale sky blue markings traced up his hand and wrist.

"What does it mean?" she asked.

"I don't know, but please don't move away. You're so warm. I thought I'd never feel warmth again."

Seraphina looked unsure. She raised her shoulder in an unspoken gesture of what to do?

Finn scooted to the side. He sat on the coffee table beside the couch. "Here, love. Sit by me"—he pointed at Marceau—"but do not move."

Marceau sipped his chai with his left hand and held the right out to Seraphina as if warming it by a fire. His chills softened and then faded away.

One by one, they removed blankets. Within an hour, Marceau was able to sit up with only a throw blanket on his legs. When he sat up, Finn nodded at the other end of the couch and Seraphina stood stiffly. She stretched and moved to sit at the opposite end of the couch.

Khat entered the room, paused, and took in the scene. "Okay, a huge pile of blankets, you are both covered in awesome glowing tattoos, and Finn's hair is standing up in every possible angle which means you really freaked him out. I hate when I miss the good stuff." She stomped over and planted a kiss on Finn's forehead and continued to the kitchen, her hands filled with bags of takeout. "We are still having movie night right? It was my turn to choose."

Marceau, Seraphina, and Finn all just stared at Khat as she unpacked container after container of food from her bags.

Khat stopped and realized no one had moved or said a word in response. "Okay, I clearly missed some *really* good stuff. Fill me in over dinner?"

"Sure, Sparrow. I'm not positive we know what happened, but maybe talking it out will help us understand," Finn replied.

Seraphina nodded. "It looks like you brought a feast." She turned to Marceau. "You will stay, right?"

"I'm starving," Marceau said with so much enthusiasm Seraphina let out an unladylike snort of laughter.

They all joined in and laughed. The tense nature of the afternoon was finally broken.

"So, what did you choose?" Seraphina asked as everyone calmed.

"Mexican food, margaritas, and *The Three Amigos*." Khat smiled and did her best Three Amigos dance.

Once they managed to stop laughing again, Seraphina said, "Perfect choice. We need something lighthearted. I'll help set everything up." She rose. "But Finn is the margarita master, so get busy, Sin Eater."

"Among my many talents," Finn teased. He headed to the bar while opening the bottle of Espolón tequila, its distinctive label ringed by playful Dia De Los Muertos-esque skeletons.

Marceau watched the others. They were so relaxed and natural with each other. He was fascinated by their little jokes and playful banter.

Khat threw limes at Finn. Seraphina ducked under the line of fire to bring the food to the table. She set up three platters of still steaming fajitas—shrimp, chicken and beef, and a vegetable assortment.

"Mm. Thanks for getting the ones with portabella mushrooms, Khat." Then Seraphina came back with chips, salsa, and guacamole.

As they sat around the table, feasting and drinking margaritas, Marceau had to agree Finn did make them well. Everyone filled Khat in on what had happened during the afternoon. They examined the matching hex pattern fading into Marceau's skin as they rehashed it all through dinner. Their only consensus was no one was sure what it meant.

Silence.

Seraphina broke the ice. "I think we could all use some time to veg out. Can we agree to let whatever happened settle the rest of the night and analyze it to death tomorrow?"

"Agreed. I'm too overwhelmed to think about anything serious right now." Marceau turned his wrist back and forth.

"Do you still see the blue marks?" Finn asked. "They've faded too much for me to see."

"Yes. Faintly now, the way I see most hexes. I can't stop staring at them. It's as if I am suddenly branded or tattooed."

Marceau helped Khat clear the plates away while Seraphina arranged pillows and readied the movie. Finn mixed a fresh pitcher of margaritas.

Marceau asked, "Do you always have such elaborate movie nights?"

"Oh yeah, at least once a week," Finn answered. "We take turns choosing the theme. It's quite serious business. The food and movie have to go together and a bad choice is rather hard to live down. Isn't it *Miss Cowboys and Aliens*?"

"Hey. At least, the chili was good," Seraphina grumbled. "And I had a thing for Daniel Craig." She winked at Khat.

"Mm. Who doesn't?" Khat waggled her eyebrows.

"Enough, ladies. You'll wound our fragile egos," said Finn. "My last choice was epic, Chinese takeout and *Ghostbusters*."

"And don't forget the Twinkies for dessert." Khat laughed. "I had a sugar rush for like two days."

Seraphina said, "Well, you did eat a whole box of them, Khat. Next time, I vote it's Marceau's turn."

"Seconded," Finn said.

"Thirded." Khat laughed.

"It-it would be my pleasure," Marceau replied. A foreign feeling made him frown. Marceau was starting to believe he belonged. He was one of them, not an outsider. For just a few moments, he relaxed. He let his careful control slip and watched his friends' playful banter. This was what freedom looked like. What true friendship and family felt like.

Finn was watching him when Marceau realized he must look like the Cheshire cat standing there smiling. He schooled his expression.

Nodding as if he understood, Finn said, "Pick something good, Marc. Oh, and for heaven's sake, do not go all *The Notebook* on me, trying to come off as romantic. Seraphina hates chick flicks anyway."

Marceau was getting accustomed to Finn's use of a nickname for him, another way to prove he was different than Max.

"True. I have a strict no-tears policy," Seraphina conceded.

"Noted," Marceau replied.

Back in his hotel room, Marceau lay on the bed and stared at his hands in the dim light of the television. Faint traces of blue still swirled across his skin.

His cell phone rang and right away Marceau's heart sank. Only Maximilian would call him at, he rolled over to look at the clock beside the bed, two o'clock on a weeknight.

Marceau was stalling and hiding everything happening here as best he could. Max was never known for his patience. Marceau had continued sending copies of the Blackthorn Grimoire transcriptions. Once when too many days passed without a transmission, Max suggested a few new inventive ways to kill Seraphina. He argued it was the easiest option. Marceau had been ready that time, though and also had a counter-argument ready. He claimed the book's curse made killing Seraphina too dangerous a gamble. The power within it could force the grimoire to disappear and never reveal itself to anyone who had participated in, or would benefit from, the death of an owner. It was bullshit, but it was convincing bullshit, at least, he hoped. No telling what Max would want this time. Marceau needed to stall him yet again.

"Hello Maximilian," Marceau said after the fourth ring.

"Marceau, how nice you answered."

Marceau sighed. Max had left a clipped voice mail yesterday, and he'd not returned the call. "I apologize for…"

"Save it, Marceau. I do not require your false excuse. Clearly, you're avoiding me, or you would have returned my call by now. So, tell me… when do you plan to return to New Orleans?"

"I am still examining the grimoire. I've been sending you the transcriptions. Surely, you recognize the complexity of translating such a book. There are three dead languages involved, not to mention the symbols and hieroglyphics."

"You would not have to waste so much time translating the book if you'd procured it as instructed in the first place," Max replied with frozen words.

"I know, Maximilian. I'm trying to compensate for my failure by providing you with as much of the book's contents as possible."

"So you have, and I'm sure spending so much time with the cursed young woman has been only academic, as well?"

"I have another appointment to examine the book today. And I'll have another email for you by the weekend." Marceau was tired, so damned tired of placating Max.

"I'm beginning to wonder if you are hiding something from me, Marceau. Perhaps I should come back to Nashville, but stay a while this time. My Ettes did seem to enjoy their time there. I could introduce myself to your fair Seraphina. Maybe after making my acquaintance, she would feel inclined to simply sell me the grimoire and end this nonsense."

Marceau's heart stopped and he leapt from the bed. It took significant self-control to keep his breathing even. No, no, no. Max had never said her name before.

"Silence, Marceau? You are usually so verbose. I am enamored with Babette. But I have been toying with the idea of adding another to my Ettes and a crimson haired Spellcaster might make a fine addition."

Marceau wanted to reach through the phone and strangle Max for even suggesting such a cruel idea. "I will not raise her into one of your playthings, Maximilian. There is no punishment or threat that could persuade me to do such a monstrous act."

"Monstrous, indeed. Tell me this, does your young lady friend know what you do for me? Would she judge you as fondly if she knew you hex the dead into my servitude?"

Marceau was already treading such a fine line here, trying to keep Seraphina safe and finding a way to release her from the curse. Max in Nashville would not be good, not good at all. He didn't take the bait. "Maximilian, I assure you…"

"Your assurances mean nothing to me. Your defiance and silences spoke volumes. I will make the arrangements and arrive on Friday."

Max hung up.

Damn. He only had four days. In four short days, Marceau needed to figure out why his skin was now marked with a hex, treasure each moment with Seraphina, find out what Finn was hiding about her death, and break the curse and free her.

Then, Marceau would leave Nashville for good and return to his life in New Orleans. It would hurt, but in NOLA, he could keep Max far, far away from Seraphina.

Max was singularly focused on the book and would punish Marceau for being otherwise, severely. But distance meant safety. Marceau would admit defeat and claim the book was inaccessible due to its curse. He could handle the repercussions as long as Seraphina was safe.

Knowing he could do nothing more tonight, Marceau grabbed the extra blanket from his closet and gave in to exhaustion. Tomorrow was going to be a big day.

Chapter Twenty-four

The next morning, Marceau woke up freezing again. He turned up the hotel room thermostat to its highest setting.

Three days before Max arrived and he had to find a way to protect Seraphina. He'd told her very little about his guardian, as little as possible, in fact. Maybe that was a mistake.

Would telling her about Max be terrifying enough to keep her from falling for his charm? Max could be quite convincing. But somehow Marceau thought Seraphina might see right through the handsome exterior to the cunning beast Max truly was inside. It was something to consider.

An inner chill shook his body. A hot shower would help warm him up. First, he called room service and ordered a pot of coffee.

After Marceau had dressed, he drank several cups and cradled the steaming mug in his hands. He missed the hints of chicory at Café Du Monde. The coffee was helping, but he had a feeling he'd not feel truly warm until he was with Seraphina this afternoon. He'd layered on two shirts and a sweater until then.

When his phone rang, he thought it strange. Seraphina always texted. "Hello?"

"Marceau, how fast can you get here?" Finn sounded frantic. He covered the phone and Marceau heard a muffled, "Get more ice."

"I'm on my way. What is it?"

Marceau grabbed his keys and was out the door before Finn replied, "Seraphina is burning up with fever. I can't get her to wake up."

Marceau skipped the elevator and ran down the stairs full speed.

"I heard a noise and found her on the floor of her bedroom. She said your name and then passed out. Hurry, Marc. Khat thinks she's at risk of brain damage if she doesn't cool down fast."

Marceau slammed open the parking garage door, ran to his rental, and peeled out of the structure. He broke the speed limit racing to Broadway and beat the steering wheel until his hand throbbed while he waited at the light. Finally, green. He floored it and wove through the morning traffic. The vehicle skidded around the right turn onto Third Avenue, turned left onto Elm Street, and took the alley to park behind the old fire hall where Seraphina lived.

Khat waited at the back door. As he flew past, she said, "Thank goodness, you're here."

Marceau climbed the stairs two at a time. He ran to Seraphina's room and skidded to a halt at the foot of her bed.

Finn had large, plastic bags of ice placed along her arms and legs. Seraphina wore only a green tank top and plaid boxer shorts. She looked so vulnerable lying unconscious on the bed. Tiny beads of sweat trickled down her flushed face. Her hair lay damp on her pillow. Her chest moved with weak, panting breaths.

"Damn it. Wh-what do I?" Marceau wrung his hands. He wanted to grab her but didn't dare.

"Come closer. Don't touch her, but come as close as you can," Finn answered. "It's like… This seems to be the opposite of how you were yesterday. You were freezing, had chills, and would not wake up. I've tried everything else I know to do and she's not responding. Yesterday, you said she was the only thing that finally warmed you. Well, it damn well better work in reverse."

Marceau took off his sweater and laid it on the floor as he crouched by the bed. He rolled up his sleeves. Finn nodded and Marceau raised his arms holding his hands over her, one centered above her chest and the other above her head.

Scrolls flared an electric blue in his hands and Marceau hissed as power cracked like a whip through his body.

Seraphina's hex reached up in a single, thin and slow winding tendril. It showed pale translucent pink. Weak, damn. She was so *weak.*

Her hex feathered along his palm to his wrist.

Come on. Wake up, flare, wrap around me, *anything.*

The hex trailed around the top of his wrist and darkened a shade.

That's it.

Another tendril raised, slowly twisting through the air toward his hand. The first one wound around his wrist again like a vine.

Seraphina took a deeper breath and another thin strand rose near his other wrist.

"What the hell is that?" Khat stood at the doorway, her eyes wide.

"Shh, Sparrow. I think it's okay. His marks are how they looked yesterday, brighter, maybe, but I don't know what the hell that stuff is coming off her, though. That's definitely new." Finn pulled Khat into the room, tucked her under his arm and squeezed tight. "But I think Marc is helping her. She is starting to breathe easier."

Marceau whispered, "You see the hex? Not only the patterns on her skin but now you are able to see the hex rising away from her too."

"Yes. Yesterday I only saw marks, like tattoos. Now, I see, I don't know what it is. Tentacles or vines or something coming from her and wrapping around you. What is going on?" Finn asked.

"Her hex is reaching out to me again. This is what I saw before, but yesterday my skin lit blue only after her hex wrapped around my wrist. Today, it felt like magic embedded in my skin called to hers, coaxing it to touch me. It's so weak, but I think the touch is making her stronger."

Seraphina rotated her head back and forth on the pillow. Her chest lifted in the direction of Marceau's hand and he quickly lifted his arm higher. She'd almost touched him with more than her hex. He hissed as the strands tightened on his wrists in response to his movement holding him in place.

Her face was still red and sweat dripped in long beads onto the pillow, but Seraphina's breathing slowed into an even rhythm.

Finn came closer and leaned down while examining the tendrils rising from Seraphina. "How do you feel, Marc? Is that thing hurting you?"

Her hex was gaining strength, darkening, and glowing. The color of the cords became more and more vibrant. Still mostly a rosy pink, but with occasional bursts of red. The scrolls and designs on her arms sharpened and spread along her shoulders toward her chest.

"No, she feels amazingly warm. I was so cold last night. A hot shower and coffee were the only things helping me this morning."

A larger tendril of color rose and stroked along his arm to the inside crook of his elbow. Caressing. Tasting.

Seraphina's eyes opened, now showing only white. Without warning, both her hands shot up and grabbed Marceau's.

Her fingers interlocked with his and Seraphina screamed as her body arced off the bed.

"Oh shit, no," Marceau yelled. His eyes bulged at their intertwined hands. Seraphina squeezed so hard, his fingers felt as if they'd break at any moment. But that was not the reason for Marceau's terror.

Khat grabbed Finn and wrapped her arms around him. She said, "Wait, Finn."

He started to pull away, but she shifted in front of him and held her arms out. Khat said, "Wait, damn it. Stop and look."

Finn's mouth dropped open.

The blue and red patterns on Marceau and Seraphina's arms were changing. The marks were joining and stretching into a new complex pattern. As the symbols entwined, they changed to a purple hue, the red and blue indistinguishable.

Seraphina's eyes rolled forward, and she looked up at Marceau. Her face was still flushed. She glanced around the room trying to figure out what had happened. "What's wrong?"

Marceau answered in a soft voice, forced calm. "You were sick. A fever. I was trying to help you."

She smiled. "I was burning up. It really hurt, Marceau. I couldn't scream. It was as if I were trapped, unable to move, while my blood boiled in my veins." Seraphina closed her eyes and shivered as if shaking off the memory of her pain. "Thank you for helping me." She took a steady breath and then seemed to really see him for the first time. "What's wrong? I'm feeling better. I think it's okay now. Why do you look so upset?"

"Our hands, Seraphina. You're holding my hands." Marceau squeezed gently.

She gasped and looked down at their interlocked hands. She instinctively started to back up, but he squeezed again to stop her. It was too late now.

Seraphina looked back up at him, terror etched on her face. "I, I'm sorry."

"No, I am. I'm so sorry. I love you, and I can't let the curse take your life." Marceau leaned closer. "This is really, really important, Seraphina. You have to do something for me. Please let the curse take me. It's okay. I've done some, well, some terrible things in my life. Let me know I saved you, let me redeem myself by saving your life."

Seraphina's eyes flared. She started shaking her head *no* and then she froze. "Wait, I don't feel anything. Death isn't pulling me. How can that be?" She stared down at their hands again. "Before, when I touched Aedan, it took only a moment. Finn and Aedan both held my wrists and I could feel the ache, the emptiness of death taking over my heart. It took hold quickly. I only had a moment to choose whether to release it or pull it into myself. To die, so they could live."

"Oh, Sera," Khat whispered. Tears streaked down her face. She still stood in front of Finn.

But Finn was on his knees.

"Finn?" Marceau asked. The sharpness of his tone caught Khat's attention and she turned around. "Finn? What's wrong?" Khat cried out as Finn began to crumple forward. She dove in front of him and tried to soften his fall.

Finn's breathing was shallow. He laid his forehead on the floor while Khat sat beside him and pulled him into her lap.

"Finn." Seraphina sat up.

"Don't let go, Seraphina," Marceau said. He climbed onto the bed with her so she could go to Finn. Their hands never broke contact.

"Finn," Seraphina sobbed and knelt beside him.

Finn was too weak to respond. He tried to focus on Khat and then Seraphina, but his eyelids fluttered closed.

"Why? Why is the curse taking him? I don't feel Death at all." Seraphina cried. She tried to let go of Marceau's right hand, but he squeezed tighter.

"You don't know what will happen if you touch him," Marceau pleaded.

"No, but I see what's happening if I don't. Let go, Marceau." She jerked a hand free.

"You could die," Marceau cried.

Seraphina looked at him as if willing him to understand. "I could save him. I have to try."

She reached out and placed her hand on Finn's chest just above his heart. Finn gasped and his eyes shot back open. The veins in his neck bulged as his body spasmed.

Finn's hex flared black and silver around him. It whipped out from his body and thick shadowy cords wrapped tightly around Seraphina's arm. She cried out in pain, but when Marceau tried to pull her away with the hand he still held, she pleaded, "No, let him."

Marceau couldn't just sit here and watch either of them die. He was a curseweaver, so maybe he could find a way. He held his breath and laid his empty hand on Finn's chest next to Seraphina's.

"You don't know what that will do," Seraphina argued.

"Well, neither did you, and I have to try too," he managed to say before crushing pressure took his breath away.

Marceau watched the three colors of the hexes unite. Blue, red, and black tendrils rose and collided between them. When they intertwined, a flash of bright light blinded him. The world fell away from him and Marceau was somewhere else.

Chapter Twenty-Five

He was alone.

Marceau rose to his feet and stood in a dark forest. The light of a full moon above illuminated his surroundings.

Confused, he flattened his palm against his chest. His heart beat loud and fast as if he'd been running. He'd been doing something important before. He was supposed to be somewhere else.

Wait, the hexes *united.*

Marceau whipped around in a circle trying to get his bearings. He had to get back before Seraphina did anything impulsive.

Stumbling in no particular direction, he tripped over winding tree roots hidden under thick piles of decomposing leaves. He had to find Seraphina. He had to save her.

A deranged, high-pitched laugh ahead pulled Marceau from his panic. He froze and focused on his surroundings. The air smelled of damp earth and familiar decay. Long swaths of Spanish moss swayed as a hot, humid breeze blew through the branches of old trees. He jumped at a sudden splash and turned his head. Behind him, low lying fog covered deep darkness and a heavy musty odor indicated a body of stagnant water.

A swamp?

Damn it. If this was one of Max's hellish games, he would…

A feminine voice echoed from the darkness somewhere to his left.

The outline of a young woman took shape as her outstretched hands glowed a faint blue. In the soft light, tracks of shadow cut across her face, and she murmured angrily, too soft for Marceau to understand. He caught a few words of French, but her pronunciations were peculiar. The light gradually intensified and he gasped as he recognized her face.

Lynette?

Her blonde hair was in a complicated bun, a flower and a pink ribbon circled her forehead. The old-fashioned dress with a delicate layer of pink lace covered a long silk slip, above a pair of small heeled, Oxford shoes.

Lynette squinted as her delicate hands cupped together, capturing a glow in her palms. She murmured, then spit into her hands and the light flared brighter. Her hands swirled around the object, shaping it into a sphere. The blue magic growing in her hands made her eyes an even richer shade of blue. No longer was her left eye the milky white to which he was accustomed. Both of her eyes were clear and her gaze focused sharply on the power expanding in her hands. Lynette's painted lips peeled back from her teeth, and she let an inhuman bark of laughter escape as the light flared again. The power no longer wisped freely; it had solidified into a ball, into a hex.

Marceau approached.

How would Lynette learn to cast a hex? Especially one this powerful? The cluttered forest floor snapped and crunched under his feet, but Lynette took no notice of him. A small animal scurried away as his footfalls disturbed its hiding spot, and an owl hooted in response to the movement of his prey.

Marceau stood before her. He could smell her familiar perfume, a unique blend of lavender and sage. When he reached for her, Lynette's head jerked up and she glared at him.

"Why are you doing this, Lynette?" Marceau asked. "This magic will cost you, will hurt you. Who could deserve such a dangerous curse?"

"Lynette? My name is Mirela. I know no Lynette. Leave me be or I'll hex you too."

Max must have changed her name too… Mirela. *Mirela?*

Adrenaline shot through Marceau's body.

A Curse Regression.

He'd done a fully corporeal Curse Regression on Seraphina's and Finn's curse. He was here and witnessing the actual weaving of their hex, but why would Lynette, er, Mirela cast such a curse?

Judge Pearce, Seraphina's father.

"Did Judge Pearce ask you to do this? Are you working for him?"

"Judge Pearce?" Mirela laughed. "That pompous, old fool thinks everyone in Savannah works for him. I took his money, but the hex is my own. I'm done playing nice. Today, I take matters into my own hands."

Marceau looked around him. He had to stop her, although he didn't want to hurt her, he couldn't just stand there either.

"I enjoyed the Judge begging me for a curse, though. Turns out *Mr. Runs the City* can't even control his spoiled rotten daughter. He gave me the key to cursing her and paid me for it too. The chump."

"Ly…Mirela, you have to stop. You don't know what you're doing, the pain you will cause.

She pulled something from a scarf tied at her waist and raised her clenched fist. "Oh, I know exactly what I'm doing. If I can't have him, I'll be damned if *she* will. The Judge gave me a lock of her hair and her most precious belonging."

Marceau looked for a branch or rock. He didn't dare touch her while she held the hex, but if he could knock her out somehow. Maybe he could take what she had of Seraphina's and stop her from…

"Before I knew who he wanted to be cursed, I said *no*. I wasn't going to be threatened, not even by him. Mirela L'Argent Dufrene doesn't bow down to any man."

Mirela L'Argent Dufrene? *L'Argent.*

Marceau covered his mouth and forced himself to stay quiet. Knocking her out was no longer an option. He needed to hear the rest.

"I'll take the life of his daughter, his precious Seraphina Pearce." Mirela sneered and her hands moved farther apart as the orb grew. The magic fed on her emotions. "She said he never loved me. She said she was trying to help me? She wanted him for herself."

The orb pulsed as a shot of red power flowed over its surface.

Mirela continued, "Well, she'll never know the touch of true love again. The Judge wanted her to love that young captain? Oh, she'll love him all right, with a ferocity that will burn in her veins. She'll love him beyond all reason, but she'll never know the comfort of his arms."

The hex burned brighter as her hatred strengthened it. Mirela reached her empty hand into the scarf at her waist again and pulled a shiny object from it.

"And Finn, that hotshot won't be driving away from me anytime soon. He thinks he's too good for me? I got a little something of his too, his good luck charm. He can either love me or suffer right along with her. His touch will determine his fate. He'd better choose wisely."

Dark magic poured over the hex like a thick, black liquid.

Marceau tried to grab her arm and an electric bolt shot from the hex, knocking him backward. His torso arched from the ground. The back of his head dug deeply into the dirt and his feet scrambled against the ground as pure, magical energy flooded his senses. He couldn't see, couldn't hear, and couldn't breathe. His body shuddered, painfully constricted as he rode out the magical current and was finally released. He fell back to the ground when his muscles relaxed.

Mirela chanted. Repeating phrases in an archaic version of French. Her neck rocked forward and back, forward and back, as her chanting grew louder, echoing away and returning. Her long, curly hair came unbound and stringy locks whipped around her sweaty face and neck. The flower and delicate ribbon fell from her head in a swaying motion to the damp ground. Spit flew from her lips as she screamed her curse upward to the sky. The glowing orb raised from her cupped hands and hovered, spinning. Blue, red, and black flashed over its surface, swirling and shimmering like an oil spill.

Marceau's chest heaved with panting breaths. The oxygen helped to clear the stars and blackness that threatened to overtake his vision but did little to clear the fog from his mind. He pleaded, "Mirela, you must stop." Marceau tried to stand but swayed, unable to keep his balance. The dark trees spun in front of him while his hands waved in the air and smacked against the ground as he tried to right himself.

Mirela wound the hex tighter and tighter by repeating their names. Seraphina, Aedan, Finn.

Then her voice dropped to a whisper. This time, Marceau recognized a French word for binding. If she was binding the curse, it was almost complete. The tithe was coming. How could he stop her? Once a curse was bound and the price paid, the process was complete.

If she really were an L'Argent… would hurting her affect him? Marceau had to stop her, even if it did. He crawled closer. The light cast by the hex moved erratically as vertigo skewed his vision, yet he tried to aim himself toward the glow.

"Death. I call on you to accept my tithe. Take my bargain. Bind my curse to Seraphina. I offer you a corpse each time she tries to find peace, to have love. I've fed my power, my love, and my hate into this hex. My tithe will bring pain, but I will endure it. Do you accept, Death?"

Pain? Death doesn't demand pain in exchange for his bargains.

"He will kill you, Mirela." Marceau tried to reason. "Don't call Death forth. You must stop this madness."

Curses required a tithe in equal proportion to their power. "If Death accepts your bargain, you will die. Death shows no mercy."

"No, not my death. I pay with my tithe. But when Seraphina touches one she loves, Death can take hold and demand a corpse. *She* will die."

Mirela opened her clasped fists. In one, lay a silver keychain in the shape of a thunderbolt. In the other, a lock of red hair and a long chain on which a unique oval shape hung. As the necklace spun, flashes of blue stones shone in the moonlight.

She raised her hands on either side of the hex floating before her and snatched it instantly from the air. "I tithe and call forth Death." Mirela pressed her hands into the magical sphere, the metal of both the keychain and the necklace glowed brightly as if being reforged by the hex's power. The sapphires and diamonds sparkled bright, shooting prisms of blue light out into the darkness. A primal growl of pain rose in her chest, but she swallowed it back. The smell of burning flesh and singed hair flooded Marceau's nostrils. Mirela's eyes were defiant as her body shook violently. She pushed and compressed the magical sphere. Smaller and smaller, its glow intensified as it concentrated and lost mass.

Blood ran down her wrists in thick, red rivulets and pooled on her pink lace sleeves. She screamed, "Seraphina."

Mirela hunched over her illuminated, blood-covered clasped hands. Falling to her knees, her head flew back as a haunting laugh bellowed from her small frame, a mixture of anguish, torment, and pure insanity.

Marceau reached her and grabbed her slick arm, wrenching it toward him, surprised by the strength in her corded muscles. Her hands did not separate. "No," he yelled.

Her head snapped down and she locked Marceau with her gaze. The left eye was now the milky white shade he was accustomed to. She curled her lip and sneered. "Death has already found her. He took my bargain."

She laughed and collapsed.

Dead.

Her mismatched eyes stared at Marceau, a grotesque smile of hatred frozen on her young face.

The buzzing melody of the swamp fell silent. The air shimmered beside Mirela's body.

Death.

Death was coming in person to collect his new prize.

Her hands lay open. The lock of hair was ash, but the necklace and lightning key chain each had a faint glow in her ravaged palms. Marceau lurched forward for them, but they disintegrated into dust and blew away in the swamp's musky breeze.

A force pulled at him, ripping him back to the present. Marceau closed his eyes as mind and body whipped away from the swamp.

Someone gripped his hand tightly.

"I love you," Seraphina whispered and the grip on his hand weakened.

Marceau opened his eyes. His vision cleared. He was back in Nashville, in Seraphina's room. Marceau peered up, trying to get his bearings, trying to figure out what happened in his absence.

Khat's shoulders quaked from her sobs. Finn lay across her lap. His eyes open and unfocused, were ringed with dark purple.

Seraphina fell forward, motionless. Marceau forced himself to look down, to face the truth.

When he regressed to witness the curse, Seraphina had wrapped her entire body around him. Her left hand was curled under her chin. She still held his hand with her right. Her torso pressed his side and her knees were curled against his back. Her eyes were open, but she saw none of his torment.

She was beautiful, even in death.

Khat laid her hand on Finn's chest. "She did it for you, Finn. I feel you still, but only a spark. Fight it. Do not let her sacrifice be a waste."

Khat bent and grabbed his slack jaw. Her glamour fell. With skin shimmering, and her breath rolling out as a thin, golden fog, she bent and kissed Finn. As her lips parted from his, a faint line of the metallic mist swirled before entering. Tiny shards of light traveled along the mist from her lips into his open mouth. Finn took a short breath and her body trembled. More power flowed into Finn's mouth and he jerked his arm. Khat's body shook violently.

"Khat, that's enough. Stop." Marceau pushed her shoulder back. Without pause, she leaned forward again aimed at Finn's lips. "Khat, his pulse. He's alive."

Marceau placed her hand against Finn's throat below his jaw where he saw Finn's rapid pulse.

Khat whimpered and closed her mouth. A final wisp of the sparkling fog escaped from her nostrils. She trembled as she bent and kissed his forehead. "Finn," Khat whispered.

Marceau asked, "Can Seraphina?"

Khat shook her head, "I don't feel her spirit. She let go of her body and pushed herself across the veil to save Finn. I'm so sorry."

Khat squeezed Marceau's free hand.

Marceau had no djinn powers, no magic spells, but he bent and lowered his face to hers. "Seraphina, I was there. I... I almost stopped her..." Tears fell in steady lines down his cheeks and onto her face. He exhaled and closed his eyes. Grief squeezed his heart until he could not breathe. "I'll never forgive myself. I love you, too. But I failed you." A lump filled Marceau's throat, making further speech impossible. He closed the short distance to her lips and kissed them gently. Reverently. Her lips were as warm and soft as he had imagined. He kissed her upper lip and then her full lower one. Leaning back for a moment, he studied her. If only his kisses could wake her, but Marceau was no Prince Charming, and this was no fairy tale.

"She's gone, Finn," Khat explained. Finn was awake and propped up on Khat's lap. Tears streamed down his face. The purple was already fading from around his eyes.

"We need to get her on the bed." Marceau forced the words out. He swallowed around the lump in his throat. For the first time, he pulled Seraphina gently to his chest and held her in his arms.

"Let me help." Finn tried to right himself.

"No." Marceau shook his head. "No," he repeated, softer. "I have wanted to hold her for so long. Let me, please."

Marceau cradled her closer. Her face rested on his chest. He carefully rose to his knees. Her arm fell and the back of her hand smacked against the floor. Marceau had a flashback to another dead girl, Babette.

If he'd known she was going to die, Marceau could have had Max here to… No. Seraphina would never want that, to be connected to a monster like Max. Don't even *think* it. His thoughts warred, as part of Marceau wished she'd died in the presence of his benefactor so he could have reanimated her.

Marceau gulped and took a deep breath. He shook his head, trying to clear images of Seraphina as an Ette.

"Let me help, Marceau." Khat waited until he nodded before she lifted Seraphina's limp arm. She laid Seraphina's hand against Marceau's heart. He looked at Khat, letting his loss and pain show in his eyes. Khat's features were blurring in and out of focus and it wasn't from his tears. Her glamour was slipping back and forth out of place. Whatever magic she transferred to wake Finn had cost her. Her eyes were sunken and she looked frail. Marceau buried his face in Seraphina's silky hair and told himself to never forget her scent. He planted his foot, standing, holding her… unable to decide what he should do next.

Khat helped Finn to his feet. They leaned against each other heavily, looking as though it took both their strength and efforts to keep the other upright.

"Maybe you could lay her on the bed, Marceau," Khat suggested in a gentle voice.

Marceau turned and stepped that direction. He leaned down and pressed his forehead to Seraphina's before bending to ease her body down onto the mattress, taking care to adjust her until she lay perfectly on her pillow. "She is on the bed. Now, what?" He laid her hands on her stomach.

"Now we find a way to bring her back, no matter the cost," Finn replied without hesitation.

Chapter Twenty-Six

Marceau didn't know what to do. Sit or stand? Scream or remain silent? Fight or give in? Call Max for help or trust in his new friends?

Khat gripped the bedpost. She swayed from weakness, and yet she repeated the spell over and over. She held her free hand over Seraphina. Weakened magic, shimmering white with a golden hue, flowed over Seraphina. It floated around her until the essence lightly encased her body.

Khat collapsed and Marceau caught her in time. He lifted her into his arms, amazed at how light she was. Her glamour was completely gone now as she fought for consciousness.

Marceau turned to check on Finn who was slumped in the antique chair beside Seraphina's bed. He stopped staring at her long enough to nod at Khat. "Thank you, Marc. Please help her to our room. She's given too much magic, but at least, she's suspended Seraphina's body. She will remain unchanged until we can find a way."

"Must rest," Khat whispered, her voice faint.

"Of course, Khatereh. You have done so much to save those you love today," Marceau answered softly. He carried her to the bedroom she and Finn shared and laid her gently on her bed, covering her with a down comforter. "Thank you for your gifts," he whispered and kissed her forehead.

Khat smiled and was asleep before he reached the door. He closed it quietly and leaned back against the hallway wall.

Marceau hesitated, not wanting to go back into Seraphina's room. He could think of only one way to bring her back and that might not even work, but he was willing to pay the price. Any price, as long as she came back. Max would finally get what he wanted. But was it too late?

When Marceau returned to the living room, Finn sat straighter on the couch and said, "I have a plan. I need the basket of candles on my bookcase and both the chalice and the dagger on the shelf above my chest of drawers. Can you get them for me while I get set up?" He staggered to his feet.

"Sure, but set up for what?"

"There is no time, Marceau. Candles, chalice, dagger," Finn repeated.

Marceau ran into Finn's bedroom to collect the items. He dropped the basket of candles in his haste and had to steady his hands as he picked them back up. Pulling the dagger from its sheath, he frowned. These runes are those for Sin Eating. Why did Finn want the tools of a Sin Eater?

Seraphina had already crossed the veil and had no evil deeds that would open her body as a vessel for possession.

Marceau slid the dagger back into its sheath and picked up the chalice. He brought the requested items back into Seraphina's room and laid them out at the foot of her bed.

Finn entered wearing a flowing, black robe and carrying a dusty bottle of wine and a loaf of the Amish baked bread they sold in the apothecary.

"Okay, here are the items you requested." Marceau gestured toward the bed. "But I hardly see how the tools of a Sin Eater will help her now, Finn."

"They aren't for her. They're for me. Set the candles all around the bed, but don't light them yet," Finn instructed.

Finn twisted a wine opener into the cork of the wine bottle. He pulled the cork, then swayed, still weak from the hex's attack. Placing his palm on her bedside table, he caught his breath. Then he pulled a chair closer to Seraphina's bed and fell back, collapsing into it.

"Are you strong enough to do whatever this idea of yours is, Finn?" Marceau asked. He placed the multicolor candles in a regular interval on the floor around the bed. The tall ones had elaborate carvings from tip to tip.

"The candles will have to fully burn and extinguish before I can begin. That will give me time enough to rally my strength for this. I'll have all the time I need to recover once she's back with us."

Us.

Finn no longer excluded him as an outsider. He finally accepted that Seraphina and Marceau belonged together, only now she was gone.

"And what is your plan, Finn?"

"I'll offer everything I have in exchange for bringing her back, but it may not be enough. Are you willing to sacrifice to bring her back too, Marc? Is your love for her strong enough you would choose her well-being above your own?"

"Yes, of course. I would sacrifice much if it meant having her back alive and well. I'd give my life if that was what it took." If Finn's plan didn't work, Marceau had already decided to make a bargain he'd swore to never, ever consider.

"Good, I have a feeling you may be asked to pay a higher price than me tonight. I don't know that I have much more to give this time."

Asked by *whom?*

"Just be careful what you promise." Finn closed his eyes. "My price was much higher than I could've ever imagined when I agreed to the bargain."

Marceau tried to decipher the carvings on the candles. Who or what was Finn planning to bargain with? "That's the last of the candles."

"Starting with the one to the left of her head, light them."

"Widdershin?" Marceau lit the first candle. "Counterclockwise opens the other realms, Finn." He bent and lit the second. "What do the markings mean? Who are the candles calling?" He lit a third.

Finn said, "Her powers are similar to the powers of Death himself. They've been so ever since this blasted curse took hold of her."

Marceau froze.

"She sees ghosts, can communicate with the dead, and if she wanted, I believe she could raise all the spirits in a graveyard at will. When she is determined and focused enough, her power knows no bounds."

Marceau stared at Seraphina. He knew she was powerful, but she rarely used her magic. She didn't even like to talk about it.

Finn continued, "It is only her innate goodness, her complete lack of hunger for power and control, that keeps her from using her unusual magic in a selfish manner. Imagine what she would be capable of if she didn't hold back? Why, if she offered to sell her services, there are many, human and supernatural alike, who would lay the treasures of the world at her feet for a chance to communicate with their dead."

"Finn," Marceau stood perfectly still. "This is vitally important. Are you calling Death here? Have you bargained with him before?"

"Death is the only one who can give her back to us now, Marc."

Marceau rounded the bed and stood in front of Finn. "Have you bargained with him before, Finn?"

"Yes. How do you think I became a Sin Eater? It was his price. I admit I didn't fully understand all those years ago, but I would do it again." Finn shuddered. "I have choked on, have relived and suffered countless sins. And for Seraphina? To bring her back? Every pained moment of my damned existence has been worth it."

Finn sat up straighter and held out his hand.

"But you can never tell her. If... *when* we get her back. She doesn't know I bargained with Death. She thought I became a Sin Eater as part of the curse. I-I let her believe that. I'm afraid it would damage her. That guilt or pain would break something in her, Marc."

Marceau stared at the candles. He only lit three. Maybe it wasn't too late to stop this. "Finn, do you know why Death demands so much from those desperate enough to accept his little bargains? Do you understand he serves only his own larger purpose in every single thing he does?"

Marceau ran both his hands through his hair. The damned *fool.*

"What more could Death possibly take from me? Look at what I have endured already." Finn responded. "So, he'll make me agree to another fifty years of Sin Eating, or a hundred. I made it this long. I paid him with fifty years of service and survived. I'll just have to find a way to keep going."

"Most of Death's Sin Eaters don't last as long as you have. I thought your extraordinary pallor was because you were a true born, you'd survived being a Sin Eater for such a long time because it was in your true nature. Almost all of them go mad, Finn. They turn violent and hurt innocents. Or their fury burrows inward until they commit suicide. That's why I assumed you were a true born."

Marceau couldn't wrap his mind around it. He'd been so sure Finn was born a Sin Eater.

Marceau continued, "I could tell you had fair hair in the regression though colors were indistinct. I thought you a Sin Eater even then, just not a well-practiced one. Figured you for one who chose to leave the Las Vegas compound and mask themselves as a Spellcaster."

Finn asked, "Why would you think I was only pretending to be a Spellcaster?"

"It was something Seraphina said before the curse, that your magic affected luck and chance. It supported my theory that you were undercover and trying to lead a normal life back then. Luck is easily manipulated. Simple hexed items can help the odds fall unnaturally in your favor. I've seen it a hundred times in my study of curses. I thought that was your big secret—that you had been a Sin Eater all along. I did not for a moment believe you were one of Death's creations."

Marceau was pacing. Again, he scrubbed his hands through his hair. There had to be something he could do. He now understood what was coming. It would make Seraphina's sacrifice to save Finn a waste. Marceau stopped and sucked in his lip. He took a few deep breaths. He was damned either way. If he told Finn what Death would demand, Death would know of Marceau's betrayal. On the other hand, if he did not warn Finn of the danger he surely faced, then Marceau was betraying his friendship to both Seraphina and Finn. Khat too, he added.

"You never answered me. What else could Death possibly want, Marc?" Finn moved to the edge of his seat. Sweat beaded above his lip and on his forehead. Though Finn did not know of his present danger, he understood the severity of Death's bargains.

Marceau winced when looking at his friend.

My *friend.*

Marceau understood in the moment that he truly was no longer alone. Finn was his to protect. He'd found what he'd always wanted most. Marceau had found true love with Seraphina. He had found true friendship in Finn and in Khat. Marceau was not an outcast here or an observer. All three of them accepted him, and at some point, they became his too.

Marceau's decision was made and he knew there would be a price, but he would deal with that when the time came. "Your soul, Finn. Death will bargain for your soul."

"B-but, Death is impartial. He's not supposed to favor good or evil. What would Death possibly need with a soul?" Finn asked wide eyed.

"Your soul has known a thousand of sins by now, right?"

Finn nodded.

"The fact that you can sit here rational and functioning is a miracle, Finn, a true damned miracle. You have a strength, a fortitude, that is extremely rare and makes your soul more attractive to Death. He's only crossed the line and collected a few souls throughout time. He's enslaved only the strongest to carry out his demands."

Finn said, "I've already followed his commands. I've eaten the sins of many after he demanded it. How is that any different?"

Marceau had to make him understand. "You would have no free will remaining, Finn. No apothecary, no home, no Khatereh. Death would make you a soldier. A minion infected by Death's own power. In my lifetime, he's never taken a Sin Eater, but he has searched far and wide for one. Death even dismissed a few true borns as too weak for whatever purpose he has derived for a Sin Eater. I've often wondered what need he has, but whatever it is, I know it will be unbearable. When it comes to Death's bargains, many wish he'd simply taken their lives. Finn, I fear you'd know no moment of rest from your servitude to Death for all of eternity."

Marceau sat on the edge of the bed facing Finn.

"He may have set his sights on you already. If so, you've been targeted. Death will go to any length to draw out chosen souls. He tricks and manipulates them, making them desperate. Then, at the moment they are most vulnerable, he takes the one thing they love most. He knows courage and strength make them suitable for his needs. The same qualities that will make them sacrifice themselves to save someone else."

Marceau turned back and looked at Seraphina. She was the key to Finn's soul. He wondered if Death already knew it?

Finn said, "I'm scared. Terrified, actually. But if that's what it takes…"

"Stop." Marceau lunged forward and grabbed Finn's arm. "Do not say it out loud. Ever, Finn. Words carry weight with Death. Just slow down. There has to be another way. Let me think."

Marceau stood again and paced. Finn was in danger. Seraphina was across the veil. What other options were there? How could he protect Finn and save Seraphina?

The biting cold of the hex still clung to his bones, and he grabbed his jacket from the floor and slid it back on, hands into the pockets where he touched the velvet bag inside.

"That's it. The Curse Regression."

Chapter Twenty-Seven

Marceau ran the few steps back to Finn. "When the hexes united, did you see anything? Did you have a flashback or a vision?"

"A memory, yes. I saw the night we were cursed. It was strange. Like I was back in my body, but I couldn't change anything. Only reliving each moment from when she suddenly loved Aedan right up until Seraphina died. How did you know? Did you see it too?"

"No, but I did have a vision from that same night. I was in a dark forested swamp. I watched Mirela weave the hex. She had more power than I've ever seen and paid for the curse's strength with a pain tithe and then with her own life. Finn, I know her, but not as Mirela. She goes by Lynette now."

"Mirela is still alive? And you know her?"

"Well, alive is not exactly the term I'd use. She is undead, a reanimated."

Finn sat straighter. "Mirela is a Possessed?"

"No, no she's not possessed. She died, but now she lives, for lack of a better verb, with only a partial soul. Lynette is a girlfriend, of sorts, of my benefactor, Maximilian."

Finn raised his hands. "Wait, Mirela is alive. But called Lynette. And she's some kind of zombie girlfriend to your mentor?"

"Exactly. In the Curse Regression, I tried my best to stop her from weaving the hex. She didn't seem to understand it would take her life when she cast it. I was thrown back by its power, but now I've seen the curse in its most basic form, I understand it better,"

Finn shook his head. "Okay, then did you learn anything new? Anything that can save Seraphina?"

"I think so. Mirela's rage and fury grew the hex to an unnatural strength and then she fed it into an object. No, into two objects. The curse made her suffer a brutal, deadly tithe. It concentrated as it fed off her pain and hatred. I've never seen a hex grow so strong. It electrocuted me when I tried to stop her. After she died, I tried to grab the objects she bound to the hex, but the magic carried them back to their rightful owners."

"Rightful owners? You mean to Seraphina and to me?" Finn rubbed the back of his neck. "What the hell did she hex? If we could somehow find them, maybe we could..."

"A necklace. A delicate moonstone cameo lined with blue sapphires and a girl who resembles Seraphina." Marceau watched for Finn's reaction. "And a silver keychain in the shape of a thunderbolt."

Finn's eyes bulged and he hissed. He shot to the edge of his seat. "I gave her that damned cameo. She'd had it this whole time. Until she..." He buried his face in his hands and shook his head.

"Donated it to a charity auction so she would get a VIP invitation to bid on the Blackthorn Grimoire?"

"Yes, and I was the one who encouraged her to do it. I thought the book was more important than an old gift. If we can find it, could we release her? Could it help bring her back?"

Marceau pulled the velvet pouch from his pocket. He tugged open the strings and turned the bag over in his palm. Finn's hands tightened on the arms of the chair as he looked at the moonstone cameo lying in Marceau's hand.

"How?"

"I overbid on it that night to make sure I won the auction. I saw her admiring and longing for it. I felt drawn to it too. It must have been the curse calling to me. Plus, I wanted to please her, even then. I've been carrying it around since we met, waiting for the right moment to give it to her."

Finn stood and reached into his pocket. He pulled out his keys, which hung from a now tarnished and battered thunderbolt keychain. "This is meant to be, Marc. I know it. But what do we do now?"

"We don't light rest of these candles, that's for damn sure." Marceau quickly blew them out. "We need the grimoire. Find a spell to communicate with a spirit."

"Whose spirit?"

"I believe the part of Lynette, of Mirela's soul, is separated from her body and may still be accessible within the veil. If we can contact her, I think I can convince her to release the curse."

Finn asked, "How will that bring her back?"

"If I'm right, Mirela will help guide Seraphina back to her body. If I'm wrong, well, there is only one other option. I will finally accept a bargain Death has tried to force upon me all my life."

Finn's head cocked, and he took a long look at Marceau. "You know Death?"

"Unfortunately, and to add to the urgency of our situation, he's arriving here in two days. Death is my benefactor, Maximilian."

Marceau hung up his phone and joined Finn and Khat in the living room. It was past midnight and they looked as if someone had dragged them around by their feet... everyone was exhausted, but none had time for sleep.

"Lynette will be here tonight. She's taking a great risk by coming. When Max realizes she has left his compound, there's no telling what he will do."

Pinching the bridge of his nose and thinking, Marceau thanked the stars he'd given Lynette his hexed key. It would get her to his apartment in the city. From there, she was on her own. It had taken some convincing, but she said she would come.

"Good," Finn said. He sat on the floor, the grimoire on his folded long legs. "This spell is the only way. It can draw a spirit to you and hold them in place."

Marceau leaned over and reread the incantation. He shook his head and said, "We've been over this. My power only works with curses. Khat can amplify powers and has limited djinn magic. And you specialize in sin. All this power and none of us has the right kind of magic for a spell of this magnitude." Marceau sighed. "Plus, we don't have enough time to make the incense it requires. We've been through the book twice now. Either we find another way or we have no choice but to bargain with Death himself."

"You said that was a last resort. We have to find another option," Khat said as she twisted strands of Finn's white hair with one finger. She lay on the couch behind Finn, reading one of Seraphina's notebooks filled with transcriptions of the grimoire.

"Ugh, this is so damn frustrating." Finn slammed the book shut and dust plumed. "Seraphina can pull any damn spirit she wants from the realm beyond at will. If only we could tap into her power, this would be child's play."

Khat shot up from the couch so fast she pulled Finn's hair.

"Ouch."

"What is it?" Marceau asked her.

"Say that again, Finn." Khat was biting her lip and staring off into space. "That last part."

"If we only could tap into her power…" Finn trailed off realizing the possibility.

Khat looked up at Marceau. "I think I can do that. I can try. I've tapped into it once before when I boosted her."

"When did you ever need to boost Seraphina's power?" Finn snapped.

"Be overprotective later, Finn, focus on the bigger picture here, will you? When she helped Rolf cross over the veil, there was a little issue with someone trying to cross back into our realm."

"You call that a little issue? Khatereh, why would you keep something that big from me?" Finn was fuming.

"Later. I promised Sera I wouldn't tell you, but she's dead. So now I can tell you, but be pissed later, k?" Khat gave him a pointed look. Finn nodded and she continued, "Anyway, I covered her with my magic while the veil was open, to protect her from the Mistress of Death's mind control juju and…"

Marceau and Finn both sucked in shocked breaths.

Khat finished enunciating each word, "…and I *felt* Seraphina's power."

Marceau asked, "Think you can still tap into it? Use it?"

Khat said, "I protected Seraphina by aligning my magic with hers. I amplified her death magic to keep her from freeing that scary ass Mistress woman. I can sort of still taste it. Magic has flavors for me." She swallowed.

"Who in the hell is the Mistress of Death?" Finn demanded.

Marceau stood and went to look out the window. "I can answer that. She is the rightful embodiment of Death."

He felt at risk even thinking about Max's past, let alone sharing it. He scanned shadows along the darkened street and then reminded himself that would do little good. If Maximilian wanted to confront him, he'd appear right in the room.

He turned his back to the window, but still felt exposed. Marceau continued, "The Mistress was Max's master. He made a bargain on an ancient battlefield to save his life and the lives of his men. In exchange, Max became her apprentice. He had a similar ability to mine, and she needed a curseweaver. I don't know many details. Only that he betrayed her and somehow found a way to seal her within the veil. He stole her position and some of her powers. There was documentation in the Conexus Library of a disciplinary hearing the Conexus held to try to punish him for his actions. Max murdered them all. Wiped out the entire ruling council. His position as the next personification of Death was never again questioned." Marceau sat down, a puzzled expression taking over. "What I don't understand is how the Mistress has any control over Seraphina or how she even knows of her."

"I may have a clue on that one." Khat frowned. "Rolf saw what was happening to Sera and tore up the apothecary to lead me to Sera's bedroom."

Finn started to say something.

"Don't ask. By the time I found her, Sera was in a trance of some kind on her knees and the Mistress was yelling at her to use more power. The veil was still holding her, but it was cracking like glass. I thought it might fail at any moment, so I coated her in my magic and found the rhythm of her power. I changed it, like changing the beat in a song, so the Mistress could no longer tap into it. The Mistress was pissed and started beating against the veil with her fists. She said she'd fed Sera her power, claiming when Sera was dead all those years in the veil that Sera had been with her. The Mistress used that time to feed Sera the death magic."

Finn's forehead wrinkled. "No wonder her powers were all tied to death when she came back. We thought it was because she'd died by a curse."

Marceau said, "Exactly what did she say, Khat? It's very important. Try to remember if she gave any indication of what type of magic she gave Seraphina."

"Spirit. She said she gave her 'necromancy over spirit,' but I don't quite understand what that means."

"If true, it means Seraphina has powers in all five elements. She's had difficulty with earth, air, fire, and water since her"—Finn paused—"resurrection. But I've always told her those powers are in her still, somewhere. She just had to get control over her new strengths to find them."

Khat said, "No Spellcaster has ever had all five elements. I thought it was impossible."

"She would be the first I've ever heard of," Finn answered.

Khat rubbed her dark, baggy eyes and said, "Then it's even more important we bring her back, right?"

"Khat, you look exhausted. You haven't had time to recover from helping Finn." Marceau's expression was one of pure sympathy.

Finn ran his hand along Khat's cheek. "Maybe he's right, Sparrow. I could try to call in the local witches. Audra might have another option if the price was right."

Marceau didn't want Khat to hurt herself, not when he had another option. Max wanted this for so long, a way to gain complete control over him. Max had punished Marceau. Max had manipulated and abused him, but he'd never managed to break him. Max could never take away Marceau's free will.

Khat squeezed Finn's hand and said, "I want to. I need to. Seraphina is my best friend. No local witch is going to be able to pull off the particular spell you found, Finn, at least not before Friday. Marceau is right, the incense recipe alone takes longer than we have. Lynette is coming tonight. We're out of time and options. I think I can help Seraphina, so I have to at least try." She folded her arms over her chest. "You understand that, don't you Finn? Have you not done the exact same thing?"

Finn studied her for a long moment before nodding. "Yes, I have and I do understand. You forget one big obstacle, though. Say Lynette makes it here and say she agrees to unbind the curse. Then, you manage to pull aside the veil, and Seraphina does reawaken. If all of those things happen, we still have the vindictive personification of Death incoming."

Marceau knew that was where he came in. He had finally found love and family for the first time in his life. But it was bittersweet because he knew beyond a shadow of a doubt, Max would never let him keep them. He would use them over and over as a weapon and they would suffer for having won Marceau's love. If he could barter with Death one last time, Marceau could spare them his wrath.

"One step at a time, Finn," was Marceau's only response.

Chapter Twenty-Eight

A faint knock echoed from downstairs.

Marceau looked at his watch and said, "Could be her, but if it is, she made record time."

Finn and Marceau clomped downstairs. Finn stood to the side of the door holding a poker from the fireplace in one hand and a glass bottle of cloudy liquid in the other. Marceau raised an eyebrow at the bottle.

"Trust me, it will slow down any supernatural." Finn grinned.

"I don't doubt it."

Finn nodded and stepped to the side as Marceau unlocked the row of deadbolts. Finn broadened his stance and raised his arms as Marceau cracked open the door.

Lynette stood outside in a black trench coat, her hair tucked up under a black fedora. "Well, I sped all the way up here. Aren't you going to let me in?"

Marceau stepped back and she stepped inside.

"I do love that car of yours, Marceau. Smooth as can be even at one hundred and thirty miles per..."

Finn stepped from behind the door and Lynette stood frozen. Her mouth agape in shock.

"Hello, Mirela."

She jumped. "I-I'm no longer that girl. Foolish, naive Mirela died many, many years ago in a swamp." She took off her hat and shook her head. Long, blonde curls fell obediently into place, and she wore more makeup than usual. The dark kohl lining her eyes made the one milky white one appear even lighter. "I am Lynette, now."

"Yes, of course. Forgive me, Lynette." Finn's words were polite, but his jaw ticked.

Marceau shook his head behind her. They'd discussed Finn's need to hold it together. Without Lynette's help, Seraphina was lost.

Lynette said, "I'd heard you were a Sin Eater. Of course, Maximilian does brag nonstop. But the effect on your appearance is even more striking than expected. Pale white suits you." She smiled up at him and started to reach her hand forward as if to touch his face.

Finn's teeth ground loudly as he jerked his chin back to avoid her intimate touch.

"I'm glad the Vanquish was to your liking, Lynette," Marceau interjected. He gave Finn a poignant look of warning. "If tonight goes as I hope, you may consider it a small token of my appreciation."

At that, Lynette's gaze finally left Finn.

Marceau held out his arm and said, "Let's go upstairs, shall we? I have a proposal to make. One I'm confident you will find mutually beneficial."

They started up the stairs with Marceau automatically placing his hand under Lynette's left elbow to help her balance. His assistance seemed to soften her defensive posture. Finn climbed the stairs behind them. Lynette's progress was slow but steady.

"You can relax on the formality, Marceau. I know you're as bored with Maximilian's requirements as I am. I don't know how much time I have before he realizes I'm gone. I am, well I *was,* his strongest and most independent in the hive mind, until Babette." She smiled. "His control over me is limited. I've had plenty of practice in shielding my thoughts, but he can still access parts of my mind through the hive. Babette agreed to keep him occupied while I'm here. She has a knack for keeping him quite entertained, but even she has her limits."

Marceau could not control his grimace. He'd wondered about the look Babette and Max had shared at the Hall of Fame, but he had tried to not dwell on it. Knowing Max and Lynette were intimate wasn't a surprise. Max never hid his high sexual appetite. It should have come as no surprise he'd taken another undead lover.

Lynette brought him out of his thoughts. "It took me most of the day to drive here despite your lovely little sports car. Time is of the essence.

I'm showing great trust in you, to risk being here. But you mentioned a plan to free me from Maximilian's control? I'd have simply laughed if anyone else made such a claim, but you are prone to a severe case of seriousness."

They entered the loft's living room and Khat stood and stepped away from the couch.

"A djinn? Really? Marceau your standards are slipping. When you claimed to be in love, I expected..."

"Can it, Lynette. She is with me." Finn walked over and put his arm around Khat. "This is Khatereh."

"She... is with you?"

Khat asked, "Why do I even bother with glamour here anymore? You recognized me as a part djinn, how exactly?"

"Um, hello? Undead supernatural? I don't see the world in the same way as the living, especially with this." Lynette pointed to her blind eye.

Marceau always suspected she saw something different through the eye Death had affected. Now he wondered why she didn't seem to notice the hex still visible on his skin.

"Your weak attempt at looking anywhere close to normal isn't going to fool me," Lynette said.

Yeah, I can't do this kissing up thing." Khat stepped in front of Finn. "So look, Mir..."

"Lynette," she snapped. "I am Lynette."

"Fine, Lynette," Khat drew out. "We don't know each other and don't have to be besties. Ever. Just for tonight, though, let's put the attitude to the side. I think I can give you what you want... I think you can do the same for us."

"I'm listening."

Lynette opened her black jacket and Marceau helped her take it off. Khat stopped talking and glared at Lynette. She wore a tiny blush pink dress. It clung snugly and shimmered, accentuating each curve.

Marceau gaped, his arms still holding her coat in the air. He'd seen Lynette in a hundred elaborate outfits, mostly in the style of bygone eras to please Max. But, he'd never seen her dressed as modern, or as provocative, as this. Closing his eyes, he wondered. *Finn.* She'd dressed sexier for Finn. "Yes, well if we could all take a seat." Marceau gestured toward the living room area.

Khat took Finn's hand and marched over to the loveseat.

Marceau laid Lynette's coat across the back of a chair and set down her fedora. Leave it to her to dress like a spy when sneaking away. She always did have a flair for the dramatic. He extended his elbow and assisted Lynette to the couch. Khat's gaze softened at Lynette's mobility challenges. By the time they sat down, Khat had looked as if she felt a little guilty for the death glare she leveled at Lynette over her dress. Lynette's beauty was striking, but her body clearly struggled to process her mind's instructions.

"Ahem, so Khatereh and I believe together we may have found a way to access what Maximilian denied you in your reanimation. Whatever remains of your spirit should still lie beyond the veil," Marceau said.

Lynette's hands flew to her torso. She pushed against her sternum and her stomach as if pressing against a void deep within. Above all else, Marceau knew she longed to feel whole, to be free of Max.

He continued, "For longer than I've been alive, you've been his unwilling companion. My earliest memories are of you and Maximilian. You were not always kind, but you did often take up for me when it counted."

Marceau hoped she desired her own release badly enough to unbind the curse. Everything… his future, and Seraphina's life… hinged on how desperate Lynette was to have her soul rejoined. If she agreed, could they even pull the rest of it off? That was the real question.

One step at a time. Breathe. *Convince* her.

Lynette asked, "And you would want what exactly? Why would you risk piercing the veil to help me regain my soul? As you said, I've been his companion a long time. You know Death's punishment for this betrayal would be severe, if you even survived it, Marceau."

This was it.

Marceau had refused to tell her over the phone. He'd demanded she sneak away and come here in person for this moment. He made sure his expression was calm, confident. "I want you to release the hex you wove all those years ago, to unravel it completely. Leave no traces bound to Finn or Seraphina, or anyone else." Marceau figured it was safer not to say how the curse had affected him until she had agreed. He didn't want her to discover an upper hand.

"Seraphina?" Lynette spat out the name as if it were poison. "She's dead. Long gone and forgotten. He's clearly moved on by now"—she gestured to Finn and Khat—"so why bring her name into this?"

"Only partially true, Lynette. She is dead…" Finn stopped and an unfiltered hate overtook his expression.

Lynette's smile beamed.

Marceau chimed in quickly, "But she died only yesterday. We want you to release her curse."

"Yesterday? She's an old, shriveled woman then? She died a lonely old hag?" Lynette giggled.

Khat's hand shot out lightning quick to squeeze Finn's knee and keep him in his seat. "Let's just have Marceau do all the talking right now, Finn," Khat whispered between clenched teeth when Finn started to respond. Her leg was bobbing so quickly, Marceau's eyes could not even track of her movement.

Marceau started again. "Seraphina has not aged. She is as you would remember her. Your hex affected her life in ways you didn't intend. To quickly catch you up to speed, she was dead for fifty years and beyond the veil. Finn brought her back to this realm through his bargain with Max. Now, once more your hex has taken her life. We are in love and it was touching *me* that activated her curse again yesterday."

"So, why barter for me to release the stupid curse then? To reanimate her like me you need Maximilian and his nasty little pet."

Marceau argued, "No, actually we need the remaining piece of your soul to help guide her back. Her magic is… unusual. She'll be able to pierce the veil and cross over."

"And how would I possibly find her?"

Marceau waved his arm at Finn and said, "You're both bound to the hex. You were a powerful curseweaver. Surely you see how it is being drawn to you. Just look."

It was true. The tendrils of Finn's hex flared with bright silver pulses of light. His threads reached for her as if desperate for her contact. Marceau took off his jacket, revealing his own arms. The hex in his skin flashed with bright blue power from her closeness, reaching out to her.

Lynette stared at Finn and then studied Marceau, but showed no reaction at all. Something was off.

Marceau frowned. "We believe Seraphina's curse will draw her to you, even within the veil."

"It cannot be done. You have endangered both of our lives by drawing me here." Lynette tried to get back on her feet though her short attire didn't help her efforts. "I will tell Death you forced me to come. I'll claim you coerced, or cursed me. I was confused."

Khat finally snapped. Her leg stopped shaking and she stomped down her foot. "Shut up and agree to break the curse. You had your revenge, not that Seraphina ever deserved your scorn to begin with. She was dead. For fifty damned years. She's never known love because of you. Finn became a Sin Eater for goodness sakes. You've done enough damage over your petty jealousy. Grow the hell up and let it go."

Lynette stopped and sat back down. "There is something you all do not understand."

"Enlighten us," Marceau responded, "please, Lynette. I know how Max has toyed with you, has hurt you, all these years. Please don't become like him. You have a choice here. You can choose to right a wrong. And you will only gain from your kindness. How can you walk away from your own chance at freedom just to punish another? Such cruelty is expected from Death, but not from you."

Lynette turned to him, "Marceau, I know what you must think of me, of my past. I was so young and had so much power. I thought I could control… I didn't really understand…"

Marceau didn't want to feel sympathy for Lynette. She had caused Seraphina and Finn unmeasurable pain. But he knew she had also suffered from Max's games and affections. He saw firsthand how naive she was when she wove the hex, just a young, love-scorned woman. "There's no need to explain, Lynette. I experienced a full corporeal Curse Regression. I watched as you wove the hex. It was clear you didn't know the price you'd pay both by dying and then your servitude to Max all these years." He paused and blinked at her. "I believe had you understood the full consequences, you would have chosen not to hurt the woman I love."

Lynette raised a brow in an unconvincing way. Maybe she wouldn't have left Seraphina alone, after all, just hurt her differently. She said, "A

Curse Regression? You went back, physically as you have theorized was possible?"

"Yes, I realize it's rather hard to believe."

"Not hard at all, actually. I always wondered if truly it was you who tried to keep me from finishing the curse. If the hex hadn't grown so powerful, you would have stopped it. I thought I'd hallucinated you, all those years I was alone with Maximilian until he brought home a raven haired little boy with those same deep, blue eyes..."

"How can you possibly remember?" Marceau stopped. It was like a time loop of some sort. This would take significant thought. How had his presence in the past affected the present? The ramifications could be...

"... the same shade of blue as my own."

That got his attention. He said, "During that night, you said your name was Mirela L'Argent Dufrene. You're an L'Argent and all these years it never occurred to you to tell me? What exactly is our connection?"

"I was forbidden from discussing it with you. It didn't serve Death's little games for you to know, but since we seem to be throwing out all the rules, why not?" She raised her chin. "I believe you're descended from my older sister, Liv. All of our family disappeared from Savannah not long after my death, but Liv was with child when I died. You favor her. She had your same dark hair and... something in your expressions, in the shape of your mouth. She would be your grandmother? Or great-grandmother, I suppose?"

Great Aunt Lynette? would certainly take some getting used to.

Lynette said, "The L'Argents have always been curseweavers. Liv and I were taught to weave small hexes even when we first learned to speak and walk. Which brings us to our next problem."

"And what is that?" Marceau thought there were more than enough problems already.

"I lost my ability to weave even simple hexes the night I died. I have no power. I've never tried to unravel one, but I have tried hundreds of times to weave and have failed each time. So, how would I unravel the hex?"

Marceau asked, "Do you see them still? Can you see the hex radiating toward you? Finn is lit up like a Christmas tree."

Lynette turned her head back to stare at Finn. Marceau held his breath, willing her to see something, anything. "I see nothing, but a paler version of the boy who broke my heart."

She didn't see the hex on Marceau either then, and there was no reason to reveal that part yet. If her power were gone, their plan would never work.

Unless.

"Wait, okay you said you lost your power upon your death, correct?" She nodded.

Marceau rubbed his chin, soft stubble grating against his fingers. Then he put it together and said, "I have a theory. If we can reunite your spirit, make your soul complete once more, you may regain your ability to work with curses."

Lynette's left hand jumped from her lap. She looked down and began wringing her hands in an attempt to hide her body's unusual response to excitement.

"But we won't know unless we successfully bring the missing part of you and Seraphina through the veil," Marceau added.

Lynette's eyes danced at the idea, but she spoke carefully, "It's just a theory, Marceau. You would all risk your lives and draw open the veil? For a theory?"

Khat scooted to the edge of her seat. "To bring Seraphina back? Yes, in a heartbeat. What do you really have to lose here anyway? You're already dead. You've lost your power. Plus, you've already come up with a way to blame all of this on Marceau to cover your own ass."

Lynette glared at Khat.

"Just try, Lynette. Try your best to help us." Khat stood. "Do that and I promise you I'll get the veil open. I will release you, or burn through every ounce of my power trying. Deal, bitch?"

Marceau's mouth matched Finn's, gaping wide open.

Lynette's head tilted to the side as she sized up Khat. A slow smile spread across her face. "There's more to you than meets the eye, isn't there little djinn? Under other circumstances, we might have even been friends... or scratched each other's eyes out." Lynette shrugged. "Deal, bitch."

Khat's face twisted into an evil smile of her own.

"Okay, so when do we do this?" Finn asked.

Marceau answered, "Tonight. Now. We have no time to waste. Death is already planning to come. If he realizes Lynette is here? He could arrive at any moment."

Khat said, "I'll go set up Sera's room. Finn, I need you to get me a large bowl of salt. Some of the incense she likes to burn would be great too since the spell in the book used incense and maybe a familiar scent will help draw her back. Besides, when she opened the veil, the air smelled gross."

Marceau asked Lynette, "Is there anything you'll require to break the curse?"

Lynette shook her head and sat back. "Oh, this will never work. I hadn't even thought about it. I'd have to have the objects I had that night. A cameo and..."

Finn stood and tossed his keys on the coffee table in front of her. They scraped across the wood as they skidded toward her. He turned and headed downstairs.

Marceau pulled the velvet bag from his pocket and poured the long chain and the cameo into his palm. He laid it gently on the table beside the tarnished keychain. "Anything else?"

Lynette stared at the objects... lost in memory.

"Lynette, do you need anything else?"

She jumped, "No, assuming the djinn can really free my soul. And supposing I can then access my curseweaving power after all these years. If so, releasing the curse should be relatively easy. Especially with the two of them together and touching the objects I used to hex them."

"Then what are we waiting for?" Marceau held out his hand to help her up.

Chapter Twenty-Nine

Marceau stood in the doorway of Seraphina's room. Someone had pulled Seraphina's large four poster bed away from the wall and into the center of the room, and with her lying on it too. Marceau's eyebrows arched, and he looked at the tiny girl beside him.

"Oh, Khat's wicked strong," Finn teased and then dropped his smile. He looked down at Seraphina.

"We'll get her back, Finn. All of this coming together the way it has? It has to mean something, right?" Marceau meant it, too.

Finn nodded.

Khat was all business. Khat and Lynette sat at the head of the bed above Seraphina's pillow, one on each side. Lynette's hands were folded in her lap. She appeared younger, and more fragile without her smug expression. Perhaps sitting next to Seraphina's lifeless body had an effect on Lynette, after all.

Khat laid her hands in a large wooden bowl of salt and rubbed them together. "Okay, light the incense, please. I'll let you know when I access her power. Lynette, that's when I'll need you to put both of your hands on Sera too. I'll need to feel your energy to help locate you on the other side of the veil. Between the energy on the cameo and from your hands, I'll find you. But do not remove your hands until I say."

Finn and Marceau approached opposite sides of the bed and lit the incense burners. Thin trails of cloying smoke rose and wound their way upward to the ceiling.

If Khat was able to find Lynette's spirit, they were relying on the magnetism of the curse and their ability to call on her to guide Seraphina's spirit back to her body.

"Here goes." Khat raised her hands over Seraphina.

"Wait," Finn said in a shaky voice, "I-I love you, Khat. I wanted you to know that before you do this. I've loved you for a long time."

"And I've known a long time, but really? Now, you finally have the guts to say it? About time." Khat's smile beamed. "I love you, too."

Lynette rolled her eyes. Marceau stifled a laugh. Khat really was something.

"Now, let's do this. It's time to bring her back." Khat laid her hands on either side of Seraphina's temples and closed her eyes in concentration.

The room went still. Marceau was afraid to even breathe too loud for fear of disrupting Khat. Her brows were pulled together and every so often she tilted her head as if listening to something.

"Got it." Khat cried out. Marceau and Finn both jumped. "Get in there, Lynette."

Lynette leaned forward. She hesitated before touching Seraphina, but then placed one hand on her shoulder and the other on her arm.

Khat sat frozen for several minutes biting her lip. She reached forward and touched the cameo Marceau had placed around Seraphina's neck. They figured Lynette's spirit should have a tie to the cameo since she died with it in her hand.

A cold, stale breeze blew through the bedroom, dispersing the smoke from the incense and blowing the curtains. The veil had arrived.

Lynette tilted her head and stared at something by the foot of the bed. "The veil is right there. I wouldn't believe it if I couldn't see it for myself. She really called it forth."

Marceau saw nothing, but he'd always suspected Lynette witnessed things usually unseen through her white eye.

Khat said, "I call upon what remains of Mirela L'Argent Dufrene beyond the veil. I call you forward. Your soul should not have been fractured, and your body awaits your return. I offer you safe passage back into the realm of the living."

Khat's voice had an unearthly, echoing quality as if her words rang out not only here, but within the veil itself.

"Mirela Dufrene, I call you forward," she demanded louder. "Follow my voice and show yourself."

The breeze turned colder and lifted Marceau's dark hair from his forehead. He looked up and saw Finn's hair was swirling in the wind too.

The instant the spirit approached the veil, every hair on the back of Marceau's neck stood. The breeze turned ice cold and he recognized the scent of Mirela's perfume from the night of the curse. Lavender and sage.

When the aroma grew stronger, a faint light hovered at the end of the bed. Lynette gasped and started to lean into the light.

"Move your hands off Sera, and I will trap it there forever," Khat hissed between clenched teeth.

Lynette froze and glared at Khat, who smiled in a deadly calm with her hands cupping Seraphina's face.

"Seraphina Pearce," Khat's voice broke. She tried again, "Seraphina, please follow the pull to Mirela's spirit. Let it lead you back to us."

"Lyn…"

Finn snapped, "Shut it, Lynette. Seraphina doesn't know you by name. You can be bitchy about what she calls you… after she's back."

Lynette closed her mouth and stared at the light growing near the end of the bed.

"Seraphina, please come forward. We're all here. Finn, Marceau, and me, Khatereh. We need you back."

Several long minutes passed, and Marceau thought the suspense might break his sanity. Finally, he couldn't take it anymore and whispered, "Anything?"

Khat shook her head. "I feel no trace of her at all. It's as though she cannot hear me. Or maybe she cannot find us?"

"Or maybe someone is stopping her," Finn added. "What if the Mistress of Death is holding Seraphina? Punishing her for not letting the Mistress out?"

Marceau hadn't even thought of that. What if the Mistress was hurting Seraphina? "No. I refuse to believe she is beyond our reach, not after so many factors coming together like this." If only he could go inside the veil to find her, Marceau looked down at his hands. If only he could reach in and pull her out himself.

Wait. What if he *could?*

Marceau's head snapped up. "Lynette's remaining spirit may not be strong enough to attract her, but the curse knows her well, doesn't it? Our hexes have reached for her every time she was near in this realm. So why not within the veil too?"

Finn asked, "That makes sense, but what do we do then?"

"Hold your hands over her." Marceau stepped forward and held his arms a few feet above Seraphina's body. Finn mirrored him. They watched, gazes intense, searching for any sign of the hex raising from their skin.

Nothing.

"I have an idea," Finn said and he grabbed Marceau's forearms. Marceau reached for his in return. "All right, concentrate. Think of her, of your love for her. This hex has fed on our emotions all these years, right? You said it was the emotional connection between you that caused it to bloom and activate the dormant portion you carried. So, focus on your emotions. Think of how badly you need her back."

Finn closed his eyes. His brow drew down tight, and he hummed a soft song to himself. One Marceau heard Seraphina hum many times when they worked on translating the grimoire.

Marceau pinched his eyes shut too. He thought of when he first saw her in the ridiculous carriage at the Schermerhorn. He smiled as he remembered how he'd practically chased her all over the building and was brash enough to take the seat beside her during the concert.

What he wouldn't give to go back to that day at the Arcade and know what he did now. If he'd known the full extent of the curse that day, he could have prevented so much heartache.

Marceau pictured her sitting there. He'd been so nervous. It was easy remembering how stray locks of her crimson hair had come free of her ponytail and blown around her face. She'd looked so natural that day. Jeans and Converse, only a little makeup. Her freckles had shown darker across the bridge of her nose than on her cheeks. Her bright green eyes sparkled with delight at each bite of her favorite lunch. She'd been playful, but wary of him. Tough and yet fragile.

"That's it," Khat said with more excitement than usual.

Opening his eyes, he noticed the complex blue pattern of the hex was traveling down his arms toward his wrists. Finn's arms were still blank.

Marceau needed her back. He'd done so many things he was not proud of. He needed to know he saved a person of such beauty and character. His hands flared bright blue. Tendrils of the hex flowed into

Finn's arms, winding around and around. Finn sucked in a deep breath. Stark black and gray traces of the hex began to form within his skin in response.

Lynette gasped. Her eyes bulged as she looked from Finn to Marceau. "I-I see it. I can see the hex now."

"We all can, Lynette, chill. This has happened before," Khat answered.

Lynette glared and said, "Wait. Why the hell is the hex in your skin, Marceau? I didn't curse you. And what are you doing to Finn anyway? I don't like this." She started to raise her hand from Seraphina's shoulder.

Khat warned, "You freeze right there. I haven't pulled the rest of you from the veil yet, Lynette. Don't push it." Khat's voice shook, but it was unclear if it was from anger or from the effort to hold the veil.

Marceau chimed in, "I carry your bloodline. I believe the curse has run through all of our family born after you cast the hex. It lay dormant in my blood until I came here. The love between Seraphina and me activated it."

"Then why didn't you just unbind it yourself then?" Lynette asked.

"I never found a way to, or, believe me, I would have."

"Enough. Focus people, please." Khat's face was no longer calm. She had beads of sweat on her forehead and her chin was beginning to tremble.

Finn stared at Khat and said, "We have to hurry, Marc. Focus on Seraphina." He started humming again.

Marceau thought of the dinner when he first met Finn and Khat. He pictured Seraphina's shy expression when he handed her the dahlias and remembered her fiery temper when she held her ground with Finn. How quickly she had eased back into laughter once she expressed herself.

They'd spent many afternoons together translating the grimoire. She was so intelligent. Seraphina had meticulously researched and translated each page. They were only partway done. She needed to comeback and finish her research.

Marceau's hex rose and twisted upward. The smoky tendrils wrapped up like a vine from a fairy tale, but in electric, pulsing blue. Finn's hex joined his and they wound around each other. Black and blue. Marceau closed his eyes and concentrated even harder. He remembered feeling so cold. His body had lost the ability to regulate itself with the curse in full power, and he thought of the warmth her closeness provided. Recalling emotions he'd experienced the night during the movie, of finally feeling as if he had found somewhere he belonged, tugged at his heart. With friends. With the girl he loved.

"Almost there," Khat whispered.

Marceau opened his eyes and peeked at the veil. The power from his and Finn's hex disappeared as if into a fog.

"You did it. You pierced the veil." Khat sat up straighter again. "Seraphina Pearce, I call you forward. Follow my voice. Come back to us." Her voice cracked. Khat cleared her throat. "Sera, come forward, please."

They waited a few minutes that seemed like an eternity.

"Do you sense her?" Finn asked Khat.

Khat shook her head. "No, how about you?"

Finn shook his head side to side.

Marceau closed his eyes. He tried to extend his senses outward beyond his skin. He imagined traveling along the power of the curse, trying with all his might to find some sign she was near.

There.

The faintest brush of warmth as if sunshine shone upon the curse. Marceau recognized Seraphina's energy. Adrenaline pulsed into his chest. "She's there."

Finn squinted as he stared at the veil.

"Are you sure?" Lynette asked.

This time, Marceau tried to push his feelings, to extend them beyond himself, to let them swell large enough to fill the entire bedroom.

I *need* you, Seraphina. Come back to me.

He heard a gasp and peeked at Lynette. Her eyes were huge.

Marceau's head whipped back to the foot of the bed. A pale, pink wisp appeared from thin air. It snaked its way closer and twisted all the while joining their hexes.

"Seraphina," Marceau said.

A pulse of red flared through the smoky tendril.

"Call her again," Finn said.

"Come back to us, Seraphina. Follow our energy through the veil. Cross back into the mortal realm," Marceau pleaded.

"Ahem, don't forget me," Lynette interjected.

"Hush, you," Khat hissed.

The power of Seraphina's hex flared bright red. The air at the end of the bed began to glow a faint red too.

Khat leaned forward. "Sera, cross the veil. I'm going to pull what remains of Mirela's spirit through. Please come with her."

The red illumination stayed at the foot of the bed, but nothing seemed to change.

"I think I can help." Lynette reached forward. "Come closer so I can touch the hex."

Finn and Marceau exchanged a look. Finn nodded and they both took a step bringing the hex within Lynette's reach.

"It's so powerful." Lynette reached out and stroked their intertwining hexes. The force intensified and the colors all sparked at her touch. "Ah, I see how it works now."

Lynette plucked the end of Seraphina's hex. It pulsed so brightly that it caused Marceau to squint. Lynette spoke a few words in same Creole French she'd used while weaving the hex as she slowly pulled.

Hope was etched in Finn's eyes. Marceau knew they mirrored his own. Their arms remained locked over Seraphina as Lynette continued pulling the red tendril of Seraphina's hex.

Khat's head shot up and her eyes were brimming with tears. "Guys, I cannot hold this much longer. We call you forth, Seraphina. Please." She sobbed.

The strand Lynette held flared a red so vibrant it burned Marceau's eyes. He looked down at Seraphina. A sudden warm rush of air blew his hair back, and Seraphina's body jumped.

She gasped a deep breath and Marceau's body shuddered in relief. More adrenaline shot through his veins and straight to his heart. He heard everyone else gasp too. They stood frozen… staring for any sign of awareness.

"It's back." Sobbing, deep and unrestrained pulled his eyes from Seraphina for a moment, long enough to see Lynette hold her hands against her chest. "I'm here."

Seraphina's voice whispered, "I promise. I promise. I…"

Marceau looked back down in time to watch Seraphina's eyes flutter open. She stopped whispering and stared up at Finn and Marceau's clasped arms above her. She twisted and looked above her at Khat, who still held her hands against Seraphina's face. Finally, she caught sight of Lynette and screamed.

"Y-you." She recoiled and scooted down on the bed.

"No," Finn yelled. "She is helping, love. Stay still."

Seraphina looked bewildered but did as he asked.

"Do you feel any power, Lynette?" Marceau hoped his theory was correct. Did her powers return when her spirit was reunited? What if they had disappeared forever?

"I'm not sure yet," Lynette spoke softly. She raised her hand and turned it back and forth in front of her.

Khat stared at Lynette's hands, eyes narrowed with suspicion. "Cut the crap and release the curse, Lynette. That was the deal we made. I held up my end of the deal, now it's your turn."

What did Khat see?

Lynette said, "I don't know. Even if I can tap back into my power, I could just let the past rest, move onward into this new... afterlife."

Finn was fuming. "This is not one of your games. You claimed you loved me once, before all this. Seraphina has died *twice* to let me live. She deserves her freedom now and to have a full life."

Marceau glanced at Seraphina. Her gaze snapped from person to person when they spoke... trying to understand.

Khat's head was lowered and her hands trembled in her lap. She was either struggling with her temper or trying to recuperate from calling forth the veil, maybe both.

"If you truly believe I'm descended from your sister, Liv, then why wouldn't you help me? I am in love with her and by some miracle, Seraphina loves me too. She's suffered all these years, and now when your own relative has found love and could have happiness? Your curse killed her again." Marceau's voice shook. "You owe her. You owe it to me, too. You will release her, or I will feed your damned soul to Death myself."

Lynette's head snapped up and her gaze locked with his. "You wouldn't."

"Don't test me when it comes to her, Lynette."

"Oh, fine. I was going to do it anyway. I just wanted you all to squirm a little."

Marceau had experienced enough games for a lifetime. He held his arm out and let the fury flow into the hex. It flared bright blue. He nodded at Finn. "Hold the key chain in your other hand, Finn, and join your part of the hex with mine again."

Finn pulled his keys from his pocket and extended his other arm. His hex flared like black flames from his hand.

"Put your hands together," Lynette said.

Finn laid his hand on top of Marceau's. Their hexes undulated around in the air surrounding their hands.

"You too," Mirela said to Seraphina.

"N-no, I can't die again. I can't. It is too much to die and come back again and again. This time, I remember. I remember everything. I couldn't move. She held me and the power… it burned. I-I will not go back into the veil."

Marceau and Finn stared at each other and then at Seraphina. What the hell had happened within the veil?

"Look at me, Seraphina." Lynette raised her hands and a deep blue glow welled from deep within. "I am going to release you. All of you. I admit it, okay? I wronged you all those years ago. You were never even in love with Finn, were you? Or you'd have never survived this long. I get it now. I was young and jealous."

Lynette turned to Finn. "You have no idea the hell my afterlife has been. I've wondered so many times what my life could have been if I'd only let you go. I hope by freeing all of you, I can move on myself, too. Besides, I did make a bargain with her." Lynette gestured her head toward Khat. "And she's not the forgiving type, is she?"

Lynette raised herself to her knees with effort. She frowned and looked down at her body. It was clear she'd thought the difficulty controlling her body would be cured once her soul was made whole again. Lynette gestured at Marceau and Finn's hands. "Put your hand on theirs."

Seraphina raised her hand and sucked in her lip. She tentatively placed her palm on top of Finn's hand. She was still careful to not touch Marceau.

Red, blue, and black twined together and illuminated the whole room.

Lynette laid her hand on top of Seraphina's and spoke loudly, "By the power of my blood, I unbind this hex. I release my claim. I free these souls."

Nothing happened.

"Oh, for the love of..." Khat smacked her hand on top of Lynette's. She squinted her eyes and a flash of vibrant gold joined the colors flowing from their hands.

"An energy boost. Now say it." Khat looked exhausted.

"I unbind this curse. I free your souls," Lynette repeated.

The hexes wound tighter and tighter until they were as thin as a thread. Then the red, black, and blue power pierced Lynette's hand.

A tugging sensation deep within Marceau's chest made him gasp. A cold burn traveled from his heart, down his arm, and into her hand. A lightness he'd never known resonated in his body. Marceau had been born into this curse and never realized how its weight affected him.

Seraphina stared at their hands. Once all the power had dissipated, first Khat and then Lynette pulled their hands away.

Lynette made a fist several times. Her brow knit together, and she stared at her hand and glared at Khat. "Mwen pa genyen? Kijan?" She was concentrating. Trying to light her hand again with power, but it wasn't working.

Finn, Seraphina, and Marceau pulled their hands away. Each turning their hands over and examining them.

"I don't see anything, but I'm no curseweaver. What you see?" Finn asked hopeful someone had an answer.

Marceau studied his own hands and then Finn's, and finally Seraphina's. Their eyes met and she smiled. A soft blush spread over her cheeks. Marceau's heart had stuttered for a moment before he looked back at his own hands and turning them over once more, just to be sure. "No traces of the hex remain. I simply see my hands."

"And on me? On Finn?" Seraphina asked.

"No curse at all."

"Of course, there isn't." Lynette pulled on the headboard for balance and stood. "I believe I'm done here. Marceau, I'll be keeping the car. I earned it fair and square. I have quite a long drive ahead of me."

Marceau asked. "Where will you go now, Lynette? Since you're free of Max's hold?"

"Why to get Babette, of course. He has no control over her anyway. She only stayed for me."

Finn held out his arm to assist her.

"I am fine. I'll see myself out," Lynette snapped, and she left the room.

Khat rolled her eyes. "I hope that's the last I ever see of her."

Marceau had a feeling it wouldn't be long before he saw Lynette again. Max would scour the ends of the earth to find her. Perhaps he could try to barter for her freedom too when he bargained with Death.

Seraphina rose to her knees in front of him. She held a hesitant hand inches from his cheek. "Is it safe?"

"Yes." Marceau nodded. "It is."

She took a breath, but her hand did not move. "I'm scared."

Warmth emanated from her hand, but it was the normal kind, nothing supernatural.

"Touch me, Seraphina." Marceau stared into her green eyes and whispered, "Please."

Seraphina lightly, tentatively caressed his cheek and they both held their breath. She bit her lip. "Do you feel anything?"

Marceau couldn't speak. He nodded yes and swallowed.

Her face fell in defeat.

Marceau grabbed Seraphina and pulled her to his chest. "I feel you, Seraphina. I finally feel the touch of the woman I love."

Seraphina laughed. "Oh…"

Marceau cut off her response with his lips. He kissed her roughly. Clutching her body against his, he cherished the feel of her mouth against his. He ran his tongue over her soft lips. Seraphina parted her mouth for him. Marceau groaned, deepening the kiss and tasting her for the first time. Reigning in his desperation for her, Marceau softened the kiss, savoring each tiny movement of her mouth upon his. Reluctantly, he pulled back and softly kissed her chin. He traced his lips across hers and they parted. He smiled, realizing her breathing was as erratic as his own. Seraphina smiled shyly. Marceau's heart felt too large for his chest.

"Uh, ahem." Finn cleared his throat.

Marceau pulled back farther, but could not look away from Seraphina's flushed face. Her lips were brighter pink. Her cheeks were covered with beautiful blush he knew so well.

Seraphina turned and said, "Um. Sorry."

"Don't be silly. What a kiss." Khat bounced up and skipped to the end of the bed. She grabbed Finn's hand. "We are going." She tugged on him.

"Wh-" Finn started.

Khat waved her finger at him. "Shush. They need to be alone and if you don't kiss me exactly like that in the next thirty seconds, I may curse you myself."

"As you wish, my bossy little djinn." Finn picked her up and slung her over his shoulder. Khat burst into excited laughter. Finn turned and muttered, "I'll, uh, see you two later. I guess."

"Less talking. More kissing," Khat demanded and she kicked her feet as Finn carried her out. She reached back and slammed Seraphina's door shut after they passed through. Her musical laughter echoed down the hallway.

Marceau laughed and buried his face in Seraphina's neck nuzzling her hair back with his nose. He left a trail of kisses up her neck and she shuddered. He smiled against her skin and small chills raised.

"Again," Seraphina whispered.

Kissing up and onto her jaw, Marceau leaned in and then stopped just above her lips. "I love you, Seraphina."

Marceau closed the distance, unable to stop kissing her. His hands cupped the back of her head. He loved the soft tickle of her hair running across his hand.

After a kiss he hoped she'd never forget, Seraphina pulled back and whispered, "I love you too, Marceau."

Chapter Thirty

Several hours later, Seraphina's head was lying on Marceau's chest. She'd finally relaxed at his touch and felt safe in his arms.

They had kissed until their lips were tired. Marceau was running his fingers lightly up and down her back when she begrudgingly nudged him and said, "Believe me when I say I want to snuggle you for eternity, but I think I'm a bit touch-drunk. If that is even a thing? I have wanted to touch you for so long. To feel you holding me now is heaven…"

He smiled. "But?"

"But I'm not used to it. My skin is tingling and my nerves are kind of freaking out. My brain is in sensory overload. And, and I am starving."

Marceau's deep laughter reverberated through his chest, bouncing her head lightly. He tightened his arms around her and bent to kiss the top of her head. "Well, technically you haven't eaten in days."

She poked his ribs, and he burst into laughter as he grabbed her hand. She loved the way his muscles flexed under his shirt.

"Hmm. You, sir, are ticklish." She looked up at him and giggled. "I will remember that."

"Just remember, turnabout is fair play." He winked.

"Oh, I'm counting on it." Seraphina's stomach rumbled loudly, causing another round of laughs. "Okay, we are going get up and head to the kitchen. However, you must hold my hand the *entire* way. Clear?"

"Clear." He nodded with a serious face.

As they entered the living room, Khat popped her head over the back of the couch and said, "I heard lots of giggling. Ooh la la." She waggled her eyebrows.

"You know she has no filter. We heard nothing inappropriate," Finn added rolling his eyes. He sat at the end of the couch rubbing Khat's feet.

"It's a djinn thing, you wouldn't understand, Sin Boy." Khat threw a pillow at him. "Dish. How was the lovin'?"

"Sin Boy?" Seraphina laughed. She felt the heat rising in her cheeks. Sometimes, it really sucked to have such pale skin. "We have decided to, um, well this whole touching thing is very new. So we are focusing on, well, the basics for a while. Kissing and cuddling are overwhelming, so… I'm starving. What's for dinner?"

Marceau stifled a laugh.

"Okay, but was it, at least, scandalous, yummy kissing like earlier?" Khat was bouncing again.

Seraphina rolled her eyes. If she didn't throw her best friend a bone, she was liable to bounce right off the couch. "Completely scandalous and infinitely yummy, okay?"

"Oh, it was. I can tell 'cause your cheeks are sooo red." Khat clapped.

"Help, Finn," Marceau pleaded.

"All right, Sparrow. Enough."

Khat poked her bottom lip dramatically.

"For now," Finn conceded.

"Okay, fine but only because I'm hungry too. With all the drama, no one has restocked the kitchen. So I guess we have to go out."

Seraphina said, "We just got a ton of groceries on Tuesday." She'd learned the hard way a hungry Khat in a grocery store was a very dangerous combination. The buggy had been so full, things had fallen out on the way to the cashier.

Khat said, "Um, hello? You've been dead. Marceau and Finn have been depressed. I used a month's worth of magic in just a couple days. Plus, you know I eat when I'm nervous."

"She's right I'm afraid." Finn smiled. "Our cupboards are bare. So I guess the question is, do we order in or go out? Seraphina's choice, since she was dead and all." He smiled and it was the old genuine Finn type of smile, nothing forced.

Seraphina laughed. "Gee thanks. Honestly, I would love takeout and a movie. So much has gone on, I just want to veg. And a shower… I really, really want a shower."

Marceau clapped his hands together and rubbed them back and forth. "I'm up. I believe it is my turn for movie night. Finn, I need a wingman. You know all the restaurants."

"My pleasure." Finn stood and kissed Khat's forehead.

"What are we having?" Seraphina asked.

"It's a surprise. It's my first turn, so I'll make it good." Marceau took her hand again and raised it to his mouth. He kissed each of her knuckles slowly, his eyes smoldering with desire before releasing her hand.

Seraphina exhaled. "I-I think I finally understand the whole knees going weak thing."

Marceau trailed his fingers down her cheek. He leaned in, bringing his lips tantalizingly close but then pulling back at the last second. A moan escaped before she could stop it, and he smiled.

Seraphina closed the distance and kissed first his bottom lip and then the bow just above his mouth. "Hurry back."

"Of course," Marceau promised, and headed out the door with Finn in tow.

"Everything is just so... so wonderful."

"You deserve to be happy, Sera. Marceau does too." Khat jumped up and hugged her. "You shoulda seen how lost that man was without you."

"I just hope it lasts." Seraphina frowned. "Death arrives tomorrow."

"Oh, Sera, please don't worry. I don't know what he wants, but we'll figure it all out. You have waited too long to be happy to let worry get in the way."

Seraphina took a breath and set her shoulders. "You are absolutely right, Khat. I have waited several lifetimes, so I'm not going waste a moment." She headed down the hall. "I'm gonna go freshen up. They'll be back soon."

The shower was heavenly. She thought about Marceau's kisses every time she closed her eyes. He meant so much to her now. When she'd first met him, she was attracted but would have never imagined how strongly she could love Marceau. Seraphina remembered those first awkward days as they looked through the grimoire. He'd been so reserved and formal, withdrawn even, when he had first arrived. Over time, Marceau relaxed and gradually began to open up as he spent time with her, Finn, and Khat. Like anyone could stay reserved around Khat anyway? She smiled.

A dark image flashed into her mind. Seraphina closed her eyes as a wave of panic gripped her. Stale air flooded her lungs. She was back on the spirit side of the veil without control over her naked body. She floated, suspended in the air, couldn't move. An ice cold hand trailed up her leg, her side, her neck.

The Mistress of Death's voice echoed through her mind, *Remember what you promised.*

Seraphina jumped and knocked over a bottle of shampoo, snapping her attention back to the present. She pressed her hands into the tile and gasped again and again until her thoughts cleared.

Don't waste a moment.

She quickly rinsed and dried off. Wrapping a large fluffy towel around her body and another around her hair in a turban, Seraphina paused in front of the door and listened to make sure the guys were not back. Finn didn't matter, he had seen her like this a hundred times before. But she wasn't in a rush to be undressed around Marceau. Even the thought made her blush. One day, though, if she survived tomorrow. She darted down the hall and into her room. After dressing in comfy pajama pants and a tank top, she was running a brush through her damp hair when she heard the door open and Finn's laughter. Her stomach growled again. She swept her hair up into a messy bun and went to see what the movie night's theme would be when Marceau was in charge.

Marceau said, "I'm gonna make him an offer he can't refuse."

Finn countered, "Revenge is a dish best served cold."

"Do you know who I am? I'm Moe Green."

"Fredo, you're my older brother, and I love you. But don't ever take sides against the family again, ever."

Seraphina giggled. Finn and Marceau were exchanging quotes like it was an epic battle of masculinity. "Leave the gun, take the cannolis," she chimed in and laughed when Marceau's jaw dropped.

He asked, "You can quote *The Godfather* movies?"

She shrugged. "Among my many skills, yes." Seraphina sniffed the air. "Please, please tell me I smell pasta."

Marceau stepped aside and she burst into laughter at no less than ten containers stacked up from her favorite Italian restaurant.

"How many of us did you order for?"

Marceau shrugged. "This is a celebration, plus I've seen Khat eat. She may be tiny, but she can out eat a linebacker."

"Darn right," Khat added as she stretched a red and white checked tablecloth on the large coffee table and lit some small candles. She placed large pillows on the floor around the table so they could sit and eat informally. It looked cozy.

"Perfect, Khat," Seraphina complimented. She went to the kitchen. "Red, white, beer? What's your fancy?"

"Beer," said Finn.

"Red," answered Khat.

"Do you have any more of the Jackelope beer?" asked Marceau.

She opened the fridge and checked. "Yep. Coming right up." She gathered the beers and opened a bottle of Cabernet to share with Khat.

The guys brought a smorgasbord of garlic bread, steaming Italian pastas, salad, and antipasto.

Seraphina sat next to Marceau and passed out the drinks. He leaned in and kissed her softly. Too soon, he leaned back, and she pouted in protest.

"Food first, then you can kiss me all you want while we watch *The Godfather.*" He smiled. "Deal? Where would you like to start?"

"Deal. Eggplant parmesan is calling my name."

They feasted. They laughed. They toasted.

Seraphina savored every moment of their newfound freedom.

Everyone ate until they could hold no more, even Khat, and that had been a sight to behold. When all four had dropped their forks, they cleaned up the table and settled in to watch the movie.

Seraphina tried to stay awake but drifted into a contented sleep halfway through the movie. Marceau held her until the show was over and then woke her by fluttering his eyelashes against her forehead.

"I always wondered what butterfly kisses felt like." Seraphina smiled with her eyes still closed. She stretched and her hip popped loudly.

"Are you all right?" he asked.

"Yep. Perfect." She finished stretching and opened her eyes.

"Just checking. That was loud."

Finn teased, "Seraphina does it a lot. She was born in 1906, you know."

"Watch it, you. You're even older than me." Seraphina threw a pillow at him. "Besides, I was dead for fifty years, so those shouldn't count against me."

Finn caught the pillow and yawned. He slid out from under a sleeping Khat and bent lifting her effortlessly. "We're off to bed. Goodnight, you two."

"Night, Finn," Seraphina said feeling suddenly nervous.

"Goodnight," Marceau said, but he looked down at Seraphina and tilted his head. One eyebrow raising in question. "You tensed up. What's wrong?"

"I. It. This is just all so new to me. You would think I'd know what to do, or at least how to act since I have dreamed of being in love for so long. Longed for it. But it is a very different thing now that I'm actually experiencing it." She picked and pulled at her shirt hem.

"Seraphina, it's actually new to me too. I have always avoided the emotional fragility of love. Please talk to me, what has you fidgeting?"

"I just, I guess I feel shy all of the sudden." Seraphina forced herself to look up and meet his eyes. Vulnerable, she needed to see his response.

"Seraphina," he said, tracing his fingers through her hair, "I understand, really I do. We made a rather huge leap in our relationship in the last few hours. Let's take the rest a step at a time, shall we? I want to enjoy, to savor every moment with you. I know..." He sat up and pulled her upright. Marceau turned her to face him and took both of her hands into his. "Miss Seraphina Pearce, of the Savannah, Georgia Pearce's, my beautiful love, will you do me the honor of being my girlfriend?"

She laughed a rather unfeminine laugh. He caught her so off guard. She was feeling nervous about if he would try to spend the night and what that might possibly entail... and here he was asking her to what, go steady? "Yes, Marceau, of course." She giggled.

"Whew." He put a hand on his chest dramatically. "Good. Now, girlfriend of mine." Marceau smiled as if he liked calling that. "I think it's time we call it a night. Walk me to the door?"

"Oh, I didn't know if... I wasn't sure." Her tongue stumbled over the words.

"Oh, I hope you will invite me to stay sometime in the future, Seraphina. But when we are both ready. Until then, I shall have to wine, dine, and romance you senseless." He stood and pulled her up against him.

"R-romance me senseless?" Seraphina asked and she batted her eyelashes at him. "That sounds… promising."

"Indeed." He leaned in and kissed her forehead.

They held hands as they walked toward the stairs. He stopped just short of the stairway and turned, his demeanor very different.

"First, we have to get through tomorrow. Max, Death, is coming. Even I cannot predict how it will go. Remember, what I told you earlier. He is charming, cunning, and utterly destructive. We must be alert. Make sure you promise him nothing, agree to absolutely nothing, without discussing it with me. He will hold you to your words."

"I won't, Marceau. We'll see what he wants and figure it out, okay?" Her heart ached at the thought of yet another hurdle to face so soon.

"Rest, Seraphina. We'll be okay. I love you."

Marceau kissed her softly at first and then it deepened. He only stopped when she was short of breath. Leaning his forehead against hers, he shook his head. "I could kiss you every moment for the next month, and it wouldn't be enough."

She giggled. "I love you, too."

"Mmm. Say it again, just one more time."

"I love you, Marceau, with all my heart."

He slid on his jacket, and they walked down the stairs in silence. "I'll be back in the morning. I don't know when Max will show up, but he is coming, there's no doubt of that. I'll need to be with you all day."

"No complaints here." She rocked back on her feet and bit her lip.

He kissed her forehead, then walked out into the chilled night air. "Goodnight, Seraphina."

She locked the door and leaned back against it, sighing as she pressed her fingertips against her mouth.

It was a perfect night. Seraphina couldn't have asked for more. She hoped for many more nights with Marceau.

But, Seraphina had a promise to keep.

Chapter Thirty-One

Sunlight warmed Seraphina's cheeks. She'd not yet opened her eyes. Instead, she lay cocooned in her blankets, replaying last night over and over. Her lips felt slightly chapped when she licked them.

So much kissing.

She stretched and wondered what time it was. Marceau said he'd be back this morning.

"Is that lovely smile for me, dear Seraphina?" an unfamiliar voice asked.

Seraphina shot up and looked at the chair in the corner of her room. She jerked her blanket to just under her neck.

A striking, handsome man sat with his legs crossed and a silver tipped cane resting across his lap. He had rugged facial features and long hair tied back in a tight ponytail, a strange mix with his formal black suit. His hazel eyes glimmered unnaturally as they caught the light.

"I assume I need not introduce myself." Maximilian thrummed his fingers on his knee.

"You assume a hell of a lot more than that. What are you doing in my bedroom? How did you get in here?"

"Ah, a feisty little one. Marceau probably finds that quality endearing." Maximilian sighed. "I, on the other hand, do not. So mind your manners, child. I find myself in ill temper to see no traces of a hex around you." He sat back and looked down his straight nose at her. "How did he do it? How did Marceau break your curse? He's put quite a damper on my plans."

"I could not care less about your plans, and I'm not telling you anything. Not until Marceau is here. And not until I'm properly dressed, for that matter. Coffee could only help loosen my tongue too if you're wondering. You come across so proper and refined, and yet you dare to sit in my bedroom uninvited? You are rude." She dropped her blanket and crossed her arms over her chest.

Death raised his eyebrows.

Okay, maybe the last part had been a *little* much.

Death let out a deep echoing laugh, and Seraphina jumped embarrassingly high. His laughter echoed around the room and rattled the pictures on her walls. A perfume bottle fell from her antique vanity and rolled, clattering across the floor.

Footsteps pounded down the hall. Marceau burst through her door so hard, she was sure the doorknob punctured the drywall. "Max, you're here. What did you do to her?" Marceau demanded wild eyed. He looked from the laughing man in the corner to Seraphina's blushing face and then back again. He stepped forward and stood between them. "Are you okay, Seraphina?" He studied her up and down.

"He scared me by being in here, but yes, I'm fine, Marceau, really." She looked around him at Death. He'd stopped laughing.

Death said, "Ah, she is quite delicious, is she not? I haven't laughed like that in years. Not without torture being involved that is," he amended.

"Could you go wait in the living room? Both of you?" Seraphina asked. "I need a minute. This is all a bit much within a few minutes of waking up. I would like to get properly dressed and well, use the facilities too."

"Of course, Maximilian, please." Marceau gestured for the man to follow him out into the hall.

"Mortals." Death sneered and faded away like dust blowing in a nonexistent wind.

"Is it? Is he gone?" Seraphina asked as she rose from the bed.

"Unfortunately not. I expect he's waiting in your living room." Marceau kissed her forehead and turned to go check. As he reached to close her bedroom door, he said, "I will, um, fix that."

Yep, big hole in the wall.

Seraphina dressed quickly and went down the hall to wash her face, brush her teeth, and take care of other necessities. When she emerged,

Marceau was speaking rapidly to their unwelcome guest. He stopped as soon as he saw her.

"Ah, Marceau is trying to convince me to leave, but I have only just arrived." Death's smile showed too many teeth for comfort.

"Coffee. I need major caffeine if I have to play head games with *The Joker* over there." Seraphina turned toward the kitchen.

Marceau's eyes bulged and his mouth fell open. He started to hold a hand up for his benefactor as if pleading for mercy.

Death laughed again, long and loud.

"Lighten up, Marceau," Seraphina said as she walked past him. She poured a cup of hot, black coffee in a mug that read, WITCH, PLEASE next to a broomstick. Returning to the living room, she sat on the love seat and patted next to her. Marceau came and joined her, but at the edge of the seat. His posture ramrod straight.

Seraphina sighed and took a sip of her coffee. Sumatra, yum. "Where are Finn and Khat? I'm sure if they were home, Mr. Giggles here would have gotten their attention by now."

Marceau said, "Seraphina, please. I don't understand how he has suddenly developed a sense of humor, but please don't push too hard. They went out to get supplies. Groceries and such."

Death said, "Nonsense. I rather like you unfiltered. I will allow you one warning if you begin to cross me too harshly."

"Thanks," she replied and took another drink.

"Am I to believe the Sin Eater's hex is gone as well?" Death asked.

"Yes," she answered.

"Enlighten me, Marceau. I had thought this one was beyond even your clever tricks and loopholes, or I wouldn't have sent you here. I bound their curse myself, after all."

Seraphina narrowed her eyes. Sent him here?

Marceau said, "Answer me this first, Maximilian. Was all of this plotted? Did you ever even want the Blackthorne Grimoire? Or did you send me here to meet Seraphina and Finn?"

Death smiled lazily and rubbed a grotesque carving on the head of his cane. A snake? A dragon? She could not quite make out what it was. The thing had fangs, though.

"I've owned the Blackthorn Grimoire for over a hundred years. I'm the one who donated it to the symphony's charity auction. I also made sure a customer just happened to leave an open auction guide on the counter for fair Seraphina as he checked out in her quaint, little apothecary. I needed her to attend the auction."

Seraphina set her coffee cup down on her leg. It had all been *planned?*

"I did not, however, anticipate your resourcefulness in bewitching the auction so Marceau could not carry out my order and procure the book back for me. I intended to lure you back to New Orleans with my handsome protégé and the promise of the spells within my grimoire."

Seraphina asked, "Why are you interested in me at all? I don't understand what you want from me." Her mind reeled. What could Death possibly want? Finn, she sort of understood. Marceau had warned her about how Death would want to enslave Finn, but why would that require *her* to go to New Orleans?

Death answered, "I popped into town a while back to peek at my Sin Eater's progress and visit an old friend. Imagine my surprise when I sensed energy similar to my own in your magic, dear. You are quite unusual. And I am very curious as to how you came to have such powers." He leaned forward. "I had originally intended to use your death to force Marceau's hand and recruit my Sin Eater's soul, but after seeing you, I realized you are quite a prize yourself." Death licked his lips. "I decided after I had their allegiances secured, I would rather keep you for myself."

Seraphina's skin crawled at the idea. Death's expression was sexual, and she'd be damned before she would ever let him touch her in any way.

Marceau reached over and laid his hand on Seraphina's knee. Great, under other circumstances, she might have found his protectiveness cute, but at the moment, she wanted Death to keep talking. He had stopped now and only stared at Marceau's hand on her leg.

"If I am such a prize, then why did you manipulate all of us to make me die?" She paused. "Oh, right. Death isn't a big deal to you."

"No, that's where things went off track actually. I planned to threaten your death to force Marceau into an accord. You see he's resisted a bargain of mine for many years. But I know how he's pined to end his loneliness. I thought his noble nature was the key to making him submit. Imagine my pleasure when I realized he actually seemed to care for you, making my plan a sure win." He shook his head. "Then you went and died for him. Your death threw a wrench in all my meticulous planning. Perhaps, if I had timed my arrival for a day or two sooner," he mused.

"I'm sorry my death was such an inconvenience."

Maximilian stared at her. "And yet, here you sit, very much alive."

Finn and Khat walked in. Finn dropped one of his bags and a peach rolled across the floor. He gaped at Death sitting on his couch.

Death looked amused by his reaction. "Sin Eater, are you not happy to see me again?"

Finn did not answer. He grabbed the dropped bag, scooped up the errant fruit, and went straight into the kitchen.

Khat stood in the doorway staring at Death. "You?" she finally managed. "*You* are Death?"

"I do prefer your true form, you know that," Death answered and winked.

Khat raised her head and walked past them. She joined Finn and both of them banged groceries and cabinet doors.

Seraphina wondered how Khat knew Death and when he had seen her in her true form? She sat back and drank her coffee.

No one spoke until Finn and Khat finished slamming things around in the kitchen. The pair of them stood awkwardly in the kitchen wondering what to do next.

"Please, do join us." Death gestured at the room left beside him on the couch.

Finn grabbed two dining room chairs and dragged them across the floor. He placed them close to his friends, and therefore, as far from where Death sat as possible. Khat nodded as though she approved and joined Finn.

"Now, where were we?" Death asked. He did not seem put off in the least by Finn's resistance to sitting close and making friends.

Seraphina said, "You were explaining how you've been manipulating all of us—you donated the grimoire to the auction, wanted me to chase Marceau back to New Orleans like a lovesick stalker so Marceau can *submit,* whatever the hell that means. Oh, and my powers over death excite you, but my actual death this week was quite an inconvenient annoyance."

Death cracked a wicked smile. "Excellent summarization."

Finn asked, "What exactly is it you expect from me, Death?"

Khat reached out for Finn's hand, and they both sat rigid in their chairs.

"When I dropped in to check on your progress, I was quite impressed. I believe you're the one I have been searching for. The Sin Eater that's strong willed enough, stable enough to become the general of my newly reanimated legion."

"Reanimated?" Marceau whispered.

"Your legion of what?" Seraphina asked.

"Why of the undead, of course. Surely, Marceau has shared with his young lady love what it is he does for me?" Death looked at the confusion on Seraphina's face and the defeat on Marceau's. He sat back and clapped slowly. "Oh, this *is* entertaining."

Seraphina said, "He breaks curses. He helps you get rare, magical items to add to your collection. I assume you make him weave some hexes too."

"There is more, Seraphina." Marceau's voice was soft, resigned.

Death said, "Oh, yes, he does all those things for me. But that's not his true talent, not even close. I could have any number of thieves steal for me. While I admit his talent for curses is impressive, it is how he uses that particular talent that makes him valuable."

Marceau snapped, "If you've somehow raised an army, then clearly I am not alone in those talents either."

"Ah, I have been very busy indeed. But you and your theories were the keys to figuring it all out." Max's gaze focused on Seraphina as if wanting to capture her reaction to his next sentence. "You see Marceau's true talent lies in reanimation."

"Reanimation?" she asked.

"Yes, I'm sure you have noticed he has quite a flare for the scientific? Well, he combines sound scientific principles with his abilities as a curseweaver to circumvent the laws of nature. You see, Marceau is quite adept at raising the dead."

Seraphina sucked air in through her teeth and stood. "It's not true. She said he did, but I didn't believe her. You're both lying."

Death's smile was long gone. "She who?"

Seraphina ignored him and looked to Marceau. "Tell me, it's not true. Look me in the eyes. You do not use your power to bring back the dead, right?"

Marceau opened his mouth but said nothing.

"Are you the one who did it to Lynette?" Seraphina demanded. "I assumed it was him"—she pointed back at Death—"or is it your fault she's still here? Why she's so different from how she used to be, so unnatural?"

Marceau closed his eyes and his shoulders dropped as he exhaled.

"How exactly do you know of my Lynette? Or how she moves?" Death asked.

Seraphina realized her mistake, but it was too late.

Death leaned forward and slammed the tip of his cane into their stained concrete floor hard enough it should have cracked. The doorknob rattled downstairs. Someone was trying to come inside.

Finn started to stand.

"Don't bother," Death said and waved his hand in the air.

The antique bell above the door rang as it opened. The distinctive click-clack of high-heeled shoes crossed the hardwood of the apothecary. Death had opened their carefully locked doors with a simple flick of his wrist.

Lynette and another blonde girl emerged from the stairwell. They wore matching baby-doll cut dresses and their hair bobbed in tight Shirley Temple style ringlets.

"Lynette, you seem to already know." Death glared at her. Lynette raised her chin, but Seraphina noticed it trembled. "Have you already met Babette, as well?"

Seraphina looked at the young woman holding Lynette's hand and said, "No, I had no idea about your zombie girlfriend collection. What is the deal with their names?"

Death smiled and then turned to Lynette. "We will have much to discuss later."

Lynette cringed against her creepy companion. Babette laid her head on Lynette's shoulder. She raised their clasped hands and licked the back of Lynette's hand closing her eyes as if savoring the taste.

"How did you come to possess a legion of undead soldiers, Maximilian? I've raised as few corpses as possible over the years." He looked at Seraphina as if willing her to understand. "I have certainly not raised an army."

"The legion, my soldier's bodies, have been lying in wait ever since I became the Mistress's apprentice. Three thousand of the finest warriors Greece ever produced. I never dreamed when I bargained with the Mistress that it would take me this long to command them again."

"I'll have no part in it. You cannot force me to reanimate that many…" Marceau stood, his fists clenched.

"Save your moral objections for someone who cares for such nonsense. Besides, it's already done. That's why it has taken me so long to come to Nashville, the reason I let you linger here. I needed you out of the way while my legion was reanimated." Max stroked the top of his cane. "Now I'm ready for phase two. Once my Sin Eater is in place, I will join their minds into a new hive and remove their shackles. The Sin Eater's mind will be linked with mine, and as my general, he will command them. I will finally be able to unleash my warriors upon humanity. The time for supernaturals to take their rightful place is upon us."

Finn glared. "I'm not leading some undead army. And you sure as hell aren't getting inside my head. I will not bargain with you again, Death."

"Not even to keep shimmery skin on your lovely little djinn?" Death laughed. "I can be quite persuasive."

Finn looked at Khat, alarmed.

It was Marceau who spoke, "It matters not, Finn. He's lying, playing one of his games. There's no way he was able to raise three thousand corpses."

"He tells the truth," said Babette. "He forced the other blue-eyed ones. Used their love for each other as a weapon. They raised corpse after corpse until they collapsed from exhaustion or death."

"Other blue-eyed ones?" Lynette asked Babette.

Babette nodded. "As a surprise, he took me to watch them awaken the final group of soldiers last night. They've been reanimating them nonstop ever since I was created."

"How is that possible?" Lynette asked. "Who has been raising them?"

Death smiled. "Your sister's descendants, of course. I took your entire family the night you died."

"No, no that cannot be." Lynette shook her head. "I would've known."

"You know what I allow and nothing more. I saw your power over curses and recognized the potential of your bloodline. They have lived in a village within the Bayou Sauvage ever since. For fear of inbreeding lessening their power, I have supplemented their numbers with fresh, powerful supernaturals with which to procreate. My experiments have resulted in enhanced powers even I had not imagined."

"They are people, not livestock. My family," Lynette yelled.

Death ignored her outburst and spoke to Marceau instead, "So you see, Marceau, I've had quite the number of L'Argent curseweavers at my beck and call"—he shrugged—"until their numbers dwindled while raising my legion, that is."

Marceau said, "You told me you rescued me from a mental institution. You said my family abandoned me. And you saved me."

"Oh, stop with the melodramatics, Marceau. I did save you in my own way. Instead of living in a secluded village in my swamp and being used as L'Argent breeding stock"—he glared at Lynette—"you were raised in the lap of luxury and excess. You never wanted for anything."

"Except love. Except family. Do I have a mother? A father? Siblings?" Marceau's fists clenched.

Death raised his chin. "Perhaps, you are a little too eager for those answers. I believe I will withhold that particular information until an appropriate bargain has been made."

Marceau started forward. "Damn you, Max. Damn you and your games and bargains."

Death's lip curled back. "Mind yourself, apprentice."

Seraphina and Lynette both grabbed Marceau's shoulders. Seraphina took his hand, twining their fingers together and squeezing.

When he spoke again, he was calmer. "Why did you choose me then? Why did you take me in as a boy? Why did I gain your favor?"

Death said, "Even as a child, your power was particularly strong and your mind was sharp. But in truth, it was a reading from a djinn. Khatereh's mother, in fact."

Khat's head snapped up.

"She prophesied the male L'Argent born with the hex visible in his skin would be the one to master reanimation, the one to aid my search for a suitable Sin Eater. I checked each babe born in the village. I knew, within minutes of your birth, you would be my champion and the key to awakening my army. I let you stay with your family until you were at a manageable age to tutor in cursework. When you were seven, I had your memory removed. The rest you know."

"My entire life has been controlled, predetermined? To help raise some grotesque army of the undead? To entrap Finn? And now Seraphina?" Marceau sank back against Seraphina. The realization wounded him. Somewhere deep inside Marceau was an echo of a young boy trying to please his mysterious benefactor. Seraphina doubted much exchange of love or affection had happened in Marceau's early years. He'd admitted as much once when she asked about his childhood. Yet Marceau struggled with complex feelings. Death had raised him.

Death said, "I've answered enough of your questions, Marceau. Now, you will answer mine. How did you break the curse?"

"I came and helped them," Lynette answered in complete defiance.

"And why exactly would you risk it? How could you possibly escape my compound? You're not exactly the generous sort, Lynette. What did they promise you?"

"The one thing I have wanted most, all these years."

Death looked at her puzzled. His confusion changed to shock. "I can no longer reach your mind. How can that be? I would have noticed."

"You've been too self-absorbed or amused by Babette to notice much else these last few weeks." Babette snuggled into Lynette's side. "But, yes, I am finally free of your damned hive. My thoughts are mine and mine alone. I am complete. You can no longer torture me with promises to make me whole or threaten to keep my soul split forever."

Death asked, "With Seraphina indisposed, who pulled aside the veil?"

"I did," Khat answered.

"You?" Max snorted. "Clever girl. I did not realize a mixed breed like yourself was capable of much more than provocative dancing."

Khat grabbed Finn's arm. With clenched teeth, she said, "Don't let him win. Do not react to that."

"And how did you separate Lynette from my hive?"

Seraphina said, "None of this matters. We're free of the curse. Finn has no reason to sacrifice himself to save me and neither does Marceau, for that matter. We just want peace. We can finally live in freedom." Seraphina prayed Death would just leave.

"Freedom," Death repeated. He looked at each of them, then laughed. "All are mine in time. Even those who court immortality can fall victim to Death's desires."

A threat toward Finn and Khat.

"I suppose you hope to remain here, Marceau? Do you really think you can abandon me so easily? I have invested too much in you. Remember, I may have L'Argents still locked away."

A threat toward Marceau and his surviving family.

"And you, fiery Spellcaster, you think I will leave you to pierce the veil and commune with my dead at your whim?"

A threat toward me.

"Enough." Seraphina stood. "Enough, Death."

She had made a promise. She would have promised just about anything to cross the veil after feeling the love from Marceau and Finn pulling her back to life. But Seraphina wasn't sure she would truly keep her promise until Death threatened everyone she loved.

Seraphina knew what it meant for her, but she could stop this madness. She would not let Death destroy the lives of Khat, Finn, or Marceau.

Chapter Thirty-Two

Seraphina held out her arms, closed her eyes, and surrendered. *I'm ready, Mistress of Death. I welcome you.*

Dark, intense magic seized her body. The Mistress had channeled even more death magic into Seraphina while she had been trapped within the veil.

Now, Seraphina invited the Mistress to share her body and align their powers. She would provide the pathway. The Mistress could harness their combined strength to destroy Maximilian, as promised. Long locks of hair floated away from her back and shoulders. Cold, resolute hatred and infinite power blanketed her while her pulse aligned with the ebbs of magic flowing through her veins. She'd opened herself fully to possession and now channeled the Mistress.

Death let out his eerie echoing laugh again.

"You mean to challenge me? Oh, what a fortunate turn indeed." His body lifted into an instant standing position. He twisted the head of his cane and a long blade shot forth.

"Venom," Marceau warned. "On his weapon."

"Finn, how much sin flows over Death?" Seraphina asked. The Mistress's voice spoke in unison with her own.

"What trickery is this?" Death demanded. "How is she speaking through you?"

Finn replied, "His sins swirl so deeply over his flesh, I can hardly see his features."

"Twice I have lingered in the other realm, and twice I have returned. My magic was of the elements… earth, air, fire, water. Never has a Spellcaster harnessed power over the fifth element, over spirit, until now.

It was your interference that corrupted my magic. In death, I garnered but a taste of the Mistress's power over spirit and yet I possess such new power. That is how I gained death magic."

Her voice changed, deepened as it combined with the voices of others in the veil's realm. The Mistress called forth all the souls Maximilian had wronged in his time as Death. She channeled their hatred and energy into Seraphina. "Now, after a second death, I drank deeply of the Mistress's power. Spirit is at my call."

Her pupils disappeared into dark, swirling gray as her eyes were filled with the fury of countless magical souls.

"Seraphina?" Marceau whispered.

She heard him speak, but Seraphina was too full of spirit to respond. Her bones ached with the weight of so much magic.

I… I'm losing myself.

Seraphina screamed and the shrieks of thousands joined hers.

Death took a step back. He tripped over the corner of the couch and had to catch himself to keep from falling. "I am the personification of Death. Therefore, I cannot die," he argued. He raised his daggered cane in front of him.

"False," thousands of voices screeched from her aching throat.

Khat, Finn, and Marceau all covered their ears in pain.

She said, "You stole your power. You embody nothing. You're nothing more than a common thief. Death is impartial. Death does not take souls or imprison the living. You have mutated Death's purpose and manipulated innocents and altered their paths to leech their strength. When they had but a shred of sanity left, you continued to prey on their nobility, their loyalty, and their love."

Maximilian argued, "The world has grown, has changed. I needed to awaken my legion. When I accepted the Mistress's deal, I asked to keep my men. I bargained to keep my army." He stared at Seraphina. "If you possess her body, Mistress, you know I speak the truth. In exchange for my apprenticeship, you said I could keep my soldiers by my side forever. And then you let every one of them fall."

"I kept my word. Their bodies remained with you, intact. But I freed their spirits. You made no bargain to keep their souls."

He yelled, "What good are their bodies to me? Empty shells. Reminders of your cruelty. If you'd let me keep my men, I would have never betrayed you. I would have been your loyal apprentice, your lover, for eternity."

Seraphina's body rocked back with the ferocity of the Mistress's anger.

Max continued, "Death should have dominion over the mortal realm. Well, now I have them back. My soldiers are reanimated. With my Sin Eater, my general, in place, I will once again have them under my command."

"Why do you need me? Why can't you lead your own damned army?" Finn asked, demanding an answer.

Maximilian snapped, "They are shackled to quell their protests until I join their minds. I need you to take command of the hive."

"Control your own damned hive then. Why me?"

It was Marceau who answered, "Because he already controls another hive. I don't think he's strong enough to control them all. He is powerful. But he could never be as strong as the Mistress, the rightful Death." He turned to his benefactor. "That's it, isn't it? You can't command your own men. That's why you have searched so long for a Sin Eater with the mental fortitude to survive the full transformation."

"Why does it have to be a Sin Eater?" Finn asked.

Marceau said, "His army was legendary for their atrocities. They ravaged the lands they marched across. If they all died at once, then their bodies are still rife with sins. You need them bound into a collective mind with a Sin Eater as a general to insure you can control them. To make sure they do not fall victim to possession."

Marceau paused before turning to Finn, "As general, you would know every movement of your men. Their bodies are eternal, but a mortal wound could send their spirit back into the veil. You would know if a soldier fell and left his body open for possession."

Finn asked, "But the soldier's bodies have been empty all this time, why are they open for possession only now?"

The Mistress answered through Seraphina, "Because I did my duty as the Mistress of Death. I let their souls cross over but sealed them from possession. This imbecile leaves corpses open for possession because he knows not, or has not, the power to protect them. The soldiers were at peace. They were no longer your legion to command."

"You brought them back to a world they will not recognize, to wreak havoc on mankind." Finn's fists clenched.

"I brought them back because they are mine," Death yelled.

Finn emphasized each word. "Then. Command. Them."

"They were ruthless, even for their time, but they were still souls worthy of passage to the other realm. Death must be impartial. All of your reanimated creations have been brought back without the freedom of choice. You ripped their souls from the veil without permission," Seraphina's strange voice said.

"And they should be led by one who respects them, one who understands they sacrifice their restful peace if they choose to stay. One who would lead them with honor." Finn's body shook with anger.

Seraphina turned and took Finn's face into her hands. She leaned in and connected their minds once more. In her voice alone, she whispered into his thoughts, *Will you accept this responsibility? Would you lead those who choose to remain? Lay the others to rest beyond the veil? My choice is made. I promised already. But I would leave you free, Finn, if you desire it. Would you serve at my side?*

"With honor, love," Finn said out loud and within Seraphina's thoughts.

Once again Seraphina spoke with the voice of many, "Then I grant you their command."

Seraphina offered her hand. Together, she and Finn rose from the floor. Ebbs of power flowed through her and into the Sin Eater.

Clouded magic swirled in Maximilian's eyes. He fought and took a blind step forward. "No, this is impossible. Stop this at once."

Seraphina raised her other hand and Maximilian raised from the floor. With an expression of fear and disbelief, he kicked his legs wildly.

Flipping over her hand, palm up, she pulled her fingers slowly inward. Maximilian threw his head back and screamed. As her fingers closed, his body curled into a fetal position in the air. When she closed her hand and brought it to her lips, she sucked in air and dark magic from the end of her fist. Then smiling, she reversed the hand as if dropping something insignificant from her palm.

Maximilian collapsed onto the floor. With shaking arms, he pushed himself up to look at Seraphina and Finn. His eyes were now a normal shade of hazel. He threw his arm out, trying to strike her down with magic, but nothing happened.

The Mistress and Seraphina laughed.

Maximilian jumped up and slashed his cane at her. Marceau dove between them and tackled Max to the ground.

Seraphina and Finn lowered back to the ground and their hands separated. Finn's eyes glowed in matching swirls of gray and black.

"General," said the voices of thousands from Seraphina's lips.

Finn knelt on one knee and bowed his head.

"Mistress Death," he replied reverently.

"No," screamed Maximilian. He writhed on the ground beneath Marceau but could not free himself. "Why can I not dematerialize? Where is my magic?"

"You're the one who is powerless now, Max," replied Marceau. He coughed and looked down, blood darkened his shirt in a spreading stain. The blade had slashed his side when he jumped forward to protect Seraphina.

Marceau managed a smile as he watched Maximilian. The cane's blade protruded from Max's chest and dark blood flowed from his wound, as well. "You're mortal."

"You're the one who is dying, not me," Max said, thick saliva frothed from his mouth tinted red with blood.

"We die together, Max, though I think the new Mistress may treat your soul differently than mine." Marceau fell forward. He coughed again.

"Seraphina. Se-ra-phi-na." Khat screamed. She ran and jerked on Seraphina's arm.

Finn still bowed before her. He raised his head now and took in the scene around him. "Marceau." He darted near and pulled Marceau's body off Maximilian.

"Damn it, you made me do this," Khat said. She slapped her palm on Seraphina's chest and scrunched her eyes closed. A blinding flash of gold magic blasted into Seraphina. She flew backward, landing on the floor. Seraphina's eyes opened in her own shade of green again.

"Marceau needs you," Khat cried as she pulled Seraphina upright.

Seraphina stumbled and almost fell on Finn. He held Marceau and pressed a throw blanket against his bleeding side.

"It's some kind of venom. He's poisoned," Finn said.

Seraphina spoke with the voice of many, but much fewer than before she shared her power with Finn. "Death shall not claim him, not today."

Seraphina bent and laid her hand on his side. A fine trail of black venom seeped from his wound. "Blood is as water, flow back to his heart. Flesh is as earth, close, and heal."

Marceau flinched and drew a pained breath as the blood reversed and flowed back into his closing wound. His eyes opened and he took a deep breath. "Seraphina, are you still mine?" he asked in a faint whisper.

Time seemed to stand still. So much hinged on that one simple question.

"Always," Seraphina answered in no voice but her own. She leaned down and kissed him.

Maximilian writhed on the ground in pain. "Mercy. Show me mercy, and I will teach you the ways of Death. I, I will mentor you," he begged.

"You can teach me nothing of Death. You bastardized your duty. You abandoned your post." She was proud of the words she'd chosen.

Maximilian turned to Finn. "Sin Eater, you must help me then. If I am to die, I cannot pass into the other realm stained with this much sin. You can feed upon my indiscretions and know true immortality from their power."

Finn crouched and jerked the cane's blade from Max's chest. He threw the staff and it clattered across the floor. "I am the general of the Mistress of Death's Legion."

Max cried out in pain as more blood flowed from the wound.

"You will receive no mercy from me. I hear their screams in my mind. I go to release the legion's bonds. Those who wish freedom will be released back into the veil. I will burn their empty bodies to ash so they can never again be disturbed." Finn locked eyes with Maximilian and completed his answer to Max. "If they so choose, I will burn them all."

"N-No, you must not."

"I will. Any who remain will never know the disrespect of your command again. Freedom from you and the freedom to choose their fate will be my gift for their loyalty."

"No," yelled Maximilian.

"Enough. Silence," whispered Seraphina. She placed a hand on Max's face. His mouth opened and eyes bulged. He looked from Marceau to Lynette and then to Babette, but his screams made no sound.

A mewling sound drew Seraphina's attention. The silver figure from atop the cane crawled toward her. Its form was an indistinct mixture of animals. Its face and body shifted so rapidly, it could barely pull itself forward.

"Come." Seraphina pressed her hand down on the floor and the silver creature transformed into a large, long-limbed spider. It scurried in her direction, talons clicking against the floor.

"Sera?" Khat called.

Seraphina didn't flinch as the metal spider leapt into her hand and ran onto her arm. She stood and peered into rows of dark eyes.

"Yes. For now, I suppose," Seraphina answered the question only she could hear. The figure melted and silver wrapped around her wrist. It formed a snake and bit its own tail, forming an Ouroboros bracelet.

Max's mouth formed repeated screams of the word "No," but no sound escaped his mouth.

Seraphina bent and laid her hand over the wound in his chest. His wound sealed closed, but she had not removed the venom. "Your veins will burn from the venom, and it will weaken you, but death will not grant you release. I am undecided as to your fate."

Babette asked in a soft voice, "May we please have him, Mistress?" She looked at Lynette and her eyes danced with the possibilities.

Lynette's answering smile was terrifying. "Yes, Mistress, we could keep him... occupied. Until you decide otherwise."

Maximilian shook his head and tried to scoot away from his former undead girlfriends. He rolled onto his stomach and across the floor on his knees and elbows, but the venom left him too weak to escape.

Seraphina nodded at Lynette and Babette and said, "Why not? I believe the two of you have much unfinished business with Max."

He sneered up at her. Yes, he did hate that nickname.

Babette clapped excitedly before leaning down and grabbing one of Max's feet. She hummed and started singing an old, familiar song,

"Tonight You Belong To Me." The girls sang in unison while grabbing Max's other foot.

They slowly dragged his body to the top of the stairs as their voices harmonized with childlike merriment. Max desperately clawed at the floor and the veins in his neck strained from his silent screams of protest.

His former Ettes turned and waved at the others, their matching pink baby-doll dresses swaying around their legs. They looked at each other and leaned in, sharing a soft, intimate kiss before resuming their song and bouncing Max along behind them down the stairs.

"Next verse…"

Thud, thud.

"Chorus…"

Thud, thud.

"You belong to… us." And their laughter echoed up the stairs and down the hall.

Max's body hit the last few steps and soon after, the bell above the shop's door rang as it opened and closed.

They all stood frozen. What was there to say after that?

Khat finally broke the stunned silence. "It may take years before my goosebumps go away from witnessing that. Creepy, undead revenge? It's damned *creepy.*"

Epilogue

Marceau sipped his coffee and looked around the familiar café, but he no longer felt his former fascination with people watching.

At one time, he had picked people and daydreamed about stepping into their lives and families. Now, he had a family of his own, some by choice, and perhaps others by blood.

Vespa hadn't been seen since her night at the AAA. And a week had passed since he'd last heard from the Ettes. They'd moved into one of the more secluded cottages Max had built in the Bayou Sauvage and kept to themselves most of the time.

Max.

Marceau hadn't seen him in weeks. Still even the mention of his name set Marceau's nerves on edge. He supposed there would always be a trace of lingering fear from the mention of his former benefactor's name, even with the stripped-down version of his powers.

Finishing his coffee, he set the mug on the table and placed a generous tip next to it. He'd come into the city to clear out the last of his possessions from his apartment. He now lived back at the main house with Seraphina, Finn and Khat, and a few thousand undead.

Finn, now more powerful than a mere Sin Eater with his infusion of death magic, was making progress in laying the soldiers who chose to forego an afterlife, to rest. Progress was slow because of the sheer numbers.

Just this morning, Khat reassured him they would get their old Seraphina back, in time. She'd been overwhelmed by her new power, the hive mind, and the responsibilities of being the new Mistress of Death. Some days, there were hints of the old Seraphina with shy smiles and playful banter. But other times, Seraphina lay in her bed crying out from the mental clutter of the hive mind. When she did leave her room, Seraphina often wandered around the mansion going from one undead to another. Touching them and seeing that they were real seemed to calm her as if she feared insanity.

Marceau had to find a way to help her… figure out a way to get inside her mental fortress. Together he knew they could overcome the challenges before them. They had already accomplished so much to be together.

But for today, Marceau was focused on another endeavor. After many messages and negotiations, the elders of the L'Argent village had finally agreed to meet with him. He had a list of items they'd requested from the local voodoo shops, a few were obscure and troubling.

Tomorrow morning, Marceau and Lynette were going to be allowed inside the L'Argent village for the first time. He was finally going to find out whether he had parents or siblings and rediscover his roots.

Marceau was patient, but soon he had to break through Seraphina's mental shields and help the woman he loved. No longer powerless, fearful of dying, and cursed, she was now the Mistress of Death itself. The supernatural world was in for big changes once the Conexus found out.

Thanks for reading *Much of Madness*. I hope you enjoyed it.

If you wouldn't mind, would you kindly leave a review? Not only does it help others gauge the book's worth, it also helps me know what I did right and where I might be able to improve. Reviews make it possible for writers to create more books! I'd be honored to hear from you.

To be notified of new releases and receive exclusive sneak peeks, sign up for my newsletter at: **sesumma.com**

Or if social media is your thing, follow me! I love to interact with readers. My user-ids for Twitter, Pinterest, and Instagram are **@sesumma**, or like my Facebook page at: **https://www.facebook.com/sesumma**

Much of Madness is the 1st full-length novel in *The Conexus Chronicles*. Upcoming books in the series are *More of Sin* (coming 2016) and *Horror the Soul* (TBD).

Want to learn more about Babette's backstory and get an introduction to new characters appearing in More of Sin? Be sure to check out the related short stories in *Debut Collective Anthologies* available in June 2016: *Secret Identity & Underdogs*

Acknowledgements

"Thank you" seems incapable of expressing the scope of my gratitude for all the wonderful support I've received. I worry I'll forget to thank someone. If you're the one, I'm so sorry. I owe you office supplies, chocolate, or whiskey – your choice!

Kathy Lapeyre, my brilliant editor, guided this story with sure-handed attention to detail and a gift for fine-tuning character voices. A few pages had enough red to excite one of my vampiric Sanguine, but Kathy's kind encouragement balanced her corrections and her insights helped me grow as a writer. Fun fact: When numerous enough, Word comments convert to dropdown boxes. Kathy taught me that. But rather than intimidating, it was thrilling to realize how spot on she was and improve my story.

Can we take a second to gawk at this gorgeous cover? Jenny at Seedlings Design Studio perfectly translated my inspiration board and delivered a fantastic cover that makes me smile every time see it.

My friend and critique partner, Robin Crawley, was the first to read my warty, plot-hole filled, original draft. She's sworn to absolute secrecy! But through every revision and my moments of neurotic self doubt, Robin magically knew when to encourage, when to laugh, and when to give me a solid and much needed kick in the ass. I look so forward to the day readers are able to devour her fantastic, action-packed stories. She ROCKS!

The Music City Romance Writers, my local RWA chapter, is a source of constant inspiration, education, and endless encouragement. I'd like to thank Stacie Wilson (the GIF Queen!) and Bethany Adams, in particular, for their support and friendship. I'll be among the first to buy their books later this year.

Last June, during the annual open keynote at UtopYA Con (now UTOPiA), I listened as writer after writer shared their goals, dreams, and fears. Realizing I'd only publish if I said it loud, often, and to others with similar goals, I created the Debut Collective the next day. Within weeks, the online group had grown to just shy of eighty like-minded members. The Debut Collective is a supportive tribe of authors (both published and aspiring), editors, formatters, and cover designers working together to foster a new generation of stories and authors. We will be publishing a series of five anthologies in June 2016 and I couldn't be prouder of all we've accomplished. Cannot WAIT to see y'all in June!

Other support included: CJ Redwine's wonderful workshops and Writer's Sanctuary Retreat, Prose Pirates, We Are Going to UTOPiA FB Group, & S.A.S.S. (Struggling Author Street-Team Service).

There is the family you're born into, others you join by marriage, and then there are those who become yours by choice. For the last thirty years, the Abernathy family has been my own through love, laughter, and times of unbelievable loss. Thank you for always supporting me.

I also have two chosen daughters, Carrie and Melissa, who read early chapters and have been amongst my loudest cheerleaders though this crazy process. Dream big and then put in the work, girlies. Life can take you in fantastical directions when you are brave. I love you both, always.

I am blessed to have a large and supportive family. They accept my personal brand of strange and roll with me when I say crazy things like, "Oh, I spend all my free time writing horror stories now." And later, "I'm going to publish my book!" I've been especially touched by the unwavering support and enthusiasm of my sweet mother-in-law, Judy Martin.

Introvert and INFJ personality types weren't as understood when I was a painfully shy, only child. Since beginning to read and write at the age of three, books have been amongst my most comfortable companions. I'm who I am today because of the unconditional and unwavering love of my parents, Ralph and Polly Summa. Thank you for always believing in me and for pushing me to step outside my comfort zone again and again. My momma's endless creativity and playful spirit developed my imagination. And yes, those bad behavior reports you made me write as a child probably helped a little too, but it was still cruel to make me read them to visitors!

My daughter Megan and granddaughter Karma are my true legacy, more than any book can ever be. I'm so proud of my quirky, creative daughter with her twisted humor, eclectic musical taste, and absolute natural talent for editing. Meanwhile, Karma has provided much needed comic relief and an abundance of hugs, noseys, and squishy faces when GiGi was being too serious. My dream for you both is to find your passion and a way to make it the focus of your lives. I love you both beyond words.

Chuck, my ever-patient husband, and our furbabies have witnessed stress-fueled meltdowns and rambling explanations of publishing woes, as often as calm confidence throughout this journey. Yet they've loved me even on my batshit crazy days. Chuck, thank you for being a true partner in life, a giving and responsible man who often puts the needs of family above your own, and after ten wonderful years of marriage, the husband I'm in love with even more now than on our wedding day.

About the Author

S. E. Summa lives in Tennessee with her husband and a menagerie of spoiled pets. After her daughter left the nest, she rediscovered her love for books and began writing. Growing up in Nashville, she always felt the city's unique culture and landmarks would be the perfect setting for monsters to play.

S. E. Is a PRO member of the Romance Writers of America (RWA) and her local chapter, Music City Romance Writers (MCRW). She graduated magna cum laude with a BBA from Belmont University.

S. E. started The Debut Collective, a supportive tribe of authors (both published and aspiring), editors, formatters, and cover designers working together to foster a new generation of stories and authors.